BORN IN A
BURIAL GOWN

—

M.W.
CRAVEN

CONSTABLE

CONSTABLE

First published in Great Britain in 2015 by Caffeine Nights Publishing

This revised and updated edition published in Great Britain in 2020 by Constable

A CIP catalogue record for this book is available from the British Library.

ISBN: 978-1-47213-264-2

Typeset in Caslon Pro by SX Composing DTP, Rayleigh, Essex
Printed and bound in Great Britain by Clays Ltd, Elcograf S.p.A.

Papers used by Constable are from well-managed forests
and other responsible sources.

Constable
An imprint of
Little, Brown Book Group
Carmelite House
50 Victoria Embankment
London EC4Y 0DZ

An Hachette UK Company
www.hachette.co.uk

www.littlebrown.co.uk

As always, this book is dedicated to my wife,
Joanne, and my late mother, Susan Avison Craven.
Without either, this wouldn't exist.

Chapter 1

It started as it always did, with a breeder. A married man with a burning need he couldn't sate at home. A married man wanting something discreet, something the boy had and was willing to sell. He'd met him in the toilets of a club in Whitehaven. Nervous at first, the man had quickly gained his confidence and let out a stifled yell as he finished. After the money had exchanged hands, he'd made the boy a proposition. In no position to negotiate, the arrangements were made quickly.

Each transaction the boy made carried a risk, he knew that. He was in the highest-risk group of what was statistically the most dangerous profession in the world, but sometimes there were no more choices left. Some breeders paid extra to bareback, increasing the risk of disease tenfold. Others hated what they'd just done and became violent. For some, violence was part of what they wanted, what they enjoyed, as if paying for sex gave them unlimited rights over someone else. The boy's profession attracted a disproportionate amount of sadists. It wasn't just the breeders he feared. Roaming gangs of youths, eager to find someone with no social value to vent their frustrations on, were a constant threat. Even the police had been known to stick the boot in.

Sometimes after enjoying the boy's companionship.

Occasionally the violence went further than a beating. Sometimes men killed to keep their secrets. He'd known four others like him who'd died before they'd reached thirty. One had been murdered, two had died from complications after being assaulted and the fourth had simply given up and hanged himself. It was a fool who thought he could beat the odds for ever, and the boy was no fool. How would his time come? At the hands of a breeder or in a hospital bed, wasting away? He thought about his own mortality often.

But he wasn't thinking about it that night.

This breeder had been different. He was kind. He'd found the boy somewhere to sleep. So, that night he was warm, he was safe, and had something to look forward to. Earlier, he'd played the game and won. Now he could enjoy the spoils.

That night he wasn't thinking about death.

Perhaps he should have been.

Kicked out of the family home at the age of eleven, when his stepfather had made his mother choose between them, the boy had spent years in various children's homes before finally being abandoned by everyone.

A friend, and despite what had happened to him since, he still thought of him as a friend, had lured him into the trade with promises of more money than he'd ever seen before.

For the first few years, his friend had been right.

He often thought of what he called his 'golden age', when the heightened value of youth meant he was in demand. He could charge what he wanted, choose whom he wanted, and always had cash in his pocket. He'd thought he was happy then. But boys in his line of work reach a sell-by date. It was a gradual decline. Previously loyal customers moved to younger, fresher products. His value decreased at the same rate his age increased and before long he was struggling to survive. Without the USP of youth, he had no choice but to drop his prices. Ten years earlier a breeder would have happily paid two hundred pounds for an hour of his time. Now he was struggling to get twenty pounds for what were becoming increasingly extreme acts.

And, like countless boys before him, he tried to blot out the violence and depravity meted out to him. As his drug use spiralled out of control, his appearance deteriorated and his value plummeted until he was reduced to selling blowjobs in dank pub toilets for a fiver a time. Unable to afford essentials such as rent or food, he became a street creature; homeless and penniless, surviving any way he could. In the previous year, he'd been strangled to unconsciousness twice, raped four times and beaten more times than he could count.

But two weeks ago, he'd had that break. The man he'd been with had offered him a place to stay during the night. Free of charge. The only cost was repaying the favour every morning.

A favour for a favour.

Somewhere warm and safe in exchange for something he'd done a thousand times before. The boy had happily accepted. He was still there. Sleeping safely at night, repaying the favour first thing when the man arrived. The boy had to leave after the act was over, forced to stay away during the day until the place was empty and he could let himself in again. A daily routine he and the man were happy with.

Earlier that day he'd scored another job and, surprisingly, the man paid more money than normal. He supposed he was new to the game and didn't know what was a fair price. With cash in his hand and somewhere free to stay, the boy bought the only thing he ever wanted these days: heroin.

He took the key the man had given him and let himself in.

Experience had taught him that carrying as little paraphernalia as possible was preferable to carrying dirty kit with trace residue. Residue was enough to get you locked up on a possession charge, and while brushes with the law were an occupational hazard in his line of work, he never took risks he didn't need to. A new syringe, citric powder and sterile water, all provided by the NHS, and an empty Coke can were all he carried. Nothing he could be arrested for. Dirty spoons, covered in heroin residue, were for beginners.

Bending the can until it was thin enough to tear in half, he used the concave base as a dish to mix the citric powder, water and heroin. With his only real possession, a Zippo, he heated it until the solution bubbled and darkened.

The real amber nectar.

Liquid sunshine.

Trembling with anticipation, he drew the brown solution through a cigarette filter into the syringe. Carefully setting it to one side, he removed his trousers.

A nurse had once described him as the most unsophisticated injector she'd ever seen and it had been a long time since his abscess-strewn arms and legs had offered up viable veins. He had to inject into his foot and he didn't need experts to tell him it was one of the most sensitive parts of the body. Flinching at the excruciating pain, he persevered and pushed the needle between his toes. He found a vein and pressed the plunger. The pain was replaced instantly by the rush.

This was what he did it for. That perfect moment when he was in his bubble, when nothing mattered but the high. When his ruined life made some sort of sense. That was what the nurses, outreach workers and probation officers would never understand. Why he would never, *could* never, quit. He didn't want to. For a brief moment in time, he could forget who he was. Why would he not want that? The initial rush was replaced by the familiar warmth and sense of well-being that spread throughout his whole body. At peace, he settled down on the carpet to enjoy it for as long as he could. Eventually, his breathing steadied and slowed.

The boy slept.

A noise woke him. For a second, he thought he'd overslept and panic set in. He didn't want to upset his breeder. He was supposed

4

to be ready and waiting, with brushed teeth and combed hair. Sitting up, he realised he was wrong. It was still dark. He didn't have a watch but instinctively knew it could only be a couple of hours past midnight. Carefully, he peered out of the window to see what had woken him.

A dark vehicle was parked twenty yards away. The headlights were off but he could hear the engine running. The internal lights didn't come on when the driver's door opened but there was enough light coming from the old hospital building for him to see the silhouette of a man get out and stretch. The boy moved closer to the window to get a better look. It was the first time anyone had ever been there after dark.

The man walked away, switching on a torch to navigate the darkness. For thirty yards he walked, casting his torch left and right as he searched for something. Whatever he was looking for, he must have found it because the torch stopped moving and shone downwards instead. Apparently satisfied, the man turned and walked back towards his car. A sixth sense, developed over years of avoiding violent punters, told the boy something was wrong and his curiosity turned to apprehension. The man walked to the back of the car, looked around carefully and opened the boot. The boy shrank back into the darkness of the room. He instinctively knew nothing good would come from the man seeing him. Apparently satisfied he was alone, the man reached into the boot and dragged out something large and heavy. Despite being twenty yards away, the boy heard a sickening thud as it fell to the floor.

It could only be one thing.

The boy gasped in recognition. His apprehension turned to abject terror.

That night, he hadn't been thinking about death . . .

Chapter 2

Detective Inspector Avison Fluke stared at the dripping blood without making a sound. It was crimson, almost black in the sub-dued lighting, and he watched as each drop grew in size until it could no longer resist the pull of gravity and fell, only for the pro-cess to start all over again.

The drips were slowing. It would be over soon. Until the next time.

Fluke hadn't used his bed in nearly a year, preferring an arm-chair as he waited for exhaustion to give him the temporary release of sleep. He was still tired and the metronomic drip of the blood had helped him achieve an almost Zen-like state. He looked at his watch and realised he'd lost nearly an hour. He felt oddly refreshed at the thought. An hour was more than he'd managed at home the previous night.

His peace was interrupted when his mobile phone rang. A nurse at the other end of the cramped ward gave him a dirty look. Fluke mouthed 'sorry'.

He looked at the caller ID: Detective Superintendent Cameron Chambers. Fluke had hoped to be left alone that morning. He stared at the phone for a moment before deciding he'd better answer it.

Chambers didn't wait to be acknowledged. 'Fluke, where are you?' He was the type of man who mistook plain-spoken for rude.

'Home,' he replied.

'Home? What the hell are you still doing at home? It's nine o'clock, man.'

Fluke didn't answer and there was an uncomfortable pause, one he knew Chambers would fill.

'Yes, well. I need you in West Cumbria. There's a dead woman waiting there for you. I'm still on this armed robbery and will be all week, so it's your case.'

Fluke had seen the bank depot robbery update on the news the previous night and watched his boss being interviewed. There was no way Chambers was giving up that limelight. He had ambitions to be chief constable and a high-profile case like that was a wet dream for him. In his mind, he was earmarked for great things. In everyone else's, he was a self-absorbed careerist. Everything he did irritated Fluke. They were going to come to blows before long.

'Who can I have?' Fluke said. Most of the Force Major Incident Team were still on the robbery but he'd need help. He also knew that Chambers equated a big team with importance so would want to keep everyone he could.

'You can have Towler, Vaughn and Skelton. Can't let you have anyone else. The robbery's at a crucial stage. Get local help if you need more. Towler's already at the scene. Get the details from him.'

Towler, that was expected. The only person people liked working with less was himself. Towler was too unpredictable, too *violent*. Jo Skelton, as a middle-aged mother of two, didn't conform to Chambers's vision of a young, dynamic detective, and Vaughn was just plain weird with his whole 'I don't like to be touched' thing.

With Fluke, the four of them represented FMIT's untouchables. They referred to themselves as the outcasts and preferred working independently when they could. Sometimes, managing them was like herding cats but Fluke wouldn't have swapped any of them. Because what Chambers failed to see was that they were all brilliant detectives. They'd have been an asset to his precious robbery case if he hadn't been so concerned with how the team looked on the evening news.

Fluke was distracted by someone pausing then looking in as they walked past the open-style ward. Whoever it was, he got the impression they'd recognised him. Before he could turn and look properly, they'd disappeared. Probably a gawper. Embarrassed to be caught looking. People often didn't know how to act round certain wards.

'And Fluke?'

'Sir?'

'Don't milk it. It's almost certainly a domestic. Identify the dead woman and arrest the husband.'

Fluke jabbed the end-call button. 'Arsehole,' he said. It had been a strange thing to say, though. What did Chambers know that he didn't? If it was straightforward, there was no way Chambers wouldn't have led on it, taking a day away from the robbery to solve a murder would, in his mind, only enhance his reputation. If he didn't want it, there was something wrong.

Fluke scrolled down his recent contacts and rang Matt Towler. He answered on the first ring.

'Boss, we've got a body, a woman. I've shut down the scene until you get here.'

'Where?' Fluke asked.

'West Cumberland Hospital, part of the site they're still developing there. She was under some mud in a foundation hole. The foreman found her at eight this morning.'

Which almost certainly ruled out a natural death or a suicide – as a rule, dead people didn't bury themselves. A concealed corpse usually meant a homicide. Murder or manslaughter. Statistically, the street was the most dangerous place for men and the home the most dangerous place for women and, as unpleasant as he was, Chambers was right: when a woman was killed, her partner or ex-partner was usually the culprit. Most of the time for the police, it was a 'whydunit' rather than a 'whodunit'. Few perpetrators of domestic homicides are forensically aware. There were always breadcrumbs to follow when crimes were committed in anger, jealousy or passion. The weapons used were chosen for expediency rather than efficiency and their murders were normally solved within twenty-four hours.

'What do we know so far?' Fluke said.

'Nothing really. Probably a relationship gone bad. Maybe premeditated,' Towler said. 'She was in a golf travel bag. It's a deposition site, not the murder site.'

So *that* was why Chambers didn't want anything to do with it. If it were premeditated, it could take time to get to the bottom of it, time away from the robbery, and more importantly time away from the TV cameras. Anything longer than a day and he risked handing the limelight over to someone else.

By making Fluke the senior investigating officer, Chambers could sit back and poke holes in his efforts. If he charged someone it would be because Chambers had delegated correctly and if he didn't, then he'd have someone to blame. He'd either take the glory or distance himself from a badly run investigation. A win–win for Chambers and a lose–lose for Fluke.

'She was under a foot of mud so couldn't be seen either,' Towler said. 'Even when looking directly in.'

'So how did—?'

'And she's only been in there six hours.'

'What? How'd you know that?' Fluke said, taking Towler's bait.

'We have a witness. They left a note.'

Fluke jabbed the assistance button above his bed until the ward nurse came to see him.

'I need to go, nurse,' he said. 'It's nearly finished anyway.' He pointed at the bag of blood that was clearly not empty.

'Marion,' she replied automatically. 'Do I call you "patient"? And you're not going anywhere. I've got a bag of plasma in the fridge for you.'

Plasma? Sod that. Plasma took even longer than blood.

After five minutes of argument and counter-argument, Fluke gave up.

'Fine,' he sighed.

As soon as she left the room, Fluke stood up. He couldn't afford to wait. The first few hours were the 'golden hours': witnesses remembered things clearly, forensic evidence was at its freshest and easiest to detect. Alibis weren't yet fully formed.

After checking he couldn't be seen from the corridor, he removed the cannula from the back of his hand. Nice and easy, just like he'd seen doctors do countless times. He didn't have a cotton swab so he used a tissue to stem the flow of blood from the puncture wound. He looked for somewhere safe to dispose of the needle. He settled for wrapping it in his hanky and putting it in his rucksack.

He knew he'd stepped over an unseen line in hospital etiquette and would be in trouble with Doctor Cooper later. She'd probably be on the phone before he'd even reached the car park but that was nothing compared to the trouble he'd be in if anyone at work ever found out where he'd really been. Arriving two hours late to your own crime scene was unexplainable. Anyway, he didn't want to see Doctor Cooper. Every time he saw her, it triggered another bout of insomnia. He'd been lying to her about his side effects for over a year now and the guilt was keeping him awake. He knew she only wanted what was best for him but the truth had to stay hidden. And the truth was that five months ago, he'd involved her in a crime. A crime she didn't even know about.

He hoisted his rucksack onto his shoulders, avoided the disapproving stare of the man opposite and walked out of the ward.

The more he went to the Cumberland Infirmary the more it seemed to tire him. Physically, he was getting stronger and stronger, but each time he had an appointment he came out feeling weary.

It didn't seem to matter how much he'd rested or how healthily he'd eaten, like a badly earthed battery, the hospital seemed to drain him of energy.

He put it down to being so sick of them that even being in a hospital tired him. Or perhaps Doctor Cooper had been right and he *had* needed the blood. He put it out of his mind and was out of Carlisle and on the A595 driving west in less than five minutes. The thermometer in his car showed 5 °C. It was biting outside. The trees were bare, their dead leaves long gone to the strong winter winds. Brown, rotten vegetation littered the verge. The countryside on the wane. A few evergreens were still battling the elements but everything else was waiting for spring. He turned the heater up.

His mobile rang and the caller ID displayed the ward's number. Fluke pressed the decline button.

A layer of fog descended the farther west he drove. Thick and white. It wasn't raining yet, but it was going to. He hoped proper forensic practices had been followed. He didn't want evidence being washed away before he got there. Chambers had the main SOCO team working the robbery so he knew he'd get whoever was left. It didn't matter. When it came to crime scenes, he preferred to be in total control. The crime scene managers didn't like having their autonomy removed but he didn't care. His case, his rules.

The drive would take at least another forty-five minutes, and without any details of the crime to think about, Fluke searched through the car's mp3 player for some music with a bit of pace and energy. He selected The Clash's *Give 'Em Enough Rope*, and turned up the volume. FMIT were responsible for investigating the most serious crimes in Cumbria, and when the county was the third largest in the UK, if you didn't like driving, you were in the wrong job.

As the opening chords to 'English Civil War' rang out – the only guitar riff he'd bothered trying to learn when he and Towler had attempted to form a band when they were kids – he smiled and started thumping the steering wheel, glad to be alive.

An hour after leaving Carlisle, Fluke arrived at the rendezvous point. Towler had set it up on some hardstanding between the main building site and the smaller site where the body had been discovered. It was where all the yellow earth-moving vehicles, which all building sites seemed to need, were parked, their enormous tyres thick with dark mud. It was also full of police vehicles, marked and unmarked, some still with their flashing lights on. He was obviously one of the last to arrive.

Whenever possible, Fluke used rendezvous points out of sight of the crime scene to ensure everyone was fully focused on what he was saying, rather than rubbernecking at the site. Towler knew that and Fluke nodded appreciatively as he saw the site's own security fences made the scene self-contained. People were milling round, waiting to start. Most of them had white forensic suits on and from a distance it looked like a convention of Scottish sunbathers.

Fluke got out of his car and stretched. A lone seagull circled overhead. It screeched and a uniformed policeman threw it the last of the sandwich he was eating. Fluke watched as it dived down to catch it. With no more food, it lazily gained height then headed off in the direction of Whitehaven Harbour. Fluke could smell the sea coming off the inland breeze. It reminded him of Plymouth and his time with the Marines.

Matt Towler, a foot taller than everyone else, was speaking to a group of suited forensic staff. He saw Fluke, broke away from the group and walked over. He could tell his friend was worried, and when something worried Towler, a veteran of a Gulf War, Sierra Leone and three tours of Northern Ireland, he also worried. Although FMIT officers weren't officially paired up, Fluke and Towler invariably ended up working together. Barely hidden disdain of anyone below their own high standards, barrack-room sarcasm and a willingness to work twenty hours a day, seven days a week when needed meant other detectives weren't exactly falling over themselves to join them. It was something Fluke cultivated rather than tried to rectify.

'You OK, Ave?' Towler said.

'Fine. Tell me about this note,' he said, as they walked towards the scene. The ground was cold and slippery and threatening to sprain his ankles. They struggled to the outer cordon and stopped.

Towler handed him a plastic evidence bag. It had a piece of paper inside.

Fluke read it.

> Look in the secund whole from the door. sum1 has put a
> body in there

It was written on stationery with a building company logo, the same logo as the ones on the fences that surrounded the site. It looked like the witness had used whatever had been to hand.

He turned it over. There was nothing on the back.

'Not exactly Shakespeare, is it?' Towler said. 'It was by the kettle in the site office.'

The poor spelling didn't necessarily indicate age. Fluke knew the average criminal had the reading age of an eight-year-old and he already had a theory about who'd left the note. He didn't know the person but suspected he knew the type.

Fluke looked at the site office and its proximity to the crime scene, easily identifiable by the forensic tent.

'Who was first on scene?'

'Dunno. But Don Holland was sticking his massive beak in when I got here.'

Fluke could see Chief Inspector Holland talking to a group of uniformed officers. They'd never really got on, although neither of them really knew why. Fluke walked over.

'Chief Inspector!' he called out.

Holland looked up, said something to the group that caused them to laugh, and sauntered over.

'What's up, Fluke? Don't tell me, you've found something to complain about already. I'd say that under three minutes is a record for you but we both know I'd be lying.'

Holland laughed at his own joke. Fluke didn't join in. 'Who set up the cordons?'

'Remember who you're speaking to, Fluke,' Holland said.

'I know exactly who I'm speaking to, *Chief Inspector*,' Fluke replied. 'Who set up the cordons?'

'I did. Why? It's all correct.'

Fluke could feel himself getting angry. 'Why's the site office not in the inner cordon?'

Holland was about to respond but saw the evidence bag Fluke was carrying and realised his mistake. The office was also a crime scene and should have been cordoned off and access controlled.

'Shit,' he said.

'I'm giving you five minutes to reset it, and in the meantime get your giggling sycophants off my bloody crime scene!' Fluke shouted.

'Now look here, Fluke, I will not be spoken—'

'I haven't got time, Chief Inspector,' Fluke snapped. 'Just get it sorted.'

'Useless wanker,' Towler said, as Holland stalked off.

There was no point reliving mistakes. Fluke needed to move on. 'Who found the note?'

Towler pointed towards a grey-haired man talking to a police officer. 'The Clerk of Works, Christian Dunn, spotted it soon as he got in. Always has a brew first thing.'

Fluke asked, 'What'd he do?'

'Had a look, saw nothing, but as it was due to be filled today, he got in with a shovel and found it.'

14

'The body?'

'No, the golf travel bag,' Towler replied. 'He opened it, saw her face and called triple nine.'

A travel bag would have to be big enough to fit a normal golf bag in it. The perfect size to surreptitiously transport a body.

'Let's go and have a word with him then,' Fluke said.

Usually members of the public who'd discovered a body were on the verge of a breakdown. At the very least, they were in shock. But if Fluke were pressed, he'd have said Christian Dunn was irritated.

He looked up as they walked over. 'Is this him? This the boss man, like?' Dunn said to the officer with him.

He strode towards Fluke, indignation all over his face. He was a small man, closer to sixty than fifty, with a weathered face. Clearly someone who spent his time outdoors.

Fluke held out his hand but Dunn ignored it.

'You the boss man? When can I get back to work?' he said. He pronounced work as 'wuk'. 'It's putting me right off my schedule, this is. I've nine tons of concrete coming soon. I need you to move that lassie.'

His understanding of personal space was about as well-developed as his awareness of volume control. Dunn wasn't exactly shouting but Fluke could feel himself leaning back anyway. Ten minutes with him and he'd be reaching for the headache pills.

'This is a murder investigation, Mr Dunn,' he said. 'The site's shut down.'

Dunn looked at him blankly. 'My gaffer doesn't pay me to sit on me arse all day with concrete getting hard in the mixer.'

'I'm sorr—'

'What she want to throw herself down there for anyway?' Dunn interrupted. 'I know it's sad an' all that, but it's selfish. If she wants to kill hersel', why can't she do it away from my building site?'

It was Fluke's turn to look blank. The idiot thought it was a suicide? She was in a bag and covered in mud.

Dunn wasn't finished. 'Look, I know you lads 'ave a job to do but my concrete's going in that hole whether you like it or not.'

Fluke didn't really know how to respond to that. Fortunately Towler did.

'Listen, you little tit,' he said. 'This is a murder investigation, your site's gonna be closed for fucking days.'

Dunn stepped back in the face of Towler's aggressive outburst.

'I'm telling my gaffer about this. You'll be hearing from Mr Johnson today, don't you worry about that. It's putting me right off my schedule this is,' he muttered.

'Look, Mr Dunn, we'll be as fast as we can but it'll go faster if you tell me everything I need to know,' Fluke said.

'How fast?'

'Maybe an hour,' Fluke lied. He saw Towler smirk as Dunn looked at his watch.

'What do you want to know?' he said.

'Tell me about the hole and the office.'

Dunn explained that the holes were due to be filled with concrete and rubble, part of the foundations for the new outpatient wing.

'Did anyone have a key to the site office other than you, Mr Dunn?' Fluke asked.

For the first time, Dunn looked uncomfortable rather than angry. Shifty even.

'No. Why should anyone else have a key? I'm the gaffer,' he mumbled.

'So you're the only one with access to it?'

He mumbled something again. Fluke failed to catch it.

'Speak up, dickhead,' Towler said.

'I said, I'm the only one who can get in.'

'You sure?' Fluke asked. He stared at Dunn.

Dunn broke eye contact first, said he was sure, then stumbled off.

'You want to bring him in?' Towler asked.

'Not yet. We'll wait and see what we find. He's not going anywhere, not when he has to "wuk".'

'If it'd been filled in today, I doubt the body would ever have been found,' Towler said.

'Not in our lifetime anyway,' Fluke agreed.

'You wanna go and have a look?'

'Yeah, but I'm not getting in just yet,' he said. 'I want to clear the site office first. Sooner we get that done, sooner it can be processed. We'll have to wait for the pathologist before we can move the body. May as well let SOCO do something.'

Fluke, like a lot of older detectives, refused to call SOCO by their new name, CSI, believing it was one more unwelcome American influence. They were Scenes of Crime Officers and always would be.

As they walked towards the foundation hole, he saw Don Holland standing outside the hastily rearranged tape. He mouthed 'fuck you' when he caught his eye. Fluke ignored him.

'He won't forget that, boss,' said Towler, nodding towards Holland. 'You humiliated him. He'll be after you now.'

'Yeah?' Fluke replied. 'Well, he'll have to get in the queue.'

'You want me to twat him?'

Fluke laughed. Then stopped. It was possible Towler wasn't joking.

'You had a look at the vic yet?' he said.

'Just to make sure we weren't pressing the button for a fucking mannequin or something,' Towler said.

'And?'

'It's fresh. I'm guessing less than twenty-four hours.'

'Any obvious cause of death?'

'Nope, and I didn't want to open the bag any further.'

Fluke didn't respond.

'I know we don't jump to conclusions, boss, but it looks well planned,' he added.

Towler was right. It was dangerous to form early opinions but Fluke was already getting a bad feeling. There was something about it that just sounded professional, nothing tangible, but it was there. It was a miracle the body had even been discovered.

'Course, it could just be a fucking nutter who killed his wife and didn't want to sit at home in his underpants talking to her till she smelled like cheese,' Towler said.

Fluke said nothing.

Chapter 3

After being met by Sean Rogers, the crime scene manager, Fluke donned a forensic suit and followed him down the route organised by the first officers at the scene.

He turned and reviewed where he was. It allowed him to get his bearings and a sense of scale. It also allowed him to assess the work that had taken place before he'd arrived. Murder investigations started with the first officer, and other than Holland neglecting to treat the office as a crime scene, everything else was satisfactory. Luckily, the building site was self-contained so there weren't going to be any egress or access problems later.

After entering the inner cordon, Fluke followed Rogers to the crime scene. As they got near, it was marked out with footboards, designed to keep ground evidence closer to the scene intact. They'd been put in properly, which wasn't always the case. Fluke had been to one crime scene on the side of a hill when the footboards were at an angle and he'd fallen off, much to everyone's amusement.

Although it wasn't raining at the site, SOCO had erected a large forensic tent. Fluke entered and looked down into the hole. It was about six feet across, roundish, and at least ten feet deep with steep sides. Fluke could see the excavation scars the digger had left. The mud was thick clay, too dark to see the bottom.

The ladder that Dunn had used was still leaning against the side of the hole. There had been some damage to the scene, probably during his scramble back out when he realised what he'd just uncovered, but Fluke could live with that. Rarely was a crime scene completely undisturbed.

He leaned over and looked down. Rogers passed him a torch. Fluke flicked it on.

The golf travel case was partially buried at the bottom of the hole and the zip had been opened about eighteen inches. It was enough to reveal the head of an obviously dead woman. Her skin was grey and frostbitten and cracking. An icy sheen clung to her, the warmth of life banished. Her mouth was open and her lips were shrinking back across the teeth in an eerie grimace. Towler was right; it was no mannequin. Fluke never ceased to be surprised at how quickly the body lost its healthy pink colour once death had occurred. It was a matter of minutes.

Some of her hair had been caught in the zip, twisting her head to the side, and Fluke thought his torch picked up the sparkle of a diamond earring. Even from three yards away, they looked expensive. Too expensive to leave. Which almost certainly ruled out a domestic. They would be far too easy to identify.

It was hard to tell, but he didn't think the victim had been a very young woman. Mid-thirties would be his guess. Like Towler, Fluke could see no obvious cause of death but he knew he was only looking at a face and an ear in a dark hole in torchlight. Things would become clearer during the post-mortem. He swung the torch round the bottom of the hole. He could see a shovel, probably the one Dunn had used to search for the body. There was nothing else. He couldn't smell putrefaction, only wet mud. If she'd been put in the hole during the early hours of the morning then Fluke was willing to bet that she'd been killed no earlier than the day before. The pathologist would give him a time of death as well as the cause.

Fluke saw no reason to get into the hole to take a closer look. It would only add confusion to the crime scene. Patience was a discipline and, after six months in hospital, it was one he possessed in abundance. The first thing he needed to do was make sure that there were no errors made in the collection of evidence, and that meant taking the time to do it properly. Together, he and the pathologist would decide how to recover the body without disturbing anything important.

He'd seen enough. He left the tent and handed the torch back to Rogers.

'What time's the pathologist getting here?' Fluke asked. Sometimes the body could be recovered without one, but it was a complex deposition site. He presumed someone had called for one.

'Should be within the hour. Henry Sowerby's coming up from Preston,' Rogers replied. 'I took one look and knew we'd need him at the scene. Sergeant Towler informed the coroner.'

'Good.'

Fluke liked Sowerby. The pathologist was extremely professional, had a good forensic brain and was as bad tempered as they came. He'd watched him reduce senior investigating officers to quivering wrecks when he felt that good forensic practices weren't being followed. Fluke had always got on well enough with him though, and he knew the bad temper was on behalf of the victims rather than any antagonism towards the police. And once an SIO had been chewed out by Sowerby for a forensic error, they never repeated it.

Fluke would wait for him, and together they would decide how to recover the body. They would agree what evidence needed to be gathered before they moved her and what could be gathered at the mortuary. Although technically Fluke would have the final say at the crime scene, it was a brave SIO who went against the advice of the pathologist, an even braver one who went against Sowerby. Fluke much preferred to reach a consensus. He knew there were genuine reasons why SIOs sometimes had to go against a pathologist's advice, he'd done it himself on rare occasions. Sometimes the need to move quickly overrode the need to collect evidence in ideal conditions. But there was no rush here. Nothing was going to change in the next hour.

Fluke turned to Rogers. 'Who's been in the inner cordon?'

'Which one?' he asked, smiling slyly.

'The first one,' Fluke replied. He didn't return the smile. It was one thing chewing out someone for an error but Holland was still a senior officer. He might be a total dickhead but he still had to be able to command his officers. In any case, Holland was going to have to provide some officer resource to do some of the grunt work. House-to-house, crime scene security, search teams and anything else Fluke needed.

'Dunn, the responding officer, Sergeant Towler and myself. And now you. Only Dunn has set foot on the bottom. Sergeant Towler climbed down to confirm it was a body but didn't get off the ladder,' Rogers replied. 'And he used a different ladder in case Dunn becomes a suspect.'

Fluke nodded. There was no way Dunn was the killer. Committing a murder would have got in the way of his work schedule. 'I'll go and have a look at the office now, then your lot can process it.'

'Matt,' Fluke said, turning to Towler. 'Can you call Jo? Tell her to base herself at HQ and set up an incident room? The robbery team have the big one so we'll just have to make do.'

Jo Skelton was the oldest member of FMIT in Penrith, a veteran of murder investigations going back twenty years, and Fluke sometimes thought she was the most valuable. She was certainly the only one he trusted to actually do the essential admin tasks: to set up databases and cross-reference intelligence without getting bored and making mistakes. She wasn't flash enough for Chambers though, which just showed what a pin-head he was.

'Will do,' Towler said, taking out his phone.

'And once she's done that, I want her checking mispers, any

female between twenty and fifty. Tell her to start with Cumbria but to do a national search if she comes up blank.'

'If she's been in the ground less than a day she may not have been missed yet,' Towler said.

'I know. Do it anyway,' Fluke said. Towler was right but they needed an ID. He couldn't afford to wait until someone started missing her.

'But wouldn't it make more—'

'Look, if we don't get someone straight away, we'll keep trying until we do,' he said. 'For all we know, she's been kept in a freezer for six months and there's a family out there who reported her missing five months and twenty-nine days ago.'

'Fine.'

'And get Alan Vaughn to act as liaison between us and uniform. Introduce him to Don Holland and let him know we're grateful for all the help he's going to offer. He won't like it but he has no choice. His lot will probably have to do a fingertip search of the site for a weapon. Doubt we'll find one but I don't want a kid finding something after we've gone. Get West CID to do the house-to-house enquiries. That'll do for now. I'll look at the office while I'm waiting for Henry.'

Towler walked off without saying anything. Fluke watched him go. They were best friends, had been since they were kids. Fluke was godfather to Towler's daughter, but sometimes Towler's attitude to the more serious cases annoyed him. He was able to look at everything dispassionately, to stop thinking about them as soon as he left work. Fluke, on the other hand, lived and breathed them. The bigger ones *consumed* him. Towler's approach was by far the healthiest but it still got on his pip occasionally.

Fluke knew Sowerby was thorough but could be slow at complex scenes. He guessed it would be at least three hours before the body could be recovered and another hour to the mortuary, which would have to be the Cumberland Infirmary in Carlisle – it was the only hospital in Cumbria that could cope with forensic examinations. Fluke would accompany it, which suited him as he could go and see how much trouble he was in after his earlier stunt. The post-mortem would take about four hours so wouldn't be until the next day. With luck, he wouldn't be late for Michelle. He didn't want another row.

Chapter 4

To avoid any cross-contamination, Fluke changed into a new forensic suit to examine the site office. Rogers opened the door and followed him in with a video camera and portable forensic kit.

Fluke had a quick look round. He hadn't noticed the type of lock but knew the door hadn't been forced. The windows were all secure and there would be no reason for them to be open in winter. Either someone had a key or Dunn was lying about the note.

He didn't really know what the insides of Portakabins were supposed to look like but he imagined they were all similar to the one he was in now: hardwearing carpet, heaters, a small sink, a computer, plastic chairs and the obligatory kettle. Site plans and Dunn's precious schedules adorned the wall. Nothing remarkable. There was no toilet but he'd seen a couple of portaloos outside. It wasn't a place to relax in, but a functional office for people whose primary business was conducted outdoors.

'The note was found here,' Rogers said, pointing at the kettle area.

The cheap plastic kettle sat on a small table ingrained with coffee stains. There was also sugar, instant coffee and a bottle of full-fat milk. Fluke couldn't see a fridge so assumed Dunn brought milk in every day. It hadn't been opened and Fluke guessed Dunn had checked the claims made in the note before he'd made himself a brew. He'd check the statement later.

Towler, having finished his call to Jo Skelton, walked in. Fluke let him have a look round. The big sergeant had good instincts.

'Key?' Towler said.

'That's my guess,' Fluke replied. Criminals much preferred walking into a building rather than breaking in. Breaking in left a forensic transfer. It couldn't be helped. Footprints, fibres, hand and fingerprints, even earprints. He'd heard recently that criminals had a new saying, 'walk in, walk out', referring to the fact that with no forensic evidence, the chances of a conviction in court were slim.

Towler said, 'According to Dunn's statement, he's still got all the keys to the Portakabin. The spares are on the board by the door. My bet is that there'll be one missing. If it was stolen, Dunn might not have noticed.'

Fluke nodded, and Towler disappeared to make another phone call. He continued looking and soon saw what he was searching for.

What he'd expected to find.

He called Rogers over and pointed to the top of the bin under the sink. The can of Coke was half-buried in the debris of everyday life on the site; crisp packets, paper towels and used teabags. 'Photograph that can for me, please?'

He waited a minute while Rogers recorded what was needed. The can was ripped in half.

Although he had rubber gloves on, Fluke took a pen out of his pocket and picked the can up through the drinking hole. It wasn't the bit he wanted but it would still have prints on it.

'So where's the other half,' he said to himself. He carefully removed more rubbish until he found it. It was photographed in situ before he removed it.

He turned it over and saw the brown residue on the concave base.

'Excellent,' said Rogers. 'Heroin?'

Fluke nodded. 'Better than a spoon. Disposable. Can't be arrested for carrying a can of pop.'

'You knew there'd be a can?' he asked.

'No, not a can. But I was expecting evidence of drug use. You'd be amazed at the places addicts call home.'

Rogers put both pieces in separate evidence bags and sealed them.

Fluke searched the rest of the office but found nothing obvious. SOCO would spend days going through it with a fine-tooth comb and gather any trace evidence. It was time to let them get to work. Fluke thanked Rogers and joined Towler who was standing outside.

'So we have a heroin addict who has a key to this place somehow. Shoots up last night and sees something he knows he shouldn't have. He does his civic duty and leaves a note. Doesn't hang around and make our lives easier, mind, but we can't have everything,' he said.

'That's my take.'

'You think he was alone?' Towler asked.

'You ever seen a shooting house? They're a mess, an absolute mess. Nope, this was one person. He's probably been here every night for a week or so, prime site like this. Out the way, warm, no chance of getting his drugs taxed by some of the thugs round here. I'd bet he's been cleaning up after himself, taking his rubbish away with him, so no one's any the wiser. Last night must've shaken him. He panics, forgets his routine and puts the can in the bin. If there were two halves of a can of Coke in the bin every morning, Dunn would've clicked straight away. He's been the only one in here for a while so everything in the bin should have been his.'

'No way his prints aren't everywhere then,' Towler said.

'Everywhere,' Fluke agreed. 'But these Portakabins aren't new. They go from site to site. It'll have hundreds of prints. We'll take them all, obviously, but we'll process the can and the note first. That's how we get him. Or her.'

He was an equal opportunities police officer when it came to drug addicts.

Someone shouted for Fluke and he turned to look. It had come from the outer cordon.

'Ah,' he said. 'The pathologist's here.'

Chapter 5

Even from a distance, Henry Sowerby was a striking man. If you were asked to guess what he did for a living, Fluke suspected a disproportionate amount would say 'mad scientist'. Apart from Towler, he was a foot taller than everyone else and was balding in a way few men do. Rather than receding, it looked more like the dome of his head had forced its way through his hair like a mushroom coming out of grass. He always wore a three-piece tweed suit and carried his equipment in a battered leather case.

Appearances were deceptive though. He was an internationally renowned pathologist. It was only his love of the Lake District and its fells that kept him from taking up a teaching position at any university hospital in the world. He had the sharpest mind of anyone Fluke had met.

He was waiting at the outer cordon, a young woman with him. *His daughter?* Fluke knew both of his children had grown up and flown the nest but that was all he knew.

'Detective Inspector Fluke!' he hailed. Others called out your name, others greeted you, but Sowerby *hailed* you. The only man Fluke had met who did.

'Long time, Avison. Glad to see you're back. You had us all a bit worried for a while,' he said.

They shook hands firmly.

'So what do we have here?' Sowerby said.

Fluke ignored the question. 'Two of you today, Henry?'

'Ah sorry, old boy, where are my manners? Avison, may I

introduce Lucy Cheesebrough? Lucy's doing her PhD in forensic entomology and is seconded to our beloved north-west office for part of her fieldwork.'

Fluke shook the hand she offered. She looked to be in her mid-twenties and appeared small next to Sowerby. She had curly hair, a serious face and wore round glasses. He guessed her pale complexion meant she probably did more labwork than fieldwork. Still, she gave him a smile, and he saw nothing to suggest she wasn't genuinely friendly.

'I want permission for her to observe me working,' Sowerby said.

'Of course,' he said. People learned by doing things so Fluke was always helpful when he could be. He'd never met an entomologist before, never mind a forensic one. He didn't think the victim had been dead long enough for helpful insect activity but it didn't harm to have another discipline looking.

'Pleased to meet you, Lucy,' he said. 'How many crime scenes have you been to?'

'This is my second. I went to a suicide in Blackburn two months ago,' she said.

'Not technically a crime scene then,' Towler smirked.

'It was by the time I'd finished,' she said. 'I told the police that the body had been dead at least two days before they thought it had been. Convinced the coroner to do a post-mortem and Henry confirmed it.'

'That she did,' Sowerby said. 'Anything to add there, Sergeant?'

Towler was trying to not catch anyone's eye.

'Yeah well, good then,' he mumbled.

Fluke liked Lucy Cheesebrough already.

'As much fun as it is watching Sergeant Towler squirm, can you tell me what's happened here, Avison?' Sowerby asked.

'We've got a body in a bag in a hole, Henry. We think the drop was witnessed by a heroin addict. Matt spoke to the coroner after checking it was actually human.'

'Good man,' Sowerby said.

Fluke knew he wasn't joking either. He'd heard the story, they all had, about a new SIO in Cheshire who had called Sowerby out in the early hours during the Easter holidays to a corpse that turned out to be a decomposed pig. The public dressing down he'd received was legendary. Fluke met him from time-to-time at the occasional conference and he'd turned into a good SIO. But later in the bar, all anyone ever did was offer to buy him pork scratchings. One of Towler's phrases had seemed apt at the time: 'If you want sympathy, it's in the dictionary between syphilis and shit.'

'Rogers has erected a tent and put footboards down. I've had a look but not been in. Other than Matt, the responding officer and the man who discovered her, no one else has been near,' he said.

'OK, let's have a chat with Rogers and see what we can come up with,' Sowerby said.

Thirty minutes later, and without any further incidents, a recovery plan was agreed.

While the SOCO team were processing the outer cordon, taking photographs and videos of the myriad tyre and footprints, the uniformed officers from Whitehaven began their fingertip search. *Nice bit of laundry for them to do, tonight*, Fluke thought as he watched them crawling through the sticky cold mud. Not one of them was smiling, he noticed. But in a command-and-control structure such as the police, not one of them was complaining either. Not openly anyway.

The ladder Towler had used was still there, and after Rogers had been down to video the scene, Sowerby followed Fluke into the hole, which was just big enough for the three of them to stand without crowding the body. The temperature seemed to be a couple of degrees cooler at the bottom. Not as cold as a freezer but colder than a fridge. It would have taken the body a long time to decompose.

'Lucy,' Sowerby called without looking up to where she was peering in. 'Keep your hands in your pockets.'

'I don't have any,' she called back down, confused. 'I've got some gloves in the car.'

'It's an expression, dear. Means don't touch anything until you've asked Avison. It's his crime scene, not mine,' he replied. He turned to Fluke and said, 'Now, let's have a look at your victim.'

He placed a thermometer beside the golf bag to take the ambient temperature. He'd use it to calculate a time of death when he had the victim's temperature to compare it to. Fluke knew in the past he'd have used a complicated chart called Henssge's nomogram but now, like everything else it seemed, it was done electronically. He probably had an app for it.

Sowerby worked methodically taking notes and collecting samples. Fluke watched him but he and Rogers had seen it done enough times for it not to fascinate them any more. He knew nothing that was happening would result in any immediate answers. They were samples for the lab to work on.

He busied himself with looking round the hole. It seemed deeper now that he was at the bottom. Looking up at the skyline, Fluke couldn't help feeling that he was in a grave.

In a way he was.

After calling out instructions for Rogers to take more samples – hair, mud, swabs and tapings – Sowerby stood and stared at the body.

'Tough one this, Avison. Can't do the rectal temperature. I don't want to take her out of the bag here, too much evidence will be lost. Can't do the intimate swabs either. Sean can do the ones on the head but that's it. Best we can do is protect the head with a bag to avoid losing anything else. Can't give you a TOD yet, I'm afraid, Avison.'

Fluke wasn't worried. He'd rather have an accurate time of death later than an inaccurate one now.

Sowerby looked at the steep sides of the hole. Fluke could tell what he was thinking. How much evidence would be lost when they removed her?

'What to do? What to do?' Sowerby said to himself. 'It's your call at the end of the day, Avison. We can risk moving her and get everything this lady still has to tell us, or we could try to do a rudimentary examination down here and almost certainly contaminate things.'

Fluke didn't hesitate. 'I want her out, Henry. I'm not leaving her in here any longer than I have to. Give her some dignity back.'

'Let's get it done then,' Sowerby said with an appreciative look. 'You'll need to call your chums in Mountain Rescue. We'll need one of their specialist stretchers.'

The body was recovered without too much damage, although Fluke and Sowerby winced at every bump and scrape as she was manhandled onto the commandeered stretcher and pulled out of her intended grave. It was taken to the vehicle that would transport her to the mortuary. A private company provided that service in Cumbria.

'I'll get someone to sit in the van with her on the way back. I'll follow in my car,' Fluke said to Sowerby.

'I'm bringing Lucy into the PM, see what her views are on this. She tells me that if a body dies in the open it only takes ten minutes for flies to lay eggs in the mouth, nose and eyes.'

'Lovely,' Fluke said.

'So, depending on what she finds, it's possible she can give us an edge on determining where she was killed. Might help with time of death too.'

Fluke turned to look for Lucy but she was heading back to the car she and Sowerby had arrived in. 'I've never worked a case with an entomologist before. I've read the manuals and been to the briefings but I'm not sure of their value yet,' he said.

'It's a tricky one, Avison. She'll be the first to admit that, from a forensic point of view, the UK still lags behind the States and mainland Europe. The science is sound, you understand, no one's disputing that. The problem is relying on it in court. Too easy for defence teams to muddy the water with their own experts.'

'Juries here aren't yet ready to convict someone on the say-so of a creepy-crawly?' Fluke asked, only half joking.

'There's a bit of that, certainly. She knows all this and accepts the limitations. She was being serious before. She overturned the police view in Lancashire about that suicide. Don't think they have anyone for it yet, but they will, now they're looking.'

'I'm not refusing any help on this one,' Fluke said.

'Excellent. Until tomorrow then. I've booked the post-mortem suite for ten o'clock.'

Chapter 6

Chambers rang as Fluke was driving back and he pulled over in the nearest lay-by. There was no point in risking a pull for using his mobile at the wheel. Gone were the days where you could flash your warrant card and be on your way. Try that and you'd be up in front of Professional Standards on a corruption charge.

As soon as Fluke pressed receive, Chambers started talking. He could hear people in the background. Chambers was on a speakerphone and would be playing to an audience.

'What's happening, Fluke?' he barked.

Fluke tried to explain the situation, how he suspected that there was more to the murder than they'd originally thought. He was starting to venture an early theory that it was a professional killing when Chambers cut him off.

'When you hear hooves, think horses, Fluke, not zebras.'

Fluke winced. It was Chambers's favourite saying and a standing joke in FMIT. He could imagine the officers within earshot cringing with embarrassment.

'We don't know who she is yet, sir,' Fluke said as if he hadn't been interrupted. 'We've only just got her out the ground and the PM's not until tomorrow. It's possible that—'

'OK, Fluke. Keep me updated.'

And with that, he rang off. Fluke stared at the phone for a second before throwing it on the passenger seat and starting the engine again. What Chambers would never understand with good detective work was that sometimes when you heard hooves the best thing to do was think zebras. That's how difficult cases were closed.

Fluke had never really understood where Chambers's antagonism had come from. Fluke knew Towler thought he made too much of it, that Chambers was a prick but harmless. Fluke suspected it was because he was a threat to his authority. Chambers was in a job that was beyond him and knew that Fluke knew. Fluke was at least one rank lower than he should have been. He'd attended and easily passed the required courses but each time there was a chance of promotion, he either said the wrong thing or spoke his mind once too often. It didn't bother him; being an inspector suited him for now, it was the optimum balance between power and responsibility. Senior enough to get things done but not so senior that he was behind a desk all day.

Normally the rudeness of Chambers didn't trouble him but this time it had preyed on his mind and he was in a bad mood when he pulled up outside Michelle's house. Three other cars were already in the drive.

Bollocks.

He'd forgotten about her big dinner party. Something to do with a new job one of her vacuous friends had just started. That was all he needed; an evening of forced conversation, enduring their excruciatingly dull chatter.

Michelle met him at the door, and although she didn't say anything, he could tell she was annoyed he hadn't bothered to go home and get changed. He still had building-site mud on his suit. She'd have something to say later, of that he was sure. She ushered him into the lounge, turning her head to avoid the offered kiss.

'Well, Avison has decided to join us at last. We can eat.'

He helped himself to a single malt whisky, drank it without bothering with ice and poured himself another. He followed everyone into her cramped dining room. Michelle was perched beside a young man in his twenties. They were already giggling together. Michelle whispered something into his ear and he looked up at Fluke before giggling again.

Fluke wondered why he didn't care.

The only seat left was beside a middle-aged man he hadn't met before. Parts of his face were losing their fight with gravity. His jowls were uneven. Fluke offered his hand but the man either didn't see it or chose to ignore it.

He reached for the red wine and settled down to ignore everyone.

An hour later his mood hadn't improved. The meal was going slowly; so far they'd only had a starter of figs and cured meats. Food he didn't understand, eaten in the company of people he didn't like. Fluke had managed to avoid speaking to anyone while at the same time drinking most of the bottle of red himself. He wasn't a big drinker and was feeling drunk.

As everybody else seemed to be engrossed with an anecdote someone else he didn't know was telling, Fluke thought about the case and what he needed to do next. Identifying the body was going to be a priority. He hoped the prints or DNA Sowerby had taken that afternoon would prove to be helpful but he wasn't counting on it. The post-mortem would be crucial. He didn't have a cause of, manner of, or time of death yet. He wanted answers to all three the next day.

He became vaguely aware that the table had gone silent and he looked up. Everyone was looking at him.

'I'm sorry, I must've missed that,' he said apologetically.

Michelle glared at him.

The man beside him, who still hadn't introduced himself, spoke. 'I was just saying, Inspector, with all these children being abducted and killed, isn't it time we brought back hanging?'

'What children?' Fluke said blankly.

'All these children in the news? The ones being murdered.'

Fluke had no idea what he was talking about. 'I'm sorry, have I missed something? I haven't seen the news today.'

'We were talking hypothetically, Inspector,' he said, rolling his eyes.

'Who are you again?'

The man held his hand out. 'Charles. We were just talking about Ian's new job as a journalist.'

Fluke ignored his hand just as his had been ignored earlier. He put down his drink. 'I thought someone just said Ian's new job was selling advertising space with the free paper?' He could feel Michelle's stare.

'It's still journalism,' the man sitting beside Michelle said indignantly.

Ian presumably. Fluke decided not to press the matter.

'No, I don't,' he said, turning to Charles.

'Don't what?' Charles asked.

'No, I don't think that we should bring back hanging.'

'You don't? I bet that's a first for a policeman. I'm sure if we asked the rest of them they'd agree with me,' Charles said.

Fluke emptied his glass and poured another. 'I don't give a shit,' he murmured.

'I'm sorry!'

'Has there been a recent spate of child killings I'm unaware of?' he asked.

'Of course, man. You only have to read the papers. Murderers and rapists everywhere, crime at record levels. It's been going up since National Service was abolished.'

He was slurring and obviously a fool, and on any other day Fluke would have let it go. Maybe it was because he'd just spent hours alongside a corpse but tonight he found he didn't want to.

'No, it isn't,' he said coldly. 'Crime's at an all-time low.'

'Nonsense, read a paper, man. Crime's rampant. Bringing back National Service would be the best thing this government could do.'

'Why?'

He clearly hadn't thought his argument through any further than the headlines. 'Discipline. Give all the scroungers a sense of discipline,' he said finally and looked at Fluke as if daring him to disagree.

Fluke stared at him. Charles tried to hold his gaze but was no match and he quickly lowered his eyes.

'Yes, well, you've obviously never served. If you had, you'd know the sense of pride you get from wearing a uniform.'

His voice dropped. 'I was a Royal Marines Commando for six years. I did two tours of Northern Ireland and fought in the Gulf War. Remind me what war you fought in, *Charlie*.'

Michelle, knowing that the quieter he got the angrier he was becoming, decided to step in. 'I'm sure we can agree to disagree. Can't we, Avison?'

Fluke paused. He was breathing heavily and gripping his wine-glass stem so hard his fingers were white. 'Fine,' he said eventually.

'But surely you agree that child rapists should be hung?' Ian said, clearly annoyed by Fluke's dismissal of his new job and oblivious to the mental weather change. 'In my humble opinion, if they knew they were going to be hung they would think twice.'

In Fluke's world there was no such thing as a humble opinion, only ill-informed ones. He noticed Ian was also slurring. Was there anyone in the room who wasn't drunk? 'Hanged.'

'Excuse me?'

'It's not hung, it's hanged. And no, I don't.'

An attractive, short-haired woman, who, to the best of Fluke's recollection, hadn't said anything all evening, decided to speak. 'Can I ask why, Inspector?' she asked softly.

Fluke couldn't sense any condescension in her question and calmed down slightly. 'It's simple actually. You've heard the expression "You may as well be *hanged* for a sheep as for a lamb"?'

She nodded.

39

'It's the same principle. I don't want rapes turning into murders because there's nothing to be gained by leaving a living witness.'

Fluke wasn't simply disagreeing for the sake of it, although the mood he was in, he would have. No one sensible in the criminal justice system thought increased punishments were a good idea. And the people who wanted hanging brought back were either too stupid or too ignorant to understand the subtle nuances of sentencing. Fluke really didn't want every paedophile and rapist locked up for life. That was what would be risked if the sentences for murder and rape were the same. Tough on crime? The only people it would be tough on would be the victims.

She said nothing in reply, and Fluke got the feeling she'd already known the answer and she was, in her own way, showing up the fools surrounding them.

'In other words, not having capital punishment saves lives. It's as simple as that,' he added.

That seemed to kill the atmosphere, such as it was. The woman raised her glass to him and winked. Fluke noticed she was drinking water.

Not everyone in the room was drunk it seemed.

The rest of the night passed uneventfully, with everyone, including the mystery woman, leaving Fluke alone. By eleven o'clock, he was feeling sober again and had the beginnings of a headache. By half-past eleven it had turned into a full-blown hangover and all he wanted to do was go to bed and get ready for the post-mortem the next day. Michelle had other ideas.

'We need to talk,' she said when the last guest had left.

That was all he needed. Another row about the same thing. He didn't like her friends and they didn't like him. Sometimes he thought that Michelle only tolerated him because it had seemed glamorous to go out with someone who investigated murder for a living. A year into the relationship though and she'd realised that there was nothing glamorous about the job or him. He was sure he'd let her down somehow. He just didn't know how. And worst of all, he didn't care enough to find out. 'Can we do this tomorrow? I've had a bit of a day.'

She was strangely calm, far calmer than on the previous occasions they'd discussed his lack of social graces. 'No, Avison, we can't. I don't think there should be a tomorrow.'

Fluke said nothing. He knew it had been on the cards. They hadn't been getting on for a while now. Looking back, he wondered if they ever had. For her, he'd been a talking point among her friends; for him, it had been easier to say yes when she asked him out than think of a reason to say no. If he was honest, he felt relieved. 'I'll take the sofa, I'll be gone by the time you wake up.'

She looked at him. The anger was there now, bubbling under the surface, ready to erupt at the slightest provocation. Perhaps she wanted one final argument. Perhaps she was angry he'd taken it so calmly, that he hadn't wanted to fight for her. 'Will you fuck,' she snarled. 'You think I want you in this house after you humiliated Ian like that? I want you out now.'

Fluke nearly replied that Ian had humiliated himself but instead he reached for his coat and left without another word. It dawned on him that he hadn't noticed Ian leave and wondered if that was the real reason she was so keen to get him out.

'And when were you *ever* here when I woke up?' she screamed at his retreating back, before slamming the door.

Fluke had a dilemma. He'd drunk too much to drive and lived too far away for a taxi. He'd have to sleep in his car. He fumbled in his coat for his keys.

'I hope you're not planning to drive, Inspector?'

Fluke turned round. The woman from the dinner party was leaning against the bonnet of her car, smoking a cigarette and blowing thick plumes into the freezing night air. She was smiling.

'Just getting something out the car,' he replied.

She obviously recognised that as the lie it was. She raised her eyebrows. 'And that was Michelle shouting "Hurry back" before she slammed the door on you, was it?'

'She's just in a bad mood is all. She gets like this sometimes,' he mumbled, embarrassed.

'What, you thought you were just going to say sorry and make up, did you? Have you not met her before?'

For some reason he felt he should stick up for her. 'She's right, I was wrong. They're her friends and I'm always rude to them. She'll be all right in a couple of days.'

'She won't, Avison, you must know that. This was a make-or-break dinner for you tonight, and you, my grumpy friend, broke it.' She was still smiling as she talked. 'I wonder why you don't seem too bothered. Is it because, apart from you and me, everyone in there tonight was an absolute arsehole?' She held up her hand as Fluke started to protest. 'Michelle's the worst one. Anyone could see you were dead on your feet and upset about something. They deserved everything you gave them.'

'Yeah, well, what's happened has happened,' he said, as if that was any sort of explanation. 'Who are you, anyway? You don't seem Michelle's usual type of friend.'

'I'm the person giving you a lift home tonight.'

Chapter 7

Fluke was woken by his hangover; drained but raring to go on the first full day of the investigation. Moving day, he called it. By the evening he hoped to have a sense of where they were going, whether they were in it for the long haul, whether he'd need more resources or whether he could release some.

He brushed his teeth, rinsed and spat. He looked down into the sink. There was even more blood than usual. Probably due to the excessive alcohol of the night before. The MedicAlert bracelet that Doctor Cooper had given him, and which he never wore, sat next to his toothpaste, mocking him. He checked the back of his hand and saw what he expected. It was heavily bruised where the cannula had been.

If his blood was that thin, he'd best avoid taking aspirin. He was going to have to tough out his hangover.

He started his coffee machine then showered. By the time he was out, the coffee was ready and Fluke poured himself a large cup, black. He took it back into the bathroom so he could drink while he shaved.

A late night and early start meant that the face he saw in the mirror was even more haggard than usual. He was only forty but his dark hair was already salted with grey. He rubbed his dark stubble before smothering his face with shaving gel.

He picked up his razor, looked at it and put it back down. He couldn't risk getting a nick – it would take hours to heal. Perhaps he should have stayed for the plasma after all. He clearly needed it. He reached for his facecloth and removed the gel. He picked up his electric shaver and pushed the on button. It buzzed into life and he looked into the mirror as he ran the whirring blades over his chin.

His most striking feature stared back in the reflection. Normal to him, fascinating to others.

Fluke had heterochromia. His eyes were different colours. One was a vivid blue; the other was multi-coloured, dark green from any distance over five feet. Sometimes he could see people looking at him uneasily, aware something wasn't quite right but not able to put their finger on it. Subliminal unease, he called it.

He occasionally used it to good effect in interviews but most of the time he simply forgot about it. At school, an older boy, trying to impress some girls, called him 'lighthouse' once. Towler had broken his nose and the nickname hadn't stuck although 'flat nose' had for the bully.

As he shaved he thought about the surreal ride home with the mystery woman. He'd accepted the lift readily, a night on the backseat of his car hadn't appealed to him. Despite asking, he still didn't know her name although she seemed to know all about him. They didn't discuss Michelle again or what had happened at dinner. Instead, they'd fallen into an easy conversation about their jobs. She was a solicitor specialising in international law. They both understood crime, albeit from different perspectives. Fluke's job was to catch criminals and hers was to get them off. His criminals were low-life scum; hers were countries. Although his head had been a little wine-fogged, he couldn't recall having had such a challenging and stimulating conversation for a long time.

It was only when they were about two miles from his house that he realised he hadn't given her any directions. She seemed to know roughly where he lived and only asked for help when the small road they were on turned into a succession of dirt tracks.

'Every time you see a smaller track, take it,' he'd told her.

Eventually, Fluke had been able to point her in the direction of his own road and she'd pulled up next to his house.

He'd got out of the car but before he could ask her in for a nightcap, she'd smiled enigmatically, waved once and driven off. When her car got to the end of his track, she honked the horn and drove away. He stood and stared, bemused, wondering if he'd ever see her again. He watched the retreating headlights until they disappeared, then pulled out his phone and rang Towler to arrange a lift into town to collect his car first thing in the morning.

He finished shaving and drained his coffee. Finding something to wear that didn't have mud on, he got dressed. Using his bedroom mirror, he fastened a cheap tie. Even he thought he looked unkempt. It wasn't that he dressed badly, it was just that anything he wore immediately looked scruffy. Losing so much weight so quickly hadn't helped. Towler used to call him a typical fat marine. He hadn't been, of course, he'd been on the right side of stocky. As an ex-marine, an elite force trained to march huge distances with heavy loads, he'd been extremely fit. Now his clothes hung from him like he was a child playing dress-up.

Back in his kitchen, he filled his travel mug with the rest of the coffee, remembering to turn off the machine. He'd lost count of the number of times he'd forgotten and come back to a solid, coffee-smelling mess on the bottom of another ruined jug. He went through five or six a year. He was debating whether or not he had time to sit on his porch and drink it when he heard a car pulling up.

Towler. They had a post-mortem to attend.

For the second time in two days, Fluke found himself at the Cumberland Infirmary. He decided he'd go and see Doctor Cooper after the PM; he wouldn't get away with fobbing her off twice in two days. He stuck his head round the door in the ward and told a nurse he'd be with her in a couple of hours. She promised to pass on the message.

The mortuary was in the basement of the hospital. He flashed his badge at the elderly man in the office and was waved through. He'd been there enough times for the staff to know him. Carlisle didn't have a dedicated forensic mortuary – there wasn't the demand for full-time specialist facilities like that in Cumbria – so one of the post-mortem suites had to be adapted each time the coroner requested a forensic examination. It didn't have the glass viewing rooms some did, so he would be in the same room as the victim.

The suite Sowerby was using was typical of all mortuaries. Fluke shivered. He could feel the air conditioning and hear the hum of the cold chambers. They were permanently turned on. The bodies could be stored indefinitely at minus 20 °C and, as the Cumberland Infirmary was the only hospital for forty miles, it was never short of business.

The room had an unpleasant personality. It smelled of chemicals and detergents. There were large sinks, drains and sluices, a room that disposed of large amounts of liquid. *Organic* liquid.

White-tiled floor and white-tiled walls; easy to keep clean and easy to hose down. Laminated notices on the walls detailed actions to be taken in the event of biohazards being discovered. It was a room where preserving the dignity of the dead took second place to uncovering their secrets.

Fluke hated it.

In the middle, under huge halogen lights, was the dissection table. The victim was already on it, still in the golf bag.

Towler was already there, gowned and with protective coverings on his feet, laughing with Lucy. Fluke didn't want to know about what. Sowerby was discussing something with the mortuary technician. Alan Vaughn was there to act as the exhibits officer, and a SOCO officer Fluke didn't recognise was preparing sample swabs and tubes. Everyone looked ready.

Fluke finished putting on his gown and foot covers, and entered the suite.

'We ready?' Sowerby asked everyone as he walked towards the body.

Sowerby was one of those pathologists who said everything out loud. Instructions, comments and observations were all recorded on the built-in digital system. After some standard introductions of who was present, what the time was and which hospital they were in, he began.

'The body was recovered yesterday at a building site adjacent to the West Cumberland Hospital, in what I am told is a foundation hole. Preliminary police enquiries suggest that the body had been in situ for no more than twelve hours. It is still in the golf bag it was recovered in. It is covered in mud, consistent with where it was found. Hopefully, whoever put her in it inadvertently left the victim cleaner than she would have been if she'd simply been interred without it. The golf bag was too big to go into a cadaver bag. I have observed the head only. The victim appears to be female. Until I have had a chance to remove her from the bag, I will not estimate age or make a statement on ethnicity.'

Fluke tuned out as Sowerby directed the technician on where to photograph and what external swabs should be taken. At that point, they would only be taking samples of what was accessible: her head. They'd already taken them at the scene but were taking them again as a precaution.

Fluke's mind went into screensaver mode as the routine part of the PM continued. He thought through what the priorities were going to be again. Identifying the body was going to be key, and Fluke hoped it would be easy. With an identification, a list of people to interview could be drawn up. And with a list of people to interview, a suspect list could be drawn up. The rest was usually a slam-dunk.

Usually.

47

Although Fluke still couldn't rule out a domestic homicide, he suspected he was looking at something different this time. It looked too professional to have been committed in the heat of the moment. While Fluke had been making arrangements to see Doctor Cooper after the post-mortem, Towler had received a phone call from Jo Skelton. She'd finished setting up the incident room and had got to work on the misper list. Early indications were that the victim wasn't a Cumbrian. Skelton was widening the enquiry to cover the whole of the UK but it would take time. Fluke would get a photo of the victim's head to help her as soon as he could.

The foundation hole was obviously a deposition site, and therefore his second priority was to find the murder scene.

Finding the person who wrote the note also needed to happen fast and Fluke expected a fingerprint match by the time the PM finished. It was unlikely that an intravenous heroin user would be unknown to the police.

After the photographs, Sowerby and the technician struggled to remove her from the golf bag. 'Some *rigor mortis* is evident,' Sowerby said. He paused and picked up some heavy-duty shears. 'Sorry, Avison. I'm going to have to cut the bag to get her out.'

Fluke nodded. It was preferable to damaging evidence on her body.

Five minutes later, she was laid out on the table and the golf bag was handed over to SOCO to process. As Sowerby had predicted, the bag had protected her from the mud of the building site and she was spotless.

'Don't forget to check the pockets of that thing,' Towler said.

Fluke looked at her lifeless face and fought the urge to reach out and brush the hair that had fallen over her milky, flat eyes. Gravity had emptied her lips of blood. Her skin was waxy, almost translucent.

48

Some detectives tried to keep things impersonal so they could maintain objectivity. For Fluke, it was the opposite. He worked at his best when he made a personal connection with the victim.

She'd been tossed away like garbage, he thought. He could feel the anger building in his stomach.

Sowerby removed her clothing, cutting everything rather than undressing her. It was the best way to preserve evidence. She'd been dressed casually but smartly in trousers and matching jacket. Her shoes were black with small heels and she was wearing stockings.

Looking down at her naked body, stiff with *rigor* and displayed like a laboratory rat, Fluke guessed she'd be in her mid-thirties. She'd clearly been attractive, beautiful in fact.

The technician fingerprinted her before taking a series of X-rays. A printer whirred into life in an adjoining room. Although X-rays were digitally viewed during a coroner's post-mortem, there were always hard copies made for the files.

Sowerby and the technician had to massage the body to counteract the *rigor* before they could start the external examination of her front. Fluke had always thought it looked obscene. He knew it had to be done but he decided to look away while they did it. He noticed Towler and Lucy were doing the same. It was a small gesture but to Fluke it was important. Anything that could be done to preserve her dignity, even in death, was worth the effort. Sowerby started talking again and Fluke turned back round.

'Slight tearing of the vagina, possible recent sexual activity. Can you take a deep swab, please?' Sowerby asked the technician.

He continued with a close examination, speaking into the microphone.

He lifted up her left hand and studied it with a magnifying glass, then put it down. The nails were painted a vibrant turquoise and were beautifully manicured. He picked up the right and did the same. 'Can you get me an evidence bag, please?' Picking up a

49

small scraping tool, he removed something from the underside of her long nails. He put it into a small plastic tube and handed it to Fluke.

Fluke held it up to the light to have a look. It was a tiny grain of something, dark brown. 'Any idea?'

'Not a clue, not for me to speculate either. That's why we have a lab.'

He went back to the body and moved the big overhead light above her head. Fluke handed the tube to the SOCO man who put it into an evidence bag. Out of the corner of his eye, Fluke noticed Lucy walk over and ask to see it.

'It's difficult to be sure, but it looks like there's some slight haemorrhaging in the eyes,' Sowerby said, looking at Fluke.

'Strangled?'

'Normally I'd say that's as good a guess as anything right now but there's nothing else to support that. No marks on the neck.'

'What then?' Towler asked.

'Patience, boy. We've only just started. We won't leave here until you and Avison have something,' Sowerby said, not unkindly. Everyone in the room had the same goal.

'Looks like she may have had cosmetic surgery at some point; nose correction, poor one by the look. If they've moved bone around, I'll know more when I open her up. Nothing else of note on the anterior.'

As the body was carefully turned over, Sowerby commented, 'She's been moved after death occurred. No uniform lividity.'

Fluke knew that if a corpse lay undisturbed, *livor mortis*, where blood obeyed the laws of gravity and settled at the lowest point, set in. If someone died on their back then the blood drained from their front and settled underneath before clotting, causing a difference in colour. White on top, purple on the bottom, like cream on raspberries. If the body was moved before the process had finished then lividity was interrupted and *livor* wouldn't be uniform. The victim on the table had purple and white patches competing with each other. She had been moved in the first few hours after her death. It didn't really help; it only confirmed what they already suspected – that the building site wasn't where she'd been killed.

Fluke noticed Lucy had finished looking at whatever had been found under the victim's nails and was back observing. Earlier, he'd wondered if she'd ever attended a PM before. Now he knew.

She was obviously struggling with being in the proximity of a dead body, and he wondered whether she'd asked to see the sample just to take time out. Her eyes were red and glistening but she was yet to cry.

Wait until the bone saw buzzes and the top of the head comes off, he thought.

In those situations some people gave up and left. Fluke had experienced it, the embarrassed pause while they walked out. It shouldn't be, but it was a walk of shame. Lucy appeared determined to stay, however. She was making notes, pages of them. Sowerby had let her have a look at the body before he started with the external examination, and she'd stated there were no signs of insect activity. Fluke would give her a call the next day, find out how she was and what 'no insect activity' meant in her world. He suspected it meant that the victim had been either stuffed in the bag immediately or it had been too cold. Probably a bit of both.

Sowerby glanced up, saw where Fluke was looking and gave him a slight nod of approval.

He bent back down. 'Gotcha,' he said quietly. 'Avison, come over here and have a look.'

Fluke did.

And the room got that little bit colder . . .

The bullet hole was in the back of her skull; partially covered by hair but still visible. Surrounding blood on the wound had clotted. It was almost black.

51

'There is a hole in the occipital bone,' Sowerby said. 'Possible GSW. Photographs, please.'

The technician moved round with his camera.

Sowerby would say nothing definite until he had the cold, hard facts to support it but he didn't need to – they all knew she'd been shot.

Execution style, Fluke thought.

A bullet hole ruled out someone covering up an accidental death. It had been a long shot anyway. FMIT officially had what Fluke had known since yesterday: a murder to investigate.

Fluke also knew that the bullet hole could reveal a lot more than simply the cause of death. It could reveal the manner by which it was inflicted. Bullets entering from an angle leave an oval-shaped entrance wound. When the gun is held against the body, the wound will be round and have burn marks from the muzzle flame. Short-range shots will leave powder residue tattooed into the skin. Longer-range shots will leave no burns or powder but the hole will be smaller than the bullet calibre, due to the skin's elastic properties. When a gun is pressed against bone and fired, the bone slows the gasses down, forcing them backwards against the skin and leaving a star-shaped wound.

Despite the dry blood and hair, the bullet hole was clearly star-shaped.

It was also small.

Which meant a small-calibre gun had been pressed against the back of his victim's head and fired. Not enough power to go straight through the head or they would have seen the exit wound. The bullet would have bounced round the inside of the skull, shredding the brain. Haemorrhaging the eyes.

A professional killer's weapon.

A professional killer's technique.

No noise, no mess and absolutely no chance of survival.

After Sowerby had carefully shaved the surrounding area and

measured and photographed the wound, he shouted across to the technician, 'Are those X-rays ready yet, boy?'

'Yes, sir.'

'Get them on the damned light board, man. Stop wasting time.'

The technician ignored the fact he'd been shouted at unfairly and put up the slide of the head.

There was no bullet.

'I don't understand,' Lucy said frowning and craning forward. 'It has to be in there.'

'Bullets don't follow straight lines, Lucy,' Sowerby said. 'It could be anywhere. Get the next slide up.'

'Saw someone shot in the knee in Somalia, once. Bullet came out his arse. Funny as fuck,' Towler said to no one in particular.

'Sergeant Towler,' Fluke said.

'Boss?'

'Shut up.'

Towler winked at Lucy but didn't add anything.

They found it on the third plate. In the abdomen.

'There you go, Lucy. Bullet's probably bounced off the inside of the skull, through the roof of the mouth, down the oesophagus into the stomach and into the duodenum. We'll get it later,' Sowerby said.

After the external examination was completed, it was time for the internal. The body was turned back over, the head raised by a body block. Sowerby was going against standard routine and starting at the head rather than the body cavity. He had a probable cause of death and would move quickly to confirm it. He knew Fluke could use the extra time.

Fluke was sure he knew what the COD and MOD would be. Cause of death would be the brain injury; manner of death would be a gunshot wound. It was more than they had yesterday, although it raised more questions than it answered.

Sowerby picked up a scalpel and made an incision behind one

ear, cutting across the top of the head to the other ear. As if the victim had been wearing a face mask, he peeled the skin from the skull in two directions. The front was pulled down, exposing the top of the skull and the face; the other was pulled back, exposing the rear. The skull was now bloody but bare.

Sowerby would remove a wedge-shaped section of bone to get access to the brain. Fluke turned away not wanting to watch. Once was enough for anyone. He found he didn't want to stay any more.

There were going to be some routine procedures for the next hour. He'd nip out and see if Doctor Cooper was back so he could apologise for leaving so abruptly the day before.

'Boss?' Towler called after him.

'I need to see someone,' Fluke replied, without turning.

The Stryker saw shrieked into life. Fluke knew that the pitch would change as it bit into the skull and he sped up. He wanted to be out of earshot before it happened.

Before Fluke had even left the mortuary he'd changed his mind. He wasn't going to be in a position to have more plasma until after the PM anyway. He decided he'd rather grab a brew in the main foyer than have a fight with his haematologist about his disappearing act the day before.

He was in the queue and about to place his order, when his phone rang. It was Towler. Fluke had only been out of the mortuary for five minutes. 'We've found something,' Towler said.

'In the brain?'

'In the golf bag,' Towler replied.

Fluke sighed, smiled ruefully at the waiting barista and headed back towards the mortuary.

The 'something' was a small notebook.

'SOCO found it in an internal pocket. There's some other stuff, electronics mainly: a phone, a tablet and a laptop. All smashed to bits and there's no SIM in the phone. The notebook's empty but it looks like the top page has been torn off,' Towler said. 'It could have been already there, I suppose, but despite it being covered in shit, the bag looks brand new to me. If the notebook was put there by the killer then it wasn't meant to be found.'

Fluke didn't know if it was evidence or not but he wasn't taking any chances. 'Right, I want the full works. Tell the lab I'm pre-authorising all the tests they want to do. Get it there tonight. Proper chain of custody. If there's anything, I want to know by tomorrow at the latest, today if possible. Get uniform to drive it down now.'

As Towler went off to arrange a fast-track forensic examination, Fluke turned to Sowerby who was just starting the 'Y' incision.

'Anything else, Henry?' he asked.

'Nothing really, Avison. We've taken our external samples now: hair, pubic hair, swabs, the lot. Got confirmation prints for you. The brown substance under her nails looks like it may have found its way into the turn-ups of her trousers as well, according to your SOCO man there. The lab will tell you if they're the same. Can't say what it is.'

'Cause of death the gunshot wound then?'

'Technically the cause of death can't be officially determined until I've finished. But yes, the bullet seems to have ricocheted around the inside of the skull causing massive trauma to the brain. That'll almost certainly be the COD. I'll have the bullet with you in five minutes if you can wait.'

'Here till the bitter end, Doc,' Fluke replied.

'Don't you have an appointment with Leah Cooper?'

'What? No. Yes. How did you know?' Fluke said, all semblance of composure lost. He looked round.

'Don't worry, no one heard, Avison. No, I popped into haematology before I came down here; the professor there is an old friend of mine. Leah asked if you were the senior investigating officer.'

'She seem angry?'

55

'Not especially, not with you anyway. She told me not to keep you too long, said you had a blood test to do before the day was out. Told her it would take as long as it damn well took. She nearly tore my head off.'

If she wasn't angry about the day before he may as well go and get checked now. 'Look, this bit is going to take about two hours, am I right? I'll go and get it over with; Towler will ring if anything urgent crops up.'

Sowerby didn't look up but waved a hand to let him know it was fine.

Fluke got to the haematology ward and asked for Leah, only to be told by the staff nurse that she'd just left.

'OK,' he said, relieved. 'Can you leave a message and say I called in, as she asked? I'll come back later.'

'Not happening, Mr Fluke. She left clear instructions that you have to have another blood test today. Very clear instructions. I'll take the blood and run it straight away. You can go after one of the registrars has had a look at it. Unless they say you can't, obviously.'

'Obviously,' he repeated, a bit too sharply.

Two minutes later, Fluke had a doctor trying to stick a cannula in the back of his hand. The first two attempts missed.

Fluke hated cannulas. Doctors always struggled to find veins, a legacy of his treatment. On the odd occasion he was having blood taken by someone who wasn't familiar with his medical history, he always ended up giving an explanation. The most common reason for poor veins was intravenous drug use and Fluke felt compelled to tell them his condition was due to chemotherapy, not heroin.

His hand would be stiff in the morning. It was getting to the point now that every time he had his bloods taken, his hand froze up during the night. Today it was the turn of a small Asian doctor he'd seen on the ward but had never spoken to, one of the multitude of junior doctors hospitals seemed to spawn.

'Sharp scratch,' she said, as she tried again.

Chapter 8

'Sharp scratch.'

Fluke vividly remembered the first time he'd heard that phrase. It was at the Patterdale Ward in the West Cumberland Hospital two years earlier. He'd thought then what an odd phrase it was, to describe a needle puncturing flesh as a scratch, and he still thought it now. And they all said it: doctors, nurses, phlebotomists, the lot. He assumed it was part of some blood-letting course. Or it could be the same as detectives picking up evidence with pens. Monkey see, monkey do. The first doctor to say it had no idea he was starting a global phenomenon.

At the time, the only thing on Fluke's mind had been getting out of a relationship that had run its course. Hayley, a nice woman, recently divorced and trying to rediscover her youth, but she needed someone younger. Someone who still wanted to go out on Friday and Saturday nights. Fluke wasn't that man.

She'd phoned earlier asking if they could go clubbing and Fluke had lied, saying he wasn't feeling well. He'd reheated the previous night's corned beef hash and settled down in front of the TV for the night. And in truth, he had been feeling a bit unwell, a sore stomach that had been bothering him for some time. Not enough for painkillers, but enough for him to go and see his GP.

But Hayley had called his bluff and turned up anyway. She took one look and called the emergency doctor's number. Fluke would never know whether she'd been trying to make a point or she genuinely thought he looked ill. He'd been using the 'too ill' excuse more and more to get out of things.

Whatever her real motivation, he'd been given an immediate appointment. Despite living in Carlisle, the out-of-hours appointment was thirty-five miles away at the old Workington Hospital. Trapped in his own lie, he had no choice but to play along and attend. Hayley had even driven him there.

Lying on a bed in a ward that wouldn't have looked out of place in a Hammer Horror film, Fluke had been expecting the standard 'I can't find anything, see your GP if it persists', a doctor's code for 'piss off and stop wasting our time'.

That wasn't what was in Fluke's immediate future however – the doctor found something. And he hadn't had to look too hard either. His lower right abdomen was as hard as iron. When he felt it, he was amazed he hadn't noticed it himself. Looking back he remembered small things though. Favouring the same side when he slept, not being hungry, heartburn.

Small things, big problems.

Admitted to hospital that same night, he was nil-by-mouth and subjected to a battery of tests. Ultrasound, X-ray, endoscopy, colonoscopy, bloods, urine, Fluke had the lot while the doctors stood round scratching their heads – they knew something was wrong but they didn't know what.

It wasn't solved until they rolled out the big gun. The dark mass the MRI found was obvious, even to the untrained eye. A dark mass that had insidiously wrapped itself round one of his kidneys and part of his bowel.

To Fluke's amazement, he was then discharged, booked in for a biopsy a week later and told not to worry in the meantime. At a loss what to do, he went back to work.

A week later, he was back, signing consent forms allowing a surgeon to basically do what he felt was best if a biopsy wasn't going to be enough when they opened him up. He confirmed to the anaesthesiologist he wasn't allergic to anything then went into surgery.

When Fluke woke he was told he'd undergone an eight-hour operation involving two surgical teams. With the anaesthetics starting to wear off, the pain began and it was through a cocktail of painkilling medication that Fluke learned he no longer had a right kidney or most of his lower bowel, and that a grapefruit-sized tumour had been removed. His wound stretched from the centre of his chest to his navel and had over fifty staples holding it together.

Two days in intensive care for pain management, two weeks on the gastro ward with a group of old men, an argument with the hospital social worker, which ended with her in tears after he told her to mind her own business, and he was discharged.

While waiting for the biopsy results, during one of the daily visits from the district nurse to look after the wound, he'd begun vomiting. Uncontrollable vomiting that lasted for two days. Nothing stayed down, not water, not the painkillers he tried to take for the terrible headaches the dehydration was causing. The district nurse finally had enough and called an ambulance.

Which was when Doctor Leah Cooper entered his life. She introduced herself as his oncologist and that she was in charge of his treatment. A serious woman doing a serious job, she sat next to the raised bed and told him what he already knew: he had cancer. Burkitt's lymphoma, she'd told him. Usually confined to the jaws of children on the African continent, it was extremely rare in the Western world.

At least they'd heard of it, he'd thought. Nobody wanted a disease named after them.

There was good and bad news. Because it was such an aggressive cancer, paradoxically, it was also very curable. The faster they grow the faster they can kill it, Doctor Cooper told him. The bad news was that the treatment was the worst there was. There was a very real chance he wouldn't survive it. And it had to be delivered, as an inpatient, in an isolation ward.

Fluke remembered barely batting an eyelid. He wasn't stupid. He wasn't expecting her to say, 'Take two of these and go home.' Cancer was a word that struck dread into even the calmest of people, yet Fluke's reaction, she admitted much later, had surprised her.

'OK, now what?' he'd said.

She'd explained that due to the complexity of the treatment, he'd have to be transferred to Newcastle, where the haematologist had a support team of specialist registrars, house doctors and senior fellows. Cumbria just didn't have the resources or the need for a team that size. She'd remain his consultant but others would deliver the treatment. She'd attend fortnightly case meetings, be consulted on all decisions and, if he survived, would deliver his aftercare for the next ten years.

'So when do I go?' he'd asked, wondering how long he'd have to tie up loose ends at work.

'Now,' she said. 'You're starting your chemotherapy tonight.'

'Hang on,' he'd protested, before she cut him off.

'No arguments. The tumour we removed a fortnight ago has already grown back to the size of a tennis ball. That's why you've been vomiting. It's wrapped round your small intestine.' There was no arguing with what she said next. 'We start fighting this thing now.'

A taxi drove him to the Royal Victoria Infirmary, known locally as the RVI, and there he'd stayed for five months.

For five months, he'd taken everything they threw at him: bright green drugs that made his hair fall out; light-sensitive drugs that had to be kept in a bag; intrathecal drugs that were injected into the base of his spine. Chemotherapy to kill him; antibiotics and antifungals to keep him alive.

Fluke took it all without complaint. He had a Hickman line

fitted directly into his chest as the chemotherapy was so corrosive it destroyed his smaller veins. For months he walked around with a yard-long plastic tube sticking out of his chest.

Each day was a learning experience on a course he hadn't signed up for.

The only way to destroy the cancer was to almost destroy him. The team took him as close to death as they dared, then stopped and let him build up his bloods and health only to do it all over again. Three courses of treatment; three times he was taken to the brink.

Finally, the scans showed that it had worked. His bloods were allowed to build up again. Physios got to work on teaching him to walk with nerve-damaged legs. Visitors were allowed in his room without wearing face masks.

He'd been a fit man when he'd been admitted, an ex-Royal Marine, and while he was never in the same league as Towler, who was a freak of nature, the job meant he had to stay in decent shape. He left hospital a shell of a man, down to eleven stone and unable to walk without crutches and splints. He was too weak to cook but that was OK as he had no appetite.

Doctor Cooper told him it was normal. His appetite would come back. The Burkitt's wouldn't.

After nearly six months in hospital and three months recuperating at home, putting up with well-wishers, genuine and nosey, he was ready to get back to work. Some of his strength had returned. His appetite was back. His legs were still troubling him but he kept that to himself.

One good thing had happened during his illness: Hayley decided that she didn't need the hassle of looking after anyone at her stage of life and had broken it off in his first month of treatment. Fluke didn't blame her, although others did.

He discussed a return-to-work date with Occupational Health.

In the past, someone who was off either ran out of sick notes and had to come back, or just decided they were fit to return and turned up.

For Fluke there were meetings with Occupational Health, with Chambers, and even the chief constable, all glad he was feeling better, all doubting he was ready. He rejected out of hand an offer of a temporary desk job.

In the end, it had taken a letter from Leah stating that he was fit to return to operational duties. Straight into the job he had nine months before: Detective Inspector, Force Major Incident Team.

Chapter 9

Fluke sat in the haematology ward's dayroom and waited for his blood test results, lost in his thoughts. It obviously wasn't the right time of day for outpatients as he was the room's sole occupant. He picked up a discarded travel magazine and flicked through it, staring at the beaches, at the five-star hotels and stunning views. It all looked so nice, a far cry from the wind and rain and biting cold of a Cumbrian winter.

A nurse stuck her head in the room and told him Doctor Cooper wanted to speak to him. She passed him a cordless phone.

'Doctor Cooper,' he said.

'Good morning, Avison. You made it, then? Sorry I missed you, but I'm on nights.'

'No problem. I was here anyway, as you know. PM on a girl found in West Cumbria this morning. I'll need to get back actually, he can't be far from finished.'

'That's what I rang for. Your results are in and they're fine. Your platelets are still low and you refusing plasma hasn't helped. Your haemoglobin's nearer where it should be, though. Your bloods are never going to be brilliant, not after what your bone marrow went through, but for now I'm happy to let you go.'

'And yesterday?'

'Already forgotten about under the circumstances, but don't do it again, Avison. If you absolutely have to go, call someone, for God's sake. This isn't a prison, we can't stop you leaving. Now, go and catch him.'

Fluke was already on his feet, trying to get someone's attention, pointing at his cannula. There was no way he was going to try to take it out himself again.

'Cheers, Doc. Do I need another appointment?'

'I'll get something out in the post but I still need to keep an eye on you for a while. It'll probably be next week.'

Fluke thanked her and put down the phone.

As he made his way back down to the mortuary, he wondered why she'd phoned him. Anyone could have told him his results.

Sowerby had finished sewing up the 'Y' cut when Fluke returned and was just calling out some last-minute remarks to the overhead microphones.

'What we got, Henry?' Fluke asked.

'I'll have an interim report with you by lunchtime tomorrow and the full report by the end of the week, but I can do a verbal now if you want?'

'Please.'

'We were right, of course, the bullet to the head killed her. I traced the path. Kept quite a neat line really; entered the back of the skull at the point of the bullet hole, obviously. Went straight through the brain tissue and hit the front of the skull just about here,' he said, pointing to his own head where the nose met the forehead. 'You'll notice this part here is quite thick. The bullet bounced down, through more brain tissue, through the roof of the mouth, as we thought. Of course, it probably started to lose shape by then so the wound on the mouth is larger than the entrance wound on the skull.'

'So she swallowed it?' Fluke said.

'Oh no, she was dead instantly. It was gravity. It probably worked its way into the stomach fairly quickly. I estimate she'd have to be upright after she was shot for three seconds at least for this to happen. When it worked its way into the duodenum is anyone's guess. Could have been immediately, could have been when she was moved.'

'Can I see the bullet?'

The bullet was in an unsealed bag as Towler had assumed Fluke would want to see it before it went off to ballistics for a possible match and a point towards the weapon used. The SOCO man carefully lifted it out with evidence tongs. It was horribly misshapen but still looked small. It had blood and other body matter on it. It wouldn't be cleaned until it got to the lab.

Fluke turned to Towler.

'.22?'

'That's my guess. And I'm not really guessing either unless it's something really exotic. No, this is a .22. Low power, judging by the shape of it.'

'How so, Sergeant?' asked Lucy.

'The British Army, along with most of NATO, use .22 ammunition in their assault rifles, only they call it 5.56 mm,' he said. 'They're high powered and have a tapered point for accuracy. A bullet like that wouldn't have bounced. At that range, it would've gone straight through her head with no deviation in trajectory. Would have carried on for another five hundred yards unless something hard stopped it. This is low-powered and the naughty end is rounded, designed for short-range work where accuracy isn't as important. The bullet's supposed to go in and stay in.'

'Any idea what fired it?' Fluke asked.

'Nah. No way of telling yet. It'll be a small weapon, even for a handgun,' he said. 'Easy to hide, deadly at close range. Not designed for deterrence, more for self-defence. This is about having the shot no one is expecting. Has to be used up close. It would probably bounce off someone at twenty yards. Easy to keep in a handbag or pocket. Ideal for a killer.'

'How do you know all this?' Lucy asked, with a look of incredulity.

He shrugged. Towler was intelligent but hid it well, and this was his area of expertise.

'Illegal in this country, of course,' he said. 'You can't get guns over here that easily, despite what the press say, and this type even less. No demand for it. The gangbangers in Manchester and London want the bling weapons, the status symbols. Why have a gun if you can't show it off? The hardcore, organised crime lot want military-grade weapons. The SIGs and the H&Ks. No real demand for a small .22. Certainly no profit in them.'

'We'll get it off to the National Ballistics Intelligence Service tonight,' Fluke said, which meant it would be sent to their Manchester hub. 'Matt, get someone to escort it there. Get traffic to take them in one of their pursuit vehicles. I want this with them in two hours. We'll see if they've seen this gun before.'

NBIS held details on all firearms and bullets recovered in the UK. If the gun had been used before, NBIS would be able to tell them.

'What else we got, Henry?' Fluke said.

'Couple of things but nothing significant. There was an absence of fall injuries, which is unusual. The momentum of the bullet should have sent her falling forwards rather than crumpling to the ground. I would have expected an injury, probably on the head, but there wasn't. No bruising on the arms, wrists or feet. She wasn't restrained or tied up.'

'Held as she was shot?' Fluke said.

'Possibly, can't say definitely, of course, but it fits the facts. It would explain how the bullet had time to travel down to the stomach as well.'

Fluke filed it away for the future. 'TOD?'

'I'm putting the time of death between thirty and forty hours ago. *Rigor mortis* was reducing. Temperature of the liver gave me a good indication. Monday was a cold night.'

Fluke knew that the body lost 1.5 °C each hour after death and kept losing it until it was the same temperature as its environment. That's why Sowerby had taken the ambient temperature when he got in the hole. If it was 0 °C, it would take the average human twenty-five hours to get to the same temperature.

So, she'd been killed between ten o'clock Monday night and eight o'clock Tuesday morning. Sowerby had said she was standing when she was shot. Fluke thought it unlikely she was killed too close to the foreman finding her and most people are asleep by midnight. His instincts were telling him she'd been killed Monday night and disposed of a few hours later. More evidence of the well-planned work of a professional.

'Anything else?'

'She'd had cosmetic surgery, but I was wrong. It wasn't a botched job at all. Quite the opposite.'

'The nose?' Fluke asked.

'Not just the nose. She'd had four separate corrective procedures. All on her face. And I'm loath to call them corrective procedures.'

'Why?'

'It was Lucy who pointed it out initially. Noticed that it didn't seem to add up.' Sowerby took off his glasses, brushed some errant hair away from his eyes and, taking a sheet of mortuary blue paper towel, wiped his face. 'You understand the basic premise of cosmetic surgery, of course?'

'I hate plastic tits,' Towler said, walking back. 'They don't wobble properly.'

'Yes, well, there's a lot of that, obviously,' Sowerby said. 'It's their core business despite what they say. They *are* in the vanity trade whether they'll admit it or not. They say they are there to improve self-esteem and to reconstruct people after accidents, but the real money is in nips, tucks and enlargements.'

'Seems a bit of a waste with a girl like this,' Fluke said. 'I wonder why she felt she needed plastic surgery.'

'She didn't. And that's the point. Lucy pointed out that the rhinoplasty, when we actually had a proper look, wasn't correcting anything, either medical or cosmetic. Can't say so in court obviously, but I'm certain the rhinoplasty was done to make her nose look worse, not better. Certainly has more of a point than it had originally.'

Fluke knew that Sowerby wouldn't comment on the relative attractiveness of someone; the defence would discredit him without breaking sweat. Between those four walls, his opinion was valid though. If he said the nose was made to look worse, then Fluke believed him.

Sowerby continued. 'This was quality work, expensive work. That's why we missed the rest on the external. You aren't supposed to see good quality work, defeats the illusion of natural youth.'

'What else was there? I can't see anything,' Fluke said, leaning forward and studying her face.

Sowerby passed him a magnifying glass.

He first pointed to her ears. 'See here, there's some very faint scarring. She's had them remodelled. I don't think they've been reduced or pinned back either, which is the normal reason someone would get them done. I think they've been made to look different.'

Fluke could see where he was going; a nose job that detracted from her looks and an ear job that she didn't need. As Sowerby talked him through a chin implant and brow lift that would have changed the shape of her face, the pattern was obvious.

Lying before him was a woman who had gone to extreme lengths to change her appearance.

'Are these reversible?' he asked.

Sowerby gave it some thought. 'I'm not an expert, you understand. Medically speaking, I see no reason why the chin implant couldn't be removed and the brow lift reversed. They've removed cartilage and bone from the ears though, so no, that's irreversible. As for the rhinoplasty, I don't know. Possibly.'

That's drastic, Fluke thought. 'Any idea when this was done, Henry?'

'At least twelve months ago. All the wounds have fully healed. Impossible to say after that. If pushed, I'll say not that long though. The scars would fade after time and they haven't. But it's not an exact science.'

'Any way to identify the surgeon?' Fluke asked.

'Not a chance. Could be anyone and anywhere. The implants don't have serial numbers. It may not have been done in the UK.'

Cosmetic surgery was one thing. There were other ways to hide your appearance. Less permanent ways. 'Was she naturally dark-haired?' he asked.

'Platinum blonde, I think Lucy called it. Light blonde to you and me. The blonde roots were just coming through. Her pubic hair was dyed the same colour as her head.'

'Who the hell was she, Mrs Potato Head?' Fluke snapped. 'What else did she have? A false moustache, a monocle—'

'Contact lenses,' Sowerby said.

'What?'

'Coloured contacts. Her eyes are blue, not green. SOCO has them if you want a look, but they're fairly common.'

Extensive cosmetic surgery. Dyed hair and coloured contact lenses. An appearance altered and not for the better. Sowerby was right: a subjective view of her beauty couldn't be recorded any-where official. Fluke was paid to make deductions based on facts, however, and there were two blindingly obvious ones: she'd been murdered and she'd been hiding from someone.

But who from?

'There's nothing common about this case, Henry,' Fluke said. He looked down at the pale body. 'Who the hell was after you?'

Chapter 10

The post-mortem finished with no new information and Fluke headed back to HQ. Twenty minutes later he pulled into his designated space at Carleton Hall in Penrith. He decided to go for a walk round the grounds to clear his head, get the smell of the mortuary off his clothes.

The sky was grey and Carleton Hall looked eerie in the pale light. A huge red sandstone building accessible only by driving underneath the A66, it was Grade II listed and had extensive grounds. It was unfit for modern policing; poor communications, not enough room and nowhere near enough parking, like a furnace in summer and a cryogenic tomb in winter.

Fluke loved it though. Loved the grandeur of it, its lines, the high ceilings, the ornate carvings on the wood panels, loved the countryside it was set in. Of course, things had been added as the years had passed. The Public Protection Unit had their own extension. Armed Response and the Dogs Unit were in separate buildings a few hundred yards away. But FMIT were in the main building.

As he wandered the gravel paths, he ran through what he needed to do. He needed to ID the witness and he expected that to happen today. It would be the first hard intelligence they got back. He'd never met an addict without a record.

He also needed to ID their victim and he wasn't convinced that would be so easy. Not after what he'd just seen at the PM. For now, she remained a Jane Doe.

NBIS could come back with a positive line of enquiry on the bullet but he wasn't sure how much help it would be. Firearms were rare in Cumbria, so it would have been obtained elsewhere in the country.

He needed someone to start working the forensic evidence. There was a lot taken from the scene. There were clothes, the notepad and the phone, and he wanted someone he trusted doing it. Jo Skelton fitted the bill.

Fluke also needed the actual murder scene now they'd confirmed what they'd suspected: that West Cumberland Hospital was just the deposition site. He knew it might not be in Cumbria and, if it was found elsewhere, there could be a jurisdiction issue.

It would almost certainly be a dead end, but someone had to chase up the cosmetic surgery lead. On top of that, all the routine stuff that had already started – the house-to-house enquiries, the fingertip searches, the passive data requests – needed to continue.

He sighed and headed back up to the main building. With two major investigations running, FMIT was noisy; half the robbery team were still at their desks.

The three FMIT officers working the murder and a couple of SOCOs were waiting for him.

Both incident-room doors were open, phones were ringing, and there was the steady babble of noise. Fluke shut their door and the sound subsided. Jo had obviously kicked out some of the robbery team to make way for them. The room smelled of takeaway food, curries and pizzas predominantly, as incident rooms always did. There wasn't a salad to be seen. Fluke's stomach reminded him that he hadn't eaten since breakfast and he picked up a spoon and an unguarded tray of chicken chow mein. It was cold, greasy and delicious.

He didn't know how much Towler had told them, but he wanted to go through it all again from the start, make sure they knew what he needed from them. He pinned up a selection of crime scene and post-mortem pictures. The mood changed instantly. It was the first time most of them had seen the victim.

'We have a white female found in a hole at the crime scene most of you attended yesterday. Matt and I have just come back from the PM and we can confirm what you'll no doubt have heard on the grapevine. She was killed by a single gunshot to the back of the head. It's likely the gun was pressed against her skull then fired, execution style. No spray and pray here.'

He paused while they digested what he'd said.

'We're working on an interim theory that it was an easily concealed, small-calibre weapon based on the entrance wound, but we'll know more tomorrow. So remember your firearms' procedures when you're closing in on suspects.

'Given her extensive cosmetic surgery it's possible she changed her appearance because she was hiding from someone. Therefore, our number-one priority is identifying her. If we can't do that, everything else will be a nightmare.'

'You want her picture released, boss?' Jo Skelton asked.

Fluke thought about it before saying, 'No, Jo, not until we understand who she was hiding from. We can't predict the consequences of releasing it.'

'We're looking at a pro,' Towler said. 'He seems to have been unlucky with a junkie tramp seeing him dump the body, but everything else has been well executed, pardon my pun.'

'Matt's right, it *was* well planned, possibly even rehearsed. It's also possible she wasn't killed in Cumbria, had never been to Cumbria, that the killer doesn't live in Cumbria and has already left the country.'

He took his time to look at the team, all faces pointed his way. A daunting task that was going to consume their lives over the next few days had been laid before them. Some looked eager and others looked resigned to the long slog.

None of them would let him down though.

Fluke thought Chambers was a moron but he *was* in charge of FMIT and therefore had to be kept up to date. He made his way up the stairs to his office. Fluke was about to knock when his phone vibrated in his pocket, letting him know he had a text message. He pulled it out, wondering if it was from Michelle. Although he was glad it was finally over, it had been a sad way to end it.

But the text wasn't from Michelle, it was from Alan Vaughn.

> Positive ID on the fingerprint on the
> Coke can, boss.

Fluke turned around and left. This was important. Chambers being briefed wasn't.

When Fluke got back to the incident room, Alan Vaughn passed him the results of IDENT 1, the national automated fingerprint system that all police forces are connected to.

'No doubt, it's him. The prints SOCO lifted were excellent quality. They got another nine hits for him from inside the cabin as well.'

'Darren Ackley. Who's he?'

Vaughn handed him a thin file. Fluke knew it would be thicker by the end of the day.

'Some scrote over in Whitehaven. There's a local DC who'll meet you and Matt at the station,' Vaughn said. 'Seems she works with those involved in the sex trade.'

'He's a rent boy?' Fluke was surprised. He'd been expecting an everyday junkie. A rent boy was exotic for Cumbria.

'"Survival sex worker", she calls him.'

Fluke grunted. Sex worker, gigolo, rent boy or survival sex

worker. He was his only witness to a murder. 'She know where to find him?'

'You'd fucking think so, wouldn't you? But they haven't got a clue, useless bastards,' a voice said from behind him.

'You up for a drive, Matt?' Fluke asked, without turning round.

Half an hour later they were on the A66 heading to Whitehaven. Normally Fluke would have asked the officer who knew Ackley to come to him, but as the day was probably going to be spent in West Cumbria anyway, they decided to drive out.

Towler drove so Fluke could read the Police National Computer and SLEUTH intelligence on Darren Ackley.

PNC showed a few convictions, mainly shop theft. He was twenty-five and all his convictions had come in the previous four years – when his addiction started, in all likelihood.

The other printout was more interesting. While PNC recorded arrests and convictions, SLEUTH recorded intelligence.

Because he worked in the sex trade, the intelligence on Ackley was impressive. Any sighting of him, any time he was searched, who he was with, the cars he was in, where he was living, it was all there.

'You read this, Matt?'

'Skimmed it. Why?'

'There's nothing for the last two weeks. Seems to have dropped off the grid. I reckon he's been in that site office since then.'

Towler paused. 'Yeah, I'll buy that. He'll be shitting himself now, though. He won't be back tonight. He's not gonna be easy to find.'

'We'll get some local help,' Fluke said.

He grunted. 'A day spent chasing a rent boy round West Cumbria. It's the fucking glamour of this job I like.'

They arrived at Whitehaven an hour after they'd left Carleton Hall. The police station was in the centre of town. They drove into the courtyard and parked up. DC Helen Banks was waiting to meet them. Neither of them knew her. They got out and introduced themselves.

'Is this related to that body you pulled from the hospital?' she said immediately. 'Because there's no way he did it, sir.'

She was in her early thirties. Short dark hair and a face that was pleasant enough, if slightly too earnest. She was dressed in jeans and a sweatshirt. She walked with a slight limp and Fluke wondered if she was recuperating from something.

Remembering her manners, she offered to take them into the station and make them a cup of tea. Fluke declined for both of them. He needed to crack on. He gestured for her to get into the back of the car then asked if she had any leads.

'I rang his probation officer before you got here, sir. She says that he's reported to her a couple of times with someone called McNab. He lives on Pinegrove. Thinks if anyone might know where he is, it'll be him.'

Towler reversed out of the yard. Fluke knew he'd worked this part of the west so would know the infamous Pinegrove Estate well.

Don Holland came to the door and smirked.

'What's that prick want?' Towler said.

'Ignore him. Come on, let's get going,' Fluke replied. Towler edged into the afternoon traffic and they headed towards Pinegrove.

Banks started telling them about Ackley's life and how he'd ended up selling his body.

'Where's he going to run to if he's not with McNab?' Fluke said when she'd finished.

She shrugged. 'I don't know. He's not a bad lad but he doesn't have many friends.'

'Guess,' he said.

She looked a little put out but recovered well. Fluke didn't care.

Ackley was a witness in a murder case. The social workers and probation officers could have him back when he'd finished with him.

'As you'll know from SLEUTH, we've not seen him for a few days. He'd normally have been arrested at least once by now for shoplifting. He doesn't even pretend to browse any more. Just walks in and runs out. All the security guards and shopkeepers know him.'

'What do you think's happened?'

'Honestly, sir? I think he's found somewhere safe out of area.'

'He's not out of area, DC Banks,' Fluke said. 'We think he witnessed the murder last night. And if he did, he'll be terrified. Any idea where he'd go?'

'There's no way he can go without scoring. Not even for a day. Even if he was scared, he'd have to go out and get some heroin. And he can't get it on tick so he'll have to pay for it somehow.'

'You think he's worked for it?'

She paused while she thought. 'Probably,' she replied. 'He's shit at shoplifting, I know that much.'

Fluke's phone rang. It was a Penrith number.

'Boss, it's Jo. I'm just ringing to let you know that the CCTV was a bust. Copeland Council turned all their cameras off months ago, part of their efficiency savings. We'll keep going with the house-to-house but there's been zilch so far. The entrance to the site doesn't face anything so there's no reason for people to take any notice.'

'OK. Thanks, Jo,' Fluke said, disappointed but not surprised. 'Any news on the bullet?'

'Not yet. It got there no problems but it may take a while. They're still trying to get something off the smashed mobile, so nothing on that yet either.'

'Any good news?'

'Not sure. The lab rang just before and said they had something from the notebook. There were prints on the cover but they all belonged to the vic. They said they can have a look for what they call "indented writing", basically trying to see what's been written on the page that had been ripped out. It's expensive though.'

'What's wrong with rubbing a pencil over it?' Fluke asked. 'Yeah, tell them to go ahead. It'll probably just be a shopping list or something but even that would be more than we know now about her. How you getting on with the misper list?'

'Nothing so far. I'll get on to the lab and tell them to run their test. Oh, and can you ring the bug lady? She says she needs to speak to you.'

'Text me her number, I'll ring her when I get five minutes,' he said.

'Will do. Where are you and Matt?'

'We've drawn the short straw, Jo. We're just about to enter Pinegrove.'

Chapter 11

Fluke knew that Cumbria was a safe county. 'A safe place to live, work and visit' was the tagline used by the authorities. There were areas of outstanding natural beauty: the lakes, fells, mountains, Hadrian's Wall, the stone circles, even parts of the Yorkshire Dales. Picture-perfect villages, castles and stately homes. A county that took William Wordsworth's breath away. A county that inspired Beatrix Potter.

But there was another side to it.

Parts of Cumbria had a lower GDP per capita than the Czech Republic. There was an underclass that was carefully hidden from tourists. Estates with third-generation unemployment. Estates, devastated by the decline of industry, where dealers and loan sharks prospered. Estates with a culture of violence and fear. Estates bereft of hope.

The notorious Pinegrove Estate was a small island, cast adrift from the town of Whitehaven. It had its own road in and its own road out. There was no reason to enter it unless you lived or had business there. It wasn't on the way to anywhere.

Like most of West Cumbria, it had a two-tier social structure: those who enjoyed the inflated wages of the Sellafield nuclear site and those who didn't. The main feature of the estate seemed to be barbed wire. The back of the pub, the rooftops of businesses, even some of the houses used it for protection. A broken ghetto, a bleak and miserable existence. The climate of fear was palpable.

Despite this, some of the streets still thrived. Functioning and legally taxed cars were parked outside houses, and gardens were well kept. People got up in the morning and went to work. They raised their families. They bought their council houses. Parts of Pinegrove had genuine community spirit. Residents on the estate tried to lead their lives, if not within the letter of the law, then at least within its spirit.

But there was a minority who had no interest in doing so.

If negativity and resentment could generate electricity, their streets would have made Sellafield superfluous. These were the streets where every other house had boarded-up windows. Cars rusted, front lawns went untended. Rubbish was piled on the street, giving the impression parts of Pinegrove had been abandoned. Efforts by Copeland Borough Council to regenerate the area were only partially successful; there were some families who had no interest in the status quo changing. Antisocial behaviour was rife, casual violence the norm. Drugs were openly sold and consumed. Children roamed the streets like feral dogs.

Pinegrove was the type of estate where some people could leave their doors unlocked while others had to barricade themselves in every night. Disagreements were settled with baseball bats instead of solicitors. Everyone knew everyone and strangers weren't tolerated. The worst thing you could be was a 'grass' – even paedophiles were safer. Police callouts were constant. The chief had long ago directed that no police officer would patrol Pinegrove alone.

'Welcome to Pinegrove, everyone, where everyone's related through incest or rape,' Towler said, as he turned into the estate. 'Now, where the fuck am I going?'

Banks wasn't sure exactly where McNab lived, so Towler parked up beside an off-licence and got out. There were graffiti-covered steel shutters on the windows despite it being open. Fluke had seen less-fortified police stations in Northern Ireland. He'd never been in the shop before but knew that all the overpriced goods would be locked in cages, nothing being handed over until the owner had the cash in his till.

In less than a minute, Towler was back with directions to Seaview Terrace, the last known address of McNab. They quickly found it.

The street was quiet. Everyone with a reason to get up had already done so. The rest were still in bed.

'It'll be one of these houses here, sir,' Banks said as they were near the middle of the wide road. 'They take the numbers off the houses to make it difficult for us to find them. Even those with nothing to hide do it. They'd get called a grass if they didn't.'

It was obvious that Seaview Terrace was one of the poorer streets on the estate. A third of the houses were derelict, a third had windows without curtains and the remaining third had curtains that were twitching. Fluke knew their presence hadn't gone unnoticed. A group of young children walked up and started looking over the car.

Towler lowered his window, and said, 'Fuck off.'

They backed away but didn't disappear.

'Right,' Towler said getting out. 'Let's knock on a few doors.'

'We'll need uniform backup before we can do anything, Sergeant. I'll call the station, get a van out,' Banks said.

'Don't worry,' said Fluke, smiling, as he followed him out of the car. 'Towler's his own backup.'

For a minute, he thought she was going to stay in the car but eventually she joined them on the pavement, looking nervous.

'Right, let's try here,' Towler said, walking up the first path and hammering on the door. There was no answer. He kept banging, looking round to see if anything else was stirring.

The occupants of the next house along opened their door a fraction to see what the noise was. Towler was there in an instant, jumping over the neglected fence without touching it.

'You McNab?' he shouted through the door, jamming his foot in the crack to stop it closing.

Fluke, having not moved from the pavement, watched on amused. Towler was in his element here. While he had finesse when he needed it, this was what he liked doing best. Getting down and dirty. Fluke didn't hear what the person behind the door replied, but Towler didn't like it.

'Wrong answer, dickhead,' he said, forcing the door wide open and walking in.

Thirty seconds later he was back out.

'McNab's at thirty-three, boss. Lives there with some local lass, has done for a couple of months. This house here is seven, so it should be twelve doors up if the evens are on the other side.'

'Wanker,' came the shout from the door behind him.

Towler ignored it.

They left the car where it was and walked up the street, counting the houses as they went. After a short discussion about whether they'd counted correctly, they arrived at a dilapidated semi-detached. The front lawn was overrun with weeds, dog faeces and empty cans. An old sofa sat on the grass underneath the window. There was a headless child's doll on the path. Towler kicked it into the garden and they walked up to the front door together.

Towler knocked and they heard movement inside, and some whispered talking.

The door opened, and a man of about thirty stood before them, shaven-headed and topless. Heavy muscles padded out a squat frame. He was covered in prison tattoos. His small eyes were dull and malevolent. Coarse black hair crept to the top of his shoulders. His body language was shouting 'I'm dangerous, don't mess with me'. He was holding a can of beer and it was obvious to Fluke that he was deliberately sucking in his stomach and tensing his muscles, hoping to give the impression that it was how he always looked.

Towler smiled, but not in a good way.

Failing to get the fearful reaction he wanted, his stance changed from intimidation to confusion. 'What the fuck do you want?'

Ignoring the insult, Fluke asked, 'Are you McNab?'

Some of the tension left his body. He gestured to his right with the can. 'Next door, mate,' he said, closing the door.

'That's him, sir,' Banks whispered.

Fluke nodded at Towler and gestured towards the back of the house. Fluke waited until he had enough time to get round the back and knocked again.

'Mr McNab, can we have a word, please?' There was no whispering but the sound of running, a door opening and then a loud crash. Someone shouted. A child's cry rose, wild and piercing, above the sound of whatever was happening at the back. The noise increased as a woman started screaming. Fluke and Banks ran down the side alley.

Banks looked shocked and a little worried. Fluke saw exactly what he'd expected to see.

McNab was on his knees in front of Towler, who had him in some sort of wristlock. He was clearly in a certain amount of discomfort and was keeping as still as possible to avoid more pain. Towler was exerting minimal pressure on his wrists, which were nearly at right angles.

A woman, no more than eighteen or nineteen, was yelling at Towler and tugging at his suit. He ignored her. She wore a sleeveless T-shirt, and fresh and old bruises were visible on her pale, thin arms.

Inside the house, the baby's cries grew louder and more urgent.

'Get her out of here,' Fluke told Banks.

Banks tried to calm the woman and persuaded her to go and see to the child. With one last look at everyone, the girl went back inside.

'Go and see if she's all right, DC Banks. And while you're at it, search the house. See if Ackley's in there,' he whispered. 'Yell if he is.'

She nodded and followed the girl in. The sound of crying stopped.

With silence restored, Towler loosened his grip on McNab who stood up warily, rubbing his wrists. He looked at Towler with a mixture of hatred and fear.

He turned to Fluke, animal cunning telling him that he was in charge. 'Bastard can't do that. I've got fucking rights, you know.' He looked round to see if there were any obvious ways out. He took a look at Towler, six feet eight and built like a whippet, and decided there was no point running. 'What the fuck do you want, anyway? I've got no charges coming up and I'm clean. Not touched smack this year, ask anyone.'

'What's your first name, McNab? And we're not the drug squad,' he said as he got out his warrant badge and identified himself.

McNab didn't say anything.

'No first name? McNab it is then,' Fluke said. 'What can you tell me about Darren Ackley?'

A brief glimmer of understanding flitted across his dull eyes.

'No comment.'

So it was going to be like that? The copper's anthem, no comment. Fluke wondered how many times he'd heard that said by someone on the opposite side of an interview room. Thousands probably. Like detectives using pens to pick up evidence and doctors saying 'sharp scratch', it was another of those anomalies that made little sense. Criminals watched the same bad cop shows as police officers, he guessed. Everyone arrested had the right to remain silent but they don't have to say 'no comment' to assert that right. Saying nothing is enough.

'You're not under arrest, fuckface,' Towler said.

McNab stared at him but looked away when he realised that Towler wasn't even looking at him.

'My colleague is right, of course. You're not under arrest. Now stop pissing about. When did you last see Ackley?' Fluke said.

'No fucking comment.'

Fluke had seen it countless times. When the police were involved in their lives they felt powerless. Refusing to answer anything allowed them to get some control back.

'Ackley's not in trouble, McNab. You're not in trouble either, unless you lie to me. Then you'll be in big trouble. I don't want to search your house but I will. I wonder what I'll find? What do you think, Sergeant?'

Towler turned to look at McNab, his contempt obvious. 'Judging by his bulk, I'd say enough steroids to put him away for six months, boss. Maybe something harder.'

The flash of fear that crossed McNab's face told Fluke that he was right. Steroid abuse. It explained his muscles and the bruises on the girl's arms. Steroid abuse and increased aggression were inextricably linked.

'We think Darren witnessed something last night. We need to know what that was.'

Another flicker of recognition passed across his face. Bingo. He'd seen him recently.

'No comment.'

Banks reappeared and shook her head briefly. Ackley wasn't inside.

'McNab, don't be a tit all your life. Tell me what you know,' Fluke said, raising his voice slightly. 'If you don't, I'm gonna have to nick you.'

Fluke thought he saw another flash of fear cross his face. So he's scared of being arrested. Why? Judging by the tattoos and the way he was talking to them he'd been arrested countless times.

'You know something, boss,' Towler said. 'I don't think he's cool enough to be called McNab. I met a McNab once when I was in the Paras. He was doing a talk on resisting interrogation. Something he'd learned when he was caught by the Iraqis during Desert Storm.'

'Andy McNab,' McNab grunted. '*Bravo Two Zero*. They made him eat his own shit.'

'Check out the military historian here,' Towler said. 'Yes, that's right. McNab. Andy McNab. And I think he's a cool bloke. A credit to his country. I don't think you should have the same name as such a cool bloke. What do you think, McNab?'

McNab glared at him but said nothing.

'I think you need a different name. From now on you're called McKnob.'

There was an immediate reaction. Anger replaced the fear in his eyes. His breathing changed, became shallow, as adrenalin flooded his body. Towler was taller but McNab had a three-stone advantage, three stones of steroid-fuelled muscle, brawn and aggression.

It would make no difference.

Fluke had seen this before. Towler would wind up a difficult suspect to such an extent that he'd provoke a primal physical reaction, which gave him every reason to meet it with one of his own.

At that point, the girl came back out. She was holding the baby.

'Ah, just in time,' Towler said. 'Can we get a cup of tea here, please, love? McKnob here is very thirsty. He's been telling us all sorts of things, haven't you, McKnob?'

The woman looked at McNab then at Towler, decided she didn't want anything to do with what was going on and disappeared back into the house.

'You think we'll get biscuits with our tea, McKnob?'

Again McNab said nothing. Being humiliated in front of the girl had turned his face and neck bright red. Fluke could tell he was only one remark away from losing it. And that would be bad for him. He could sense Banks fidgeting beside him, wanting him to stop the deliberate provocation but Fluke didn't have time to explain what was happening.

Towler then delivered the final straw.

'How'd your missus get those bruises on her arms, McKnob?' he said.

The 'quick and dirty signal', scientists call it. A survival trait where the thalamus allows the body to react without speaking to the rational part of the brain. In dangerous situations, it saves several seconds. If you know what to look for, there is a subtle change the split second before someone switches from flight to fight. With McNab, it wasn't that subtle. With a bellow, he charged and swung a giant hairy fist at Towler with a force that would probably have killed him.

If he'd been where McNab thought he was.

He wasn't.

Chapter 12

Fluke was no stranger to violence. He'd been a Royal Marines Commando for six years and a police officer for eighteen. From pub brawls to full-blown riots, from the fully mechanised war in 1990 to women pulling each other's hair out in Carlisle city centre, he'd seen good fighters, brave fighters, psychotic fighters and any number of others.

And then he'd seen Towler, and Towler was in a category all on his own.

He wasn't a martial arts expert and he wasn't the biggest dog in the pack. It was a combination of absolute confidence, controlled aggression and an utter lack of fear that made him so formidable.

·During the part of Parachute Regiment basic training known as P-Company, all recruits are required to undertake a particularly brutal test called 'milling'. Two recruits of equal size are paired against each other, and for the longest minute of their lives are forced to go head-to-head in a version of boxing not seen anywhere else. Having a solid defence is frowned upon. Fancy footwork is frowned upon. Boxing skills are irrelevant and not scored. The object of the test is to demonstrate that the recruit can stand up to violence, that they won't let their head go down. That they can take a pounding and still come back for more. That they are in control of their aggression. That in battle, when they are pinned down by effective enemy fire, they will have the character to get up and fight.

The spirit of Wireless Ridge and Goose Green.

During one of the rare times their leave coincided, Fluke had met up with Towler and a mate he'd brought up from Aldershot who he'd been going through P-Company with. After several beers and a couple of hours of Marines versus Paras piss-taking, Towler had gone to the toilet and his friend had told Fluke about their experience of milling.

Already having a reputation as a hard man, the recruit Towler was paired with was terrified. Correctly guessing that the instructors were not looking to see him simply bullying and humiliating his opponent, he opted for a different approach.

For virtually the whole minute, Towler kept his arms by his sides and his gloves down. He looked straight at his opponent and allowed him to rain blow after blow on his head. His nose broke immediately. A cut above his eye restricted his vision. Still he kept his arms down and allowed himself to be beaten. With the sixty seconds almost up and the point clearly made, with a lightning quick jab, which seemed to come from nowhere, he laid his fellow recruit out cold.

When he was finished telling his story, they sat in silence. Fluke didn't doubt it was true. It had that paradoxical mix of violence and compassion that made Towler who he was.

A fight wasn't the best way to describe what happened next. A fight implies two people engaged in violence with a shared aim of hurting each other.

McNab never got to lay a finger on Towler, but in trying to, he'd run into the wall, punched it twice and hurt his neck with a missed headbutt. Fluke thought his right hand was broken and there was a nasty cut on his forehead. He was drenched in sweat. Every time he lunged at Towler, he missed.

Fluke watched dispassionately, moving out of the way occasionally, as Towler allowed McNab to beat himself into submission. With the aid of some fairly basic defensive moves, Towler used McNab's own strength and lack of control to make him hurt himself.

Eventually McNab ran out of steam and he stood with his hands on his hips, gasping for breath and looking with hatred at Towler, who hadn't broken sweat and was watching him with an amused look. Fluke thought that he might have had enough. Until Towler taunted him again.

Putting on a terrible Michael Caine accent, he told McNab he was big but out of shape.

Fluke groaned. 'Stop pissing about, Matt, and finish this, will you?'

At the point of exhaustion, McNab charged one last time. Towler sidestepped again but, as if putting an animal out of its misery, his right arm darted out like a striking viper. It firmly connected with McNab's solar plexus. He collapsed to the ground, gasping. He moved onto his side and vomited noisily. He wasn't crying yet but he wasn't far off.

Towler and Fluke casually discussed the previous two minutes while McNab writhed on the ground, panting. Banks looked shocked and Fluke didn't blame her. She asked if they needed a van to come and get McNab. She assumed they'd be arresting him. Fluke didn't think it would be necessary and said so.

It took a full five minutes for McNab to get his breath back, which was followed by five minutes of threats of violence and legal action and tears.

'Just in case you were wondering, McNab, this isn't going well,' Fluke said. 'You know I can arrest you now? Take you in for assaulting a police officer. Well, trying to anyway.'

Towler snorted.

McNab looked at them, sullen, defiant, planning a revenge he wasn't capable of. There was vomit on his chin, the side of his face and matted into his chest hair. He carried on muttering under his breath, Fluke heard the words 'filthy bastards' but chose to ignore them. He shivered. Adrenalin extracting its payment in all likelihood. Nothing was free.

It dawned on Fluke that they were maybe looking at it from the wrong angle. McNab was scared. Not scared for Ackley. Fluke doubted he'd give two shits if something happened to him. He wasn't protecting Ackley for any altruistic reasons, he was doing it for himself.

But Fluke needed to know what he knew. Time to do to him psychologically what Towler had done to him physically.

'Look, McNab, if Ackley really is your mate then you need to speak to us. He's in trouble. Not legal trouble. Proper trouble. Tell us where he is and we'll leave. Don't and you're gonna have to come with us.'

Fluke's gaze softened.

'And you know what Whitehaven's like; it *will* get out that you're helping us,' he said.

McNab stopped sobbing and looked up, his eyes red, his nose running heavily.

'We know he saw something, something that scared him.'

Like a punctured tyre, McNab deflated in front of them.

He looks terrified, Fluke thought.

'Not out here,' McNab said, looking round.

He led them back into the house and they took seats in what Fluke supposed was the lounge. The sofa in the front garden looked cleaner but Fluke was wearing a machine-washable suit. Before they started, Fluke asked Banks to go and stay with the woman and make sure she was OK. He wanted to keep it as restricted as possible.

'Ackers came by yesterday morning,' McNab said, lighting a cigarette and using an empty beer can as an ashtray.

'What time?' Fluke asked.

'Dunno, but it was still fucking dark. I was in me bed. Kept

91

bangin' on the door. Ignored it to start with, thought it must've been a smackhead looking for some gear and I don't do that any more.'

Pinegrove wasn't a long walk from the deposition site so it fitted in with what they knew.

'So what did you do?' Fluke asked.

'I got fuckin' sick of it, didn't I? I've been good lately, haven't really been up to much. Doing weights and that. Hoping to get on the doors in town. Good money and it's cash in hand.' He stopped and looked up, aware that he'd admitted to benefit and tax fraud.

'Go on, we're not bothered about that. What happened next?'

'I sent Siobhan down, didn't I? She was gonna be up anyway feeding the larle 'un.'

'You're a modern man, McKnob,' Towler said.

Fluke winced. Sometimes Towler's off button malfunctioned. He had McNab talking now. He could do without it kicking off again. He flashed Towler a warning look.

McNab continued, 'No, it made sense for her to get the door. She's got a fuckin' mouth on her anyway. You heard her before. She's lived on the estate all her life and knows how these things go. If I'd went down and it'd been a couple of dirty smackheads I'd have fuckin' killed 'em and I'd have got lifted.'

'But it was Darren?'

'Who? Oh aye, it was Ackers. Darren. Funny that, I'd forgotten what his proper name was. I know he sells 'is arse an' that, but he's a good lad really. We were in the same children's home when we was little. He came in, crying his eyes out. Said he'd seen a big fucker dumping a body up at where the new hospital's gonna be. Said he'd left a note but wished he hadn't. He'd been staying in the site office for a few days. Siobhan won't have him in the house with the larle 'un because of the needles. She thinks he's got AIDS or hep B so won't even make him a brew in case we catch something off the cup.'

'What else did he see?'

'Dunno, didn't fuckin' ask him. Told him I didn't want to know any more. Sounded proper scary, it did. Didn't want any fuckin' part of it. Ackers was fuckin' brickin' himself like. He wanted to get out of Whitehaven.'

'And you helped him?'

'Did I fuck. What could I do? Don't have a car and he wanted a hundred fuckin' quid to get to Newcastle. I don't have that kind of money and even if I did, I wouldn't let him have it. I know he's a mate 'n' all, but he's a smackhead. He'd have just fucked off with it. I'd not see him for six months and then he'd deny ever fuckin' borrowing it. I gave him a fiver from Siobhan's purse. Just to get him to fuck off. I didn't want anyone finding him here.'

'So where is he now?' Fluke asked.

McNab burst out laughing, a low guttural sound. He looked at Towler. 'You may be hard, mate, but you're a thick twat.'

Fluke looked at him, tendrils of apprehension creeping over him. He was laughing at them. What did he know that they didn't?

'You fuckin' stupid bastards,' he said, some of his earlier bravado returning. 'He's with you lot.'

Fluke's confused expression caused McNab to burst out laughing all over again.

McNab continued. 'He's at Whitehaven nick.'

Fluke was furious. Furious at Banks, who'd only just come on shift and hadn't read her emails, and furious with himself for not believing Holland would retaliate by deliberately interfering in a murder investigation. His smirk made sense now. He knew why they were there and he knew who he had in his cells. And he knew that at some point, Fluke would find out.

McNab had told them he'd been arrested for shoplifting that morning. He'd walked into Tesco, picked up a DVD player and, according to the arresting officer, simply waited outside until the police arrived.

93

Towler phoned the station immediately but it was too late. 'They've already taken him to court, boss. Magistrates remanded him. He's in the back of a G4S van, on his way to Durham. No way of stopping it.' He slammed his fist on the steering wheel. 'No one thought to fucking check why we were here? What did you think we were doing, buying fucking ice creams?' Towler shouted into his phone.

Fluke felt the same but let him rant. He knew he'd calm down soon enough. Banks was sitting quietly in the back, chastened. It wasn't her fault any more than it was Towler's. Fluke blamed himself. If he hadn't humiliated Holland at the crime scene Ackley would be in their custody now. He asked Banks what she thought the shoplifting meant.

She looked surprised to be asked.

'I can't say for certain, obviously, but all the regulars at court know what the remand threshold is at any one time in case they need to get off the streets to escape a drug debt. It sounds like he passed it deliberately. He's never done it before.'

Fluke sighed. Michelle's friends would never be able to understand that for some people prison was the best they could hope for in their lives. Auntie Betty's B & B. Warm and safe, all the food they could eat and free healthcare. For some people, prison was a sanctuary.

The custody sergeant at Whitehaven obviously wasn't prepared to take any more grief from Towler and was giving as much back. Towler rang off and threw his phone down in disgust. 'Prick.'

They dropped Banks back at Whitehaven, and Towler drove out of the station car park without saying goodbye. Fluke gave her a weak smile as they drove past her.

At least they knew where Ackley was.

As Towler got back on the phone to organise a prison visit, Fluke remembered he hadn't phoned Lucy, the bug lady. There was no time; he wanted to go back to the crime scene to make sure it was still secure and that SOCO had everything they needed. Towler drove through Hensingham and parked in the same place Fluke had the day before.

The crime scene was still being processed. Fluke knew that the reality of forensic work was methodical, painstaking and laborious. It took days rather than hours, popular TV shows giving a false picture of what the actual job entailed.

He could see that there were journalists and a TV crew there. Word was out.

A shrine of flowers and soft toys had built up. There were candles as well but the wind had blown them all out. A crowd of onlookers had gathered and some were being interviewed by the press.

Fluke turned and surveyed his surroundings after he signed into the outer cordon. It was as he thought: the old hospital was the only building that overlooked the site. A combination of trees and the screens the building company had erected interrupted the view from everywhere else. It couldn't be seen from the road. He didn't really know what to make of that information. He was working on an early theory that the killer wasn't from Cumbria. Professional killing wasn't a trade Cumbrians normally moved into. So how did the killer know about the deposition site? Other than being unlucky enough to have actually been observed disposing of the body, it was perfect. He took one last look at the old hospital. It was still operational, the new one wasn't due to open until later in the year, but even to his untrained eye it looked as though it had had its day. It was grubby and it was old-fashioned. Not old-fashioned in the grand architectural style of the Royal Victoria Infirmary in Newcastle, more the prefabricated type favoured in the seventies. It didn't look nice then, and it looked worse now. But had their killer been there? Had he stood in that old dilapidated building and seen what he must have thought was the ideal deposition site?

95

He walked up to the uniformed sergeant, who eyed him warily. Word had obviously got out about how he'd taken Holland to task.

'Sergeant. Can you move those ghouls back another fifty yards? I don't want a suspect placing themselves here on purpose so they can claim that's why their forensics were found later.'

The sergeant walked off to arrange it.

Fluke took one last look at the crime scene. There was nothing more he could do here. He turned his phone on to check his emails while he had a signal. There was only one that mattered. The NBIS report on the bullet was back.

Chapter 13

Fluke was back at FMIT an hour later, reading the report from the National Ballistics Intelligence Service. As he read, Alan Vaughn précised it.

'Matt can probably give you more info, boss, but there's good and bad news. The good is that ballistics were able to make a positive ID. It's a .22 LR.'

Fluke nodded, it was the calibre Towler had said it would be. 'LR?'

'Stands for long rifle apparently. Not really sure why as it was almost certainly fired from a handgun. Matt, you got five minutes?' he called out. Towler walked over. '.22 LR?'

'.22 long,' Towler replied. 'Fuck. Just about the most common bullet on the planet. In the States you buy them by weight rather than number, they're that cheap. Used as a practice bullet. Not too bad for vermin from a rifle, shit from a handgun. Range is terrible. Ideal for our man, though. No way is that coming out the other side of the head. It's rimfire as well. Quiet.'

'Rimfire?' Vaughn said.

Distracted as he read the report, Towler said, 'Means the firing pin strikes the side of the bullet rather than the back. Makes it less accurate, I forget why.'

While Towler familiarised himself with the report, Fluke asked Vaughn what the bad news was.

'They've run the bullet through their database and it's from a virgin. Nothing at all on their system.'

'Anything good coming out of this?'

'Not really. He said if we wanted, he could give us a list of gangs and individuals who may deal in this sort of thing, but it was going to be sixteen pages long and none of them are Cumbrian.'

'If he's as professional as we think he is, he's not going to buy from a gangbanger,' Towler said. 'He's going to use someone we don't know. No way he leaves breadcrumbs that way.'

'Agreed, but check it anyway,' Fluke said. 'You're right though, we won't catch him through the bullet. He's left us no forensics. Even though he can't have expected us to find the body, I doubt he'd have left the bullet if he knew it was traceable.'

'I'll get the list, boss, see if there's anything that sticks out,' Vaughn said.

'No way to tell what type of weapon we're looking at, Matt?' Fluke said.

'Nope. Any number of handguns fire it, any number of rifles fire it.'

'Best guess then.'

'I'd start with revolvers, that's what I'd use. Never jam and no brass to police. There's some nice reliable ones being made now. Nice and small too. But, even if we narrow the search to those, we'll still be looking at hundreds. The rifling on the bullet may help narrow it down but not much.'

'Dead end then,' Fluke said.

'Yes and no, boss. It tells us a bit more about him. If you want to kill someone quietly then this is the ammo to use. A small gun, a subsonic load in the .22 LR and it'll make more of a pop than a bang.'

'You think he put the gun to her head to make sure he hit her?'

Towler thought about it for a second. 'Nah,' he said. 'The bullet'll penetrate the skull at twenty feet but only just, but you could be reasonably sure of hitting her at ten. There'd be no need to get up that close. Why risk the forensic transfer?' he said thoughtfully. He paused, looking at the report. 'Unless . . . unless he used her head as a silencer.'

There was silence as they thought that through.

'That's . . . disturbing,' Vaughn said eventually.

Fluke nodded in agreement.

'The skull's full of liquid, you see?' Towler said. 'Press a small gun against the head and fire it and you won't hear anything. Not even if you're in the next room. The prick knew what he was doing.'

'An ex-squaddie?' Fluke said.

'If he is, he's special forces,' Towler said, without any trace of admiration. He was simply stating the facts as he saw them. 'Normal grunts don't get this type of training.'

'What else we got, Alan?' Fluke said.

'Second thing's a bit weird, boss. That test you ordered on the notebook came back with some writing.' He looked down at his notes. 'They used something called an electrostatic detection device. Apparently it can find writing several layers below the top sheet, years later. Found only one thing, clear as day. They've made the assumption it was one layer above the top sheet as there was no other writing, although they can't rule out someone has just rested another bit of paper on the notebook to write.'

'Name and address of the killer?' Fluke said.

'Numbers,' Vaughn replied, missing the irony, 'Weird ones. Jo and I have started running them and, so far, we've come up with squat.'

'You got a copy?' Fluke asked.

Vaughn handed him a bit of paper. Towler bent over his shoulder to look.

2.3 – 8.7 – 92

'Ah, a puzzle,' Towler said. 'Fucking love it when they leave us puzzles.'

'Nothing on the phone?' Fluke said.

'Nothing yet,' Vaughn said. 'The lab's sent it off to another lab, though. Hoping to try some sort of ghost system retrieval, whatever that means.'

'Means they're looking for two systems running side-by-side,' a voice said.

Everyone turned. A small man was leaning against the doorframe. He was grinning.

A cheer went up.

Jiao-long Zhang had joined FMIT on secondment from the Beijing Municipal Public Security Bureau a year earlier, on a UK/China exchange programme. Why he ended up in Cumbria had been a mystery until Fluke learned of his childhood obsession with Beatrix Potter. According to the chief constable Jiao-long had begged the programme manager in the Met to be attached to Cumbria. Most of his spare time was spent in the heart of the Lake District exploring the landscape that inspired the books. He knew more about Peter Rabbit, Jemima Puddle-Duck and Mrs Tittlemouse than anyone else in the building, including Jo Skelton, and she had young children. The rest of his spare time was spent mucking about with Towler, and they could often be seen leaning against each other as they staggered from pub to pub at weekends, one nearly seven feet tall, the other barely over five. The odd couple, Vaughn called them, but only when Towler couldn't hear him.

Normally, Longy, as he quickly became known, would have been expected to do time in an area CID team before joining FMIT. However, he had computer skills no one else in FMIT came close to having. Even the High-Tech Unit deferred to him. Finding hidden information, easy. Recovering information from damaged machines, no problem. Smartphones weren't safe; he could unlock them and retrieve every text and email ever sent. Every photo you'd ever taken.

In the past, Fluke had had him hacking into suspects' social media accounts, breaking passwords and retrieving information that had been hidden or deleted. He was also the best person on the team for tracking suspects across Carlisle's myriad of CCTV cameras. He knew where they all were. The council's as well as the privately owned ones.

Chambers, who was against the whole idea of Chinese secondments, never used him, so Jiao-long worked with the outcasts. Fluke found him to be one of the nicest men he'd ever met. Nothing was too much trouble, his manners were impeccable and he did everything with a huge smile on his face.

He'd just come back from a trip home and he looked exhausted. Fluke knew that he'd insist on diving straight into the investigation, however, and didn't insult him by asking him to go and get over his jet lag first. 'You OK to do some work, Longy?'

'Of course. I've only been up twenty-four hours, boss.'

He handed Vaughn's piece of paper to Jiao-long. 'Run these numbers through every database you know of. I need to know what they are by the time we start again in the morning.'

'And don't worry, Longy, jet lag's all in the mind,' Vaughn grinned.

'And someone needs to make sure he doesn't fall asleep and buy him something to eat around midnight. Thanks for volunteering, Alan,' Fluke said.

Vaughn's face fell. He hated spending money.

'And *proper* food, Alan,' Fluke said. 'Nothing out of a supermarket skip.'

He went back to his office, wanting to sit quietly and reflect for an hour. Let his mind go over what they had before he went home. All he had so far were questions. Who was she? Where was she killed? *Why* was she killed? Why had she changed her appearance? Were the mystery numbers important, or were they a red herring?

Also, he couldn't shake the feeling that there was something he hadn't picked up on yet, something obvious. There was no point forcing it though; when flashes of inspiration came, they never came head on. They always slipped in from the side, usually when his mind was preoccupied with something else.

He turned on his computer and checked his emails. There were the usual ones he received as a senior manager, along with some from HR and the policy unit. One from Professional Standards reminding staff that any gifts had to be declared. The usual twaddle.

There was also one from Chambers demanding Fluke come and brief him on the murder. Fluke wrote a quick response summarising where they were, which was basically nowhere. He knew fobbing Chambers off with an email wouldn't last for ever but he wasn't ready to talk to him yet. Chambers had never had an original thought in his life and didn't trust those who did. Going to him with a half-formed theory about a professional killer was too risky. He'd either ridicule it and replace him with one of his lackeys or, worse, he'd take it seriously and want to manage it himself. Either way, the killer would never be caught.

He turned off the computer and opened the file he'd made up on the murder. He was re-reading Christian Dunn's statement when he was interrupted by a knock on the door. Fran Miles, FMIT's civilian administrator, stuck her head inside.

'You and Matt are booked on the ten a.m. slot tomorrow at Durham, boss.'

'Thanks, Fran.' Fluke yawned. Another early start and he was already tired. No wonder his blood was playing up. There was nothing more for him to do so he picked up his coat, packed a file to read and headed home.

Chapter 14

Fluke had left hospital craving solitude. Before his illness, he'd lived on a nice new-build estate in west Carlisle. After he was discharged, he'd found it claustrophobic. Too much noise, too many children shrieking, too many dogs barking. Where he'd once enjoyed neighbours coming round for a beer or a coffee, he found himself ignoring the doorbell.

Doctor Cooper told him he was suffering from post-traumatic stress disorder but Fluke dismissed it. He'd fought in wars, been shot at in Northern Ireland. If he was going to get PTSD, it would have been then. But she persisted with her diagnosis and carried out something she called 'watchful waiting'. Basically, she was waiting to see if he was going to become suicidal. Fluke didn't, but he found his tolerance of idiots had become even lower than it had been. And it hadn't been very high before. Chambers especially wound him up.

After a massive argument with him over something trivial, Fluke had driven home and sat up all night nurturing a beautiful anger. For the first time, he considered whether Doctor Cooper could be right. He didn't have the energy to carry on. He needed a change. He needed a place away from the masses. He could cope with the human debris his job threw up during the day if he could get away from it at night.

He decided he either had to make a change or wallow in self-pity for ever. Luckily, a solution presented itself in the form of an insurance cheque. A critical illness insurance cheque to be precise. Enough to pay off his mortgage.

Fluke had sold up and headed for the middle of nowhere: the fells above Ullswater. Despite clearing nearly three hundred thousand, prime real estate was still out of his reach. He needed something cheap and that meant something no one else wanted. He bought an acre of woodland high up on the side of a hill that the Forestry Commission were selling. The holiday home company that owned the adjoining land had been holding out for a lower price and Fluke had nipped in and stolen it from under their noses.

It was on a sharp incline, had too many large rocks to make logging profitable and was barely accessible. Fluke was sceptical. Until he saw the view. Although some pine trees partially obscured it, he could see down the entire length of Ullswater. With selective pruning, he'd have a vista that rivalled any in the world.

He applied for planning permission for a holiday home. He spent the rest of his money on a luxury log cabin, which he imported from Finland. Made in the Scandinavian style, it was designed internally around a large open living space. Two bedrooms and a bathroom were off to one side but that was it. But it was the external features Fluke bought it for. A covered terrace encompassed the front and one side of the house, which meant the outside had almost as much floor space as the inside.

The civil engineer from Carlisle he'd initially contacted had told him he was a fool and had wasted his money on the land but the firm who supplied the house also provided the expertise to site it. Engineers from Finland. For them it was a minor project. They were used to working in denser woods and on steeper inclines. They felled a dozen trees and moved some boulders. After two days, they had an area they were satisfied with. They didn't need to be told to site the house facing Ullswater. When they were finished, they even started to clear the trees that blocked his view. Only one of which Fluke insisted on keeping where it was.

It was here that he lived most of his life. He ate outdoors, he read outdoors and, during the summer months, he slept in his hammock. He loved his monastic existence and rarely missed company. His neighbours were creatures of the night. Foxes prowled, owls hunted and the occasional deer came to nibble on the tender shoots of young trees.

He spent the weekends and summer evenings making improvements to the surrounding area. The road, previously a mud track for logging vehicles, had to be upgraded and the backbreaking work gave Fluke a sense of achievement he'd not felt since he'd left hospital. He made a carport out of an old sail to keep pine needles and the worst of the weather off his car. His hands became gnarled and heavily calloused from chopping wood for the fire pit and wood-burning stove. He wasn't yet a third of the way through the trees that the Finns had cut down. When he'd burnt them, he'd earmarked a couple of pines that, if removed, would open up the view further and let in more light. Not too much, though. He didn't want to advertise his presence. Once the cabin had been sited and the trees cleared, he'd taken a trip on one of the Ullswater 'Steamers', the old passenger vessels that cruised the lake, to see if his home could be seen from the water. It could, but only if you had binoculars and knew where to look. The engineers from Finland had known what they were doing.

His wood ran all the way down to the shore so technically he had a lakeside property and one of the jobs he'd planned for the coming summer was to put a series of steps down the treacherous slope. He was toying with the idea of getting a small boat. A couple of nice pubs had their own jetties and, although they were a twelve-mile drive, they were just ten minutes away by boat.

Fluke approached the mud track that led to his home. The sign on his American-style postbox showed he had mail. He slowed, opened his window and retrieved it. A minute later, he'd parked under the carport. As he did every night, he paused for five minutes to take in the view.

The fell on the opposite side of the lake was lit by the moonlight, the bare, splintered bones of shattered rock gleaming. The network of dry stone walls seemed to have grown directly from the land. It was a beautiful night. Fluke strongly believed that where he lived was as much a feeling as a physical location. He couldn't explain it any more than he could explain why certain pieces of music evoked such strong emotional responses.

Despite it being winter he decided to have his supper outside. He put logs on the fire pit and lit it before going inside to prepare some food and get a cigar. He browned off some lamb, chopped onions, added spices in measures he knew by heart and let the curry simmer. He'd leave it until the meat was tender, about two hours.

While he was inside, he opened his mail. Nothing of note until the last one. His stomach sank as he recognised the postmark. He sighed and opened it. It was another letter from the council. The tone wasn't pleasant.

When he'd bought the wood, the planning permission Fluke had applied for was for a holiday home, not a main domicile. He'd assumed that as no one knew it was there, no one would know that he lived there permanently. He'd assumed wrong. The county council knew. Fluke suspected it was the holiday home company owners who'd told them. Six months before, he'd returned home and found a letter in the postbox. They wanted to discuss two things. The log cabin wasn't of the type on the original planning permission and it appeared to be his only home. They needed evidence he was living somewhere else in winter. It was all in an apologetic tone making it clear that the fault was all theirs and if he could provide what they needed, they would stop bothering him. Fluke wasn't surprised when a letter from the holiday company arrived two days later, offering to buy his land.

He ignored them both.

Six weeks later, a second letter from the council arrived. Bureaucracy wasn't quick, but it was thorough. The tone was no less apologetic but, right at the bottom, it mentioned court. And they'd continued to come with depressing regularity, each more threatening than the last. However, the latest was the first letter that actually had a court hearing scheduled.

He walked outside and pushed the letter into the fire pit, waited until it caught then lit his cigar with it, throwing it back in when he was done. He watched as the letter curled and blackened in the flames. The path he was on with the council only had one way of ending. He'd be made homeless with his savings decimated. He'd own a stunning bit of land that was next to useless. He doubted he'd even get permission for a caravan now.

He smiled. It was strange but he worried about it less than he worried about lying to Doctor Cooper.

He settled into one of his numerous outdoor seats and blew smoke out towards the lake. The mingling smell of the cigar smoke and curried lamb coming through the open door was pleasant and comforting. He relaxed, the tension of the previous twenty-four hours gradually leaving his body.

As the meat cooked and his cigar shortened, he thought about the investigation. Best-case scenario was that when they interviewed Ackley the next day, he'd have either recognised the killer or could give them a workable description. He wasn't hopeful though. Ackley was a doped-up smackhead and it seemed he was scared stiff.

He thought about the seemingly random numbers again. He had Jiao-long feeding them into every database he could legally access, and some he couldn't. He hoped he'd have an answer by the morning; all they'd done so far was increase their ignorance. He resisted the temptation to ring Jiao-long and check on his progress. If there were anything significant, he'd be contacted. During murder investigations, his phone was never turned off.

As the curry continued to simmer, Fluke finished his cigar and watched the bats that lived in the wood ducking and diving as they chased the insects drawn to the cabin's light.

Insects.

He'd forgotten to ring Lucy.

Helping her with her thesis would mean he was owed an ento-mological favour in the future, and he had nothing to do while his curry cooked anyway. He retrieved the text with her number and pressed dial.

But Lucy Cheesebrough didn't want a favour, far from it. She wanted to do Fluke a favour.

'Coffee,' she said when pleasantries had been swapped and Fluke had asked what he could do for her.

At first, he thought he was being asked out by a woman fifteen years his junior.

He was wrong.

'During the post-mortem, Mr Fluke—'

'You don't work for me, Lucy. You can call me Avison.'

'Yes, well. Anyway, during the post-mortem you may have noticed that I was interested in the brown substance Henry found under the victim's fingernails, as well as the stuff SOCO recovered from her trouser turn-ups?'

Fluke remembered. He still hadn't heard back from the lab on what it was.

'I'd thought they might have been blowfly puparia,' she said.

'Remind me what they are, Lucy. It's been a while since my PhD in flies.'

She laughed. 'Sorry. The blowfly is usually the first insect on a corpse. It's also the one that colonises the body in the greatest numbers and for that reason it's been studied the most.'

Fluke paid attention. Henry had told him that, as well as help-ing with the time of death, insects could also help with where the victim was killed.

She continued, 'There are four stages in a blowfly's life cycle. An adult lays eggs and those eggs hatch into maggots, which go on to feed on the flesh of the corpse. We can accurately measure that part of the life cycle.'

'But there weren't any maggots on the body.'

'No, but there was that brown substance. The next stage of the maggot is to turn into a pupa. This is the cool bit when the maggot actually turns into a blowfly.'

Fluke resisted saying her 'cool bit' was everyone else's 'disgusting bit'.

'The shell it forms during this transformation is called a puparium. You'll have seen them, they're dark brown and barrel-shaped. They're actually made of the dead skin of the maggot, it sort of hardens around itself,' she continued.

'And they're brown?'

'Exactly. Now, no way does your crime-scene guy fail to identify a fully formed puparium and no way does one fit under someone's fingernail. They're about five or six mills big and easily recognisable. However, when the adult fly has broken out of the puparium, it leaves it in pieces, and sometimes they get broken up further. That's what I thought the substance under her nails could have been.'

'So it *was* insect activity? I'd have bet a month's wages it had been too cold that night.'

'No, no, you misunderstand, Avison. It wasn't bits of puparia at all. She hadn't been dead long enough for that kind of activity. And if she had, there'd have been much more it.'

'Oh. So what was it?'

'I told you: coffee.'

'Coffee,' Fluke repeated.

'Coffee,' she confirmed. 'Ground-up coffee. I had a look at it under a microscope. Henry was kind enough to arrange for me to have supervised access to your lab. There's no doubt.'

Fluke thought for a moment. 'So our vic liked coffee. That's something else I know about her, I suppose. Doesn't help much though. Doubt the brand could be identified and even if it could, I don't see where it would take us.'

'I have more,' she laughed.

Sometimes it's the most inane thing that opens up a case. Sometimes you need that little bit of luck. The police officer who stops a killer for having a brake light out. The man arrested for drink driving whose DNA matches a rape twenty years earlier. Was Lucy going to be his luck on the case?

'I can't tell you what the brand was because it wasn't commercial. These were fresh beans, freshly ground.'

'So?' Fluke asked impatiently. If there was a point he wanted to hear it.

'I'm a coffee lover, Avison. I'm a coffee snob if I'm being honest, although to be fair I'm not a snob about anything else. But I do like my coffee and I know a lot about it.'

'So you *can* identify the bean?'

'Nope, of course not, no one could.'

'That's what I thought,' Fluke said, lying.

'But what I can tell you is that the substance found under her nails and in the turn-ups of her trousers wasn't pre-ground. The beans weren't even ground in a shop. She ground them herself.'

'How can you possibly know that?'

Fluke got up and walked into the house. He wanted to take notes. He wrote down 'coffee beans' and circled it.

'Because the grinder she used was worn. Most coffee enthusiasts use electric grinders. They give a uniform grind although I personally think the friction heats the beans too much.'

'Or?'

'Or they have a manual burr-mill grinder.'

'Burr-mill?'

'Looks like a small sausage maker. About eight inches. That's what I use. I have an old one my dad gave me.'

'And you think that's what she used?'

'I do. What a manual grinder, especially an old one, will do is give an uneven grind. The gears wear down and the burrs rotate unevenly. You don't want an uneven grind. Uniform grinds make a purer cup of coffee. The water is in contact with each grain for the same amount of time. So the only reason you would keep a grinder that didn't work properly is—'

'Because it's personal to you,' Fluke finished.

'Exactly. I don't care how uneven my grinds get, I'll never get rid of my dad's burr-mill. I love it too much. And only coffee lovers would get sentimental about a grinder.'

There was a weird kind of logic to that. It was eccentric but entirely believable. If they ever found where she lived, Fluke would give short odds on there being an old coffee grinder in her house.

'OK, still not seeing how this helps. There must be thousands of coffee enthusiasts in Cumbria.'

'Tens of thousands probably, but the vast majority get their beans pre-ground at the supermarket. Why wouldn't they? It's decent quality and most of it's fair trade. You can even get whole beans there now but there's far less choice.'

'Where do you buy yours, Lucy? From the supermarket?'

'No, I don't. I have my favourite bean and I grind it as I need it. The oils in the bean are at their freshest then. They start to dry as soon as they've been ground. Keeping ground coffee in the fridge helps but it's always best to freshly grind.'

Fluke knew where she was going. 'And a fiver says you can't get your favourite bean at a supermarket?'

'Nope.'

'Another fiver says you have to go to a specialist coffee shop.'

Chapter 15

Fluke was back at Carleton Hall at seven in the morning, still wiping sleep from his eyes. The other early bird was Jo Skelton. Jiao-long was nowhere to be seen but a message on his desk said the computer search of the numbers had turned up nothing. He'd gone home for some rest but would be back later. Fluke joined Skelton in the incident room. He summarised the previous night's call from Lucy and the possibility that their victim may have been buying coffee from a specialist shop.

Fluke left to check his emails. After he'd finished, he came back into the interview room to find Skelton with her face buried in the *Yellow Pages*. Intrigued, he walked over.

She looked up as Fluke approached. 'Was the bug lady sure it was specialist coffee, boss?' she asked.

'As sure as she could be, I suppose. Says she might have been a regular customer. Every other week at least, Lucy reckons. There can't be many of these shops, surely.'

'Loads,' she said. 'I've trawled through *Yellow Pages* and cross-referenced what I found with a search on the internet.'

'How many?'

'Almost eighty.'

Fluke winced. Eighty wasn't manageable. Not without bringing in more staff and he wasn't prepared to go to Chambers with something that flimsy.

He needed to reduce the list somehow.

Working on the assumption that a snob would avoid the

international coffee chains, he removed them from the list. That left a smaller, but still unwieldy list of thirty that primarily sold what he imagined was gourmet coffee.

'We need to triage the shops,' Skelton said.

Fluke had been thinking the same thing but didn't know how to go about it. He'd been considering looking at the ones nearest the murder scene first then expanding outwards but decided that wasn't scientific enough. 'Go on,' he said.

'We'll have to search the Whitehaven area, obviously, that's where the body was found.'

'Agreed.'

'Common sense would suggest that we would then widen the search in an expanding radius around the body. Do all of Copeland, Allerdale, South Lakes next, then Barrow Eden and Carlisle last.'

'Yep.'

'But the killer's a pro. You said it yourself. So if he transported the body to the deposition site, it's likely that the actual murder site was where she was living.'

'Agreed,' Fluke said.

'I'm going to take a guess at something now. The killer knew about the deposition site in advance. Means he's either been there before or had been talking to someone who had.'

'Yep, I was thinking that yesterday. You can't see the hole from the road,' Fluke said. 'It doesn't help with locations though.'

'Doesn't matter. All we're trying to do is triage the search rather than rule anything out.'

She was right. It didn't matter what order they searched, they were just trying to guess where was most likely. 'What you thinking then, Jo?'

'I'd do South Lakes and Barrow last. Neither are in West Cumberland Hospital's catchment area.'

'Nor is Carlisle,' Fluke said.

'Agreed, but if you were planning a murder and were looking for a deposition site, what would you look for, other than the quality of the site itself?'

Fluke thought about where she was going. Tried to think his way through the question.

I've killed someone. The murder site's not in the same place as the deposition site. I have less control over the murder site presumably as the victim has to be present so to a certain extent I'm bound by her movements, but I can choose where I dump the body. I need to transport the body from the murder site to the deposition site.

'A safe route,' he said finally.

'Exactly. He needs a straightforward drive from A to B. It's possible he knows our back roads and if he uses them, he'll never get stopped by us. But he knows driving them in the dark isn't easy, there are blind corners after blind corners. They're narrow, only wide enough for one car in places so you have to use passing spaces. You have to crawl past each other.'

'And someone may remember you,' Fluke said. He thought about it for a while. She was onto something. 'He'd also want a decent escape route if it all went wrong.'

'I hadn't thought of that, but you're right.'

'So we rule out the back roads. Now what?' he asked.

'The next thing I considered was where point A could be. Where she lived. Matt says the bullet used would have been quiet and that he may have used her head to quieten the shot further.'

'Correct.'

'And that you think she was hiding from someone. Only reason for the type of cosmetic surgery she had.'

Fluke nodded. 'Keep going.'

'If she were hiding in Cumbria, she has two options. She can keep her head down in an isolated village or hamlet. We're a rural county, it's possible to disappear. Some of these places aren't even marked on the map.'

'Risky though. They all talk to each other in these places. Strangers stand out like pepper in salt.'

'That's what I think. I'm ruling it out for now. The other option she has is that she moves into one of the big towns. Tries to blend in.'

'She hides in plain sight,' Fluke said. 'Uses people to hide in. Somewhere big enough so she doesn't stand out. Carlisle or Barrow basically.'

'Carlisle, sir. Not Barrow. The road from Barrow to the deposition site is terrible. You ever been over Corney Fell in the dark? The road's a nightmare. Tiny, narrow, up and down, and, because it has common grazing rights, no one can put up a fence, which means there are sheep on the roads at all times. Even the locals avoid it at night. He'd have to take a massive detour to use semi-decent roads. Too much exposure.'

Fluke knew she was right. During the day, it was a lovely drive but better suited to fell walkers than drivers. It took about half an hour, and even on a good day, it was exhausting. It wasn't the route to take if you were transporting a body.

'So I think we focus on the shops around Whitehaven and Carlisle first,' Skelton said.

Fluke thought about it but not for long. The victim was perhaps more likely to be attracted to Carlisle than Whitehaven if she was the sort of person with a taste for the finer things in life. After all, he got his own coffee from a specialist shop in Carlisle.

'OK, Jo, you've convinced me. We'll run with it, but we should do Carlisle first. I'll need you to arrange it though. I'm going to be away until mid-afternoon with our witness. Can you take the morning briefing? Focus on the coffee lead. Send a photo of the vic to all area CID teams but make sure it's an E-FIT. I don't want cops turning up at posh little bistros with a picture of a corpse.'

'Requested it last night, boss,' she said.

Fluke thanked her and smiled to himself. That was what Chambers would never understand about Jo Skelton. She may not

115

look the part but she was better than any detective working the robbery. She'd had ten minutes to think about Lucy's theory while he'd checked his emails and she'd developed a plan to triage the coffee shops. All his team had initiative. Admittedly sometimes it backfired, like the time Towler had used initiative to give everyone a long weekend after they'd charged the farmer who had drowned his wife in slurry. Fluke had come in on Monday to find the FMIT office empty. But by and large, all you had to do was give them some general direction and they'd do the rest.

'One more thing, Jo,' Fluke said. 'Can you make sure we keep trying to figure out what the numbers mean? Get hard copies for everyone and hand them out at the briefing. If it's a code, I want people thinking about it. Let's get some lateral thinking going on.'

'Clever stuff,' Towler said, after Fluke had explained the coffee lead. 'Might not turn up anything, but at least we're being proactive, for a change. All we've done so far is chase fucking shadows.'

Fluke nodded. He felt the same. The previous night, he'd found Lucy's theory interesting. After speaking to Skelton, he'd upgraded it to promising. He lapsed into silence and reread the preliminary post-mortem report. Something had been bothering him but he'd drawn a blank. Something Skelton had said that morning had made him revisit it, and he'd been thinking about it since they'd turned onto the A66. As the main road connecting the west to the east, they'd travelled it often. The wind buffeted the car and Towler had to grasp the steering wheel with both hands.

Towler was talking about something his daughter had said to his mother the previous night but he wasn't really listening. Towler doted on his daughter and wasn't afraid of showing it. If anyone took the piss, they only did it once.

'You remember the PM, Matt?' Fluke interrupted. 'There was something Sowerby said that I thought was a bit odd.'

Towler briefly took his eyes off the road. 'What?'

116

'The bit about there being no fall injuries,' he replied. 'You're a professional killer, right? You have a gun that will kill at . . . what distance?'

Towler thought for a few seconds. 'Like I said yesterday, ten feet to be safe. You shouldn't miss the head from that distance. Not if you know what you're doing.'

'So why kill her with a contact shot?'

'Told you, contact shot with a subsonic bullet. The liquid in the skull acts as a silencer. Quiet, very quiet.'

'So why not just use a silencer? He has the contacts to get the gun, yes? So why not get a silencer at the same time? Do it from a distance of what, say six or seven feet? Still kills her but there's no chance of forensic transfer. Why stand right next to her?'

There was only one obvious answer. 'He had to catch her. Wherever he was, he didn't want her falling to the floor. Why though?'

'That's been bothering me as well. Didn't even know it had, but Jo got me thinking about the victim differently. About how she must have hidden herself. About the two options. Now, if she's hiding in a remote cottage then so what? He walks up to her and shoots her. No one is going to hear that, and even if they do, so what? Guns are common in the country. More importantly, no one would hear her fall. No dramas.'

'Makes sense. No point getting close to your victim unless you have to,' Towler said.

'Exactly. I think he killed her up close as he had to catch her. I think that if she'd fallen, someone might've heard. I think she lived in a flat.'

They discussed the case for the rest of the journey, everything they knew and everything they didn't. Fluke struggled to remember a case with so little to go on after forty-eight hours. Numbers in a notebook, an untested coffee theory, a worthless bullet and that was it. The rest was conjecture and that was dangerous. It was worrying. An unknown victim, an unknown killer and unknown motive. Chambers wouldn't stand for that for too much longer. He'd want progress soon or he'd start moving resources around.

'Been thinking about what you said yesterday,' Towler said, as they passed the army ranges at Warcop. 'I think the killer probably is ex-military.'

'It could just as easily have been a paintballer.'

Towler snorted. 'Bollocks.'

Towler pulled into the Old Elvet area of Durham, and parked as near to the prison as he could.

As they walked up the hill, past the barristers' chambers towards the entrance gate, Fluke said, 'Matt, don't wind up the prison officers this time.'

Durham prison was deceiving. It looked old. It *was* old. An ancient cathedral of human misery. But until a couple of years ago, it had been part of the high-security estate so had state-of-the-art gate facilities. They had their fingerprints taken at the gate with a biometric scanner, and photo IDs were printed before they moved to the search area. They sat in the metal chair that detected anything concealed inside the lower body and moved on to the queue to be physically searched.

As they waited, Fluke read the imposing Prison Service signs on the wall. White writing on a blue background. They listed prohibited items, along with the penalties for smuggling. Mobile phones, keys, money and cigarettes. None of it could be taken inside. They'd been on enough prison visits to know what they could and couldn't bring in, and after Towler had left the car keys in a locker, they went through to security.

Fluke made Towler go through first. The previous time, he'd gone second and Fluke had been unable to stop the commotion that followed.

Towler objected to the treatment of police officers by prison staff. Always had. He objected to being fingerprinted. He objected to queuing with solicitors and prisoners' families. He objected to having a chair check his anus for drugs and mobile phones.

But most of all, he objected to being searched.

It was a clash of egos, and prison officers seemed to be able to sense when they had a police officer who was going to provide some entertainment. He'd been refused entry on at least two occasions: once for refusing to hand over a mobile for safekeeping – it had contained evidence he wanted to show a prisoner – and another time for refusing to take off his belt. This time, he went through with no problems and Fluke breathed a silent sigh of relief.

They were directed up the stairs and through a couple of security doors. If the prison had still been a Cat A, they would have been escorted everywhere but, as a Cat B, they were just given the directions to the official visits suite.

'Suite' was a grandiose term for what was essentially a series of dirty boxes. Eight each side of a wide corridor, sixteen in total. The rooms were clear Perspex on three sides to ensure the prison officers could observe everything. The corridor had an entrance at either end: the prisoners' entrance and the visitors' entrance.

'You're in suite seven,' the prison officer told them.

'Cheers,' Towler said. 'Can you send him in?'

Each suite had a table, four fixed chairs and nothing else. They were stark. The smell of disinfectant was invasive. It was the sort used when cleaning needed to be quick but thorough. A smell only found in institutions. More signs on the wall listed the suite rules.

'Here he is, lads,' the prison officer called out.

'Jesus, look at the state of this,' Towler said as Ackley came through the prisoners' entrance.

Chapter 16

The sallow, skeletal figure standing in the doorway looked like the picture in his file, but only if he'd been dead a week. The word 'gaunt' popped unbidden into Fluke's head. He clearly hadn't showered or washed recently and a sour stench immediately permeated the room. Neither Fluke nor Towler commented on it. Long, lank hair framed a pallid face. White gunk had formed at the corners of a mouth surrounded by spots. His teeth were brown. A sheen of cold sweat glistened on his forehead.

Fluke wasn't up on the rates for rent boys but he guessed that Ackley was working the cheaper end of the market.

Despite being a remand prisoner, and therefore entitled to wear his own clothes, he was in standard prison-issue clothing of tracksuit bottoms and a green sweatshirt. The prison had probably decided the clothes he'd arrived in were a health hazard and removed them. He stood in the doorway, looking at them, vigorously scratching his arm.

'Come in, Darren,' Towler said.

As soon as he sat down, he started to shake. Fluke initially thought he was scared. He was, but that wasn't the reason for the shakes.

He buried his head in his hands. 'I'm clucking, man.'

Fluke looked at him blankly. He knew most Cumbrian phrases but that was a new one.

Towler interpreted. 'Means he's withdrawing, boss.'

Fluke didn't respond. Towler would lead on the interview.

'Bastards won't put me in the hospital,' Ackley mumbled.

'Darren, look at me.'

Ackley looked up, his bloodshot eyes squinting in the pale light of the flickering fluorescent tube.

'Do you know why we're here?'

Ackley shook his head. 'Nah, man. Leave us alone.'

'Where were you Monday night, Darren?'

There was no surprise on his face, just resignation.

'Fuck off, man, I'm badly.'

'I don't give a shit,' Towler said. He waited until it was clear Ackley wasn't going to say anything.

'Look, Darren, we know what happened. You saw a man dump a body. You left a note and now you wish you hadn't.'

Ackley doubled up in pain. A stomach cramp, no doubt. Fluke wasn't sure how long they'd be able to carry on. He didn't look well at all. If he were in police custody there was no way the doctor would allow him to be interviewed.

Towler continued, 'Do you know what an Osman Warning is, Darren?'

Ackley shook his head.

'It's where the police have a duty to warn someone that they're in danger. When you're released, I will personally serve the Osman Warning on you. And then I'll walk off and not give two shits about what happens next.'

Ackley sniffed and wiped his nose on his sleeve. He said nothing.

Towler stared at him. Ackley held his gaze for as long as he could but soon put his head back in his hands and rocked back and forth.

'Look, I'll lay it out for you. Someone dumped a body. They seem to know what they're doing, so it's likely they've done this type of thing before. But this time, he's seen. And he'll know by now because there's cops all over that building site. How long before he starts looking for the witness? How long before he finds out it was Darren Ackley who saw him?'

It was clear Ackley had been thinking about that a lot. He trembled again and Fluke didn't think it was just withdrawal symptoms this time. It was often the case that those who had so little to live for clung on to life so fiercely. Towler thought that too it seemed.

'You got yourself remanded so you'd be safe,' Towler said. 'And I understand that. If I were in your position, I might have done the same.'

Ackley looked at them both. His eyes screwed up and he wept.

Towler pressed his advantage. 'But how safe are you in here, really? We both know people can be got to in prison. There are people in here with nothing to lose. They're never getting out. They'll do pretty much anything for a pack of cigarettes or some drugs. You know this, Darren.'

Ackley sniffed up some snot that had been making an escape, and wiped his eyes with his sleeve. 'So what do you want me to do?'

'The only thing you can do, Darren,' Towler said. 'Help us catch this bastard.'

Towler picked up his pen and opened his notebook, a signal that he was ready to work and that he expected Ackley to do the same.

Ackley told them everything. They prodded and poked, and were eventually satisfied that they knew everything he did. It wasn't much and most of it they'd already guessed. By the end, they were no closer to moving the case forward. The only thing that happened was they'd softened towards Ackley. He was a tragic figure.

He told them how he'd met a man in a Whitehaven club and they'd had sex in the toilets. Afterwards, he'd offered Ackley a place to sleep. The office on the building site of the new hospital. It was warm, it was safe and no one knew about it. He'd jumped at the chance. He'd been sleeping there for two weeks by his reckoning, but he had a junkie's attitude to time, so it was only a guess.

'This good Samaritan – did it for free, did he?' Towler asked.

That got a reaction.

'Did he fuck. He was there at seven o'clock every fuckin' morning wanting sucked off. Fuckin' twat never even paid me after the first time. Just came in, got his tiny cock out and stuck it in me mouth. Soon as he shot his load, I had to fuck off. I wasn't allowed back till it was dark again.'

'And that was every day?' Towler asked.

'Near enough. There was one day, must've been a Sunday cos he brought some food with him, that he came in the afternoon. I was supposed to be grateful.'

'And you weren't?'

'Was I fuck. The dirty bastard didn't give a shit about me. Soon as I finished, he went and got a blow-up mattress from his car and he fucked us on it the rest of the day. He got fifty quid's worth of sex and I got some scabby chicken and minging cabbage.'

'This man, what did he look like?' Fluke asked, the first time he'd spoken since Ackley had arrived. He thought he knew the answer but wanted to hear it first-hand.

'Old bastard. Shorter than you. He was from Whitehaven, I'd seen him hanging round the club a few times. Shittin' himself most of the time. Fuckin' typical. Wants cock but won't leave his wife to get it.'

Christian Dunn. The site foreman who'd called the police. No wonder he'd looked shifty. Seemed he was using his office as his personal shag-pad. Nothing wrong with that, each to their own. But he'd lied to Fluke about not knowing who'd left the note and, for that, he was going to be arrested. He couldn't do anything about the way Dunn had treated Ackley, but Fluke would make sure he never lied to the police again.

Ackley's concept of time caused them problems. He told them what he saw: a car had woken him, he'd watched as a man walked onto the site with a torch before returning to get something from the boot. But he had no idea what time it had been, only that it was still dark. Towler pressed him for more details but it was clear that fear was the only thing he was remembering.

'How'd you know it was a body he got out the boot?' Fluke asked. 'We know you didn't go down and check.'

'I just knew. What else could it have been, man? Middle o' the fuckin' night, he turns up with a shovel and torch. What did you think he was doing, planting a fuckin' tree? Nah, man, it was a body. Anyway, it sounded like one when he grabbed it from the car and it hit the deck.'

'Then what?' said Towler.

'He picked it up, didn't he? Carried it t' hole an' skopped it in. Shovelled shite on top for ten minutes then got back in his car and pissed off.'

'Where were you?'

Ackley looked at Towler like he was an idiot. 'I was in the office, like. Haven't you been fucking listening?'

Fluke hid a smile.

'I meant, were you hiding the whole time or did you get a proper look, dickhead? In other words, are you guessing what he did or did you see it?' Towler growled.

Ackley looked at Towler and then to Fluke for some help. He didn't get it.

'No, I seen it all. I stuck me head back up after a while and when I did, he was carrying the bag in a fireman's lift. Still had the torch on, that's how come I could see. Fucking shitting mesel' the whole time, mind.'

'What did he look like?'

'Big. Maybe not tall as you, but not far off. Had a suit on, I think. It was pitchers, like, so I cud only see an outline.'

124

'Car?'

'Dunno. Not mad for cars, never 'ad one. Me mate Macca's the one for cars. He'd tell ya what it was from the outline, nee bother like.'

'Macca?'

'Me mate. Davey McNab. I went t' him to get a loan, like. Was gonna naff off to Newcastle for a bit till it calmed down. He could only spot us a fiver, like. Not enough for a bus and not enough for a bag o' smack. Scared shitless of that woman he's with. She said no t' lending us the cash, like. I could hear 'er.'

'So you went to Tesco?'

'Aye, it was the only thing I could think of. Knew I could get mesel' locked up if I took summat big enough. Had to wait by the door or the fat guard wouldn't 'ave caught us.'

'Why'd you not come to us? Or to your probation officer, for that matter?'

'Them twats. What's the point? They do nowt for ya. "Piss into this, Ackley; do this, Ackley; stop having unprotected sex, Ackley; stop taking drugs, Ackley." Fucking knobs, the lot of them. I tell you, probation can go fu—'

'The car?' Towler said, cutting him off.

'I dunno. It was a fuckin' car. Had a boot rather than a hatchback, I suppose. Biggish. Looked like a dark colour.'

Towler realised that was all he was going to get. 'Why'd you leave the note?'

His demeanour changed. Fluke could have sworn he saw colour rising on his pale cheeks. He doubled up. He seemed to be shaking again. Fluke thought that the stomach cramps might cause him to vomit. He was wrong, he wasn't cramping, he was crying again.

Ackley looked up. His eyes were red and wet. Tear tracks glistened on his grimy cheeks.

'I'm a piece of shit,' he sobbed. 'I mean, look at the clip of us.

Nee family. Nee friends apart from Macca and he's a cock most o' the time. Been on the streets over ten years. When I was larle, I was getting two hundred quid a go. Now I'm lucky to get a fiver. Who's gonna give a shit when I die? Fucking no one, that's who. Who's gonna call the police when someone puts me in a hole in the ground?'

'It just seemed like the right thing to do?' Towler said gently.

Ackley nodded.

After that, there didn't seem to be anything else left to discuss. As they left the interview room, Fluke turned and looked at Ackley, waiting there for a prison officer to collect him. Shivering in his own private hell.

Fluke didn't think he'd seen anything so sad in his life.

Chapter 17

When Fluke got back to their car and retrieved his phone, there were missed calls and a text. All from Skelton.

He called back and she answered on the first ring. 'Jo, what's up?'

'We've got a hit on the E-FIT, boss.'

Fluke could hear excitement in her voice. 'Christ, that was quick. I've only been gone four hours,' he said.

'I sent it off to Whitehaven and Carlisle first thing. Carlisle CID got it just in time to get it on to the shift-change briefing. I thought, if we got it out early enough and followed up with detectives later, we would cover a lot more ground. See if there was anything immediate.'

'And there was.'

'Yes, sir. John Watt & Son. She was there a week ago.'

'You're joking? In Carlisle?' His pulse quickened.

'You know it?'

Fluke couldn't believe it. Other than Brucciani's, where he bought his Cuban cigars, Watt's was probably his favourite shop in Carlisle. He bought coffee from there if he was ever passing and knew the owners well. Although they would have to confirm it with a proper photograph of the victim, it was their first real breakthrough.

He felt a buzz of excitement, the first he'd felt since finding the body. Skelton was from Ulverston so Fluke knew something she probably didn't.

'Watt's is on Bank Street,' he said, 'and that place is crawling with CCTV. If it's her, we have a place to start. Get Longy back in. I'll need him to work the cameras. We may even be able to track her to her house.'

Poor Jiao-long. Only back twelve hours and he's stuck with another major task. Couldn't be helped, though. He was the best chance they had of navigating their way through the city's cameras.

They arrived back at the incident room to find it full. Everyone was waiting for Fluke, waiting to be tasked. They knew the investigation had taken a turn and things would now speed up. Before, they'd been casting their net wide; now, there was focus. If they could find her house, they could start piecing her life together.

Find out how the victim lived and you'll find out how they died.

A mantra drummed into him by an instructor on his SIO course, one that he still filtered every decision through.

Fluke went straight into tasking.

'Longy, if we confirm she was at Watt's, I want you on the CCTV. Go and base yourself wherever you need to be; probably at the council's control room initially. How many people will you need?'

He'd obviously been thinking about that as he answered immediately. 'Just me to start with, boss. If I find her and she disappears, I may need help tracking down other sources of film.'

'OK. Hopefully we'll get a description of what she was wearing last time she was there as well,' Fluke said.

Jiao-long left to make the arrangements. Fluke knew he'd go straight to the council and, despite their objections, take over their suite. He knew his way round their machines better than they did.

Fluke remembered something. 'Longy,' he shouted to get him back. 'She may live in a flat.'

He briefly explained to everyone the theory on why she was shot at point-blank range. There was no dissent, which Fluke took as a good sign.

128

With Jiao-long gone, he continued with the rest of the tasks. As he did, Skelton handed out something to everyone. When he got his, Fluke saw it was a business card printed with the numbers found with the body. The logo on the back told him they were from a local printer. She must have paid for them herself. He was impressed. Carrying it about in your wallet or purse meant it was always to hand.

'Right, Matt and I will go to Watt's. See what we can get from them.'

He stood, ready to leave. Everyone did the same, eager to get going. A break in the case was better than a double shot of espresso for getting the energy levels up.

'Jo's also just handed out some cards with those numbers on. Longy came back with zilch which means the answer's not on the internet. I want you thinking about this every spare minute you have. Spread them around. They must mean something to someone.'

He made a show of putting his in his wallet and noticed most of the others did the same. He had a sudden thought.

'Go to the university, Alan,' he said. 'See if there's a cryptographer in the maths department who might be able to help with them.'

'Does Cumbria University even have a maths department?' Vaughn asked.

'Alan, go to the university and find out if they *have* a maths department,' Fluke said, to laughter. 'If they don't, go across to Newcastle University. I know they do.'

'Will do, boss.'

'What about the cosmetic surgery lead, boss?' Skelton asked. 'Do you want me to follow that up?'

'No, I'll do it straight after I've been to Watt's,' he said. 'No point everyone going into Carlisle. You stay here, keep HOLMES up to date and coordinate the intel as it comes in. I want to know everything in real time.'

With the major tasks allocated, Fluke walked back to his office and checked his emails.

There was nothing on the system that needed his urgent attention. He leaned back in his chair and stared out of the window. The weather was changing. The light was poorer than it had been that morning. Rain was on its way. Fluke didn't mind. His office view encompassed fields and sheep. He liked the rain. It gave the landscape a northern quality.

Without realising he had, he'd removed the card Skelton had given him from his wallet. He'd been shuffling it between his fingers like a magician. He stopped and studied it.

2.3 – 8.7 – 92

It wasn't on the internet. Fluke knew if it had been, Jiao-long would have found it. Or if it was on and he hadn't found it, then it wasn't meant to be found. He was good, but there were some systems he couldn't access.

Instinctively, Fluke thought it would be something normal rather than something exotic. Something obvious. Something that made you cry out, 'Of course.'

2.3 – 8.7 – 92

The key to it all or just random numbers that would end up costing the taxpayer thousands of pounds in police hours?

Fluke read them again. Were they familiar? He thought they might be, but had no idea why. He thought the most likely explanation was a password to something online and, if it was, they may never find out. He took one last look, but they stubbornly refused to reveal their secrets. A noise outside, getting louder, told him that Towler was on his way.

Time to go and get some coffee.

John Watt & Son had been selling coffee in Carlisle for over one hundred and fifty years. Starting off as general grocer's in 1865, they traded for nearly a hundred and thirty years until the challenge of out-of-town supermarkets forced them to change to tea and coffee specialists. They were more recently known for stocking coffees and teas that were simply not available anywhere else in the county. They had a small café in the shop and Fluke often stayed for a piece of cake and a chat with the owner if he had time.

The journey from HQ took less than half an hour. Towler double-parked on Bank Street, walked over to a traffic warden, who was just starting the street, and explained who they were. The man didn't seem to want to get into an argument and Towler was soon back.

'Sorted,' he said.

It was a strange street. There were half a dozen high-street banks, half a dozen charity shops and a pet shop. In Fluke's experience charity shops and banks never normally rubbed shoulders. It was a contradiction. Shops for the poor alongside the organisations that *made* people poor.

And right in the middle was Watt's.

Fluke and Towler entered.

The smell hit Fluke immediately. The scent of exotic coffee beans, acrid espressos and cinnamon lattes mingled to create a heady bouquet that made his mouth water.

The bank of jarred beans behind the counter told you everything you needed to know about Watt's. Over a hundred varieties, enough to tempt the fussiest connoisseur. Beans from Brazil, Vietnam, Peru and Ethiopia. A United Nations of coffee growers. The day's special offer was from Costa Rica. The big glass jar sat on the top of the rich mahogany counter next to the till and a selection of fresh cakes under a glass cloche.

The huge grinder whirred as another customer had their beans freshly prepared, ready to be taken home and enjoyed later. Fluke hadn't bought a bag of Watt's coffee since he'd moved and he vowed to stock up before he left.

He didn't recognise the woman serving behind the counter.

'Hello, Avison. We were wondering if it'd be you who'd turn up,' said a cheerful voice on his right.

Fluke turned. A middle-aged woman was in the café section, serving a group of office workers. They were all wearing the same name badge. Civil servants by the look of things. They looked glad to be out of the office.

'Hello, Barbara. How are you? Was it uniform you spoke to earlier?' Fluke asked.

'I'll come over,' she said. 'We can go in the back.'

After they'd settled in the small office, she answered. 'Yes, it was me initially. I've seen the poor girl a few times but it was Kath who saw her last.'

'I'll need to speak to Kath as well then,' Fluke said.

'She's gone home, Avison,' she said. 'She was a bit upset.'

'I'm sorry, Barbara, I really am. But we'll need to speak to her today, it's very important.'

'I made sure she wrote everything down though,' Barbara added triumphantly, pointing at a piece of paper.

'We'll get onto that in a minute,' he said.

From his conference folder, Fluke produced a photo of the victim's face taken at the post-mortem, and put it upside down on the table. 'Barbara, I want to show you a picture and it's quite upsetting. But I'd like you to look at it nonetheless.'

She smiled. 'I was a nurse for twenty years, Avison. If you need to show me a picture of a dead body, go right ahead.'

A sense of relief flooded through him. Getting someone to actually look at the photo had never been a given. He turned it over. A glossy photo of the victim's face, ghostly white under the post-mortem lights, stared up at them.

'This woman shops here?' he said.

Barbara took a pair of reading glasses from her cardigan pocket and picked up the photo. She didn't appear fazed.

'Yes, she did. Nice girl, quiet.'

Fluke was prepared to accept that as a positive sighting. He had a place for Jiao-long to start. 'We don't yet know who she is. Is there anything you can help us with? How long has she shopped with you?'

'Not long, a couple of months, maybe. But she was in every week.'

'Can you remember anything about her?'

'Not really, she didn't stick out. Always paid cash. Always bought a three-bean blend. One hundred and fifty grams of South American Mountain for flavour, one-fifty of Sumatran for strength and two hundred grams of Costa Rican for depth. Always the same, even when we had specials on. Always the same amount, a five-hundred-gram bag. Never had the beans ground instore. I assume she had her own grinder. A lot of our regulars do.'

Well done, Lucy, Fluke thought. *She hasn't got a thing wrong yet.* 'You wouldn't happen to know when she was here last, would you?'

'Last Thursday, ten past twelve,' she said. 'We checked the till roll. Kath served her. And the reason we know it was her is because she only served two people that morning. The rest of the time she was doing the tables. More fun, you see, you get to talk with the locals. She hates the till. But if we're jammed, she'll help out. She remembers her because she's never made her blend before.' She pointed at the statement Kath had written. 'It's all on here.'

It was written on Watt's stationery. Attached was a photocopy of the receipt as well as a description of what the victim had been wearing.

'This is excellent, Barbara,' Fluke said. 'She seems to have a real eye for detail.'

'Yes, well. Kath's a bit of a clotheshorse. If it had been me on the till you wouldn't have got this much detail. I wouldn't know my Prada from my Primark.'

'You've no idea how helpful this is going to be,' Fluke said. He passed the statement over to Towler. 'Seems Kath remembered what she was wearing as well.'

'She didn't speak to her?' Towler asked.

'No, no one ever did. She always seemed to come when it was busy, around lunchtime. People rushing in and out.'

Fluke and Towler exchanged glances. Another way of making sure she wasn't noticed. Another indicator she'd been hiding from someone.

'Matt, can you give Longy a bell and let him know what she was wearing, along with the date and time,' Fluke asked. Towler left to make the call. 'This will save us hours of work, Barbara.'

While he waited for Towler to come back, he looked at the photo again. A pretty woman, no more than a girl really. A life snuffed out for reasons he hadn't even started to unravel yet. Towler returned.

'All done. He's gonna give us a live update.'

Fluke turned to Barbara. 'Thanks again for all this. You won't believe how much help you've been.'

'My pleasure, Avison. Now can I get you something while you're here?'

Fluke studied the shelves. Millions of coffee beans waiting to be ground, waiting for their oils to be released and for hot water to be added. A custom the same the world over. A custom older than Carlisle.

'I'll tell you what, Barbara. Make me up a bag of her blend, can you?'

'Of course. I'll grind it right up for you.'

'Don't, I'll take a grinder as well.'

Find out how the victim lived and you'll find out how they died.

134

Chapter 18

Towler parked at the Cumberland Infirmary. They were in Fluke's car. Towler lived in Carlisle so would walk home.

Fluke walked through the huge revolving doors into the open-plan foyer. The clack of keyboards, the squeal of wheelchairs and the low voices of staff, patients and visitors combined into a cacophony of sensory confusion.

As he headed towards oncology, Fluke was reminded how much the foyer looked like an airport departure lounge. It was huge. It had opened to criticism that it took up too much valuable space and when it transpired that ward corridors were so narrow that two beds couldn't pass, the criticism appeared justified.

'Is she in?' he asked the nurse on the reception.

'I'll call her, Mr Fluke. Take a seat.'

Fluke elected to stand. While he was waiting, he took the business card out of his wallet and stared at it. Willing the numbers to change, to make sense. He even tried squinting, tried to look through it as though it were a magic-eye picture. Nothing. But the nagging feeling persisted. They looked familiar.

'And to what do I owe this pleasure?' Doctor Cooper asked, entering the reception area.

She looked tired but then she always did. Fluke's job carried a huge responsibility but, in between major cases, he at least had some respite. A chance to recharge the mental batteries. Consultants never had that luxury.

'I need your help,' he said.

'OK,' she said cautiously. 'Am I going to like this?'

'It's nothing bad, I promise you. I just want your advice on this case. Maybe a name I can call.'

'We'd better go to my office then.'

'Thanks, Doctor Cooper.'

'Look, this is ridiculous, Avison. Will you please call me Leah? We've known each other long enough now.'

'OK,' he said carefully. Fluke was one of those people who felt uneasy calling a doctor anything other than 'doctor'. He didn't know why that was. Probably a class thing.

He followed her into her office and took a seat.

'OK. What's it about?' she asked.

'This is going to be a bit left field, but what do you know about cosmetic surgery?'

She looked nonplussed and stared at him for a few seconds. 'Nothing, of course. I'm not a surgeon. I'm certainly not a *cosmetic* surgeon. And there aren't any private clinics in Cumbria. Any patients requiring it for medical reasons have to go out of county.'

'That much I already know. I just want the basics. Where would someone go to get some surgery done? How long it takes? Would it be possible to get multiple procedures done at once? How long to heal, that sort of thing?'

'Is this something to do with that woman they found on Tuesday?'

He paused before deciding she deserved to have some background.

'Yes,' he said. 'At the PM, Henry found extensive cosmetic surgery. Bit of an enigma. Very high quality but it made no sense. Medically speaking.'

'Oh. Go on. Why?' she said, her medical curiosity obviously piqued.

'She didn't need it, for one thing.' Fluke held his hand up, knowing she was going to launch into something about how men had no right to decide what women did to their bodies. 'No, all the changes she made detracted from her looks rather than enhanced them.'

She folded her arms. 'Says you.'

Fluke had neither the time nor the inclination to get into an argument on feminism.

'Says me, says Henry and says Lucy. Says . . .' He was going to add Towler but he remembered his remark about plastic tits not wobbling and decided against it.

'Who's Lucy?' she said unexpectedly.

'The bug lady,' he said, without thinking.

She said nothing. Continued to stare at him with her arms folded and her lips pursed.

'An entomologist. A PhD student working with Henry for a few weeks. She's been a big help, actually.'

'You have a theory about the cosmetic surgery?' she said, changing direction.

'She was altering the way she looked for a reason. We think she was hiding.'

Leah leaned forward. 'Were there any other supporting factors?'

'Yes.'

'What?'

'Her hair was dyed. Platinum blonde to brown.'

'Anything else?'

'Coloured contacts.'

She leaned back in her chair. She flicked some hair from her eyes, stood and retrieved a book from the bookcase beside her desk. She flicked through it. She sighed and closed it.

'Look, I'm not an expert on this but I know the laws on cosmetic surgery are constantly changing. It used to be an entirely unregulated business. There were more regulations governing toothbrush manufacture than there were on liposuction, believe

137

it or not. All changing now, of course. Breast implants saw to that.'

'The exploding ones?' he said without thinking.

She smiled. 'At one point, there was more money being made repairing them than there was fitting them. Did she have hers done?'

'Nope, strictly above the collar. Nose, ears, chin and brow.'

'And the rest is easy to hide with clothes,' she said straight away.

'Exactly.'

They discussed what procedures she'd been through and Leah eventually agreed that Fluke's theory was possible. Probable even.

'I take it you'd like to speak to the doctor who did the surgery?' she said.

'If possible.'

'Not a chance. There's hundreds of surgeons who do this sort of thing in the UK. You can add three noughts to that if you include Europe and the States. Breast implants have serial numbers now but with the procedures she's had, there'll be nothing to check.'

Fluke knew she was right, and had known it before he'd left HQ. Still, another potential lead had been crossed off. Negative intelligence was *still* intelligence. Detectives were taught to use an acronym: TIE. Trace, interview, eliminate. It was meant for suspects and witnesses but worked just as well for potential lines of enquiry.

'Look, I know someone in London who may be able to help. I'll call him tonight, see if he can get you a number to ring,' she said. 'You can at least hear from someone who knows what they're talking about.'

'Thanks, Leah. Anything at all will be more than we have on her so far.'

She returned the book to the shelf and sat back down. 'How are you, Avison?'

'Can't complain,' he replied, his mind already on the next task.

'Avison. How are you really? You look exhausted. How are you sleeping?'

Fluke shrugged. He wasn't comfortable talking about things like that.

'Look, it's common to feel this way. It would be extraordinary if you didn't. You weren't expected to live, remember? No one gave you a chance when they saw the size of the tumour. Whether you'll admit it or not, you had PTSD. That's why you were so angry with everyone. The world didn't change when you were in hospital, Avison. You did. At first, I thought moving out of Carlisle to live on your own in the middle of nowhere was a mistake, but I have to admit, you knew more about how to heal yourself than I did.'

Fluke looked at her. He didn't realise she'd been paying that much attention. He rubbed his hands over his eyes, tried to remove some of the grit that came with fatigue. The truth was he was no longer reliving his illness any more. For a few months, he'd suffered badly from flashbacks. He'd dreaded sleep, dreaded waking up sweating and trembling. If it hadn't been for his thin blood, he'd have used alcohol as a numbing agent.

'I'm doing better, Leah. Much better,' he said finally.

It was no longer the reaction to his illness that kept him awake. It was what he'd done to her. A secret he couldn't share.

'Good then. Now we just need to stabilise your bloods and we'll be fine. How was dinner the other night?' she asked.

He paused. 'I'm sorry,' he said eventually. He had no idea what she was talking about.

'Dinner at Michelle's. I gather it didn't go all that well?' She laughed at his expression. 'Sorry, bit naughty of me. It's just that you met one of my friends. She says she gave you a lift home.'

The mystery woman was her friend? It seemed unlikely that Michelle and Leah ran in the same social circles. Leah was intelligent and reasonable; Michelle's friends were right-wing bucketheads. She must have been reading his mind.

'Don't worry, she doesn't normally run with that sort of crowd. She knew someone called Charles and he'd invited her. She was going to say no, but I convinced her to go.'

'I thought you said she was your friend,' he said. 'Who was she?'

Leah smiled. 'Wheels within wheels, Avison. Wheels within wheels.'

The drive home took just under an hour. It had started raining, only lightly, but enough to bring the visibility right down. He was bone tired when he made it through his front door and just wanted to go to sleep. When he'd lived in Carlisle, he'd have reached for the takeaway menus he kept in a kitchen drawer. Out here, he was on his own. He was debating whether he should reheat some of the previous night's curry, or cook an omelette, when the phone rang. He looked at the clock on the oven, briefly thought about ignoring it before deciding he couldn't.

'Boss, it's Al Vaughn. We've been trying to get hold of you for an hour.'

Shit.

He'd muted his phone at the hospital and had forgotten to turn the sound back on. He hadn't even checked in with Towler on how things were going.

'What's up, Al? I'm only just in and I'm knackered. Gonna have some food and get some kip.'

'We've got him, boss.'

'Got who?'

'The man who killed our vic. Long story and we haven't actually got him, but we're nearly there. We know which family he's from.'

'I'm on my way,' he said, hanging up and reaching for his coat, all thoughts of food forgotten.

As soon as he was off the dirt track and on to a safer road, he phoned Towler for an update.

'That E-FIT Jo circulated was doing the rounds at Carlisle CID and one of the DCs recognised her. She'd reported being raped last week.'

'In Carlisle?' Fluke asked.

'Yep. Looks like she was roofied or something. Says she went out for a drink, woke up the next day with no memory of the evening. Thought she'd been raped and the doc confirmed there were date-rape drugs in her system. There was also some skin under her nails and a couple of foreign pubes. Got DNA from all of it, results came back this morning. Their case was a few days before ours, obviously, and there was no reason for anyone to link them.'

He went on to explain that the DNA was an interfamilial, rather than a direct match. The rapist wasn't on the National DNA Database, NDNAD, but a blood relative was. Ten years before, that wouldn't have been possible but with more and more people on the database and technology retrieval methods never better, hits like this were increasingly common.

'Where'd she get examined?'

'Preston SARC.'

Good, Fluke thought. The Sexual Assault Referral Centre at Preston was the best in the north-west. 'Name and address?'

'Name's Samantha Farrar, but there's a Kay Edwards, the DC who accompanied her, who wants to speak to you about that. And we don't have an address for Farrar – she wouldn't give it.'

'Why not?' Fluke asked. Victims of crime didn't have to give their addresses but it was unusual.

'Dunno. Scared of reprisals, possibly? DC Edwards is at HQ waiting for you. I've put her in your office.'

His team knew that Fluke always preferred to question witnesses himself wherever possible. He felt at his best when the information was coming to him raw. Reports and witness statements sometimes lacked things such as non-verbals or the emotional state of the person being interviewed. How upset or angry they were. Whether they could remember a smell or a sound. Murders had been solved on such things.

'Tell me about the DNA hit.'

'Nathaniel Diamond? Nothing to tell really. Just a fucking thug. Twenty-nine years old. From a big family that seems to think they run Carlisle. Live mainly in Meadowby. They bring in small amounts of heroin and cocaine. Run a few women, massage parlours, that type of thing. Bit of rural crime. We think they do loan-sharking and payday loans as well. He's been arrested just the once. A Section 18 GBH. Never went anywhere. Victim refused to press charges.'

Fluke had vaguely heard of the Diamond family. They'd never come to the attention of FMIT, so his knowledge was sketchy. He'd never heard of Nathaniel but Grievous Bodily Harm was a nasty assault. The Section 18 signified there'd been intent. It carried a maximum sentence of life. The next charge up was attempted murder.

'They big?' he asked.

'Hard to say, boss. There's intel suggesting they're bigger than they let on. They certainly don't flash the cash, so the National Crime Agency have never got involved. But there was a snout last year who said all the other crime families around here have to pay to play. Give up a percentage of everything they do. They can't sell anything but Diamond drugs apparently. Drugs team mounted an operation but got nowhere.'

'If it's interfamilial DNA, it's not him we're looking for. Who's in the mix? Who are the likely suspects?' Fluke asked.

'Nathaniel's the younger of two brothers. Wayne's the elder, doesn't have a record. Never been arrested.'

'You think it's him we're looking for, though?'

'Can't rule it out but I'd be surprised, boss. Drugs team say Wayne's not really involved in anything any more. Happily married. Seems to be a gentle bloke. Doesn't like violence.'

'Anyone else then?'

'There's the dad, Kenneth. Probably the brains of the family. He lives in a big detached house in Stanwix. Bit of a show place, apparently. Never been arrested either.'

'Wider family?' Fluke asked. He knew interfamilial DNA was far reaching, it pointed at more than just the immediate family. It was its advantage and disadvantage. Uncles, aunts, cousins, illegitimate children, they would all need to be tracked down and eliminated.

'Fucking mess, boss. You know what these lot are like. They're everywhere. Some are related, some aren't. They all shag each other, so the children's heritage is anyone's guess.'

'How many do we have on the database? I'm assuming they're being ruled out as we speak? I don't want to bring in twenty people who we know aren't in the frame.'

'Looks like about half of them have been arrested. The brighter ones tend to not go near the drugs at all. They have an army of mules and dealers working for them. Intel suggests that most of the wider family are enforcers and foot soldiers. They think Kenneth Diamond is the main man. Nathaniel is probably his number two.'

'You got a theory on the murder?' Fluke asked, knowing he would. He had his own, but liked others to voice theirs first.

'On paper it looks straightforward. Our victim finds herself with the unwanted attentions of a Diamond. Most of the local girls would just put up with it for the night, shut their eyes and wait for them to finish. "Pull my nightie back down when you're finished" type of thing. Better than refusing and having the shit kicked out of you. But she doesn't know the family and she says no. Our man goes to plan B. Being in the drug trade, he has access to Rohypnol. Slips it in her drink. Takes her back to his cave. Rapes her. Dumps her somewhere. Thinks he's golden. How am I doing?'

'Same as me so far.'

'But she wakes up and knows what's happened. Reports it. There's DNA evidence and traces of the Rohypnol still in her blood. Our man finds out and panics. They track her down and kill her. Might have been the rapist, might have been a team effort. But one of them bastards did it.'

Fluke agreed entirely. He'd keep his mind open until they had definitive proof but he couldn't see any other explanation at present.

'Works for me,' he said. 'I think she came back home to hide from someone. Can't see any other reason for the cosmetic surgery. Might have been here a few weeks, might have been a year. But she was hiding. And then she runs into a Diamond and she has a whole new set of problems.'

'You want a hard arrest?'

Fluke considered it. Towler's hard arrests were something to witness. Professional Standards had investigated him three times over them but they were all above board. Sort of. All three of them had involved child sex offenders, all the victims the same age as Towler's daughter. Fluke thought they'd got off lightly.

'No, but I want it coordinated. We'll do it by the rules, but we go in early and fast. Get them all in before they can warn each other.'

'We won't get them all. We don't know who they all are. They're like a virus. Spread all over the fucking city. Best we can do is get as many as we can, take their DNA and then sweat them for the rest if our man's not in the first trawl. Longy's got some new genogram software he wants to try out. He'll plot out their family tree as we go along. Make sure we don't miss anyone.'

'Shit, Longy. How's he getting on? I've forgotten about him. My phone was switched off after I'd been to the hospital,' Fluke said.

'He's still got her. Says he wants to speak to you. Thinks she's surveillance-aware. Illogical routes, doubling back, the works.

Her face isn't on camera, not really. Only long shots, where she has no control. She's on foot though, which is making it easier.'

'But he's still following her?'

'Yeah. He's had to change systems a few times and commandeer a couple of private ones. Thought he'd lost her down by the station but one of the takeaways on the Crescent had an outward-facing camera. They'd had some bother with racists and were scared of getting their windows put through. Anyway, he picked her up heading towards the viaduct.'

'Tell him this is a no-go-home situation. Anything he wants. All overtime. I need an address,' he said.

Towler rang off just as Fluke pulled into HQ. Dark skies, light rain turning heavy. A cold wind grumbling its way down from the fells. Fluke was hungry and he was tired.

He'd never felt more alive.

Chapter 19

Fluke spoke to Jiao-long and caught up with the passive data search. Jiao-long hadn't seemed to notice the hours he'd put in – he was another member of the team who would keep going until the job was done. Fluke's apology for not checking in on him was waved away. He confirmed what Towler had told him. The victim seemed to be surveillance-aware. He'd nearly lost her a couple of times but the city was saturated with cameras and Jiao-long knew them all. It annoyed him that he had to ask permission to view private CCTV without a warrant but his winning personality normally got him through the door.

Jiao-long made him laugh sometimes. The only real culture clash they'd had since he arrived was over the rights of the public. He couldn't get his head round the fact that people weren't legally obliged to help the police. He couldn't get his head round criminals getting free legal and, more importantly, *independent* advice. He couldn't believe the UK police had so few rights. Fluke got the impression that in China, being a policeman was a little different. He also got the impression most of FMIT envied Jiao-long.

DC Kay Edwards from Carlisle CID was waiting for Fluke in his office. A woman whose age he wouldn't be able to get within ten years of. One of those women whose hair had turned grey before she wanted it to but she still managed to look youthful. Probably never occurred to her to dye it. Good for her. Coppers, male and female, who were too bothered about their looks got on his nerves. It was an outside job predominantly. Save the makeup and the highlights and the hair gel for your nights off.

She stood as he entered his office. She reached for his offered hand with a smile that showed confidence but not cockiness. Her handshake was warm, dry and firm.

'DC Edwards. May I call you Kay?'

'Of course, sir.'

'You've heard what we have so far?'

'Yes, sir.'

'It looks like you're one of the last people to have seen her alive. What can you tell me I don't already know? Half an hour ago I didn't know her name. Now I have a name and a suspect.'

Edwards took out a notebook but spoke without referring to it. Good, if you couldn't be bothered to memorise facts before a briefing then you had no business *doing* a briefing.

'On paper it seemed fairly straightforward, sir. She said she went out for a quiet drink last Thursday. Wasn't meeting anyone but was sick of being on her own. She can't remember anything at all about the night. Doesn't even remember leaving home.'

'Did she say home or flat?' Fluke asked. *Little details*, he thought. Good detectives had an eye for them. Little details solved crimes. For the first time, she looked through her notes.

'Flat, sir. She said, and I quote, "I had no recollection of leaving my flat." Is that important?'

'Might be,' Fluke said. 'Go on.'

'Next thing she knew, she was waking up in her bed with no idea how she got there. Said her vagina was sore. Knew straight away she'd been raped. Walked into Durranhill first thing Friday and reported it. I was on duty. Just going off actually, but I've been trained to work with victims of sexual assault.'

Durranhill was Carlisle Area's headquarters. He made a mental note to let Jiao-long know; some of the businesses there might have cameras he could use.

147

'Had she been assaulted?' he said. 'Apart from sexually.'

'Didn't look like it. Me and a colleague took her straight to the SARC.'

'In Preston?'

Sexual assault referral centres were fairly new concepts and all Cumbrians went to Preston. They were basically one-stop shops where victims could access everything they would need but where a forensic chain of custody was in operation at all times to support any subsequent prosecution. Doctors, nurses, counsellors all worked from the SARC and it was open twenty-four hours a day.

'And she was examined there?'

'Yes, sir. The doctor confirmed she'd had sex recently. There was slight tearing in the vagina and the swab for semen was positive. There were foreign hairs recovered from her pubic hair and she had skin under her nails. It's possible she'd scratched her attacker. Something to look out for anyway.'

Fluke nodded for her to continue.

'The doctor took bloods and they came back this afternoon. Same time as the DNA hit, as it happens.'

'Why take blood? Is that routine?'

'It is, sir. They have to test for STDs and HIV. It's a victim's number-one fear after a rape. That, and pregnancy. With date rapes being so common, and her saying she had no recollection, they screened her for all the common drugs. Came back positive for flunitrazepam.'

'Rohypnol?'

'Rohypnol's a trade name for flunitrazepam, yes, sir. They aren't the only manufacturer.'

'I didn't know that,' Fluke said. Most officers, himself included, used Rohypnol as a generic name the same way people used Hoover to describe vacuum cleaners and Sellotape to describe sticky tape, regardless of who made it.

'Anyway, it's not the best drug to use for date rape. Stays in the system for three days so it's not used that often any more. GHB or zolpidem have the same effects as flunitrazepam but they only stay in the body a few hours. Gone by the time the victim wakes usually. Makes drug-facilitated rape much harder to prove.'

He grimaced. Even rapists were evolving. No wonder Towler's sex offenders always seemed to 'resist' arrest.

'OK, so we got lucky. We were due something. What else?'

'Very upset as you can imagine. Said she came to Cumbria because of the low crime rate. Was the first time she'd been out and this happened. Wouldn't give me her address and didn't have to. Rape victims are entitled to anonymity, as you know. Said she'd report to the station as much as we wanted her to. I didn't want to push it.'

'You check on PNC or DVLA?'

'Wasn't really supposed to, sir. I'd been asked by the victim to not take down her address.'

'That's not what I asked,' Fluke said.

She paused and Fluke knew that he'd find out what kind of cop she was. Whether she was curious enough to go beyond her statutory responsibilities. There was no such thing as a detective being too nosey.

She looked directly at him, gauging what she should tell him. Whether she could trust him.

'Nothing, sir. Nothing that fitted anyway. Plenty of Samantha Farrars. Plenty of Sam and Sammy Farrars too. But they're either too young or they were too old. Checked for a credit rating but she didn't have one. Checked every database I have access to. Even checked Facebook, Twitter and a dozen other social media sites. Nothing. Either she gave me the wrong name or she lives off the grid.'

Fluke said nothing. Living off the grid was virtually impossible in the UK. The only real way of doing it was to have more than one identity.

'Can I speak freely, sir?'

'You're in my part of the building now. Everyone's allowed an opinion here.'

'Something didn't quite add up, sir. She was upset, yes. And I'd never put this on paper, but she didn't seem upset enough. I've been to maybe a dozen of these and every reaction's different so maybe it was just her way of dealing with it . . .'

'But?'

'But there was just something about her, sir. Intangible almost. She was given a leaflet when she arrived explaining what would happen but I didn't see her read it, and I was with her the whole time. I dunno, there was just something not quite right. Like when you're watching a film and the sound's slightly out of sync.'

Fluke had learned to trust people's instincts and he was impressed with Edwards. Good insight and only once had she needed to check her notebook. Time to bring her inside.

'We'll keep that in mind, Kay. As you're going to find out, nothing about this case is straightforward. The first thing you should know is that what she gave you was almost certainly a false name.'

She looked at him. Expecting more, knowing she'd passed some sort of test but not sure how.

'The second thing you should know is that she's had extensive cosmetic surgery, all done to drastically change her appearance. Blonde hair dyed brown, coloured contacts. The CCTV that one of my detectives has her on shows she's surveillance-aware. We have a working theory that she was in hiding, and chose Carlisle.' He explained what they knew and what they thought they knew.

'We know who she's hiding from?'

'Not a clue,' Fluke said. 'But if you're in hiding, you don't give your real name, no matter what's happened.'

'Then why give it at all?'

'Too odd. Raises suspicion. Address? Understandable not giving that out, but your name? No, better just to give a false one and hope no one checks. Anything else you can think of?'

She looked at her notes. She shook her head. 'Not really, sir. Some of her answers did seem a bit evasive but I wasn't interrogating her, you understand. I talked to her on the way down in the ambulance. We're supposed to. Theory is that the more you can get them to talk the less they will dwell on what's happened. We're part of the healing process, according to the course instructor. Don't know if it's true or not but I've never seen any reason not to try. I asked where she was from, what she did, how long she'd been here, that type of thing. Looking back, all I got were superficial answers. No depth to any of them.'

'You think she was telling the truth about the rape?'

'Again, not sure. I think she was raped, definitely. Hard to come to any other conclusion really.'

'Did she ever report back to get an update on the investigation?' Fluke asked.

'No, sir. I asked her to come in on Monday but I never saw her again. But then again she may have been murdered soon after.'

'Times don't work,' Fluke said. 'We have a TOD we're happy with, and there's four days between the rape and the murder. There was no evidence to suggest she'd been abducted. We think this was a hit. In and out, same night. But I think you're right, there was something she wasn't telling you.'

'If you say she was in hiding then why did she even go out at all?'

The same thought had occurred to Fluke. He was in no doubt that Samantha – Fluke would think of her by her first name, it helped remind him the crime involved humans and was more than just an intellectual exercise – had been scared of someone. Surveillance-aware, extensive cosmetic surgery, false name, no address. She was doing everything right to stay hidden.

And then she goes out.

In a public place. Not to meet someone. Just out, on her own.

Said she was lonely. Fluke doubted it. Women that scared didn't get lonely.

'That, Kay, is a detective's question.'

He thought quickly. He'd have to take over the rape investigation and absorb it into the murder. No point in having the two running parallel. The original team would have to stay on the rape but he'd need liaison between both. He needed someone working from FMIT who knew the rape.

'I'm going to bring you across to my team for the rest of this investigation, Kay. I'll clear it with your super. Go back over the night she came in. Speak to the ambulance driver that took her down to Preston. Go to Preston and speak to everyone who saw her there. It's a murder investigation so don't worry too much about hurting anyone's feelings. Get as much footage as you can. I want to see if she is as aware of cameras when she's suffering from trauma. See how controlled she was. I need to know more. Before you go, though, read the murder summary. Sergeant Towler will give you a copy.'

Find out how the victim lived and you'll find out how they died.

After Edwards left, Fluke looked for something to eat. When night ops were being planned, there was always plenty of it lying around and he found it in the incident room. Towler was there, in his element. An extension of a military operation, it was something he excelled at. Yelling and organising. Classic sergeant tasks. Military or police, the role never changed. Every officer reporting was given a number and a briefing pack and was told where to be and at what time. As Towler was doing all the briefings himself, they were all at different times. Some officers were therefore able to disappear again for a few hours. Most didn't, however. The chance of closing off a rape and a murder in one noisy dawn raid was a caffeine shot to the heart.

There was a contingent of armed response officers standing in a group on their own, dressed in black combats and peaked baseball caps. They would draw their weapons from the armoury later. As a firearm had been used in the murder, each arrest team would have armed response securing the premises.

The air smelled of fried food. A few years earlier, it would have been thick with cigarette smoke as well. Phones were ringing and keyboards were clicking. The closer an investigation got to being solved, the faster people typed. The faster they answered the phone. The louder they got.

He wandered over to see Towler to make sure they were both in the group that was taking down Nathaniel Diamond. On paper, he was the most violent, the most likely to resist and Fluke wanted to make sure he was taken down quickly and efficiently. Although not a suspect for the rape, if one of the Diamonds had killed Samantha, then Nathaniel would know who. He may have even authorised it. Emotions ran high during early-morning arrests and unguarded comments sometimes slipped out. If they did, Fluke wanted to be there.

Towler saw Fluke approach.

'With you in two, boss. Just sorting through this crap. Got one man reported sick this evening so one of the teams is gonna be light.'

'How many do we have going out?'

'Around eighty in total. We also have half of every TPT on standby to provide urgent uniformed assistance if we need crowd control. They'll be in reserve, dotted around the city in vans.'

Territorial Policing Teams were the bobbies on the beat, but could be drafted in to support operations when extra resources were required. Fluke knew they would have a better knowledge of the city than FMIT did. If things went wrong, their help would be crucial.

'Longy's not going out, is he? I need him working on her address.'

'No, and you know what he's like. Kicked up a right stink. Probably wanted to try some kung-fu shit. Told him you needed him where he was but he wouldn't have it. Says he's going to speak to you about it. Told him to stop bitching like a fucking marine.'

Fluke smiled, refusing to take the bait. The rivalry between the Royal Marine Commandos and the Parachute Regiment was infamous. The Royal Latrines and the Parasite Regiment were the nicknames they'd bestowed upon each other. In reality, they were both elite units, and there was nothing to choose between them so Fluke always took Towler's piss-taking in the manner it was given – lightly. He'd never intended to be a career marine, saw it as a job, something he had to get out of his system before he settled down and did something normal.

Towler, on the other hand, had been serious about being a para. He'd served most of his time with 1 Para and had been part of Operation Barras, when the Paras and the SAS had fought the West Side Boys in Sierra Leone before rescuing the five Irish Rangers being held hostage.

For Towler, SAS selection seemed inevitable. Fluke had assumed he'd do the full twenty-two years, finishing on a decent special-forces pension before going into the lucrative close protection business. For a couple of years' work, ex-SAS troopers were earning seven-figure sums. Fluke had thought it entirely possible he'd never see his friend again until they were old men.

And then Abigail came along and changed everything. One cold night, the rain lashing down sideways, the way Cumbrian rain did sometimes, Fluke's doorbell rang. Towler was standing outside, soaked. He wasn't alone. Far from it. He was holding a baby. His baby.

'I need a job,' were the first words he said.

To this day, Fluke had never found out where Abigail, Abi to everyone who knew her, came from. Only that her mother wasn't around any more and Towler had needed to come back up north so his family could help him raise her. He'd asked Towler once, but he'd replied, 'I'll tell you when I've told her.' Fluke had never asked again.

Towler had given up a career he loved for someone he loved even more and he'd never regretted it.

He'd joined the police a month after returning to Cumbria and passed everything he was asked to. The fitness came easily enough. The restraint classes were more difficult. The police taught defensive techniques; the Paras taught exclusively aggressive techniques. By the end, his instructors passed him as they didn't know what else to do. He could do everything they asked but what he knew was better. He applied himself with a dedication that had surprised even Fluke, and was soon on the beat as a probationary officer. Posted to the isolated village of Cleator Moor, a terrifying prospect for all but the hard of understanding, Towler single-handedly reduced antisocial behaviour by 50 per cent within a month.

He passed his detective's exam and was immediately posted to Fluke's team at both their requests. Towler was one of nature's sergeants and it came as no surprise to anyone when he passed his exam a year later and was immediately promoted.

But Fluke knew Towler sometimes missed the Paras, knew that the action was tame compared to what he'd been used to. He had a skill set he wasn't using and, although he didn't regret making the sacrifices he'd made, Fluke knew he was sometimes frustrated by the constraints the law imposed upon him.

But here he was in his element. Some organising to do, some action to come later.

Fluke went back to his office to email Chambers and the assistant chief a summary of the progress made that day. For the first time, he was able to say the investigation was actually moving forwards. And by doing it late he could guarantee they wouldn't receive it until it would be too late to interfere.

Chapter 20

Electricity coursed through Fluke's veins, fuelled by adrenalin. He could tell he wasn't the only one. The action was always where the boss went, where the key arrests were made, and in the back of the van, the armed response cops fidgeted with nervous energy. Towler seemed fine though. He was chewing gum and had his eyes closed.

The smell of gun oil in an enclosed space brought back vivid memories of the Saracens they'd used in Northern Ireland. Fluke remembered sitting in the back with seven heavily armed marines as they drove down the Falls Road in Belfast. He'd felt invincible back then. How times change. Not being able to rely on his own body had forced him to face his mortality for the first time. The tumour had succeeded where the IRA had failed. He'd have laughed if they weren't all staying silent.

They drove to the staging area in a convoy of vans and unmarked cars. No lights, no sirens. It was a covert operation. As it was 4 a.m., Carlisle was asleep and the journey was quick. The staging area was in an empty car park on the Durranhill industrial estate, close enough to Carlisle Area HQ that the modern glass building could be seen. There were still lights on as police officers on nights went about their business. It was a big operation but that didn't mean policing the city stopped.

Each call sign knew where they were going and the route they would take. Some were doubled up in vehicles if their targets lived close together. Towler had decided that quarter to five was late enough to ensure the targets would be at home but early enough so that the few with jobs weren't up and about.

Ten minutes to go and the vans moved into their forward areas. Fluke's van crept along the deserted streets of Meadowby as quietly as the engine's throaty growl would allow. Although he couldn't see where they were, he assumed they'd arrived when the van stopped and the driver cut the engine. Fluke felt a bead of sweat work its way down the back of his neck and under his shirt. He shivered.

There was no rush as they disembarked. Stealth was more important than speed. Fluke was last out. He didn't know this part of Carlisle so was relying on others to find the correct address.

It was still dark. More of a dirty grey than black. It wouldn't be daylight for another three hours. After the regeneration of the infamous Raffles, Meadowby had become the most rundown estate in Carlisle. Like Pinegrove, efforts had been made to improve it and, like Pinegrove, there were still streets where the residents just didn't care. It was a different kind of estate to Pinegrove though; more urban, more suffocating. On Pinegrove the houses were all two minutes away from fields and open spaces; on the Meadowby there was just more Carlisle.

All the housing officers and community policing in the world weren't going to get some residents to tidy their gardens. Or paint their doors. Or fix broken windows. Some people don't want to be helped. And some people don't want others to get any help either. One thug could turn a whole street bad. There were few cars. Sensible residents parked in a different area.

Repairing street lamps was a never-ending job for the council in Meadowby, but there were enough working for Fluke's team to make their way to the target address. They got to the house one minute before the go order was scheduled. A large blue Mercedes was in the drive. It was less than two years old and was spotless.

The house was on a better street than the two they'd passed

through to get there. Cheap cars were in the rest of the drives but they all looked legal. A street that believed in working, in breaking the benefit trap. Or maybe it was just that a street with a Diamond in it kept itself tidy. A dog barked in the distance and Fluke wondered if one of the other teams had been compromised. Doubtful, though, not at that time. There was a reason they did raids at those times: humans are naturally at their lowest at 5 a.m. Dogs, not so much.

'Leaders report in with a click,' Towler said over the channel, a specific one that wouldn't be used by cops on other jobs.

A succession of clicks could be heard over the radio. No voices. At that point, Towler and Fluke would be the only ones breaking radio silence.

'We're set, boss,' Towler said. 'OK to go?'

'Go,' he said.

'Right, on my order. Thirty seconds to go. In position, please.'

The officer selected for the breach was a short, stocky man Fluke didn't recognise. He carried the metal battering ram like it was made of balsa wood. It was painted red but was chipped and scuffed in places. Clearly not the first time it had been used. He was allowed space to move to the front. He got into a position he was happy with, raised the battering ram and waited. He stared at the point he was aiming for. The armed officers took positions behind him. They would be running forward as soon as the battering ram was in motion. They bunched up close. Their knees pressed into the back of the knees of the person in front of them. Fluke knew there were two reasons for that. It meant they could form up in tight spaces. More importantly, as soon as the go order was given there could be no hesitation. The movement of the person behind meant the person in front was going into that house whether they liked it or not.

Techniques developed by special forces now being used by civilian law enforcement. A fully militarised police force was inevitable. It had happened in the States and the UK was never far behind, particularly when it came to aping more self-destructive trends.

Other than the lone dog, there was no sound. Towler wouldn't count down the thirty seconds, only the last five. Fluke could sense an increase in his team's rate of breath. A team confident in what they were doing. Confident that they had enough to overcome whatever was on the other side of the door. Confident that they would soon be back at Durranhill catching up with friends from other teams, swapping stories. But there was always going to be some nerves just before they went through a door.

Towler caught Fluke's eye and winked. He was still chewing gum.

Time slowed. Fluke counted the thirty seconds in his head. He got to zero and checked his watch. He was ten seconds out.

Towler's voice came loud and clear over the airwaves as he started the countdown. 'Five.'

Fluke breathed in and held his breath.

'Four.'

He heard clicks as the armed officers moved their safety catches to fire.

'Three.'

Another bead of sweat formed at the nape of his neck.

'Two.'

The officer with the ram tensed.

'GO, GO, GO!' Towler screamed down the radio.

The secret to any breach is speed, aggression, surprise. Carried out correctly, the suspect has no chance. Before he realises what's happening, he's face down with police officers sitting on him.

The breach officer hit the door six inches above the handle. It was no match for the cold steel battering ram. Instead of opening, the door flew off its hinges and into the hall. Before it had landed, the armed officers were through.

The noise was incredible. A combination of nerves, the release of tension and legitimate tactics to disorientate the criminal meant that every officer was shouting as loud as they could.

'Armed police! Armed police! Armed police!'

Fluke waited outside with Towler while the house was secured. There was more noise as the shouts of armed police were joined by the shouts of frightened occupants. The noise reached a crescendo then abruptly stopped. He looked down at the ruined door and noticed it still had a takeaway flyer through the letterbox. An Indian Fluke had used when he'd lived in Carlisle. The thought of sharing a takeaway with Nathaniel Diamond bothered him for some reason. He briefly considered confiscating it.

'House secure,' came the shout from upstairs. Fluke entered.

He had a quick look around the hall. He was surprised, and then he was embarrassed that he was surprised. The house was spotless. He'd expected filth. Diamond's house was cleaner than his own home and far more tasteful. It seemed his surprise was shared by the rest of the team. Noisy and aggressive on entry, they'd quietened and he could hear some of them picking things up.

Fluke could hear screaming upstairs along with some muffled swearing. An armed officer walked down the stairs and approached Fluke.

'He's upstairs,' he said.

'Who's the woman?'

'Follow me, sir,' he said. 'I think our intel on Nathaniel Diamond was incomplete.'

Fluke followed him up the stairs.

Like the hall, they were tastefully decorated. No flying geese in this house. Prints and maps of old Carlisle on the way up; a black and white photograph of Dixon's Chimney, the tallest in the country when it was built, where the stairs turned left. Fluke wondered if it had been specially commissioned or whether someone in the house had taken it.

He could hear muffled cursing coming from the bedroom. He followed the sergeant in and stared at the scene in front of him.

Nathaniel Diamond was face down on the bed. Plasticuffs bound his wrists and leg straps meant he couldn't kick out. Fluke looked at the person next to him: the screamer, also bound with plasticuffs and leg straps.

'Oh,' he said.

Chapter 21

The person secured next to Nathaniel Diamond was a man. A good-looking, slender blond man. He was naked. So was Diamond.

Fluke stood on an open condom wrapper. He bent down to pick it up. Saw two more.

His immediate reaction was that he was looking at another rent boy. Two in one case would be a record for him, the previous high score being zero. It was his first thought but, as he studied the rest of the room, he immediately dismissed it. There were photos spread around the bedroom, and the blond and Nathaniel Diamond were in them all. It was clear that they were a couple and, judging by their expressions, a very happy couple. It was also evident they'd been in a relationship for a while as they'd aged together. They were taken in different locations: Las Vegas; New York; another looked like Paris. Another was shot on safari somewhere, probably Africa, possibly Australia. There was one taken at a pavement café in a European city Fluke didn't recognise.

Nathaniel Diamond looked like a thug in the one photo they had of him and in truth, he looked like a thug trussed up on the floor. Shaved to the bone, his skull wasn't smooth and shiny, it was rough, like sandpaper. He obviously tried to keep on top of it with a razor but the hair kept winning.

Black tattoos covered his arms and back. He was heavily muscled but not in the steroid-induced way McNab had been. They were like the muscles Towler had. Built for stamina and

162

speed. He looked dangerous. He was watching Fluke calmly, the anger replaced by curiosity.

Gay men living together in Meadowby wasn't unheard of but it was unusual. The estate wasn't exactly known for embracing diversity. People who were different didn't go unnoticed for long. The fact that Nathaniel and his boyfriend were in what now seemed likely to be an openly gay relationship was testament to the reputation of him and his family. For anyone else, it wouldn't be a tenable way to live.

Fluke wondered why the intel on Diamond didn't have that he was gay. There was always some little scrote who'd pass on information like that to curry favour with the police or to get charges reduced.

It suggested the family had far more influence over the criminal class than anyone had imagined. As Fluke stared into Diamond's cold, intelligent eyes, he had no problem believing it.

Nothing was going to get sorted there though.

'Take them to Durranhill,' he said. 'Separate cells.'

There weren't enough cells at Durranhill, so some of the Diamond family were transported to outlying stations. Detectives were interviewing them; SOCO were swabbing them for DNA and sending samples off to the lab.

It was going to be close. Fluke had the power to hold his suspects for twenty-four hours and the DNA results would start coming about the same time.

It was possible, probable even, that when they matched the DNA found on Samantha to the DNA they were scraping from the insides of the cheeks of the Diamonds they'd just gathered up, they'd have their killer. However, there wasn't a superintendent in Cumbria who'd authorise an additional twelve hours detention if all Fluke had was 'It could be any of them, sir.'

Fluke needed something more. Enough to convince a senior

officer to extend their detention to thirty-six hours. By then, all the DNA results should be back.

Of all the suspects arrested that night, Fluke thought Nathaniel Diamond was most likely to slip up. When he found out the reason for his arrest – that he *wasn't* a suspect in the rape – Fluke hoped he'd get cocky and make a mistake. He was hoping to do mentally to Nathaniel what Towler did physically to McNab.

Nathaniel *was* in the frame for the murder but he wouldn't know that yet.

Along with Nathaniel, Fluke had wanted his brother, Wayne, and his father, Kenneth. The three believed to be in control of the family business. Wayne had been picked up without incident, but their father had disappeared. The team raiding his house said it didn't look like he'd been there for a few days, judging by the mail that had built up. They'd collected a toothbrush and a comb and were confident they had enough for the lab to get a DNA profile that either ruled him in or out. Everyone else on the target sheet was in custody. A good night's work.

It was unusual for anyone above sergeant to conduct interviews but Fluke always liked to do the big ones himself. He also preferred to interview with Towler, who had the knack of unnerving suspects without actually saying anything.

But first, he needed something to eat.

'How we gonna play it, boss?' Towler asked, through a mouthful of bacon sandwich.

Fluke shrugged, his own mouth also full. It was an interesting question. If their dad was the brains of the outfit, there was no doubt that Nathaniel was the enforcer. Everything about him screamed it. The fact he lived with a man on the Meadowby estate was proof enough of the fear he instilled. He was probably bright enough to not be the triggerman but he'd know who had been. Even if they'd brought in someone from outside the family to do the actual hit, it was inconceivable he wasn't involved in the decision.

'Dunno yet. Play it by ear to start with. See how chatty he is. Is he lawyered up yet?'

'Yep, they all are, the waiting room looks like a right wankers' convention.'

Nathaniel Diamond was wearing a paper boiler suit. He'd been allowed half an hour with his solicitor. When Fluke entered the interview room, they were hunched over, talking quietly. Actually, the solicitor was doing all the talking, Fluke noticed. Diamond wasn't saying anything.

Fluke took a seat, then spent a minute setting out various photos and documents. Diamond's solicitor was trying to read them upside down. At this point, Diamond would have no idea why he was there. It could have been any of their criminal enterprises. He'd be concerned but not worried. Fluke assumed there were firewalls against the main players having to do anything too incriminating. He glanced up at Diamond and found him watching him with an amused expression. He ignored the documents Fluke had laid out.

Diamond was an interesting-looking man. Although he was of average height, power leeched from him. It was clear his solicitor was scared of him. From a distance, Diamond looked exactly like he did in the few photos the police had of him. He kept his ginger hair short, shaved it every day, Fluke guessed. He had heavy stubble but no one had had time to shave that morning. He knew some heavy gold rings and a thick gold chain had been taken from him as part of the booking-in process. The custody sergeant had told him that they were not the usual cheap rubbish habitually favoured by criminals. They were the real deal. Thousands of pounds' worth, he estimated. Not a bad way of carrying currency around with you if you needed cash in an emergency.

Nathaniel Diamond was undoubtedly a thug. A bouncer with attitude. A violent man in a violent business.

But that didn't mean there wasn't more.

It was the eyes that gave it away. The photos didn't do them justice. There was intelligence behind them. They were watching Fluke shrewdly.

Although there'd been a press release on the murder, the press pack released to the *News & Star* did not include the victim's photo or E-FIT. Fluke wanted to gauge Diamond's reaction when he saw it for the first time. It would be the key moment in the interview. Diamond had been there enough times to keep quiet but human reactions aren't so easily controlled.

Fluke sometimes used an unapproved method when interviewing suspects.

Some years earlier, after attending a multi-agency public protection meeting in Liverpool, Fluke had been having a coffee with a forensic psychologist and had idly asked him what he was working on, more for something to say than anything else. The kind of thing said when two people who don't know each other are thrown together.

The psychologist had told him that he'd been commissioned to develop a two-minute interview for airlines that had flights leaving the UK for the States. They wanted staff interviewing passengers in the check-in queue but they needed it to appear as if it were a casual conversation. They were looking for signs of deception before they progressed to the formal security checks.

He explained they'd been encouraged by the early results of a technique they'd been piloting. The member of staff would ask a series of questions so normal it would appear the interviewer was simply killing time. Questions designed to put the passenger at ease. But they didn't want rehearsed answers. They wanted honest answers. And the best way to get honest answers was to ask questions so mundane there would be no reason to lie.

'But terrorists plan for this, don't they?' Fluke had said. He'd never worked counter-terrorism but had a rough understanding of it. 'They have legends that they memorise, they know which schools they went to, they know where they were last night and what they watched on television. They certainly rehearse the "did you pack your own bag?" question.'

'Can I ask you something, Mr Fluke? What was the last supermarket you shopped at?' the psychologist had asked.

'Er . . . Sainsbury's, I think,' he said. 'Why?'

The psychologist looked at him. 'This is the type of thing we ask. We ask mundane questions, but questions that can't possibly be predicted and rehearsed.'

He'd gone on to explain that the human brain wants to tell the truth and, in the absence of a reason to lie, *will* tell the truth. When they answered, the passenger's facial micro-expressions, essentially very brief movements, contained what he called truthful indicators. If those micro-expressions changed when answering questions that the passenger could expect and rehearse, it indicated possible deception. A far more rigorous security check would then follow. The two-minute lie detector, the psychologist called it. Passengers don't even realise they've had one.

Fluke had adapted and refined it to the point where he believed he could tell when someone was lying to him almost every time. It was virtually infallible. He couldn't remember the psychologist's name and had never seen him again to thank him.

After the usual formalities were covered – who was present, an explanation of how the digital recording worked, and what happened to copies afterwards – they began.

Fluke had checked. Diamond had been arrested and interviewed eight times. To date he'd never been charged. He'd read the interview transcripts and he always went no comment. Not the McNab no comment: Diamond never actually said anything. Eight times, from the point of arrest until he walked out with no charge, and he'd never said a word. That took discipline.

'Who was that you were in bed with, Nathaniel?'

For a moment, Fluke thought the interview was going to go the way of all the others. He'd planned for it, which was why he had a whole range of photos with him. They were going to be his questions.

'Mathew.'

Fluke looked up, surprised. He honestly hadn't expected Diamond to answer.

'And who's Mathew?'

'He's my boyfriend.' There was no defiance in his voice. He'd simply stated it as the truth.

'And how long have you been together?'

'Look, Inspector. I really don't see what my client's personal life has to do with this,' Diamond's solicitor said.

Fluke ignored him. Diamond was looking at him carefully.

'Eight years,' he said.

The solicitor put his hand on Diamond's arm. He leaned in to whisper something but Diamond said, 'Get your hands off me.'

He delivered it quietly and without turning his head. The solicitor snatched his hand back as if he'd been burnt. He reddened but said nothing. Fluke heard Towler snort. The solicitor's face flushed red, embarrassed he'd been spoken to like that but too scared to protest. Fluke almost felt sorry for him. Almost. He chose to represent the Diamonds and in his own way made a living from human suffering just as surely as they did. Guilty by association. He reached into his suit, took out a silk handkerchief and dabbed the back of his neck.

'What does Mathew do, Nathaniel?' Fluke said, looking at the solicitor as he said it, daring him to interrupt. Everyone knew who got the last lick of the lolly in that room.

'He's a photographer. He's good. He took the photos in our house.'

168

Fluke nodded. 'I saw them.'

Diamond's expressions had all been neutral but he was sure he was telling the truth. Fluke had watched his micro-expressions carefully and thought he'd recognise any changes that might indicate deception. He wanted to ask one more though. One that would ordinarily illicit an expression of anger, but if answered would be truthful.

'Where do you buy your condoms, Nathaniel?'

The solicitor couldn't help himself. He exploded out of his chair. 'That's it, Inspector! This is outrageous. My client has been here two hours and so far—'

'Shut the fuck up, fat man. You work for me. Speak when I tell you to.'

Delivered in the same flat tone. Diamond turned to face him. The solicitor sat back down, visibly shrivelled.

'I don't know why you called me if you're not . . .' He petered out under Diamond's gaze.

'Sorry about that, Inspector,' he said. 'The Co-op on London Road.'

'What's that?' Fluke said, nonplussed.

'Our condoms. The ones we used last night were bought from the Co-op on London Road. We don't always get them from there, obviously, but I assume you only want me to go back so far.'

Fluke knew that the real skill in interviewing was knowing when plan A wasn't working. Diamond was too calm, as calm as anyone Fluke had ever sat opposite. His answers were delivered as the truth. He seemed to be hiding nothing. Fluke had planned to ask about drugs next, see what he looked like when he was being deceptive but also to keep the real reason for his arrest hidden. But he wasn't convinced Diamond wouldn't see straight through that. He was getting the impression that Nathaniel Diamond was far more intelligent than anyone had imagined.

Fluke had been on the back foot since the interview started and that hadn't happened for a long time. He was considering his next move when Diamond took the matter into his own hands.

'You have heterochromia, I see, Inspector.'

His doubt about Diamond's intelligence left him in an instant. Leah Cooper hadn't even known the correct term for his different-coloured irises and she was a doctor. She'd had to look it up and even then it took her three goes to pronounce it correctly. Towler called them his 'fucking weird eyes'. Fluke couldn't even spell his own condition, it was that rare.

A full minute passed before he answered. He could feel Towler stirring beside him. The big man was also getting uneasy.

'Yes, I do,' he said.

Fluke re-evaluated. He briefly considered stopping the interview so he could regroup. By revealing his intelligence, Diamond had thrown him. It hadn't been accidental either, it had been deliberate. He couldn't have made it clearer if he'd come in with his IQ certificate.

For some reason Diamond wanted him to know how intelligent he was. And the fact he'd hidden it for so long meant it was for something significant.

Something was happening here, something Fluke didn't yet understand.

There was nothing to be gained by playing games. Nathaniel Diamond might have been the most intelligent criminal he'd ever met, he might even be a genius, but there was one thing outside his control: his micro-expressions.

It was time to see if he was involved in Samantha's murder.

It was time for the photo.

Fluke took it from the folder and placed it face down on the table. He stared at Diamond. They both knew the whole interview had been leading up to this moment.

'Have you seen this woman before, Nathaniel?' Fluke said.

He flipped over the photo. It was an 8 x 10 inch colour glossy of

Samantha's head on the mortuary table. Diamond glanced down then back up at Fluke.

Fluke studied his face. He saw what he'd been hoping for: recognition.

A tiny change in his expression, there for a fraction of a second, but it was enough.

Diamond had seen her before.

Fluke smiled. They were getting somewhere. The Diamond family were involved.

'Why would I have seen her before?' he replied, calmly.

Even liars don't like to lie. Before answering questions of any consequence a liar will at first try to avoid answering it at all. Replying with a question was a classic reaction.

With no warning, Towler shouted. 'Answer the fucking question, dickhead!'

Diamond didn't flinch; his solicitor nearly fell off his chair. Fluke didn't move a muscle. He'd been expecting it. He'd planned it.

'No, I haven't seen her before, Inspector.'

There was no emotion in his answer but Diamond was no longer holding his gaze. He was looking slightly above his eyeline. His micro-expressions were different. The difference between his truthful and deceptive indicators were bigger than Fluke would have expected in someone so intelligent but, as the psychologist had told him, people have very little control over them.

He was lying.

Fluke felt it was the first time he'd actually gained anything from the interview. He was ahead and didn't want Diamond to have an opportunity to claw back the advantage. Time to change the rules. Fluke had always believed that it was best to do what the criminal least expected.

Fluke stood up and put everything back in his file.

'Thank you, Mr Diamond. You've been very helpful.'

'He can go?' the solicitor asked, surprised.

Diamond was watching Fluke, the same small smile he'd had at the start of the interview playing across his lips.

'Of course I can't, you fat idiot,' he said. 'I'm a suspect in a murder.'

'You should listen to your client. I'm keeping hold of him for a while longer,' Fluke said.

'I won't be paying for your services today, Mr Potting,' Diamond said. 'I don't think you've been of any help. Would you agree?'

That got the solicitor's attention. 'My advice is only useful if the person listens—'

'I asked if you agreed?'

For a moment, Fluke thought the solicitor was going to stand his ground.

But he didn't have the balls. 'Yes, of course,' he said quietly.

Diamond stared at Fluke throughout the whole interaction.

They left the room.

Fluke had new things to consider now. Diamond was highly intelligent. He was used to command. Serious command. When he spoke, he expected to be listened to. It had been like a game of 'Simon Says' with the solicitor. He also knew that Nathaniel Diamond was involved with Samantha. Whether it was her murder or something else he wasn't ready to speculate on.

He rubbed his eyes.

He needed some rest. He needed to regroup.

Chapter 22

They drove back to HQ, and Fluke slept on the couch in his office for a couple of hours. He woke, still feeling tired and with a headache. He checked his emails. There was one from HR on Jiao-long – he'd applied for an extension to his secondment – as well as information on current investigations: a street robbery in Ulverston; a social worker in the council's fostering department who'd been found with indecent images of children on his computer; and someone had been impersonating a police officer in different parts of the county. Nothing that FMIT needed to get involved in. He yawned and looked at his couch.

Instead of going back to sleep, he went looking for Towler. He found him sleeping in a hard plastic chair in the incident room. Towler had the soldier's knack of being able to fall asleep anywhere, and under any circumstances. The room was busy and noisy as Jo Skelton coordinated the updating of HOLMES 2 with the morning's raids and the subsequent interviews taking place around the county. People were shouting for things: links to computer files, passwords, codes, but Towler slept through it all. Fluke envied him. Towler and sleep were best friends; Fluke and sleep weren't even on speaking terms.

Fluke shook him gently by the shoulder. He woke instantly, immediately alert. Fluke was reminded just how close Towler had become to being one of the world's top soldiers. Fluke asked him to get the team together for a quick update.

* * *

Jo Skelton, Alan Vaughn and Towler crowded round the table in Fluke's office.

'So, what do we know?' he said.

'Nathaniel Diamond was involved,' Towler said.

'Nope,' Fluke said.

Fluke remembered once discussing with a probation officer whether the rehabilitation of criminals was really possible. The PO had told him part of his job was equipping offenders with reasoning and consequential thinking skills. Skills most people took for granted. The programme facilitators would start with a scenario before asking the group certain questions. They would then ask whether each answer was a fact, opinion or guess. Fluke had never thought about things that way before but knew several detectives who could have benefitted from separating the three.

'We know he's seen her before. I'm happy enough after the interview to call that a fact. That he was involved is a guess. What else do we know?' he said.

Skelton got up and drew a table with three rows on his whiteboard. She entered what they'd discussed up to then.

'Who raped her?' Fluke asked. 'Do we wait for the DNA results to come in or do we keep looking and interviewing?'

Vaughn was first to speak. 'Most of the family are in custody. We've questioned and released those who aren't blood-related and taken DNA from the rest. We've identified three family members we didn't know about and there were four who weren't in. There's something to be said for hanging on until the results come in.'

'There is,' agreed Fluke. 'But we aren't after a rapist, we're after a killer. We need to keep investigating. There will also be countless blood relatives and illegitimate children that we *don't* know about. Theories, anyone?'

He liked to hear others thinking out loud. It helped him poke holes in his own theories.

Towler gave his version of what happened. It was remarkably close to Fluke's own thinking.

'I think one of the Diamonds raped the victim, boss. Used roofies, and thought he'd got clean away. Word gets out that she's reported it. The Diamonds don't like that and want her silenced. They don't know if they're being watched though – the drugs squad must be parked outside their houses every night. So they bring in outside help from Manchester or Liverpool, probably Liverpool given their links with the drugs trade. Then they sit back and work on their alibis.'

'Anyone got anything to add to that?' Fluke asked.

There was silence. Intelligent minds went to work on pulling the theory apart. No one could, it fitted the facts.

'No one? OK, let me add something then. The family is big. After that interview with Nathaniel, I think they're bigger and better than we thought. They're not on a par with the gangs from the north-east, Manchester or Liverpool, but they're big for Cumbria. And I'd be very surprised if young Nathaniel isn't their number one. It's been a long time since I interviewed someone that bright. Other than some slight surprise when I showed him the photo, he was in total control for the whole interview. His brief's terrified of him.'

Fluke looked at them all in turn. Towler and Vaughn were looking into space, concentrating. Skelton was nodding. Psychology 101. Men nod their heads to show they agree, women nod their heads to show they're listening. He clearly hadn't convinced them of anything yet.

He continued. 'Even so, hiring a professional to kill someone is a big move. Not cheap either. So, either the rapist is important to the family – a close relative, someone they care enough about to spend money on protecting – or they're a key figure in the business. Key enough for their supplier in Liverpool to send someone up to fix their problem.'

Nods from round the table.

'I'm thinking it's someone who isn't expendable. Someone who the suppliers thought was worth protecting as well,' Vaughn said. 'I doubt they'd send a cleaner just because Uncle Bob's in trouble again. Not unless Uncle Bob makes the trains run on time.'

'There's still Nathaniel's dad,' Skelton said.

Shit. Kenneth Diamond. Fluke had forgotten about him.

'Sorry, Jo, you're right. He potentially fits who we're looking for. Nobody really knows what his role in the family business is. Where do we think he is?'

'Nobody knows. We don't think he's been home for a few days though, judging by the build-up of mail. Looks like he lives on his own,' she said.

There was a short discussion about whether the UK Border Agency should be informed, but they agreed it was probably pointless. If he'd fled, he'd have already left the country. Jo Skelton said she'd inform them anyway. Fluke decided he'd only get seriously interested in Kenneth Diamond if the DNA they'd taken from his toothbrush or comb matched the semen taken from Samantha. It didn't mean they couldn't start looking for him, though. He put Towler on it.

'In the meantime, let's get back into those interview rooms. See who else we have, and see who's important to the family. Speak to someone you haven't spoken to yet. And let's get working on that family tree. I want to know who else is out there with Diamond blood running through their veins. I'll have another run at Nathaniel. Anyone got any questions?'

They were all staring at him. No nods this time. Something was different, something had changed.

Towler looked uncomfortable. 'Boss, your nose is bleeding.'

Fluke refused to go to hospital, and after a few minutes with his head tilted back and toilet paper stuck up his nostrils, the blood flow had at least slowed. Towler had, without appearing too urgent, cleared the room.

'You look fucking awful,' he said, as he closed the door.

'I'm fine,' Fluke had replied.

'You're fucking grey, mate. The victim's got more colour than you.'

Fluke ignored him. He busied himself getting clean. He opened a drawer and took out the new shirt he always kept for emergencies. It was still in the wrapper. He threw the old shirt in the bin then examined his tie. Decided it was salvageable.

'See, good as new.'

It didn't put Towler off.

'And these hospital appointments you think we don't know about. They're nearly every week now.'

Fluke's stomach lurched. He thought he'd been discreet. Made sure they were always first or last thing. He hadn't wanted HR or Occ Health knowing about them. Or worse, Chambers.

'How'd you find out?' Fluke asked.

'I didn't. But you've just confirmed it,' Towler replied, holding his hand out to stop Fluke's protests. 'Look, I'm not an idiot. You're always knackered, you've got eyes like a racing dog's bollocks and now you're having fucking nosebleeds. That's the fourth one this month. Something's gotta give, boss.'

'I'm fine,' he repeated.

'Whatever,' Towler said. 'Keep going like this and I'll go and see what that doc of yours was playing at letting you come back so soon.'

Fluke knew it was an empty threat. The concern was genuine but Towler would never rat him out.

'Who else knows?' he said.

'No one. But you're leaving breadcrumbs bigger than teacakes. Won't be long before Chambers has figured it out.'

'Soon as this is over, I'll take a holiday. Get some proper rest. Honestly.'

Towler nodded. 'OK then. But until then, take it fucking easy, will you?'

They were interrupted by a knock on the door. Jiao-long stuck his head in.

'Found it, boss.' A massive grin split his face.

'Found what?' Fluke said, still on the back foot.

'Her house. Her flat actually. You were right.'

Fluke stood up so quickly that he spilt his drink all over his new shirt. He ignored it – a coffee stain he could live with.

Chapter 23

They took Jiao-long's car to Carlisle city centre. On the way he briefed him on how he'd tracked down Samantha.

He'd followed her on CCTV across the city. She was sneaky but Jiao-long was sneakier. She knew where most of the cameras were. He knew where they *all* were.

He'd watched as she walked towards the west of the city, not always taking logical routes. She'd eventually turned down a small street sandwiched between the River Caldew and the railway viaduct. Viaduct Estate Road had little on it and was most often used as a shortcut to the Royal Mail sorting office on Junction Street. She should have reappeared. She didn't. The council had no cameras facing down the road.

Jiao-long still had a few tricks left, however. Knowing that the buildings opposite were all student accommodation and that there'd been a spate of cycle thefts, he checked whether the university had put up cameras of their own.

They had.

One of the buildings had installed a high-tech machine. During daylight, it faced outwards, covering the area where students parked their bikes. At night, when all bikes were chained up or indoors, it pointed down, and was used as a safe-entry camera for the front door. The daytime angle gave an uninterrupted view across the dual carriageway and down Viaduct Estate Road.

Jiao-long had watched Samantha entering the only block of flats on the street.

He'd watched the remaining hours before the camera moved down at about 7 p.m. to check she hadn't left. She hadn't.

Fluke asked him if there'd been sight of anyone who might be their killer.

'Nothing, boss. It only points that way during the day. There are people going in and out of the flats, obviously, but no one stands out. If there's an entrance to the back then it's in a blind spot. We can check when we get there.'

Fluke was banking on her flat being the murder scene. If it wasn't, he wasn't sure where he could go next. He had no more leads. Jiao-long told him that he'd viewed footage from the surrounding cameras for twenty-four hours before and after, and had seen nothing. Either she hadn't left her flat and had been killed there, or she'd somehow evaded Jiao-long.

They assembled in the flat car park. There was one designated space per resident. None for visitors. At that time of day most of them were empty but they'd been filled with the various police vehicles.

Fluke got out of the car and smelled gingerbread. It was coming from the nearby biscuit factory. It reminded him that he hadn't eaten recently. He arched his back and got his bearings.

On the other side of the dual carriageway was the most besieged castle in Britain. During its thousand years, Carlisle Castle – once described as the ugliest in Europe – had been a Norman stronghold, a royal garrison and a frontier fortress in the border wars between Scotland and England, and its red sandstone walls were soaked with blood and history. Clinging to a small hill like a rusty limpet, it looked as formidable now as it had done all those centuries ago. Fluke sometimes walked round it if he had half an hour to kill.

He turned away from the castle and viewed the flats. He wanted to get in quickly and was glad to see the breach team was already there. The same man who had smashed Diamond's door that morning was back with his discoloured battering ram. A two-man armed response team was also waiting. Fluke knew they wouldn't have been involved in that morning's raids; there were tight controls on how many hours an armed officer could do before there was compulsory downtime.

The flats were modern and privately owned. Fluke had been thinking on the drive up about how to identify Farrar's but decided that simple was best; knock on doors and show the E-FIT until someone recognised her and told them where she lived. Then go in with armed response. He thought it extremely unlikely that the killer would still be there but there was no point taking unnecessary risks.

They got lucky straight away.

'Quiet girl, polite, lives in number five upstairs,' a middle-aged man said when they knocked on the first door. 'What's she done?' the man asked.

Fluke told him to go inside and lock his door. They made their way upstairs and quietly gathered in the stairwell below her flat.

'I'm going to knock first,' Fluke said. 'I'm fairly certain there's no one in. But if no one answers we go in hard. You two first,' he said, pointing at the officers with the H&Ks slung over their shoulders. 'Secure the flat, but remember, this is probably a murder scene so the priority is to preserve forensic evidence. I don't want to get excited about a print, only to find out it's one of yours. Got it?'

They affirmed they had indeed got it.

The short stocky officer with the battering ram worked his way into position.

Fluke knocked twice, hard. The sound was in sharp contrast to the silence that had preceded it. They waited, holding their breath, straining to hear the slightest noise, anything that might point to the flat being occupied.

Fluke knocked again. Louder.

A door opened behind them making them jump. The two armed officers swung round, flicking their safety catches off as they did. Fluke saw their response before he saw who was behind him. They lowered their weapons, flicked the safety catches back on.

'Sam's not in,' a young man said.

A nerd, as Towler would have called him, stood in the doorway of the other flat on the landing. He was wearing a faded Captain America T-shirt and looked paler than Fluke. Myopic eyes stared at them through modern glasses. He pushed them up his nose nervously. He had untidy hair and was stick thin but otherwise seemed normal enough.

Fluke identified himself. 'How do you know she's not in?' he said.

The man looked sheepish. 'I watch out for her.'

'What do you mean, you "watch out for her"? Do you mean you look out for her, or do you mean you spy on her?' Towler said. 'What's your name? What do you do?'

'William, sir.'

'Speak up!'

'William Robinson, sir. I work at DEFRA. I keep their software running. I meant I like her. I speak to her sometimes. I notice when she leaves her flat.'

'When did you last see her, William?' Fluke said. He could hear armed response getting restless behind him. Tough shit, they could wait.

'Not for a few days, sir. But that's not unusual. She often doesn't leave her flat. I knocked and offered to pick something up when I went to Sainsbury's one night but she said no. Said she didn't need anything. She actually goes out less than I do. And I hardly ever go out.'

'You don't say?' said Towler.

'You hear anything suspicious a couple of nights ago, William?' Fluke asked. 'It would have been late, in all likelihood.'

'I'm up until about midnight most nights. I sometimes see the light in the corridor change when her door opens but I can't remember when I last saw her. I haven't heard anything suspicious though.'

Fluke needed to keep moving. He'd come back to William later. He needed to get inside Samantha's flat and see if it was the murder scene. And it wasn't lost on him that he had armed police standing round in a public area doing nothing.

'OK, William. A police officer's going to take your statement. I need you to go back inside. We're going to have to break the door down so don't worry if you hear something loud.'

'You don't have to break in, sir,' he said. 'I have a key.'

'Excuse me?'

'I have keys to all the flats. The landlord gives me money off my rent if I take care of the building's systems. They're all computerised, you see. I need access to reset heating and electric timers sometimes. Not often – our electricity's quite good as we're on the same grid as the hospital.'

'Could you get me the key, please, William?'

William disappeared into his flat and returned a minute later with a box of keys. He sorted through them and handed Fluke one on a red plastic key ring, bearing the number five.

After standing down the officer with the battering ram, Fluke quietly unlocked the door. The two armed officers, in total contrast to the earlier raids, moved in quietly. Towler followed them in. Fluke held his breath. They were back out before he needed to exhale.

'All clear, boss,' Towler said. 'Nothing obvious.'

Fluke was disappointed but not discouraged. A great deal could be missed on the first sweep. He'd have preferred a big pool of blood but, even without one, he was convinced it was where Samantha was killed. He thanked the armed response unit and stood them down. It was now a detective's job. On the off chance a weapon was recovered, he and Towler were more than capable of making it safe before it was bagged for evidence.

He called everyone together. 'Right, I'm treating this as a crime scene. That means full forensic protocols. No exceptions. When's the CSM getting here?'

'Downstairs now, boss. Just waiting for your nod,' Jiao-long said. He looked pleased to be out of the office.

'Good. Tell him to come up. I'm having a quick look round but no one else is to go in. Matt, make sure we set up entry cordons. Two, please. One at the door and one downstairs. Longy, get a list of residents; the rest of you, start knocking on doors. I want to know what the rest of the building knows. And someone take William's statement. By the looks of it, he's got a bit of a thing for her so may know something about her movements and habits.'

Fluke struggled into the forensic suit and covered his shoes with the protective slippers. Putting on his face mask, he entered the flat. There was a worn and sad 'Welcome' mat on the inside. The walls were painted a neutral cream. He knew, from his old flat, that most building companies used cream. It showed empty rooms at their best, apparently. The landlord obviously hadn't bothered to change the colour scheme.

The first room off the hall was the kitchen, and Fluke saw the coffee grinder immediately. He laughed out loud. It was exactly as Lucy had described; like a small sausage machine. He couldn't believe their conversation two nights ago had paid off. He owed her a great deal. He'd ring her later.

He opened the fridge to check something. He knew it would be there but wanted peace of mind anyway.

The bag of coffee from Watt's sat on the top shelf. The same blend as he now had in his own fridge.

He opened the bag. Shiny brown beans, waiting to be ground. He thought about them and felt a little sad. The care and attention of the coffee farmer who grew them. The way they'd been picked, dried and sold to a trader. How that trader had sold them on and eventually, probably three or four stages later, they'd found their way to a gourmet coffee shop in Carlisle. Bought by someone who appreciated them. And now they were evidence. It didn't seem fair. He put them back so they were in the right place for the videos and photographs.

The rest of the fridge was bare. He opened the cupboards in the kitchen. Nothing of interest. Some stock ingredients: rice, pasta, tinned tomatoes, a half-eaten packet of crisps. Nothing that couldn't be found in a million homes across the country.

Fluke wandered through the rest of the flat. It was tasteful but impersonal. The only thing that wasn't generic was the coffee grinder. No photos, no flowers, no ornaments and no pictures. He'd have to check to see if the flat was furnished or unfurnished. His money was on furnished. It looked like the flat-packed stuff you got from IKEA. Not bad quality but you wouldn't spend too much money on it. The TV was a flat-screen but fairly basic. No satellite dish, no DVD player.

He entered the bedroom. The bed was made up with a plain cover. There was a glass of water on the bedside cabinet. A charger for something was plugged into the wall. He opened the bedside cabinet. There were a number of books in there and an e-reader, which would possibly explain the charger. He checked. It fitted. There was another charger, the lead neatly wrapped around the plug. He'd check if it fitted the mobile they found with the body later.

He opened the wardrobe and found it half full of expensive-looking clothes.

The curtains were shut and Fluke lifted them to see what type of view she'd had. Something out of place caught his eye. There was a small pile of coins on the window ledge. He looked across at the other window and saw there was another pile there as well. Two-pence pieces, carefully balanced on top of each other. Fluke made his way out of the bedroom and checked the rest of the windows. They all had piles of coins on them.

On a hunch, he walked back to the front door and lifted the welcome mat in the inner hallway. He thought he'd heard something as he stepped on it. He lifted it up. There was broken glass underneath. A broken light bulb unless he was mistaken. Thin and curved. Very fragile. Noisy when stepped on, especially in the confined space of a hall.

Coins on window ledges. Glass underneath the mat, covering the flat's only entrance. Crude, but extremely effective anti-intruder devices, designed to alert whoever was inside that someone was trying to get in.

Everything he knew about Samantha told Fluke that there would also be an external device. Something to tell her that someone was inside waiting for her. She was too careful for there not to be one.

He went back out onto the landing she shared with William. Towler had cleared it to make sure the inner cordon was secured. He was on his own.

Fluke groaned involuntarily as he got down on his hands and knees. He found he was doing it more and more. He knew it wasn't just his age – he was still only forty – but that he was just weaker now, plain and simple. He hoped that some of his strength would return in time but he knew he'd never quite be the same again. A serious illness, the inevitable march of time and a secret only he knew about. *Still*, he thought, *I'm too young to be feeling this old.*

He knew from his Northern Ireland training that security devices were invariably at ground level. They were easier to set up and harder for casual observers to spot.

In the movies all you needed was a folded piece of paper wedged into the doorframe – if the paper's on the floor, the door's been opened. But in reality, that's far too easy to see, far too easy to replace and everybody knows the trick anyway. It was the same with a strand of hair. Fluke thought that if she had an external device, it would be far more subtle. Something that wouldn't look out of place. He cast his eyes over everything at ground level but couldn't see anything. He stood back up and checked the top of the doorframe. Again, nothing.

He stepped back, still convinced he was right. If she was being hunted, as was still reasonable to assume, he knew she'd have some way of telling if someone was already inside. She wouldn't go to all the effort of plastic surgery, false names and counter-surveillance precautions just to walk into a trap.

There were two options: either a device that he couldn't see, or the killer had removed it and taken it with him. Fluke doubted the second. Why would he bother? Removing it before she arrived was the same as triggering it, and removing it after he'd killed her served no purpose. There was a third option: that she didn't have one, but he dismissed it immediately. There was something there, he just hadn't found it yet.

Fluke stepped farther back to get an overview, to look round the rest of the landing, see if there was anything different about her entrance compared to everyone else's. The door was the same colour as William's and the same as those he'd passed on the way up; dark blue. Each spyhole was in the same place and the flat numbers all came from the same pack. Even the external doormats were the same; a dark brown that the landlord probably hoped wouldn't show up dirt, there to encourage people to wipe their feet before standing on his carpets. There was a light on each landing, equidistant between the two flats.

Fluke stared at the open doorway, convinced he'd missed something. He heard someone coming up the stairs and held his hand up to stop them. He wasn't ready to share the scene yet, knew he stood the best chance of catching the killer if he could get inside Samantha's head – if he could think like her.

He tried to imagine how she'd have done it. It would have to be quick to set up; nothing that would keep her on the landing for too long. It would also need to be quick to check. And it needed to be completely reliable, had to work every time. To fail even once would be unthinkable. Fluke started again. But everything was made of solid stuff, designed to withstand a transient population. No room for individual expression anywhere on the outside. The only thing they could even move would be the doormats. Everything else was fixed solidly in place.

He sighed. It was time to let SOCO in.

He hadn't seen anything to suggest it was the murder site but he instinctively knew it was. It had to be. Science would prove him right. It was time to add chemicals and powders and special lights to things.

As he stepped away from the door, he moved the mat slightly with his foot. He paused. It was heavy-duty, designed to get mud and grit off shoes and boots but Fluke had moved it by accident, far easier than he should have been able to. The friction of his shoes had been enough to move it as he turned. Frowning, he bent down and lifted it up at the corner. It had been modified. It had been hollowed out. Scraped and cut away from all but the edges. A rough job, but effective. What was originally a heavy-duty item was significantly lighter. From the outside it looked like all the rest in the complex. With the inside removed it left a gap of at least half an inch, the half-inch she needed.

Underneath the mat were some crisps. Two of the crisps were crushed into small pieces. This was it, this was her alarm system. Cunningly simple and incredibly clever.

It also explained why the bag of crisps hadn't been finished. Fluke was a crisp addict and knew there was no way he could open a bag and not finish it. Family-size ones, yes; single bags, not a chance.

'Clever,' Towler said, appearing at his side and instantly

recognising what he was seeing. They stared at her ingenuity in silence.

'Who are you, Samantha?' Fluke said, eventually.

He couldn't be sure if the crisps had been broken before they got there or whether the size twelves of armed response had crushed them. There was no way of knowing but if she'd arrived back and saw broken crisps there was no way she'd have entered her flat. She'd expect to see them unbroken, dreading the day she didn't.

'But which cleverer bastard circumnavigated it?' Towler said, putting words to exactly what Fluke was thinking.

Fluke had the same crime scene manager, Sean Rogers. They quickly devised an evidence recovery strategy. It was far easier when there wasn't a body. No pathologist to wait for and argue with.

Fluke needed to see blood. There wouldn't be much but with a gunshot to the head, even a small one without an exit wound, there would be some. It wouldn't be visible to the naked eye but it would be there. If there was no blood, it wasn't the murder site.

And if it wasn't the murder site the investigation was effectively over.

They agreed which route would be taken by SOCO and put down stepping plates. A tech went first and videoed the flat, followed by the photographer who snapped everything that Fluke and Rogers thought relevant. Next, they went in with luminol. Fluke knew that when luminol came into contact with blood, the haemoglobin oxidised and went through a chemiluminescent reaction, a reaction that would be visible in the dark.

The curtains were drawn and the blinds pulled down. With the flat in darkness, Rogers sprayed each room methodically. Fluke followed him. The reaction would only last for thirty seconds but that would be more than long enough.

There was nothing in the hall and nothing in the kitchen.

Rogers sprayed the bedroom and again there was nothing. The small bathroom was the same. There was only one room left.

The living room.

Rogers sprayed the room and Fluke saw an immediate flare of light. There wasn't much, a few flecks on the carpet, spread over a circular patch a yard in diameter, but it was enough. Flecks that glowed. Beautiful and eerie. Mesmerised, Fluke stared until the luminous blue light faded and disappeared.

As the room returned to darkness, Fluke felt a lurch of excitement. Up until then, he'd been three steps off the pace in the investigation. Everything they'd achieved had been through sheer luck, it seemed.

But regardless of how they'd got here, he was standing where the killer stood and where Samantha had died. He'd taken a massive step forward.

I'm coming for you, he thought.

Fluke had his murder scene.

Chapter 24

Fluke left Rogers to process the flat. He and his team would go back in when the forensic evidence was secure. He went outside to ring Chambers and tell him they'd found the murder scene. Chambers's frustration at the lack of pace in the case seemed mollified with the latest news. In fact, Fluke was surprised at the way Chambers had spoken to him. Gone was the antagonism: he actually seemed happy for once. Fluke didn't like it.

After he'd finished, he wandered over to where FMIT had gathered. Alan Vaughn had been to the nearby Sainsbury's to get food for everyone. Fluke looked at the selection on offer. He'd been to the reduced section judging by the yellow stickers plastered over the price labels. A man on a budget. Fluke grabbed a duck in hoisin sauce wrap and a bottle of water. He refused the bag of crisps he was offered and noticed Towler did the same.

Fluke idly listened to Vaughn and Towler arguing about the reduced-price food.

'Fiscally conservative, my arse,' Towler said. 'You're a fucking tight bastard, mate. That's your problem.'

Fluke smiled. Some things never changed.

He'd just finished his wrap when Rogers came back out. 'We've done a preliminary sweep, sir. Your team can go in now, but there's something you need to see.'

Fluke nodded his thanks and prepared to go back inside, but Vaughn signalled he wanted a word first.

'We've just taken William's statement, boss. I asked if he'd ever seen her put down crisps, to see if there was anything to support your theory.'

'And?' he said.

'He saw it, boss. He bloody saw it. Every time, I reckon, or near enough. I think he was obsessed. He thought she was putting her keys under the mat when she went out. Said he never checked and I believe him.'

'No chance it was him?' Fluke said, doubting it.

'Nah. He's been here since the block was built. Bit of a loner but not all loners are serial killers. Likes his games, likes his films, but I didn't see anything that made me nervous.'

'OK, tell him we'll need him at the station at some point but for now we focus on the flat. Make sure Jo updates HOLMES. And don't forget to put through the receipt for the food.'

'Will do,' he said, walking off.

Rogers had been waiting patiently out of earshot. Fluke beckoned him over. 'What we got, Sean?'

'I can take you through the video. It's all logged. Easy job really. You'll have noticed there was nothing there other than the blood.'

'Yep, nothing personal anyway. If it wasn't for the coffee grinder, I'd bet the flat looked the same as it did the day she moved in.'

Rogers nodded. 'You seen the film *Heat*, sir? When De Niro says you shouldn't have anything in your life that stops you from just walking away? It reminded me of that. There was nothing personal. Nothing at all, not even utility bills. It's for you to decide how important that is, obviously, but it stood out to me.'

Fluke knew what Rogers meant; there was none of the usual debris of life.

'Anything else?'

'There was one thing, sir.' Instead of telling him, Rogers led the way to the evidence van. All portable items potentially of interest were bagged and tagged there. He reached in and pulled out a larger bag. He signed the seal and tore it open, then held it out for Fluke to inspect. 'Found it under the bedside cabinet.'

Fluke had no idea what Rogers was holding. It seemed to be a two-part device. One part was a control unit of some kind. The other looked like a plastic heat pad, the sort used to keep pet snakes warm. It was flat, flexible and about a foot squared. It had a wire leading from it, which fitted into the control unit. Fluke took it from him and looked it over. He couldn't even begin to guess what it was.

'You don't know what this is?' Fluke said.

'Not a clue.'

'Longy?' he shouted.

The cry went up and Jiao-long was soon with Fluke, the irrepressible grin still there, despite the lack of sleep. He'd have to make him go home soon.

'Boss?'

'Glove up and find out what this thing is, Longy. I think that's a part number on the side of the battery pack.'

As Jiao-long took out his smartphone and began checking, Fluke asked Rogers when he could expect an inventory.

'Within the hour, sir. I'll send it up to Durranhill to be typed. I'll email you as soon as it's done.'

Rogers walked off to continue the supervision of his SOCO team. They still had work to do even though the initial excitement had worn off. Cases were won or lost on how thorough SOCOs were.

Fluke mentally recapped while Jiao-long surfed the internet. There were at least three crime scenes. The murder site and the deposition site were now his. The third crime scene was the car the killer had transported the body in.

He also still had some numbers stubbornly resisting identification and a mobile phone that the techs were trying to recover data from.

While he waited for Jiao-long, Fluke got out the card Skelton had produced for everyone and had another look at the numbers. Sometimes sneaking up on a puzzle was the best way. He stared at them but the answer remained rigidly out of reach. He'd noticed his team picking up their cards and staring at them when they had downtime, discussing it with their colleagues when they were having a brew. Just like Fluke was. A bit of paper that you had to take out of a file or unfold wouldn't get the same attention. Fluke reminded himself to thank Skelton. It was something he'd probably replicate in future investigations.

He turned his thoughts to Samantha. It was clear she was obsessed with secrecy. The only sensible answer was that she was hiding from someone. Someone serious. She was well resourced, that was obvious. Expensive surgery, nice clothes. Refined taste with the coffee. But he had nothing else to go on. Rogers was right, she seemed ready to leave at a moment's notice. She'd have left if the crisps were broken when she returned. She'd have regretted leaving her coffee grinder but would have left it nonetheless. There was nothing else in the flat of note except some weird gadget.

Was it the killer she'd been hiding from? Fluke wasn't sure. Common sense said it was. It had taken a professional to find her. If all the cosmetic surgery was relevant, someone was looking for her long before the Diamonds entered her life. So who had killed her, the Diamonds or someone else? That was the key question and one that wouldn't be answered until the DNA results from that morning's raids were in.

Best-case scenario was that the killer was one of the Diamonds or someone connected to them. That a Diamond had sex with her was beyond doubt. Avoiding a rape charge was more than enough motivation for some men to arrange a murder.

Worst-case scenario was that the DNA hit was unconnected to the murder. Fluke might struggle and secure a rape conviction but that would be scant consolation if Samantha's killer remained undetected.

He rearranged his thoughts into a logical SOE, sequence of events. He dismissed the order in which things had been discovered – it had little relevance to each piece of the puzzle's importance, and was misleading. There were four to reorganise: first there was Samantha getting surgery. Then there was the rape. The rape was followed by her murder. The murder was followed by the body deposition. Everything else would fit into that timeline somewhere. Something must have preceded the surgery, something that could have happened years earlier.

Now he'd seen her flat and the extraordinary lengths she'd gone to to protect herself, something was nagging him, a slow insidious thought and one that he couldn't share. If he did, he'd leave himself wide open to a Professional Standards investigation and an article on the front page of the *News & Star*.

If she was that scared why did she report the rape at all? Why risk the exposure?

Fluke had attended all the relevant training and took rape investigations very seriously. They were horrendous crimes, a personal violation from which most victims never fully recovered. But report it she did. Fluke was prepared to believe that the rape had been so unacceptable to her, so abhorrent, that she'd put her personal safety at risk to see justice done, but he wasn't closing his mind to the possibility that there were other factors at play here, factors that he didn't yet know about. He wouldn't share it with anyone, not even Towler. He wasn't even comfortable thinking about it himself.

Jiao-long interrupted his train of thought with a satisfied shout. Fluke leaned over his shoulder to see what he'd found. There was a photo of the device on his phone. Newer, with a different coloured control unit, but essentially the same.

'What the hell is that?'

'A bed-wetting alarm, boss.'

Fluke hadn't known what to expect but it certainly wasn't that. 'Does that mean what I think it means?'

'Yep, here, read the description on the manufacturer's site,' he said, handing his iPhone over.

There was a photo of a smiling child but the corresponding text was too small for him.

He handed it back, 'Just read it out, Hawkeye.'

'Basically, this flat bit here,' he said, pointing at the part Fluke had thought looked like a heat pad, 'that goes under the sheets, and you lie on it. If you start to have a piss, it sends a signal to the control unit which triggers the alarm here.' He pointed at the squarish box. 'It's supposed to wake you after the first few drips.'

They walked over to the van and retrieved it from the evidence bag. They put it together and worked out the mechanics of it all. Fluke was satisfied Jiao-long was right.

'So it's exactly what it sounds like then. Why would she have one? Wouldn't this type of thing be for kids? Who wets the bed at her age?'

Fluke mentally reviewed the post-mortem. There had been no medical problem in the preliminary findings that he could recollect. Of course, some of the tests weren't back, so he'd need to ring Sowerby and check to be sure. As someone who suffered from nightmares himself, he believed that Samantha had demons in her head, demons that came out at night, causing serious psychological problems.

Towler had walked up and caught the last part. 'What's next, boss?'

There was nothing urgent and Fluke wanted to rest before he went back in with Diamond. He'd been caught off-guard last time – it wouldn't happen again.

'Wait for the DNA results to come through, I suppose,' he said.

'You want me to drive you somewhere?'

He looked at his watch. It was still the middle of the afternoon and despite having been up for hours, it was too early to go home. He had a couple of calls to make. 'No point going back to HQ just yet, Matt. We'll head back to Durranhill.'

196

The phone rang half a dozen times before a gruff impatient voice answered. 'Sowerby.'

'Henry, it's Avison Fluke. You got two minutes?'

Fluke was in a temporary office at Durranhill.

He could hear noise on the other end of the phone. Metal on metal. Sowerby was probably in a mortuary somewhere, prepping for another post-mortem.

'As long as you don't mind being on speakerphone, Avison. I've already scrubbed up. I have Lucy with me.'

Fluke's second call was going to be to Lucy to let her know what a help she'd been with her coffee theory, so he quickly brought her up to date and thanked her. She sounded pleased but Fluke could tell she'd rather it had been entomological evidence that had led to the breakthrough.

'Anyway,' he continued, 'did you find anything in the PM, Henry, that would have made her incontinent?'

'Incontinent? Don't think so. Why?'

'I've got evidence she was a bed-wetter.'

Fluke explained what they'd found.

'You mean adult nocturnal enuresis then,' he said.

'Do I?'

'Just the doctor in me coming out, Avison, don't worry. I'll check my notes but there was nothing I can remember. I'll have the report finished by the end of tomorrow hopefully. It's being typed now. I just need to proof it.'

Sowerby's voice faded in the distance. Fluke was used to it; he frequently forgot he was talking on a speakerphone and drifted off, assuming everyone could still hear him.

'He's gone to find his notes, Inspector,' Lucy explained.

'Thanks, Lucy. And thanks again for that coffee link. We wouldn't have found her without it.'

'How's the investigation going otherwise?'

'Honestly? Nowhere. Well, not nowhere, but we don't seem to be able to get a bead on this bloke. It's taken me nearly four days just to find out where the victim lives. I'm not sure I even have her real name yet. I've found a motive to kill her, I'm just not sure it's the *right* motive.'

'Oh, dear. Surely finding the murder scene is going to help?'

'Hopefully, but so far every time I find something, all I end up with is more questions.'

They were interrupted by the sound of shuffling papers as Sowerby came back in range of the speakerphone.

'No, nothing here, Avison. There was very little wrong with her when I got inside. Liver had a little scarring. If she drank, it was minimal. No evidence of drug use. Bladder normal. Bloods showed nothing of note. I can re-check them for levels of the ADH hormone if you'd like?'

'In English, Henry.'

'The antidiuretic hormone. It's a signalling hormone that tells the kidneys to produce less urine at night. Don't ask me how it works – I'm dredging this from med school. I've certainly never come across it in this field before. You want me to run the tests?'

Fluke thought about it. The shotgun approach to forensic evidence gathering had its uses but he preferred the targeted approach wherever possible – asking for forensic evidence when he knew what the answers were going to be. Never ask a question you don't already know the answer to, his first SIO had told him.

What would a hormone deficiency prove one way or the other? That she wet the bed. So what? That she had a bed-wetting alarm to manage her problem. So what? And if it wasn't a medical problem, then it was the type of evidence that only made sense after the fact. It wouldn't move the investigation forward. The samples would be there if he needed tests later.

'No, thanks, Henry. I was just curious. I can't see how it's relevant. I'm not wasting taxpayer's money finding out why a woman wet the bed.'

Fluke had just put down the phone when Jo Skelton stuck her head round the door. 'Early DNAs are back, boss.'

As the results were computerised, they came in by email to the investigation address that linked directly to HOLMES. Fluke could see that there were at least ten emails from the lab. As each one linked to a different suspect, they were coming in one at a time. The top one was red, and the time next to it indicated that it had only just come in. All the rest were black, telling him that Skelton had read them.

'Anything?' he asked.

'All negative so far, boss. Everyone we locked up this morning has been cleared, including Wayne Diamond – his was the third result in. The ones we're waiting for are the samples taken from clothes, combs and toothbrushes.'

She pressed F9, the refresh button. Another red email appeared. As she opened it, Fluke leaned forward, as if being closer to the screen meant he'd get the result quicker.

He read it to himself as it flashed on the screen. Although there were several attachments with photos of evidence labels, scientific graphs and other indecipherable bullshit, Fluke was only interested in the second line. The name the sample was taken from and the result: a cousin who was in HMP Durham but had been out at the time of the rape. An interfamilial match but negative. Fluke leaned back, disappointed. He made a note to contact HMP Durham and ensure Ackley and the cousin were kept apart. Last thing he needed was Ackley getting shanked.

'How many are interfamilial?' he asked.

'Everyone bar one, boss. They're all related to the sample we have, apart from Uncle Jonna or whatever it is he calls himself. My guess is he's one of those family friends who's been called uncle from such an early age, it becomes fact. I bet if you asked any of them they wouldn't know he wasn't a blood relative.'

Fluke knew it was likely. He also knew it wasn't a class or criminal thing. Towler's daughter, Abi, called him Uncle Avison. With extended and complicated families like the Diamonds, just identifying who was who was going to provide valuable intel for years to come.

Another email came in. Another negative.

'This could take ages,' Fluke said. He decided he'd go back to his temporary office and ring Chambers to let him know where he was, in case Fluke was needed at HQ. He rang and was put through to Chambers's PA. After they exchanged some banal pleasantries about Fluke's health, she asked him to wait while Chambers finished a call. As Fluke was listening to the hold music, he got a text. It was from Towler.

'Got him!'

Fluke put down the phone.

'Old man Diamond,' Towler said, when Fluke got to the room the team had colonised at Durranhill.

Fluke was genuinely surprised. Kenneth Diamond was the only one of the family who seemed to be an upstanding citizen. He was a businessman. He had the big house in Stanwix. When compared to the rapist profile Fluke had in his head, Kenneth was twenty years older than he'd imagined. 'Wasn't he away at the time of the rape?'

'Dunno, boss,' Skelton said. 'He's been away for a while now, no one seems to know where he is. He's supposed to have distanced himself from the family though. Disowned the lot of them. He did it publicly, if I remember. We only checked his house to rule him out and to see if anyone else of interest had been there.'

'Are we sure the sample's definitely from him?'

'Sure as we can be. Until we actually take a sample from his mouth, we can never be one hundred per cent.'

'Good enough,' Fluke said, eventually. 'Until we know anything otherwise, our number-one priority now is finding Kenneth Diamond. Find him and we're a step closer to finding the killer.'

Chapter 25

By the time Fluke had organised teams to search for Kenneth Diamond locally and sent a nationwide alert out to all territorial police forces, he was exhausted. Luckily Skelton had already warned off the Border Agency. He left Towler to organise searches into Diamond's personal and business life.

As Fluke left the building, he smiled to himself. Towler had done exactly what he'd have done: he'd shouted for Jiao-long. It looked like his plan to send him home for some sleep wasn't going to be a reality for a while yet. With the investigation in full flow and a manhunt being organised, Fluke felt he should really stay but he reminded himself that the nosebleed earlier had most likely been caused by overworking. It was time to go home and get some rest. His car was still at HQ so he got a lift home with uniform, and arranged for someone to pick him up first thing.

It was still light enough to sit outside for a while and he opened a bottle of beer, poured it into a pint glass and sat on the porch of his log cabin. He stared out across the lake. Long shadows were forming on the fell on the other side. He marvelled at the heat and pressure it must have taken to force it up from the earth's crust, only for rivers of moving ice to chip away at it, eventually forging a way through. Ullswater, the permanent reminder of a glacier so big it cut a mountain in half.

He lit a cigar and opened the file he'd brought with him.

Years before, Fluke had discovered his brain worked best looking at things in isolation, in small batches. That way, when he came to look at the thing as a whole, he knew he had an intellectual grip on everything. So instead of taking everything home, he'd only take the things he either hadn't read or wasn't sure he fully understood yet.

That evening, he'd taken the evidence log from Farrar's flat. He also took out the card with the numbers and clipped it to the top of the file. The list was short and there was nothing that stood out. The SOCO officer had obviously started in the bathroom.

> Toothbrush, electric, still charged.
> Toothpaste, half-empty.
> Floss.
> Assorted toiletries and makeup, used.
> Hand mirror.
> Coins, from window ledge.
> Paracetamol, bottle, 15 tablets remaining.
> Birth control pills.
> Toilet paper, two rolls.

The list continued, going from room to room. Her clothes were listed and Fluke's first suspicions were right. They were all brands he knew to be expensive. SOCO had attempted to separate out her personal items from items that were part of the furnished flat. Efforts were underway to get hold of the landlord in London for an inventory, up to then without success. They would need to know how long she'd lived there, as William had been vague. Fluke also wanted to know how she was living there without any bills being paid. He suspected she'd paid the landlord a large amount of cash to keep it in his name, but Fluke needed confirmation.

Despite the cold, Fluke felt his eyes closing. He shut the file. He wasn't in the right frame of mind and it would do more harm than good to persevere. He relit his cigar and finished it, drained his beer and went to bed.

For once, he wasn't disturbed by nightmares.

It was still dark when Fluke's alarm went off and he opened his eyes. In that halfway state – not asleep but not yet awake – he was able to remember the last thing he'd dreamt of. It had been the inventory. Something in his subconscious had been bothered by it. But as his mind cleared, so did any chance of remembering. It would come back; there was no point forcing it. He knew how his mind worked.

Fluke had no qualms about telling everyone they were working Saturday but felt that when he did, he should be in first. He debated whether to put on some fresh coffee but decided to have one when he got to work instead.

He got to Carleton Hall to find the incident room deserted. He put a fresh filter in the coffee machine and started it off. Towler was already in but had gone to find a newsagent in Penrith to buy some milk. As the machine hissed and gurgled, Fluke thought about what he wanted to achieve.

First, he needed to check with the custody sergeant that everyone other than Nathaniel Diamond had been released. Fluke wanted another go at him. Although he wasn't a suspect in the rape, he knew something. Plus his dad was now in the frame. He'd task the first DC to arrive to go and get an additional twelve hours from the on-call magistrate to question Nathaniel. The advantage of asking in the early hours was that the magistrate would be woken at home and less likely to say no.

While Fluke waited for the coffee machine, he opened his file from the previous night. He stared at the list, willing that night's thoughts to come back but there was nothing. Apart from the bed-wetting alarm, it was still a list of everyday items. He'd mention it at the morning briefing. He turned to the photo of the alarm. It was bothering him as well. He couldn't help feeling there was something else on the list that made sense of it. The previous day, he'd thought she was running from someone and was having nightmares because of it. Now he wasn't so sure.

There was also the question that Kay Edwards, the DC who had travelled with her to the SARC, had raised. If she was in hiding, why had she even been going out for a drink at all? Fluke had initially thought it had been a fair question but it had slipped his mind before he could seriously consider it. Put alongside his own unasked question of whether anyone that scared would report a rape, it took on greater significance. He had the feeling that Samantha still had secrets to be revealed.

Find out how the victim lived and you'll find out how they died.

Fluke enjoyed these rare moments of solitude where he was surrounded by the fruits of the investigation. He liked looking at things in isolation at home but in the incident room he could look at everything. It was his wide-angled lens. The board with photos of the two crime scenes was full. The previous day, photos of the different Diamonds had been staring back at him. That night, someone had replaced them with a single photo of Kenneth. It had been cut out from a newspaper article about a new business venture he was involved in. One other photograph was on the board: the cold, lifeless face of Samantha Farrar. It was up to Fluke to find out if the link between them was a straight line or whether there was still another photograph to go on the board.

The coffee machine had quietened down and Fluke poured himself a large mug. As he blew on it, his mind drifted from one photo to the other, taking in all the pictorial evidence.

His peace was interrupted by another of his team coming in. Jo Skelton walked through the door. Surprised to see him, she was even more surprised to find that there was already a pot of fresh coffee. 'There's no milk yet, Jo. Matt's gone for some.'

'No organisation, you two,' she said, pulling a carton from her bag.

She grabbed her 'World's Best Mum' mug and filled it. She walked over and perched on the edge of the table, next to Fluke. 'You get any kip, boss?'

'Some. You?'

'Not much, nasty one this. I let Tom sleep in. He can take the kids to football today. I may struggle to come in tomorrow, though.'

Fluke nodded. Skelton's husband was in a band. Not like the short-lived band that he and Towler had formed when they were kids, Tom was in a proper band. They played lots of weddings so he normally worked weekends. 'No gig tonight?'

'Nope. Bookings are down nearly thirty per cent. People just want discos and hog roasts these days. He's enjoying the extra time with the kids, though. I've been thinking about everything we have, trying to make some links but I can't get my head round it all yet. Can't remember the last one we had that was this complicated.'

'Same here. That inventory is bugging me,' he said.

'Why?'

'The birth control pills, for one. If we accept that she was in hiding, why did she need to take them?'

Skelton shrugged.

'Women take them for more than just birth control, boss. Sometimes they're taken for health reasons,' she said. 'They can make periods more regular and less painful. Reduce the risk of cysts and ovarian cancer.'

Fluke accepted that being a woman was far more complicated than being a man. If Skelton said avoiding pregnancy wasn't the only reason to take the pill then that was good enough.

'Was that it?' she said.

'No, there was something else,' he said. 'I just can't put my finger on it yet.'

Fluke had worked with Skelton for long enough to know that she was a 'plodder'. He'd mentioned that to Chambers once, and he'd asked if he wanted her replaced. Fluke had needed to explain that it wasn't meant as an insult. His team worked best when there were hares *and* tortoises. He needed officers who could methodically plough through hours and hours of evidence, who wouldn't get bored doing repetitive tasks, who wouldn't miss things, who would take care to set up and maintain HOLMES. The ACPO *Murder Investigation Manual* stated that the office manager of an incident room should be either a detective sergeant or a detective inspector but Fluke chose Skelton every time. She never complained and knew she was valued highly, fully accepting her role in the team. Police work was 99 per cent perspiration and 1 per cent inspiration. A cliché, yes, but some clichés were clichés because they were true.

'You'll get there. How's your health, boss? You've been looking pasty the last couple of days.'

Some officers had earned the right to ask questions such as that and she was one of them.

'I'm tired, Jo. Weary. Can't seem to shake it off.' He pointed at the evidence boards. 'And this one's a bad one. There was nothing personal about it. Every murder I've ever worked has had anger at its core, whether it's about money, sex or jealousy. At least there's a spark of humanity. Not this one. This was cold. Someone probably rang a number or sent an email, and an emotionless sociopath came up, shot her and threw her in a hole. How can you make sense of that?'

She blew on her drink. 'We'll get there, boss. We always do.'

They finished their coffees in silence as the incident room filled up.

Fluke appeared alone in his concerns over the list. No one else had given it a second thought, but as he sometimes made links that others couldn't, he knew they would all look again. No one had anything new on the numbers either. Not a dead end. Just dead. He was prepared to accept that they meant nothing, but there were too many random things in the investigation already. They were all potential leads.

The rest of the briefing was spent allocating tasks for the day, most of which were about the search for Kenneth Diamond. That was Towler's speciality: running people to ground. If he were still in Cumbria, Towler would find him.

With Towler busy, Fluke took Vaughn with him to re-interview Nathaniel Diamond. He took his own car and Vaughn took the pool car. Fluke needed to be mobile. He wasn't expecting anything to break early on and if he got time he'd decided he'd go and see Leah, and check if she'd found someone to talk to about cosmetic surgery.

Fluke and Vaughn arrived at Durranhill within minutes of each other, and an hour later they were sitting opposite Nathaniel Diamond. The custody sergeant told Fluke that, despite spending twenty-four hours in a police cell, Diamond still looked calm. His only reaction had been when his solicitor was served the notice granting an additional twelve hours' questioning time. Apparently, he'd looked at the camera and raised an eyebrow.

The previous day, Diamond had been in control. Fluke had detected deception when shown the picture of the victim but other than that he'd remained calm.

This time Fluke wasn't leaving until he had something he could use.

Vaughn had asked if he should bring Diamond up from the cells, and Fluke was about to tell him 'yes' until he realised it would just be a continuation of the previous day. He needed something more, some sort of leverage. It was going to be a battle of intellectual heavyweights, and Fluke needed to land the knockout blow. Instead, he turned to Vaughn, 'No, Al, I want to review yesterday's interview first.'

For an hour, Fluke pored over the footage. He watched it with the sound and then without. Vaughn, a brilliant detective in his own right, looked over his shoulder but said nothing.

Fluke watched himself reveal the photo of Samantha to Diamond. There'd definitely been recognition. He watched from the beginning again. He saw himself enter. He saw himself open his folder.

And he saw what he'd missed the first five times.

Chapter 26

Fluke stared at Nathaniel Diamond across the scuffed table and studied him. Really studied him. On the face of it, he was what he looked like. A thug. An intelligent thug, yes, but a thug all the same. Yet, as Fluke looked closer things cleared. The tattoos were a little too well done. No prison ink there. Expensive black tribal sleeves on both arms. His tracksuit, before it had been removed, was also expensive, according to the young officer who had bagged it. They'd also taken an Omega watch from him and that wasn't cheap. It also wasn't garish like some of the more expensive watches could be.

After what Fluke had just witnessed in the footage, he no longer thought of Diamond as an intelligent thug. He thought of him as being one of the most gifted men he'd ever met.

Fluke now suspected his image was completely cultivated. It suited him at that moment and, like a chameleon shedding its skin, he would swap it for another when the time was right. The more Fluke thought about it, the more he came to view Diamond as the head of a large business – an illegal business, but a business all the same. No business survived for long without a business plan and without a CEO. And the CEO had to look the part. On Wall Street, the bankers, moneymen and oil analysts wore their pinstriped suits. In Carlisle, the crime families wore tattoos, tracksuits and heavy jewellery. Occasionally, a dangerous dog was thrown in for good measure. It was still about projecting the right image, though. Two extremes, but the principle was the same.

Brains wouldn't have been enough in Diamond's business, however. He would've had to spend some time establishing himself among some pretty rough competition, competition that would undoubtedly have included his own family. The fact that he was the younger brother but the head of the family spoke volumes. Violence was just another business tool, to be used when needed but only then. As well as being highly intelligent, Nathaniel would be a genuinely frightening man to get on the wrong side of.

Fluke had met hard men all his working life. The Royal Marines recruited exclusively from that gene pool. Some were bullies, some weren't. A few were psychopaths, and some were the nicest people you could ever wish to meet. During his time as a police officer, Fluke had met men who were arguably harder. Men who were psychotic. Men for whom violence was a daily occurrence.

What they all had in common, though, was that there was always someone harder round the corner. Someone younger and quicker coming up through the ranks. Someone just a little bit more mental. Just a little bit more fearless.

Violence would have got Nathaniel to the top, and his brains would have kept him there, but not indefinitely. The X-factor would be ruthlessness. That would be the trait that kept him in charge and made the Diamonds a viable option for outside investment.

A ruthless man could organise a murder if his business were threatened.

The previous day Diamond had been in control.

Today, it would be Fluke's turn. At first, he'd thought he was imagining it. Part of him still didn't think what he'd seen was possible. He'd had to watch it over and over again until he was sure.

Diamond held his eye as Fluke stared at him but it wasn't a battle of wills. Just as Fluke was weighing him up, he got the sense Diamond was doing the same to him.

Fluke broke the silence. 'Just how clever are you, Nathaniel?'

Diamond said nothing.

'You see, I think you're very clever. Far more intelligent than my colleagues in Carlisle have given you credit for. Far more than I'd given you credit for.'

Diamond watched Fluke. There was something going on that Fluke was still unaware of, some context to the investigation that he was yet to see. Diamond could see it, Fluke was sure of that. Would he share, though?

Time to take a risk.

'When did you learn about the airline's interview technique, Nathaniel?'

Still nothing. But Fluke sensed there was movement behind his eyes, as if the neurons in his brain had suddenly had to change direction.

'You see, very few people know about that technique, Nathaniel. It's still being piloted. It's still a university project for now. I'm the only person who uses it in Cumbria. I may be the only police officer in the country who uses it. But you knew what I was doing all along. So I have two options. You either knew about the technique or you were able to work out what I was doing. I think you worked it out, Nathaniel. You want to know how I know?'

Diamond raised his eyebrows slightly. He was curious. Fluke had grabbed his interest.

'It's because I fucked up,' he said. 'You knew what I was doing. You knew I was asking control questions. You reacted to every question as I'd expected. As you had wanted to. You never lost control. Even the little burst of anger at your solicitor was part of it.'

Diamond said nothing but Fluke knew he was right.

'I had my control questions. Now I had to ask *the* question. The one question that it had all been for. But I messed it up, didn't I, Nathaniel?'

Diamond continued to stare. Just as Fluke was about to continue, he nodded slightly.

'You were playing along. You were expecting the question, weren't you? You were expecting the surprise, if you'll forgive the oxymoron. You were watching me as carefully as I was watching you. I showed you the picture of my victim. That was my big surprise. But it was no surprise, was it, Nathaniel?'

'No, Inspector, it wasn't.' The first words he'd said since the interview had started.

'No, Nathaniel. Because when I went through the interview footage again, I noticed that when I took my papers out at the start of the interview, I had mistakenly left the photo of the victim in view for nearly two seconds.'

Fluke took the photo back out of the file and placed it on the table in front of him.

'This one, in fact. But you noticed. The footage shows you noticing. You hid your surprise well. I watched it five times before I spotted it, and I had to watch it another five times just to be sure.'

Fluke picked up the photo and studied it. It was the question that was going to break the case. Sometimes it wasn't just about asking the right question, it was about asking the right question at the right time.

'So my question, Nathaniel, is this. I have you on tape fully in control of your micro-expressions. I have you on tape letting me see what I was expecting to see on my control questions. I know you'd seen the photo before I showed it to you. I know you weren't surprised by it and that you were expecting it. You could easily have cast suspicion away from your family.' Fluke stared at him. Crunch time. 'But for some reason you didn't. You feigned surprise. Subtle, yes, but enough so I wouldn't miss it. You made sure I'd know your family's involved somehow. Nothing that will stand up in court but enough to keep me interested.'

Diamond was watching him carefully. There was a game being played here but only one of them knew the rules.

'I want to know why, Nathaniel? I want to know why you want me investigating your family for murder?'

The room was silent apart from the sound of something dripping. There were no taps, radiators or pipes in interview rooms so Fluke assumed it was coming from internal plumbing in either the walls or the ceiling. He counted the drips and got to thirty before Diamond spoke.

'Are you investigating my father for rape, Mr Fluke?'

Of all the responses he'd anticipated, that wasn't in the top hundred. He had to be careful. 'Why do you say that, Nathaniel?'

'I hear things,' Diamond said.

'And what do you hear?'

'I hear you have a dead girl. I hear she was raped. I hear you think whoever raped her, killed her . . .' he said quietly, staring directly at Fluke. 'Or arranged to have her killed, which is the same thing really.'

Fluke thought for a moment. 'I hear that too.'

If they were being open with each other, he'd play along. For now. He paused. He had the feeling Diamond was trying to tell him something, something he wanted Fluke to work out. Something he couldn't say on tape.

Fluke wondered if he wanted to snitch but immediately dismissed it. Being a snitch would end his business. None of the bigger gangs would deal with him. No, that wasn't it.

Diamond stared at him. He wanted Fluke to get the message. Needed him to understand the subtext. Fluke stared back but it wasn't a pissing contest, just two people trying to communicate without speaking.

'You're going to need to give me something, Nathaniel.' Fluke felt rather than saw Vaughn turn to look at Fluke, not understanding what was happening but knowing not to interrupt. The solicitor didn't understand either but was too scared to speak.

Fluke saw Diamond look down and think, saw him deciding

what he could tell Fluke and what he couldn't. He knew that the investigation was either going to stall completely or progress fast in the next few seconds.

Diamond looked up. 'The girl. You need to look at her again.'

For the second time in five minutes, Fluke was surprised by Diamond's response. There was no bone being thrown here. No suspect was going to be thrown his way. No vehement denial of involvement. Just another riddle added to the embarrassment of riddles they already had.

This was different though. Diamond wanted him to go in a direction he wanted to go anyway. Until now, a direction he'd not dared to. To do so would have been unthinkable.

Fluke understood.

Nathaniel didn't want his family investigated. He wanted Samantha investigated.

Find out how the victim lived and you'll find out how they died.

'Why do I need to do that, Nathaniel? What do you know that I don't?'

'I can't make it easy for you, Mr Fluke. If I tell you what I know, you'll stop looking. You'll take what I give you, and the investigation will end right here, right now. And the outcome would be, shall we say, unacceptable to me. I can't have that.'

Fluke believed him. 'We've looked at her pretty hard, Nathaniel. What am I missing?'

Diamond leaned forward. Planted his elbows on the table.

'Look harder, Mr Fluke,' he said. 'Look harder.'

Chapter 27

Fluke had lied to Diamond. They hadn't looked at Samantha that hard. They'd looked at her as a murder victim. They'd looked at her as a rape victim. They'd looked at her as someone on the run. But they were the only lenses they'd looked through. They hadn't touched the surface on *why* she'd been murdered, *why* she'd been raped and *why* she'd been on the run.

Diamond knew something but for some reason he couldn't tell Fluke. It would stop the investigation, he'd told him. He told him he needed to focus on Samantha.

And Fluke already had suspicions, unshaped and unshared.

He gathered his team.

'I'm changing the focus of the investigation,' he told them. 'The hunt for Kenneth Diamond goes on but our number-one priority is now the girl. We need to know everything about her. Nathaniel Diamond knows something we don't. Something he can't tell us. I want to know what that is.'

Towler walked over to the whiteboard, ready to list the allocated tasks when Fluke called them out.

'We know she was hiding from someone,' Fluke said. 'I'm now convinced it wasn't someone in the Diamond family. So we need to know more than we do now. Where's Kay?' Fluke had kept DC Edwards on secondment to FMIT and now was the time to use her.

'Here, sir,' said a voice from the back.

'Go through the rape again with Jo. Get everything down. Nothing's irrelevant. The pair of you are to go back to the SARC at Preston. Retrace everything.'

Towler wrote down the task on the board along with the initials of the two assigned officers.

'I'll go back to the Cumberland Infirmary and see if they have a cosmetic surgeon for me to speak to yet. I'll do that on my own, Matt. Longy, I need you to look for her online. Anything. Use the name she gave. Use her DNA, fingerprint, surgery scars, anything you can think of. And don't limit yourself to UK databases. I want Interpol tapped up. The States. See if you can speak to the FBI. Check with their border security, if she's been to America she'll have been fingerprinted on arrival.'

'Will do, boss,' Jiao-long confirmed.

'Al, I want a bulletin made up. Don't piss about with the E-FIT, use a post-mortem photo. I want it sent to every force in the country. Let's see if anyone else has come across her. I also want you to start on her financial footprint. She was paying cash for the flat but she had to have a source of income. Work with Longy and find it.'

He looked up from his notes. Everyone was waiting for him to dismiss them, waiting to get on with it. Energy had been renewed.

It was time to let them do what they did best.

Half an hour later and Fluke was back on the M6. With no tram or underground system and a limited bus service, he seemed to spend half his life on Cumbria's major motorway. In a big county with a small population, driving was the only real option. The Yanks had a term for it: freeway therapy. When someone was causing trouble but not enough to be sacked, they would be based as far away from their home as possible. Their options were move or spend hours driving.

Fluke didn't mind though. The amount of driving he'd done over the previous few days had been largely self-imposed and, as he was using his BMW X1 rather than the pool car, he wasn't getting mileage. He didn't care; using his own vehicle gave him flexibility. Plus, you couldn't smoke in the pool cars.

He put on a Ramones album and turned up the volume. He needed to clear his head of all previous preconceptions about the case, and loud fast music was the best way of doing that. He was soon singing along to 'Beat on the Brat'.

He'd already checked with the ward that Leah was on duty. Anyone could have done that but he wanted to keep busy, to keep moving. He debated telling her about his nosebleed but decided against it. He knew it was down to over-exerting himself, and she'd only tell him to slow down, or worse, that he needed more plasma.

He searched for a parking space but couldn't find one. Even the overflow car parks were full. Fluke knew that you either got there at eight o'clock or you entered the parking lottery. He and a black Saab prowled the main car park for a while before he eventually gave up and parked in the staff section, leaving a note on the dashboard that he was a police officer on official business. It didn't give him any right to park there but it might fool an idiot.

The ward nurse asked him to take a seat in the dayroom while she told Doctor Cooper he was there. There was only one other person in the room – a middle-aged man watching the highlights of a rugby match on the flat-screen TV. The volume was muted. He wore a baseball cap to hide his hair loss. Tubes went from a portable drip stand to under his T-shirt. A Hickman line no doubt. Surgery to attach it to a major blood vessel, surgery to remove it. Fluke subconsciously rubbed his chest where he knew his own scar was.

A nurse came in and asked the man if he needed any pain medication.

'Aye, lass,' he said in a voice that had little fight left.

'One or two?' she said, removing a blister pack from her pocket.

'Two, lass. Unless I can have three?'

'Away with yer,' she replied, with good humour. 'More than my job's worth.' She popped two pills and placed them into a thimble-sized container.

Fluke frowned. He had the strangest feeling that he'd just witnessed something important. He replayed the innocuous exchange, but there was nothing. It was probably nothing. Too little sleep and too much coffee. He was overthinking everything.

The man watching the rugby sighed as the wrong team ran in a try. It seemed nothing was going right for him.

A healthcare assistant stuck her head around the corner.

'Doctor Cooper will see you now, Mr Fluke.'

Doctor Cooper and *Mr Fluke*, he thought. Very formal.

He knew the way to Leah's office but the HCA led him there anyway.

'If you can just wait outside, Mr Fluke, she's finishing a telephone call.'

Fluke took a seat, perplexed. Normally Leah would come and grab him, and they'd have a cup of tea together. Even when he was being treated, it was never that formal.

He'd been a copper long enough to be on his guard. Something was different this time.

It was over five minutes before Leah's office door opened. By then Fluke had taken Jo Skelton's card out again. He didn't need it any more; the numbers were imprinted on his mind. They continued to elude him. He'd rearranged them. Added them. Subtracted them. Ignored the decimal points. Nothing.

He was reading them when Leah walked out. She saw him and walked back into her office without saying a word. She sat behind her desk and stared at him. The second time someone had done that to him that day. Nathaniel Diamond had been a master of it. Fluke knew behind his eyes was pure danger, eyes that knew a thousand dirty secrets. But this was worse, far worse. Leah looked angry. Angry and disappointed.

Her desk was empty except for a letter. He could see it had a stamp on it, the sort admin used to show the date it had been received. He didn't want to try to read it upside down, she was angry enough. She picked it up and pretended to read it.

Fluke started to feel scared. Scared and uneasy.

She hadn't found out, surely? How could she? He knew that at some point he was going to have to come clean but he'd not once considered she might find out on her own. He wasn't sure there was any way she actually could. This must be about something else.

'Did you find a cosmetic sur—' he started to say.

She cut him off. 'Do you know what this is, Detective Inspector?' She was holding it at such an angle that he wasn't meant to see it.

Fluke looked back at her face and was astonished to see a tear running down her cheek. She made no attempt to wipe it off.

'No, Leah, I don't know what's on that piece of paper.'

'Are you sure? Your name's all over it.'

The unease was replaced by dread.

'My name, how? Can I see?' he said.

More tears ran down her face. She let them.

'It's from Carleton Hall. An official request for a copy of the letter I sent your Occupational Health department confirming you were fit to return to full duties.'

Fluke slumped in his seat. It had happened then. She'd discovered his secret. His complete betrayal of her trust.

His crime.

There was nothing he could say. Nothing he could do to excuse himself. He'd known that if it ever became known he'd be thrown off the force.

He looked up. Her tears seemed to have stopped. Their tracks had dried, and left marks on her lightly made-up face.

'Perhaps you can help me out here?' she said. She spoke coldly, no emotion in her voice despite the tears and her obvious distress. 'Perhaps the great Detective Inspector Fluke could explain how the letter they want a copy of, the one I'm supposed to have written and signed and sent on hospital stationery, is a letter I'd never fucking heard about until this afternoon.'

Chapter 28

Fluke had left hospital a shell of a man. After major surgery, he hadn't been in the best physical shape to begin with and the consultant in charge of his treatment had told him there would be times he'd hate them for what they would be doing to him. He tried to be polite to the doctors and nurses but at times it had been hard. The chemotherapy protocol for Burkitt's was the most aggressive they did, and the effects on his body were catastrophic. It caused him pain like he'd never experienced before, like his blood had turned acidic sometimes. He stopped eating and lost a third of his body weight. Simple things like washing and shaving became a chore. He left hospital a different man. Different physically, but also different mentally.

Buoyant to be out and cancer free, he just wanted to get on with his life. The police had organised Occupational Health to assess when he could return to work. He'd realistically thought it would be two months of eating well, getting some uninterrupted sleep, regaining some strength and completing the course of physiotherapy organised for him.

What he hadn't known was that some of his side effects were irreversible. He was left with thrombocytopenia. His body wasn't producing the right amount of platelets. It was manageable and it wasn't dangerous unless he was wounded. In most jobs it wouldn't have mattered but Fluke knew that the police was one of the jobs where it did. They couldn't put him out on the street knowing a small stab wound could be fatal. That his blood no longer clotted properly, that he could bleed out before help arrived. That surgery had to be carefully planned, the right blood had to be stocked up in advance, specialist surgeons had to come in. It was a condition that would end his police career. He might be allowed to ride a desk but as far as he was concerned that was the same thing.

Leah had explained it was a seldom-seen side effect. Determined to get back to work, he decided not to tell the Occupational Health nurse yet. See how long he could get away with it. So he hid it from everyone. And apart from the occasional easily explained nosebleed and bruising, there were no obvious external signs.

Gradually, his strength returned. It was nowhere near the level he'd previously enjoyed, but enough to give the appearance he was fit. His hair grew back and he put on weight. He might not be ready to go back to work but he *looked* ready.

But he still had a problem. Occupational Health had to state he was ready to return to work. He thought about ways round it but came up against a brick wall. Occupational Health would only say he was ready when his doctor said he was ready – they didn't have their own doctors, all they did was summarise medical reports and make a recommendation – so everything came back to Leah. He briefly considered asking her to lie but knew that she wouldn't and that he had no right to ask.

He became distant and withdrawn, and for a while took it out on those around him. And increasingly, his thoughts turned to how he could circumnavigate the NHS. Nothing legal sprang to mind.

So, inevitably perhaps, he started thinking about the illegal ways he might circumnavigate them. He justified it by saying the force was better with him in it. A half-fit Fluke was better than any other fully fit detective. That the people of Cumbria deserved him, *needed* him. He told himself he was being altruistic, not selfish.

He was lying to himself but he didn't care.

The semblance of a plan came together. But he needed help. He paid ten pounds to have his medical records copied, as anyone was entitled to do. He sent them to a struck-off doctor he'd found online advertising his services. Two hundred pounds got him a comprehensive report detailing everything he'd been through but omitting the thrombocytopenia. It was delivered on a memory stick. Fluke had a report full of medical terminology that gave him a clean bill of health. But he still needed a credible way of getting it to Occupational Health. One that would get him back to work with no more questions asked. One that would avoid the need for a genuine NHS report.

For days, Fluke struggled with how to do it. Every scenario he went through failed. The police weren't irresponsible employers, they weren't going to let him come back to work without a report from his consultant, and his consultant couldn't give him one. Whoever he pretended the letter was from wouldn't stop Occupational Health from demanding a full report from Leah. The request would go directly to her, and although he would get a copy, she'd send the report direct to them.

Fluke knew he would have to do Leah's report himself. For a month, he did nothing. He couldn't bring himself to pay the price. He decided that he wouldn't do it. He'd take his chances with the truth, hope for a restricted duties job where he could still have some input into investigations. Maybe after time they'd forget and let him outside every now and then.

But it was a routine blood check when the opportunity presented itself. Leah had been discussing results with him on the ward. The curtain around his bay had been closed, as if a plastic sheet gave any real privacy. In Fluke's experience, any time a curtain was closed, everyone else on the ward strained their ears to hear what was happening.

She'd been discussing how his platelet count had been higher than the previous few visits and that she was pleased with his progress, when the crash alarm had sounded. Every member of staff ran out of the ward. Fluke was left alone.

With his file.

He looked at it for a while. He became nervous about what he knew he was about to do. His mouth went dry and the vein in his neck pulsed. He opened the file and went straight to the back where he knew the patient details stickers were kept, the stickers that went on every vial of blood, on every wristband he wore.

On every letter.

They had his name, address, and more importantly, a barcode.

As if on autopilot, he removed a whole page and put it in his jacket.

He spent the next couple of days preparing his letter. He went to a local printer and got some good quality copies of a blanked-out page of one of his own medical letters. He then tried various options with the text on the memory stick. Different fonts and letter sizes to try to find the ones the Cumberland Infirmary used. He amended some of the language to fit in more with Leah's style. He spent several hours trying to forge a natural signature. Like anyone who signed their name several times a day, Leah's was little more than a scrawl. Eventually though, he was confident he had a passable enough forgery. He had enough colour copies of the stolen letterhead to get the text in the right place by trial and error. He affixed one of the stickers and forged Leah's signature. The process of stealing the stickers to having a fully forged document had taken just three days.

He'd stared at the final version for nearly an hour in silence. What he was about to do was wrong. Very wrong. A betrayal of someone who had only ever had his best interests at heart. It was a betrayal of Cumbria police who had stood by him during his ill health. And it was a crime. Fraud, making a false instrument, obtaining a pecuniary advantage by deception, misconduct in a public office; take your pick, just a few of the charges he could face if he was caught.

At best, he'd be thrown out in disgrace, at worst he'd do jail time. But most of all, it was a betrayal of himself, of his own values. He considered himself a moral man. A man who stood up to bullies, who gave the vulnerable a voice and spoke for the dead. If he sent the letter, he could no longer stand on the high ground looking down. He was just another dirty cop.

The last stage of his plan involved sending the letter from the hospital so it would have NHS franking marks on it. He ran several scenarios but settled on just looking for an opportunity.

It came the next time he was getting his blood checked.

He had to wait at the receptionist's station on the way out while they sorted out his next appointment. As a frequent visitor to the ward, the staff knew him well and always had a chat. As she read out the next available appointments, Fluke pretended to lean over to see the computer screen. As he did, he slipped the letter into the middle of the outgoing mail.

It was addressed to the Occupational Health department and on the way out he rang them to say he was fit enough to come back and that he'd asked his consultant to send them a letter detailing his current condition, which he hoped would support his application to return to work.

A month later, he was back at his desk in Carleton Hall. He'd spent two weeks doing a phased return at the insistence of Occupational Health, and one week receiving a handover from the temporary DI they'd installed. Nine months after being diagnosed with Burkitt's lymphoma, he was back on the Force Major Investigation Team.

For how long was now out of his hands.

Chapter 29

'You bastard!' Leah shouted. 'You utter bastard. How could you?'

Fluke wasn't surprised by her reaction. He decided to say nothing. There was nothing he could say. No point denying it; no point explaining it. He was categorically in the wrong and had no choice but to ride the lightning.

'Well?' she asked.

Still he remained silent. He was at her mercy now. Later, he'd be curious why the original letter had been requested by HQ but right now it was irrelevant.

He had consequences to face.

He had the betrayal of a friend to face.

Leah had stopped crying. Her eyes, normally so friendly, so warm, were cold, devoid of anything but hurt and disappointment.

'Well?' she said again.

Fluke still didn't know how to respond. Anything he could say would appear trite and self-serving. *Was* trite and self-serving.

Honesty was his only option.

'I'm sorry,' he said.

She held his gaze until shame got the better of him. He broke eye contact.

'Sorry? You're sorry? Oh, well, that's all right then. The great Avison Fluke is sorry. Do you know what you've done? Forget the fact that you've risked your health, forget the fact that you've probably broken the law, you've put my job at risk. Why, Avison?'

'I had to, Leah.'

'No, you didn't – you *wanted* to.'

'I felt that in the circumsta—'

'You selfish prick, don't you dare try to justify this,' she snapped. 'You did this for you, and you alone. If you mutter one feeble fucking excuse about the greater good or some other crap, we're done here. Done, Avison. I'll hand over your case to a colleague and we'll never see or speak to each other again.'

The excuse died on his lips.

'You're right, of course,' he said. 'I wanted to go back to work. The job was all I had. And I lied and I cheated to do it.'

She glared at him.

'I've been wanting to tell you for a while,' he added.

'And what exactly am I supposed to do now?'

Fluke shrugged.

'I know what I should do, what I'm *required* to do. I'm supposed to go straight to the trust board and tell them everything. Anything else and I'm complicit.'

'Of course. You should do what you think is right,' he said, wanting to punch himself in the face the moment it left his mouth.

'Oh, piss off, you patronising arsehole. Don't speak to me like that. I thought we were friends. This is me you're speaking to. What do you think I should do? What do you *want* me to do? I've already lied once for you this morning. I'm not in the mood to do it twice, not if you don't care enough to act like a grown-up. I'm not the headmistress, and you're not a schoolboy, Avison. What do you want me to do?'

She'd lied for him once already? What did she mean by that? Things were moving so quickly he was struggling to keep up.

Fluke rubbed his eyes. He was tired, bone tired. He'd been leeching energy like a badly earthed battery, he just hadn't realised.

But there was also a sense of relief. The lying had been

debilitating. Lying wasn't what he did. He wasn't used to it. To keeping secrets he shouldn't have.

'I don't know, Leah. I'm not trying to be coy, I'm really not. I don't want to lose my job, of course I don't. But the last thing I want is to get you into trouble. I need you to believe that.'

Her expression softened.

'It may be out of my hands anyway,' she said.

Fluke looked up.

'No, I haven't said anything to anyone. Not yet anyway. But how do you think I got this letter, Avison? What in your addled mind do you think is going on here?'

Fluke said nothing. It was a letter. Letters got posted.

'Oh, you stupid man. It was hand-delivered.'

'Hand delivered?' Fluke said. 'That doesn't make sense. Why would HR hand deliver it?'

'A police officer brought it. Someone called Fenton, Alec or Alex Fenton. He showed me a letter they received. Wanted to know if I remembered writing it.'

Fluke gasped. He went numb.

Alex fucking Fenton.

This was bad. Very bad. As bad as it could get. He tried to speak but couldn't. His mouth had turned to ash.

Leah's expression changed. Anger turned to concern.

'Avison, who is Fenton? What does he do? How did he know about this letter?'

Fluke put his head in his hands and didn't answer immediately. He was in serious trouble. *Prison* trouble.

'Alex Fenton is the superintendent in PSD,' he said eventually.

'I'm not a policeman, Avison,' she said. 'What's PSD?'

'Professional Standards Department,' he said, already resigned to his inevitable fate. It was as certain as death.

She looked confused.

'*Quis custodiet ipsos custodes?*' Fluke said.

'I only know medical Latin.'

'They're the cop's cops, Leah. Alex Fenton is from internal affairs.'

'I don't understand. How did—'

'I'm screwed, Leah. There's no need for you to get into trouble now. No need to cover for me. I would never ask you to anyway. I don't even think I could bear you to risk anything for me at the minute. I don't feel worth it today.'

'That's not what I was going to say, and you can cut the martyr bullshit. I'll decide what I'll do about this, not you. And certainly not Alec Fenton.'

'Alex.'

'Piss off. No, what I was going to say was, how did he know about this letter?'

'You've seen *Line of Duty*. They have access to all our personnel files. PSD can poke their nose where they like. And someone of Fenton's rank can speak to who he wants *when* he wants. He can challenge anyone, investigate anyone.'

'I'm not on about how he physically got hold of it. I mean, how did he know to ask for the original? If it wasn't for the fact that I know I didn't write it, it would have fooled me. It looks genuine. Nice job, by the way; I'd be impressed if I didn't think you were an absolute shit for doing this.'

Fluke didn't know why Fenton had known to request the original. Something to brood on later. His time was going to become limited soon and he didn't want to waste it thinking about his future. He needed to focus on the case. Leah, it seemed, did want to continue thinking about it.

'So, tell me. Why did he ask for it? You must have done something to raise suspicions?'

Fluke thought about it. PSD wasn't the pariah that Internal Affairs was in the States. For most officers, it was something they moved to in routine inter-departmental shuffles. It wasn't anything to be feared. Do it well and it was a good career move. Nobody was castigated for being in PSD.

Apart from Alex Fenton.

Because Fenton enjoyed it. Enjoyed the infamy of being the one member of PSD that wanted to stay. Enjoyed being feared. Enjoyed being able to hold grudges, and act on those grudges. He'd tried to be a CID detective but had no aptitude for it, so he hated those who did. He was an arsehole, an isolated careerist, but he did play by the rules. So if he'd asked for a copy of the letter then he had something concrete on Fluke. He wouldn't be fishing. This was the start of a formal investigation. It might even be the *end* of a formal investigation, one that had begun months ago.

There was no way to tell.

He thought about what had given him away. There was only one thing.

'I've been having nosebleeds,' he said. 'Someone outside the team must have noticed and told my boss. He's been after me for a while. All he'd have had to do was fake concern, go to PSD with his suspicions and they'd do the rest.'

Fluke decided it would have to wait.

He needed to focus on what he'd come for. Forget Fenton, forget the shit storm brewing in PSD.

'Sorry to do this, Leah, and I promise we can talk about the letter later, but did you find me a cosmetic surgeon to talk to?'

Leah held his gaze for a moment,

'I went one better actually,' she said. 'And I'm sorry to kick you when you're down but it's not good news. From what you described, and from the photos you provided, I was able to email my friend in London. He confirmed what I suspected: there's little chance of identifying the victim through her surgery.'

Fluke hadn't really been hoping to get anything but he was disappointed anyway. 'Did you ask if all her procedures could have been done at the same time?'

'Not a chance, I'm told. I didn't think it was likely but you asked me to check. He tells me that because they were all in the same area it wouldn't be possible. The face swells too much to attempt more than one at a time. Sorry.'

Fluke said nothing. That was that then. He knew he should get back to HQ and make sure the hunt for Kenneth Diamond was progressing properly, but he didn't want to leave things like they were. Leah also said nothing. She was no longer looking at him. She was looking at the card with the numbers on. He'd put it on the table when they'd been talking.

He picked it up and put it into his breast pocket. 'Sorry.'

'What was that?' she said, the edge to her voice returning.

'What, this?' he said, pointing at his pocket. 'Nothing, just something to do with the case. Something we're trying to work out. It's become a sort of unit puzzle. That's why we all carry them.'

'No, I mean where did you get them? Tell me you didn't steal them from me, Avison. It's one thing forging that ridiculous letter but I have a duty, an absolute duty, to protect patient confidentiality. Please don't tell me you've also stolen a patient file?'

Fluke's fatigue disappeared instantly.

He took the card back out of his pocket and handed it to her. 'Leah. Listen to me very carefully. What do these numbers mean?'

She folded her arms and scowled.

'I'm not telling you anything, Avison,' she said. 'Not until you tell me where you got them.'

Fluke made a decision. Sometimes case integrity had to go out of the window. 'We recovered them from the deposition site. They were on a notebook left with the victim. I didn't steal them from you, of course I didn't. I know this sounds strange coming from someone who spent three days practising your signature but you have to trust me. Now tell me, what do those numbers mean?'

'Well, they're blood count results, obviously,' she said. 'A full

232

blood count, the main three. Anyone can see that. *You* should be able to see that. You've had enough of them, for goodness sake.'

Fluke couldn't believe he'd failed to see it. These were numbers he should have instantly recognised. Leah was right. He'd been twisting the answer in his hands for nearly a week, looking without seeing.

He didn't even need Leah to explain them.

The 2.3 was the white blood cell count, 8.7 was the haemoglobin and 92 was the platelet count. The numbers were low. Not as low as Fluke's had been during his treatment, but lower than a healthy person. These numbers were from someone who was ill.

Fluke handed the card over and leaned forward. 'Is there any way we can find out who these belong to?'

Chapter 30

Fluke arrived at West Cumberland Hospital less than an hour later. Leah was with him. He'd tried arguing it was police business, that a murder investigation was no place for a doctor, but she'd insisted.

He'd asked Leah to run a data check on the NHS's medical records but blood test results didn't work like that apparently.

'Look,' she'd said, 'although everything is computerised, the analyser machines that run the full blood counts in Cumbria's haematology departments are on standalone systems. There isn't a database that *can* be searched. The blood would have been taken by a phlebotomist, entered into the analyser and a report printed out. That report would then be given to the department who'd asked for it and they'd record the results on the patient's file. Searching for blood test results can only be done manually, and unless there's some way of narrowing it down, it'll take ages. Days, even weeks – and we still have to get round patient confidentiality.'

The last part was potentially the biggest problem. Fluke couldn't see any way he could reasonably ask a magistrate for permission to go through an entire department's patient records, even for a murder investigation.

'It isn't just haematology who ask for full blood counts, Avison, you know that, don't you?' she said. 'West Cumberland will do hundreds of FBCs every single day.'

Fluke didn't respond. She was right but he had a few things in his favour. He knew the results weren't Samantha's. Until she'd been shot in the back of the head, she'd been physically healthy. The notebook from which they'd recovered the numbers had been dumped with her body and that meant that they were probably the killer's.

He ran through what he thought was the likely sequence of events. The killer arrived at Samantha's flat, circumnavigated all her security systems and waited for her. Before she'd returned, he either received or made – and Fluke's money was on received – a phone call about his blood test results. He wrote them down on the nearest thing to hand, a notepad Samantha had lying around. He then tore off the top page and left the notepad with the body rather than leave it in the flat, fearing exactly what had happened – that the numbers would be retrieved by some smartarse technician in a lab.

The second thing in Fluke's favour, and why he went straight to West Cumberland Hospital, was that he now thought it unlikely that the deposition site had been chosen by chance. Fluke was sure the killer had seen the building site while he was at the hospital for personal reasons. He fully expected to be able to see the deposition site from the ward the blood test came from.

The third thing, and the reason he'd relented and agreed to Leah coming with him, was that she knew every haematologist in the county, and the haematology department ran phlebotomy in all hospitals. If they didn't order the test themselves, the request certainly went through them.

'It'll be easier if I go in and have a word with Nick Weighman, West Cumbria's consultant, first,' Leah said. 'There's no way he'll ever give you open access to his files but he might give me a nod in the right direction.'

On the journey to West Cumbria, Fluke had explained the case in as much detail as he dared. She impressed him by only asking the questions she needed answers to and respected there were things he couldn't tell her.

Before they arrived, he told Leah something that had been nagging at him for the previous quarter of an hour. Something she might be able to help with.

'I don't think he's a Cumbrian, Leah. Samantha was in hiding. She'd spent a lot of time, effort and money in making herself invisible.'

Leah said nothing, but he thought she could see where he was going.

'And then she just happens to move to within forty miles of a professional killer?' he continued. 'I don't think so. I think he tracked her here.'

'You're wondering how he was able to get a blood test done in a Cumbrian hospital if he's not from here?' she said.

He nodded.

'It's not a problem, Avison. There are many people in the UK who have to move around with their job. Or their lifestyle. Or even a holiday. Some of them need ongoing treatment. We don't turn them away.'

'What about private patients? Do we have them here?'

'Yes, we have them here. Lots of doctors also have private contracts. Pays more and it's a much nicer way to work. More time with the patient, no waiting times. You'll have seen the private patient rooms at our hospital.'

Fluke nodded. He had. 'Would a private patient be able to walk in off the street and demand a blood test?'

She considered it for a minute. 'No. They'd need a doctor somewhere leading on their care. But it would be simple enough for that doctor to ring and ask for continuation treatment for a specified timescale. Cumbria gets nearly twenty million tourists a year so it's not unusual. Sometimes getting away on holiday is worth the inconvenience of swapping doctors for a bit.'

'Can you ask Doctor Weighman if he's had any new patients with blood test results like that in the last few weeks?' Fluke said.

'That should narrow it down. If he won't give you a name, at least try to get him to confirm he actually has someone who fits the description. I can maybe get a warrant on that basis.'

Still discussing the best way to approach Doctor Weighman, they entered the main foyer and headed towards the Henderson Suite, where haematology was situated.

While he waited, Fluke called Towler and asked him to get Jo Skelton on to drafting two warrants: one for West Cumberland Hospital's CCTV coverage, and another to access an as yet unnamed person's medical records.

'Can you see the deposition site from the hospital, boss?'

Fluke had been so wrapped up in the task in hand he hadn't thought to check.

'Going for a look now,' he said.

He left the waiting area and walked along the corridor, looking for a window. The walkway that led to phlebotomy had windows but they overlooked the roof of a lower part of the hospital. Fluke could see air-conditioning units and a dead seagull, but not the building site.

He went back to the waiting area and spoke to a nurse, flashed his badge and was briefly allowed onto the ward.

He walked towards the window. Half the beds were occupied and most patients were sleeping. Fluke had spent a lot of time on a similar ward in Newcastle so knew the kind of fatigue they were feeling. They'd be wearing it like a heavy coat.

The windows were south-facing and they afforded a perfect view of the new development. Fluke could see the yellow police tape and a lone uniformed officer guarding the crime scene. Fluke took out his smartphone and snapped some photos.

Instead of returning to the waiting area, he carried on along the south side of the hospital to see if any other wards had similar views of the crime scene. Only the dental department received patients and the building site couldn't be seen from their ward.

The rest of the floor seemed to be administrative and storage. He considered taking the stairs to the floor above but decided he'd wait for Leah. He took the same seat in the waiting room. An elderly couple were seated near him and they smiled. He smiled back but said nothing.

He never knew what to say to people on a cancer ward.

Fluke took out his phone and composed a brief email to Towler. He attached the photos he'd just taken and pressed send.

An office door, offset from the ward, opened, and Leah beckoned him over.

Fluke was introduced to Nick Weighman who wasn't at all what he'd been expecting. Closer to seventy than sixty, he had a mass of thick white hair. He was a tall, thin man. On his desk and on the walls were mountaineering photos. He was in them all. In most of them, he didn't look much younger than he did now. Some were of him in cold-weather gear on mountain ranges Fluke knew weren't in the UK. A serious mountaineer then. No prizes for guessing why he lived here. Some of the most challenging rock climbing in the UK was to be found in the Cumbrian mountains.

Leah summarised what they'd discussed and, at the end, Doctor Weighman gave Fluke the bad news.

'Can't do it, I'm afraid. Patient confidentiality is the absolute bedrock of the profession. There's just no way round it. And no way will you get permission to go through my files either, no court will allow it. If you had a name, maybe. But an entire ward's files? Forget about it.'

It was what he'd expected. At best it had been a long shot. He hoped that Doctor Weighman had been able to give Leah a nod in the right direction though. Something off the record that couldn't come back and bite either of them. He glanced at her to see if he could get a read on it. She was watching him. Waiting for him to look at her, he thought. And she didn't look deflated either.

In fact, she looked as though she had something she wanted to share.

'Do you want a coffee, Inspector?' Doctor Weighman said.

Fluke could have used one but he wanted to speak to Leah alone. He was about to decline when he noticed she was still staring at him. She nodded.

'You do, don't you, Avison?' she said.

He agreed that he did.

'I have some things to sort out here. I suggest you go to the fresh coffee cart in the foyer and get yourself a cup, it's rather good. Get me a doughnut while you're there, will you?' Doctor Weighman said with a slight smile. 'Oh, and if Penny is on, you may want to ask her about the tall American gentleman she seems to have quite the crush on.'

Fluke stood there stupidly. 'Excuse me?' he said.

'Come on, Avison. Let's go and get a cup of coffee,' Leah said, guiding him out of the office and back through the ward before he could ask anything more.

'What the hell just happened?' he asked as they headed towards the foyer.

'Not here,' she said.

'Fine,' he said. He'd let whatever was happening play out.

There was a small queue at the cart, one of the fake wooden ones that nevertheless seemed to produce excellent coffee. Fluke and Leah stood in silence while they waited. The vendor was a middle-aged woman, Women's Institute or WRVS by the looks of things. One of those women who volunteer. Cumbria seemed to produce armies of them. If even half of them withdrew their services, the county's infrastructure would collapse. She was chatting to every customer as if they were friends she hadn't seen for months. When it was their turn, Fluke ordered three coffees and a doughnut.

'You wouldn't be Penny, by any chance, would you?' Fluke asked.

'Yes, I am, my dear.'

Fluke asked if she had served an American recently. Said that Doctor Weighman had suggested she might have. Luckily, Penny seemed to have been blessed with the ability to read between the lines. She readied their coffees, put up a 'Back in five minutes' sign, and found an empty table for the three of them.

Fluke briefly told her what he could; that he was looking for a man and he may be American. He added the little he'd been able to get from Darren Ackley.

Penny immediately knew who he meant. She described him as in his forties and around six feet tall.

'Looks like he spends a lot of time outdoors. Spent time abroad as well judging by his complexion. Weather-beaten and brown.'

'And he's definitely American?' Fluke said.

'He didn't have a strong accent but I've been to the States a few times as my daughter lives in New York. We travel when Geoffrey and I go over. I couldn't place him so asked him where he was from once. He was a bit vague actually. Just said, "The east coast," if I remember correctly.'

Fluke asked her to tell him everything she could. There wasn't much. It wasn't that Penny couldn't remember, it was more that there wasn't anything that stood out. Handsome, polite, always put his change in the charity jar, always had a black coffee. Dark hair, cut short. Unremarkable clothes. No earrings or visible tattoos.

It was clear that Penny liked him.

'There was a melancholic quality to him, Inspector. He always had a smile for me but it was like the smile on a clown. It seemed to hide sadness. I assumed he was very ill.'

'Why was that?' he asked.

'The Henderson Suite isn't a place where babies are born,

Inspector,' she said. 'I always make sure I give everyone a smile when they come from there; I'm aware they're all going through terrible experiences.'

'Did he have a name, Penny?' Fluke said.

She thought for a while. 'Do you know something, I don't think he ever offered it.'

Fluke and Leah got up and they all shook hands. He asked her if it would be OK for a police artist to come and work with her. She agreed.

Fluke had walked halfway out of the dining area when he turned and ran back to Penny. She'd just reached her cart.

'Sorry, Penny, one last question. How often is that charity jar emptied?'

'Ah, excellent,' Doctor Weighman said when they handed him a cup of coffee and a doughnut. 'Never get time to eat properly these days.' He looked down at what he had in his hand and seemed to recognise what he'd said. 'Oh, well, one doughnut's hardly going to kill me.'

The three of them sat in silence. The coffees weren't cool enough to drink. Fluke took the lid off his and blew gently on it. The sooner he finished the sooner he could get away. He could feel himself getting closer to their killer and every moment was precious. He could talk to Leah on the journey back.

Doctor Weighman stood up suddenly. 'Well, I can't wait for this to cool, I'll have to take it with me. I have patients to see, managers to harass, nurses to frighten. I'll be back in about twenty minutes, Inspector.'

Fluke stood.

'No, please stay here. Finish your drink. It's the least I can do. I feel as though I've not been as helpful as perhaps I could.'

As he put on his jacket and opened his door to leave, he turned back round.

'Twenty minutes, Inspector,' he said. 'Leah, there's a patient I wouldn't mind a consultation on if you have the time?'

'I'd be delighted,' she replied.

Before Fluke had a chance to say anything they'd both left Weighman's office. He stared at the door.

What the hell was all that about?

He sipped his coffee. Thought about what it all meant. He'd not been told anything so it wasn't that he had to sit and think. So, it was something he was meant to *see*. Something in Weighman's office. He stood up. There was a desktop computer on his desk. He wondered if it had been left unlocked for him. Perhaps that was it? Perhaps he wanted to be out of his office when Fluke searched it. The NHS logo filled the screen. He touched the keyboard and was asked for a password. Not the computer then.

But that wasn't the only thing on the desk. There was also a file.

A *patient's* file.

What if . . .

Fluke opened it.

Chapter 31

'Dalton Cross!' Fluke shouted. He listened to Jo Skelton on the other end of his phone to make sure she'd got everything. 'Yes, that's his name. Don't ask me how I got it. I want a full search. Every database we have. Every database we *don't* have. Get Longy on it. I want an update in fifteen minutes. I'm coming back in now but I need to go via Carlisle first. And I want a SOCO team standing by. I may have his fingerprints.'

He finalised his immediate plans and ended the call.

He'd spent the full twenty minutes with the file, only stopping when Doctor Weighman knocked on the door and waited a strategic ten seconds to ensure he didn't see anything untoward. By that time, Fluke had read it cover to cover. Snapped as many pictures as he could.

The man's name, or the name he was using anyway, was Dalton Cross. He had dual citizenship – American father, English mother. He'd had to go through a bureaucratic process to get treatment in the UK, but as he was technically a Brit it was never in doubt. There were reports and documents from hospitals in different parts of the UK. Manchester, London, Norwich, Glasgow, Plymouth as well as West Cumbria. No obvious pattern with the locations or the dates. He'd been zigzagging across the country.

Or hunting.

Ironically, Fluke also knew what he looked like, but only from the inside. MRI scans, X-rays and sonograms, they were all in his file.

Dalton Cross had leukaemia. He had just finished his treatment. The last entry on the patient notes were handwritten by Doctor Weighman. They included the blood test results from a sample taken that Monday.

Fluke had the same numbers on his card.

A nurse had called Cross with his results and the time fitted the timeline Fluke had in his head. It was as he'd thought: she'd called while Cross was waiting in Samantha's flat.

He'd given an Allerdale address when he'd arrived in Cumbria two months earlier, and had been allocated to West Cumberland Hospital. A quick check revealed the address's real occupants had never heard of him.

Despite all the internal photos, Fluke still only had Penny's and Ackley's vague descriptions of what he actually looked like. Patient files didn't have pictures. Jo Skelton would arrange for some photofitting with Penny but he wasn't holding his breath for anything useable. It seemed no one could remember what he looked like. A trained grey man.

There were other phone numbers in the file but he expected Jiao-long to tell him they were all burners and were no longer in service. He would probably get a new one every time he moved. He assumed the most recent was the one Doctor Weighman's staff called him on, the phone that had been smashed to pieces and buried with Samantha.

Fluke had asked Penny if he could take the charity jar if he promised to put twenty quid in when he returned it. It was half full but Fluke was hopeful that at least one coin would produce a useable print. With a print, he could check more databases. Might even get a photograph.

Without the fingerprints, he wouldn't be able to get a warrant for the file. Although he knew beyond all doubt he had his man, he couldn't reveal how he'd linked the blood test numbers to a particular file without exposing Doctor Weighman.

He'd worry about that later though. His number-one priority was catching Cross before more people died. Having a legally sound case was a distant second. He was pulled from his thoughts when his phone rang. Jo Skelton.

'What you got, Jo?'

'Nothing yet, boss. Longy's still doing his stuff. But we do have news. We've found Kenneth Diamond.'

Fluke's spirits soared. When cases broke, they broke fast. Kenneth Diamond wasn't the killer but he was involved. Nathaniel had as good as told him. He'd do the interview himself.

'Right, Jo, listen to me carefully. Nobody interviews him until I get there. Nobody. And he doesn't get to speak to his brief until I say so. We need to do this right.'

'Won't be a problem, boss.'

A sixth sense stopped him asking why. 'He's dead, isn't he?'

Chapter 32

Fluke arrived at Kenneth Diamond's Stanwix address within half an hour of getting the call. He parked at the side of the road. He'd already dropped off Leah and promised to call in when he could. She hadn't said anything about the forged letter and he hadn't been able to read her expression.

Police and SOCO vehicles were there in abundance. In the dimming light and glare of emergency lights, Fluke could see his team milling round waiting for him.

The crime scene was the house next door to Diamond's. The team that had gathered his DNA had been two brick walls from his corpse.

Fluke took his bearings. Stanwix was a prosperous part of Carlisle and the houses on Diamond's street were all detached and large. Mock Tudor, or similar.

Towler was waiting at the drive entrance, which had been set up as the external cordon.

'How did he die, Matt?' he asked as he signed in.

'Screaming,' Towler said.

Fluke followed him into the house. The entrance vestibule had an umbrella stand and a coat rack. He could see a kitchen at the end of a long hallway. A middle-aged man was sitting at a breakfast bar, talking to a uniformed officer. The owner of the house, he presumed.

'The owner?'

'Yes.'

'Get him interviewed outside, please.'

'On it, boss,' Towler said. 'And it's down there.' He pointed towards a door under the main stairs. It opened onto more stairs descending to a cellar.

Fluke walked down them carefully. Sean Rogers, the crime scene manager, followed him down. They stood at the bottom of the stairs and looked into the basement.

The owner was using it as a wine cellar, a gym and a workshop. The basement was lit by a bank of fluorescent tubes. Fluke could hear the buzz of the starter motor as one of the lights flickered. The basement had bare brick walls but seemed dry. A rowing machine was in the middle of the floor. A towel hung from one of the handles. Tools were on a large shadow board above a workbench with a vice and a bench drill. There was a half-full wine rack on the wall on Fluke's right.

Fluke didn't know much about storing wine but he was fairly sure that clean air would be a prerequisite for any cellar. And if that were the case, then the owner's collection was ruined.

Kenneth Diamond had been dead for some time.

The stench of his decomposing body was oppressive and cloying. Fluke's mouth flooded with saliva, the first warning of nausea. He swallowed and continued into the room.

Towler hadn't been kidding: Diamond had not died well. He had a bullet hole in the centre of his forehead but Fluke didn't need a pathologist to tell him he'd also been brutally tortured.

'Shit,' Fluke said to himself, as he circled the body, not getting too close. The scene hadn't been processed yet and the corpse was now evidence.

Diamond was tied to a high-backed wooden chair, probably taken from the kitchen. He was naked apart from a tea towel covering his groin. It was soaked in dark blood. A pool had congealed on the floor underneath the chair. Blood and urine. Some faeces.

Diamond had swelled as bacteria in his body formed gases that had nowhere to escape. His skin appeared slimy. Blisters had formed on his torso and some had burst. His eyes were sunken, dry and milky grey.

Fluke looked at his legs. The blood, following the laws of gravity, had settled there and turned them purple. Kenneth Diamond hadn't been moved. This was where he died. In that room, tied to that chair, in unimaginable agony.

The smell was appalling. Thick, sweet and cloying, it seemed to get into the very mucus of his nose. Fluke knew he'd be smelling it for a long time.

A lone fly buzzed and settled on something organic leaking from his ear.

Fluke knew dead bodies broke down quickly but he estimated Diamond had been in the basement for at least a week, possibly longer.

When the pathologist got there, he hoped it was Henry and that he had Lucy with him. The corpse had been there long enough for her to find insect activity. He was watching one of them now.

Diamond's face was swollen. Fluke couldn't tell if that was due to decomposition or the beating he'd had. Threads of clotted blood still hung from his gaping mouth. His lips had shrunk back and Fluke saw that some of his teeth were missing. He looked down and saw white, bloody fragments scattered around the base of the chair.

Fluke walked round the back of the body and saw he'd been secured using wire coat hangers. The swelling of his wrists had enveloped the wire against his skin but he could see it joining his hands together. He thought he saw something and bent down for a closer look. Diamond no longer had any fingernails. He looked at the floor again but couldn't see them scattered among the teeth.

'Fingernails?' he said to Rogers, who until that point hadn't said a word.

'Over there,' he replied, pointing towards the workbench.

Fluke looked up, squinted and walked over. On top of the bench was a pair of pliers. Even Chambers could have worked out what they'd been used for. Lined up in two rows of five, were Diamond's fingernails. Fluke looked back to check something and confirmed that his chair was facing the bench. Someone had been making a show of it, letting him see how many he had left to go.

The bench had two other tools on it: a hammer and long-bladed knife. Both were bloodied. There was also a plastic bottle containing a clear liquid.

It was easy to see what the hammer had been used for. Diamond no longer had knees. With tremendous force and accuracy, his kneecaps had been reduced to a pink, jelly-like mush. Fluke forced himself to look closer. He could make out the indent of the ball-peen end. He looked down at his feet. They'd been reduced to the same bloody pulp as his knees.

Fluke put on a pair of gloves and carefully lifted the tea towel covering Diamond's groin.

It wasn't there for Diamond's modesty. It had been put there to stem bleeding. His testicles had been smashed beyond all recognition.

'For fuck's sake,' he said out loud.

He was looking at something that would haunt him for years but he forced himself to continue. Fluke had assumed the blood that had pooled on the floor was from Diamond's groin injury but he noticed that there was also a deep smear of blood going from his mouth and down his bare chest. His mouth or throat had suffered major trauma.

He doubted having his teeth ripped out would have caused him to lose that much blood. He took out his penlight and shone it into Diamond's mouth. He bent forward and peered inside. It was filled with blood. Fluke angled his torch down and saw what had caused such massive bleeding. He jerked back in revulsion.

His tongue had been cut out.

Why though? Cutting out his tongue wouldn't have stopped Diamond screaming. Screams don't work that way. They come from a much deeper part of the body.

Uneasily Fluke looked back across to the workbench and the bottle of clear liquid. Not willing to believe it was possible, he forced himself to pick his torch back up and look into Kenneth Diamond's mouth again. This time he looked past the gaping wound where his tongue used to be. He angled his penlight further down the throat until he saw what the liquid had been used for.

Diamond's throat, including his larynx, had been completely destroyed by chemical burns. Fluke leaned forward and lightly sniffed, recoiling instantly from the sharp smell. It wouldn't take Sherlock Holmes to work out what had happened.

Kenneth Diamond had been forced to drink acid.

Diamond hadn't died screaming in agony, Fluke thought; Diamond hadn't screamed at all.

Fluke had no doubt this was the work of the man who had killed Farrar, but he wanted confirmation before he acted on it. He shouted for Towler. He appeared within seconds and Fluke asked for his opinion.

Towler circled Diamond slowly. He didn't have the same reaction as Fluke, but he hadn't expected him to have. Fluke had witnessed some bad things in the army but knew Towler had witnessed worse. He also knew he'd be cracking jokes about it later while the rest of them were drinking to forget.

'Poor fucker,' he said finally.

'Who found him?' Fluke said.

'Mr Dawson. Came back today from a two-weeks sailing holiday. Him and his wife. Came down to get some wine and walked straight into this. Least he'll have something interesting to tell the neighbours, I suppose. Probably for the first time.'

Fluke guessed Diamond had been snatched from his own house and dragged next door for privacy.

He stared at the corpse.

'Punishment beating?' he said.

'For the rape?' Towler said. 'If so, it went wrong.'

'Possibly. Or maybe for something else.'

'Could have been a plain and simple information extraction, I suppose,' Towler said. 'But if it was, I doubt Diamond had what he wanted. Don't care who you are, no one stands that much pain.'

Fluke had seen the results of sectarian beatings in Belfast when he'd been in the Marines. They were invariably rushed, had little finesse and had no discernible pattern. Both sides tended to focus on kneecappings. Shotguns, electric drills, blow torches, they'd all been used for what became known as their signature punishment the world over. Hundreds of Catholics and hundreds of Protestants would never walk again because of the Troubles.

Diamond's ordeal had been different. It was methodical. No area had been wasted in the infliction of pain. The killer had taken his time.

This wasn't a simple punishment beating.

This was a message.

'You think this is Dalton Cross's handiwork?' Fluke said.

'Hard to tell. The head's swollen but the bullet hole looks the same calibre. Yeah, it's Dalton Cross; I'd bet me bollocks on it.'

He looked down at Diamond's groin.

'Looks like he's already bet his.'

Scratch that, Fluke thought. Towler was already cracking jokes about it.

Fluke let Towler supervise the forensic process while he went outside to think. He had the beginnings of a headache. One of those that starts behind one eye but eventually feels as though it's

251

drilling its way out the back of the head. He pinched the bridge of his nose. It made no difference.

Someone arrived with a dozen cups of takeout coffee. Fluke took one. He didn't want it, and it wasn't going to make his headache go away, but it gave him an excuse not to talk to anyone for a while. He wasn't ready to discuss what he'd just seen.

He was spared forced conversation by the arrival of Henry Sowerby. The big pathologist got out of his old Jaguar. Lucy got out of the passenger side. Despite the awful scene he'd just left, Fluke smiled. Although it had been less than a week since they'd all stood on that cold building site he was glad to see them again.

Sowerby's voice boomed, causing a uniformed officer to spill his coffee. "I'm hearing things," I said to Lucy. "The great Avison Fluke back on the force and Cumbria has two murders in less than a week. Surely not," I said.'

He left Lucy by the car and walked over. They shook hands.

'What do we have?' Sowerby said.

While Fluke briefed them on what he'd seen, Sean Rogers walked over, ready for the crime scene briefing. They agreed his team would go in and record everything before anyone else went down. After Rogers had left, Fluke sighed and rubbed his temples.

'Are you OK, Inspector?' Lucy said.

She was standing slightly apart from the group being briefed. She wasn't formally part of the investigation and hadn't been invited in yet. Fluke beckoned her over. They wouldn't be where they were without her.

'Bit of a headache, Lucy, that's all. I'll be fine.'

She reached into her handbag, pulled out a box of paracetamol and threw them. He caught them and opened the box.

Fluke pulled out one of the blister packs.

He stared at it.

It was a standard paracetamol box. Two blister packs. Two rows of four in each. Sixteen pills in total. The maximum allowed in any one box in the UK. Part of the government's suicide prevention strategy.

There were only five tablets left in the one he was holding.

Neurons fired. A memory stirred. The man watching the rugby. For some reason it was important.

'What's up, Inspector?' Lucy asked.

He stared at the blister pack but said nothing.

Sometimes Fluke could have answers maddeningly out of reach for weeks. The harder he looked the deeper they seemed to hide. Invariably he'd need a prompt.

Like a blister pack with five tablets remaining.

The answer to what had bothered him about the inventory from Samantha's flat rushed out to greet him like an old friend.

He knew what Samantha's secret was.

He knew what Nathaniel Diamond hadn't been able to tell him.

Chapter 33

'Having all your ducks in a row' sprang to mind. It was what Fluke could do that HOLMES couldn't. Putting seemingly random bits of information together, making the irrelevant relevant. He sometimes called it the key code. That one bit of information that made everything make sense.

'Lucy, why are there only five tablets in this blister pack?'

She looked confused. 'It's not new, it's just one I carry round with me.'

'No, sorry, you're not following. I mean why are there *three* missing? Why not two or four? I've never taken just one paracetamol in my life. They're nearly always taken two at a time.'

'My sister came over last night with my niece and the poor thing had a headache. She's only eight, so she just had the one,' she replied, still bemused.

'Exactly,' he said. 'A child may be given one. Someone with medical issues may only take one. But like Samantha, you seem healthy, Lucy – have you ever taken only one?'

She thought for a while. 'Actually, I haven't.'

Fluke directed the same question at Sowerby and Towler. 'Have either of you ever only taken one paracetamol?'

They shook their heads.

'And you never take more than two because it damages your liver, right?'

Sowerby nodded. 'What are you getting at, old boy?'

'Something that's been bothering me for a while, Henry,' Fluke said. 'Didn't even realise what it was until just now.'

'What is it, boss?'

'I think I know what Nathaniel Diamond was hinting at. What he couldn't tell us. I think we've been looking at it all wrong. Samantha Farrar wasn't a rape victim and that poor bastard in there isn't a rapist.'

Silence.

Sowerby broke it.

'I think you'd better tell us what you know,' he said.

'That bed-wetting alarm was a clue but it was so random, so unexpected it threw us all. But put that together with a bottle of paracetamol with fifteen pills in it and it starts to make sense.'

He looked at them all. It was clear they hadn't caught up yet.

'I'll bet everything in my pockets against everything in your pockets that those pills aren't paracetamol,' he continued. 'I'm betting they'll turn out to be Rohypnol.'

Nobody said anything. It was the type of silence that said, *Let me process that*.

'Do you not see yet?' Fluke said. 'The stupid woman was drugging herself. She was drugging herself then crying rape.'

Fluke left a Carlisle CID sergeant and Sowerby to manage the recovery of the body. It was against protocol but he and Towler needed to get back to HQ. He ignored the speed limit and it took him less than twenty minutes. Alan Vaughn, Jo Skelton and Kay Edwards were waiting for him.

'We're working on a new hypothesis,' he said. 'We think she was operating a blackmail scam. She targets wealthy men with no criminal record. Men with no DNA on the system. She has sex with them somewhere. Goes home, takes her *own* Rohypnol then goes to bed. In the morning, she reports a drug-facilitated rape. Goes through the sexual assault process.

Evidence is found and logged. No one doubts her, the Rohypnol is conclusive.

'I'm guessing the next part, but I think she then approaches her victim and tells them that she's reported a rape. Presents them with the facts, that the police have their DNA, that there is an active rape investigation. That fifty grand or so makes her disappear. Fail to pay and she starts to remember little bits of information. Doesn't have to be much. Just the name of the bar they met in would be enough for us to find them. Their DNA and her Rohypnol would make a conviction inevitable. How many rich men would pay? Particularly if they're married.'

'Why risk the stigma of a rape trial when you can afford not to,' Towler added.

'Exactly,' said Fluke. 'When they pay, she simply moves to another town.'

'And if they don't?' Jiao-long asked.

Fluke thought through what might happen if a victim wasn't in the mood to be blackmailed. He decided it was unlikely she'd go through with it.

'There'd be nothing to gain by going ahead with a prosecution,' he said. 'I think she'd probably walk away. She won't win every one but she won't need to. Even one a year would be a decent payday.'

There was silence as they absorbed the new theory. There were no holes in it. It didn't mean it was correct, only that they couldn't yet rule it out.

'The bed-wetting alarm is part of it, I'm assuming?' said Edwards, eventually.

Fluke had kept her on the team, finding her insight into rapes invaluable. And he knew she'd take this personally, knew she'd be a terrier for him.

'She'd have to take the Rohypnol the same night she had sex or it would have been too concentrated when her bloods were taken. I think she probably had accidents in the past. It fits anyway.'

'In other words she was sick of waking up drenched in piss?' Towler added.

'Well put, Matt.'

Crude, Fluke thought, but essentially spot on. She'd found something to wake her if it happened.

'It also means she wouldn't be remembered by landlords when she left,' Fluke said. 'Mattresses are expensive to replace.'

'How does she find her victims, sir?' Edwards asked.

'Good question. We're assuming that she had information provided to her. She'd need to check her victims weren't on the DNA database. The only way this works is if she has time to blackmail her victim. DNA results come through fast now. It wouldn't work if the victim *was* on the database. We'd make an arrest before she could get paid. That's one of our new lines of enquiry. Who'd she get her information from? Longy's going to work with IT to quietly take a peek at who's been looking at Kenneth Diamond.'

Jo Skelton, who'd said nothing up until now, spoke. 'If we assume she approached Diamond and demanded cash, why didn't Nathaniel say that when you interviewed him? His dad was a victim in all this. It would have got him off the hook.'

'Would it?' Fluke said. 'Think about it for a second. We wanted him for rape and murder. Nathaniel saying she was falsely accusing his father of rape still gives him a motive to kill her.'

She nodded. 'Murder's murder. Doesn't matter what the reasons are.'

They accepted other ideas; Fluke liked that about his team. Especially when they accepted his.

'It's a perfect scam,' Towler said. 'Ingenious, really. As long as she chose her marks carefully, she could have done this indefinitely.' His brow furrowed. 'She was still in hiding though, boss. Who from and why? And why come to Carlisle? It's slim pickings here millionaire-wise. There must be easier places for her to work than this.'

'Anyone?' Fluke said.

There was a moment of silence. Vaughn broke ranks first.

'She was hiding from a previous mark,' he said. 'Got to be. She targeted someone she shouldn't have. Someone with the resources to find her.'

'And then *end* her,' Towler added.

'That's what I'm thinking,' Fluke said. 'And that person, ladies and gents, is the person who hired Dalton Cross.'

'She's done this before then,' Edwards said. Not a question, a statement.

'Probably several times,' Fluke said.

'How can we be sure, sir? How do we know this wasn't her first time and she got it wrong?' she asked.

'I think it comes down to Matt's point; why was she in Carlisle at all? He's right; this isn't Mayfair. Millionaires aren't bumping their Bentleys into each other round here. Her surgery wasn't cheap so we know she had access to money. I think she came here to hide and started running low on funds. Probably planned to tap Diamond for twenty grand then move on.

'And that's the second line of enquiry. We need to know where else this has happened. Jo, work on a bulletin and get it out nationwide. Work with Kay and make sure every rape team and SARC in the country gets it. Look for drug-facilitated rapes where the victim disappeared then cross-reference the results with cases where they had clear DNA evidence but no hits on the system. I doubt that'll be an unmanageable number. Get photographs where they have them. Let's see how many times she's done this.'

They nodded.

Vaughn frowned. 'Where does Diamond's murder fit in, though? It must be related?'

'Must be,' Fluke agreed. 'I think the killer's been tracking her for a while. But this time she makes a mistake and targets someone we can trace through his son's DNA, someone who also has the resources to search the city at street level. Kenneth Diamond might have been clean but the family isn't. They would have found her eventually. Every low life in Cumbria would have been looking for her.'

'How'd Cross find her though, boss?' Towler asked.

'How would you do it?' Fluke said. When it came to tactical planning there was no one better.

Towler considered it for a moment.

'He probably copied what she was doing,' he said. 'That's what I would do anyway. Monitor the intelligence databases for drug-facilitated rapes until he comes across a case that fits her MO. He's only looking for rapes where the suspect's DNA isn't on the database. As soon as he gets a hit, he races over and starts doing what Longy's doing now. He searches local intelligence systems to see who's been looking at names with no criminal records. That's her target. It also becomes *his* target. That's how he found her – through her own target.'

Fluke nodded. He'd come to the same conclusion. It was a game that was only ever going to end one way.

Towler finished it off. 'Cross finds out it was Diamond she's blackmailed. Grabs him, tortures him and finds out where the blackmail drop is supposed to be. He stakes out the drop site and then follows her home. The rest we know.'

'He would've had to move quickly though,' Vaughn said. 'When Diamond didn't show to pay, it would be time to move to a new city. We've all seen her flat; she could pack and be out of there in two minutes. She wouldn't hang around; nothing to gain, potentially everything to lose.'

A natural silence settled over the team.

Fluke thought about Samantha. What had made her choose a life like that? Where her job was accusing innocent men of rape? A life where she set out to ruin the lives of others?

For money.

And then the sudden realisation that she'd got one wrong. That she'd targeted someone too powerful, too well connected. Someone who had no intention of being blackmailed. Someone who had more than one way to resolve problems. And the hunter becomes the hunted.

Fluke imagined her panic when she realised someone had gone a step further than call her bluff. The urge to flee must have been overwhelming. But she didn't. She took the time to prepare. Either that or she had a contingency plan. Cosmetic surgery, some superficial alterations and she became a ghost, moving from town to town, from city to city, always looking over her shoulder, never daring to settle. And eventually, she ends up in the northernmost city in England. Carlisle.

The end of the line. Literally and figuratively.

He thought about Nathaniel Diamond. He suspected that if he'd found Farrar before Cross, she'd have quietly disappeared. Or perhaps not. He was intelligent enough to see the whole board. Perhaps he would've thought paying her off was the cautious move. He wouldn't have known about the extensive things she'd done to change her appearance, but he may have felt that there might have been a bigger player at the table. That she worked for someone, someone who hadn't yet declared their hand. Why risk cancelling someone's asset? Starting an unnecessary feud.

The office phone rang.

Jo Skelton answered it.

'I'll tell him,' she said, putting the receiver down.

'You were right, boss; the tablets in that paracetamol bottle were Rohypnol.'

No one smiled, no one punched the air. All the call had done was confirm their very worst suspicions. Fluke would much rather he'd been wrong.

Towler stood up and stretched.

'She was born in a burial gown,' he said.

He didn't expand and Fluke didn't need him to. He was right. It was a term he'd heard once or twice in the Marines, referring to someone who seemed to have a death wish. Someone who relished doing the things other people were terrified of. They were the first through the door and the last one to take cover. They appeared fearless, even reckless. And maybe they were.

People who didn't know him thought Towler was like that. The truth was the opposite. Towler had fears. He'd told Fluke one night over a couple of cigars. Abi was his greatest fear. He was terrified that something might happen to his daughter. He brought his fear home every night.

Perhaps someone he'd put in prison. Nurturing a grudge during the twenty-three hours a day he was in his cell. Blaming Towler for his predicament. A twisted revenge fantasy that wouldn't go away. Eating at him, keeping him awake. Towler knew he had a reputation and knew it was fully deserved. His daughter would be a much easier target.

That was Towler's fear.

Fluke had heard a rumour a few years ago. A rumour he'd deliberately not looked into. Towler had just joined the police and Abi was still an infant. A drunk in Cleator Moor had thrown a bottle at him while he was on nights. Towler was busy putting him into the back of the van for a night sobering up in the cells – he hadn't even intended to charge him. The rumour was, that in the morning as the drunk was being let out, he'd turned to Towler and told him he knew where he lived. A none-too-subtle threat. Towler had ignored him.

Three days later the same man had turned up at A & E with two broken legs and two broken wrists. He refused to name his attacker. Fluke had no way of knowing if the rumours of a big man seen walking on the back roads of Cleator Moor on the night of the attack were true, and he wasn't going to ask.

No, Towler had fears like everyone else.

Nathaniel Diamond had been released. Fluke left instructions for the duty officer to try to locate him. He wanted to speak to him before anyone else did. He'd know about his father by now, secrets weren't easily kept in Carlisle, but they had a statutory requirement to tell him anyway. With their father being a widower, Nathaniel or Wayne would have to formally identify the body.

Fluke would ask him to do it from the neck up.

He drove back to Carlisle and the crime scene but Sowerby and Lucy had left with the body. Fluke hoped the PM would be the next day. Towler could attend on his behalf. The investigation was moving fast and he needed to be in the thick of it. Jiao-long would have information on who'd accessed the database to check the name Kenneth Diamond soon. It didn't matter what user level you had, every system left footprints, even if you didn't want it to. Each time you logged on it was recorded.

The bulletin to rape teams and SARCs across the country had been sent. Fluke was hopeful it would get a response, although he didn't know how helpful it would be. He was convinced he knew what had happened in Cumbria. He might help other forces close some open cases but it wouldn't move his own forwards.

The photofit artist was interviewing Penny first thing in the morning. There was decent software available now but a good artist was always preferable. Someone who understood the way faces were structured. They would have something to send out with Dalton Cross's name by lunchtime hopefully.

Fluke left the crime scene and called at the Cumberland Infirmary. He needed to thank Leah for her help. He also needed to see where he stood with his forged letter. He was going to ask if she could wait until the end of the following week before she reported it. He'd know one way or the other if there was going to be an arrest by then.

She'd gone home. Fluke wished he had such luxuries.

His phone rang. It was a Penrith number. Police HQ but not one in his contact list. He answered it as he walked back to his car. A nasal voice spoke when Fluke answered.

'Ah, Fluke. It's Alex Fenton from Professional Standards. I wonder if we can have a few words.'

He'd been expecting the call. Fenton wasn't the type of person to let an opportunity pass. He would need to tread carefully.

Fenton outranked him but was universally despised throughout the force, which evened things up a bit. Fluke's earlier despondency lifted. If Fenton had definitive proof the letter to Occupational Health had been forged, he would've arrested him. The prick would have probably done it at HQ, in front of everyone.

Fluke couldn't afford distractions at the moment though. He would have to communicate clearly that right now wasn't the best time. That his interview would have to wait.

'Fuck off, Fenton,' he said.

He'd deal with him when it was finished. He turned off his work phone and sent a group text from his personal phone telling his team to use that number for the next couple of days. He immediately got one back from Jo Skelton. The hospital warrants were ready and she was driving to the duty magistrate's house now. A warrant for Cross's file and a warrant for the CCTV tapes. If they were signed, Skelton would collect everything from West Cumberland Hospital herself, make sure nothing was missed.

He sent a text back to her:

Buy Doctor Weighman a doughnut if he's in

Then he got back into his car and headed home.

He'd just finished boiling some pasta when his phone rang.

Half an hour before, he'd looked in his fridge for something healthy to eat. There was nothing. Fluke's kitchen was functional.

No decorative bottles of olive oil on the window ledge, no fancy plates, no ornamental scales. The food in his cupboard was chosen for longevity rather than taste and he only ever bought fruit and veg to see how long it took to go off.

After spending the day with Leah, he thought he'd better try to have a healthy meal. He settled on pasta and a ready-made sauce. He defrosted a Cumberland sausage link to add some protein. He told himself he'd need it the next day, although he knew he'd ignore the pasta and only eat the meat. He was basically having a sausage for tea.

He picked up the phone and pressed the receive button. It was Jiao-long.

'Got him, boss. Gibson Tait. He's not badged; civvy in charge of IT.'

Fluke was surprised. It could have been anyone with clearance, which meant every officer and half the civilian staff. The head of IT?

'Are we sure, Longy? Big name to accuse. And you can't discipline civilians for anything without their unions getting involved.'

It was a constant gripe of police officers everywhere that their civilian colleagues had the protection of a union in work-related matters whereas they themselves were banned from joining one.

'Yeah. No doubt. He tried to hide it. Used different machines and changed his password enough times to try to confuse matters, but it's him.'

'When?'

'Three times in total. Once was a PNC check. Diamond's not on so he logged out straight away. Went to a different machine and logged back in. Checked SLEUTH, but there's not much on there either. Lots on the rest of the family but Kenneth Diamond seems clean.'

'And the last time?' Fluke asked. He suspected he knew the answer.

'He checked them both again the day before she made the rape allegation, boss.'

So, she *had* had someone on the inside, someone who could check a potential mark for her, make sure the police wouldn't be able to identify him before she had a chance to get paid. Once the target was identified, Fluke assumed she'd go to work. Research and prepare. One final check of the system to make sure nothing had changed, and she'd go for it.

Careful. Clever.

It had also got her killed.

'For Cross to find out who the target was in Cumbria though, he'd also have to find out who's been searching for names without getting results. Can we check that?'

'Already on it, boss. That'll take a while though. I'll have to write a program. It probably won't be a Cumbrian. I assume he has a contact in the police somewhere. It'd be a bit of a coincidence if it was Cumbria.'

'We got an address for Tait?' he said. 'I may go out now.'

Tait's address was suspicious enough. Bassenthwaite village. Picture perfect. Unspoiled. Sitting at the top of Bassenthwaite Lake, it was out of the price range of the average working man unless you were lucky enough to inherit property there.

'Anything I need to know about him, Longy? I've never met him.'

'Nothing I can see, boss. He's not been here that long. He may not be in though; the system has him on leave all week.'

'Bollocks,' he said. 'I may have a run across and see if the bastard's in anyway. It's only an hour away and I have nothing pressing. What's he look like?'

'No photo yet. Not been here long enough. I had a quick look on social media but all his accounts are private and his profile pictures are all of the band logo.'

'Band? What band?'

'I spoke to someone in IT and they say he's in a local band.'

'Like Jo's husband?'

'Don't know, boss. I can find out more if you want.'

'It's OK,' Fluke said. He checked his watch. 'Right, I'm setting off now. I'll ring the duty officer with an update. I imagine Tait will deny the whole thing. If I nick him, I'll send for a van.'

'You sure, boss? Have you seen the weather? It's going to turn bad.'

He looked out of his kitchen window. Jiao-long was right: this was a job that could wait until the morning. Tait didn't know they were on to him. He then looked at the pasta congealing in the pan.

'Yep,' he said. 'I'm going.'

Chapter 34

It was a foul night. Cold, dark and spitting. Heavy clouds grumbling overhead in anticipation of the storm they were readying to unleash.

After ten minutes, the light rain turned into a monsoon, raindrops exploding on the road like small grenades. Fluke knew he should go home. The hidden dips and bends, dangerous enough in good light and fine weather, were making driving treacherous. He also knew there was a fair chance the road would flood. He slowed and looked for somewhere to turn around.

But then he thought about Samantha, lying in a grave of wet mud and clay. She may have ruined lives but no one deserved to die like that. He set his windscreen wipers to double speed, gripped the steering wheel and drove on.

After an hour's nervous driving, Fluke turned onto the narrow, twisting lane that lead to Bassenthwaite village. His double beam picked up the sign for the Christian retreat. A sign warned drivers to watch out for red squirrels. A bicycle with a wicker basket leaned against a wooden fence.

The trees were so close and the road so narrow that they formed a canopy overhead. During summer it would be like driving through a green tunnel. In winter, the entwined leafless branches gave Fluke the impression he was driving into a funnel-web spider's trap.

The trees thinned after half a mile and his headlights illuminated one of the most picturesque villages in Cumbria. Despite the weather, it still looked like a scene from a postcard, a scene unchanged for hundreds of years. If McNab's Pinegrove represented the very worst of Cumbria, Bassenthwaite represented the very best.

It was largely unspoiled by tourism. It didn't really have streets in the traditional sense, it was more a collection of whitewashed cottages that just happened to occupy the same stunning landscape.

It sat at the edge of Bassenthwaite Lake and nestled in the shadow of the imposing Skiddaw – Fluke knew the property prices were out of the reach of most people. They could save for a hundred years and never be able to afford to live there. Properties were rarely put up for sale and when they were competition for them was fierce.

He checked his phone for the directions Jiao-long had texted him. He had to drive through the village. After one hundred yards, Tait's house would be on the left, on its own. It wasn't a well-lit village, most of the old Cumbrian villages weren't, but after a couple of wrong turns, Fluke eventually found it.

It was set back from the road at the end of a long drive. Fluke estimated it was about sixty yards. Few houses in Bassenthwaite had numbers and Tait's was no exception. Two large, slate pillars flanked either side of the entrance, remnants of what would have once been an impressive gate. 'The Lodge' was engraved on one of the pillars, the letters filled with whitewash to highlight them.

Fluke had planned to park at the side of the road and approach the house quietly and on foot, but with the rain beating a drum the way it was, he couldn't see the point. Instead he drove up the drive and parked right outside Tait's front door.

He turned off the engine but left the headlights on while he surveyed his surroundings. It was a cottage in every sense of the word. Single-storey with a whitewashed, ivy-covered front. Big wooden door and a front garden that would be filled with flowers later in the year. There was one other car in the drive. Fluke looked for a bell but couldn't find one. He used the large brass door knocker.

The wind made it impossible to hear if anyone was coming so he was surprised when the door opened immediately and warm light spilled out into the cold winter darkness.

He stared.

Gibson Tait wasn't what Fluke had expected.

Fluke tried not to have preconceptions of what people should look like but when Fluke heard 'head of IT', he expected an older version of Samantha's neighbour, the nerdy William. Tait looked as if he should be hosting survival programmes on TV instead of working in an office.

He had dark hair and dark eyes and was wearing typical Cumbrian fare: checked shirt and strong denim jeans. He looked at Fluke with mild curiosity. There was certainly no panic. He smiled encouragingly.

Fluke introduced himself and showed his warrant card.

Tait said, 'Come in, you're getting soaked.'

Fluke guessed the cottage was at least two hundred years old. It had the low ceilings and doors favoured by previous generations who statistically had been shorter. He had to duck through a doorway as he followed Tait into the kitchen. It was small but surprisingly modern.

Tait asked him if he wanted a coffee. Fluke was going to say it was too late, but having one would give him an excuse to stay a bit longer if he needed to.

'Thanks, Mr Tait. Black, no sugar.'

'Please, call me Gibson or Gibb, Inspector. I'll fire up the machine,' he said, as he filled up an expensive-looking coffee maker, and slotted in an espresso pod. It was soon spitting it out and the room filled with the aroma of fresh coffee. He topped the cup up with hot water from the kettle and handed it to Fluke. He slotted in another pod and repeated the process.

Fluke placed his steaming mug on a coaster.

'Do you know why I'm here, Mr Tait?' he said.

It was an informal interview but as Tait could end up on the wrong end of a conspiracy-to-murder charge Fluke wasn't prepared to use first names just yet. He might have to arrest him later.

He took a sip of his coffee before answering. 'I haven't the faintest idea, Inspector. I assume something's happened at work.'

Fluke couldn't quite place his accent. It was English but not Cumbrian.

'How long have you worked in Cumbria, Mr Tait?'

'Just over six months,' he said. 'I was sorting out Sussex council's waste management software before moving here. I wanted to live somewhere with fresh air and mountains. This job came up. I applied, I was appointed.'

Tait's lack of nerves was making him uneasy. He should have been scared and Fluke should have been ready to take him down. Instead he wanted to buy him a pint, talk to him about mountains and lakes and walks. He gave himself a mental shake. Because of Tait, Samantha was thrown in a hole and Kenneth Diamond had been tortured and forced to drink acid. That Samantha would have found someone else to help her didn't lessen what he'd done.

'What's this about, Inspector?'

'We've traced your unauthorised use of police databases.'

'Oh?'

'You checked a name twice on PNC and twice on SLEUTH. That person's now dead. Murdered.'

'When am I supposed to have done this?' he asked.

'I can't remember the exact dates. A month or so ago, then again a few days ago. The woman you passed them to is also dead.'

Fluke decided enough was enough. He knew he had him, time to stop playing nice. He put down his cup.

'And you, Mr Tait, are well and truly in the shit. You decide if you sink or swim in it. Tell me what I need to know and I'll keep a conspiracy charge off the table.'

Fluke thought there was surprise in Tait's expression, but the fear he'd been expecting still wasn't there. If it was, he was hiding it well.

'I'm assuming this last date wasn't when I was on leave? I've been off for nearly a week. Band rehearsals.'

'You were at work,' Fluke said, hoping Jiao-long had triple-checked.

Tait didn't answer. He drained his coffee and put another pod in the machine. 'Sorry, I won't sleep tonight now. May as well give myself some fuel. Can I tempt you?'

Fluke declined with a quick shake of his head.

'We have a problem, Inspector. I haven't accessed PNC or SLEUTH, lawfully or unlawfully. There would be no reason for me to go on either system. I manage the IT department but I do very little hands-on IT work.'

'The computer doesn't lie, Mr Tait.'

'No, it doesn't. But it doesn't always tell the truth either. All it can tell you is whose log-on name was used. It can't tell you who actually used the name.'

He was right, of course. All Jiao-long had was Tait's username and password.

'No one would hand out their password for this exact reason, Mr Tait. I bet you don't.'

Tait nodded. 'True enough. No one hands out their passwords. Even writing them down is against regs.'

He paused as the machine finished, he picked up his full cup and turned and faced Fluke again.

'What do you do if you can't log on?'

It had been a while since his computer had locked him out. 'Hasn't happened for a few months now.'

'But it has happened?'

Fluke nodded.

'And what did you do?'

'I can't really remember. I'll have called IT, I suppose.'

Fluke wasn't sure where Tait was going with this, but he had a feeling his lead was about to go bad.

'Exactly,' Tait said without triumph. 'You'll have rung my department. What they'd have done is accessed your account and reset it.'

'I suppose,' Fluke said.

'How many people have access to police systems in Cumbria, Inspector?'

Fluke did a quick calculation. There were thirteen hundred badged officers and nearly a thousand police staff. 'Just shy of two and a half thousand,' he said.

'Say each person needs IT's help twice a year,' Tait said. 'That's five thousand calls a year. What's that a day? Fourteen nearly? On top of everything else we have to do. And I think that's what I'm getting at. We can access anyone's account. We have access to everyone's details. We know everyone's passwords. We have to; if we didn't, the whole system would crash. Software develops glitches, people forget their passwords or go so long without logging on that the system resets itself. It's bread-and-butter work for my department.'

'So you're saying th—'

Tait interrupted him. 'And that's not all, Inspector. Have you heard of a master-access level?'

Fluke hadn't. He suspected he was about to be taught a lesson in what happens when your intelligence hasn't been stress-tested.

'A master-access level is something all systems need to have. All secure systems anyway. It means there's one person, normally the head of IT, who has access to every part of the system. And in Cumbria, that's me. What I'm saying is that I can access all parts of our system and use anyone's name. And that's not all. I have access to the system's histories. In other words, I can delete my footprints as I go along.'

Fluke sighed. He'd need to confirm what Tait had just said but it sounded like he should have been the first person they ruled out. The person they actually went to for help.

'Here, come with me,' Tait said.

Fluke followed him into one of the spare bedrooms, the one he used as his home office. An expensive-looking Apple desktop computer sat in the middle of a tidy workstation. A trackpad and a notebook were on the left of the keyboard; a glass paperweight with a corporate logo Fluke didn't recognise was on the right. A souvenir from some event, no doubt. A heavy-duty laserjet printer was underneath the desk along with a wi-fi router, its blue light flashing. His bookshelves were filled with IT manuals, books and DVDs.

Tait tore off the top sheet of the notebook and wrote something down. He handed it to Fluke. It was a password.

'I shouldn't really do this but if you give this to your guy it'll give him the same access that I have. He'll see that everyone with this password has oversight of the entire system. I've been away from the office for a bit but I think it's current. If it isn't, give me a call and I'll get you the new one.'

Fluke pocketed it. He'd pass it to Jiao-long on Monday.

'Thanks,' he said. 'If you don't mind, I will have that coffee now.'

Tait grinned. They returned to the kitchen.

'And I'm truly sorry, Mr Tait,' he added. 'The only defence I have is that my IT guy has been working around the clock on this and he's still suffering from jetlag.'

Tait shrugged. 'Don't worry about it. I'd rather help than put in a complaint, if you'll let me.'

It was more than Fluke deserved and he knew it.

'If not you, any ideas who?' he said.

Tait looked thoughtful. After maybe twenty seconds he said, 'Someone in my department, unfortunately. The thing about the master-access level is that it has to be known to all the tech guys.

It's more of a departmental password than an individual one. If something is urgent, then whoever's on duty will use it. A system reboot or a software update, that type of thing.'

'How many people are in your department?' Fluke asked. It was Cumbria, so it wouldn't be a massive number.

'No more than a dozen at any one time. They're all vetted, obviously, but no system's foolproof. I can get a list to you first thing Monday if you want. Make a few calls.'

Fluke thought about the best way to do this. He had twelve potential suspects. Thirteen if you counted Tait, and Fluke supposed he couldn't rule him out just yet.

'There's definitely no way to tell who's searched using this master-code thing?'

'Sorry. We all use it.'

'So, we'll have to do it the old-fashioned way. My team's going to have to hit your department next week, Gibson. Everyone will need to be interviewed, and interviewed hard.'

Tait shrugged. 'Can't be helped. If one of my lot's dirty, I want to know.'

'Can I send someone round to take a statement after the weekend? Save you coming in when you're on holiday? I'm not doing it now, I've wasted enough of your time.' Fluke took his mobile out but he had no signal. 'I can probably log it now? I would need to use your landline though, there's no reception on my mobile.'

'Nor mine. We're too close to Skiddaw. I don't know of any network that gets more than one bar. I have to go all the way past the Sun Inn to get any signal at all. Price you pay to live here, I suppose. It's OK, you send someone when you can. I'll be in.'

'Thanks. I'll have someone up as soon as possible. And Gibson?'

'Yes.'

'You can call me Avison.' Fluke stretched out his hand and the two men shook.

Fluke stayed to finish his coffee. They moved on to their shared passion for music. They liked some of the same bands and they talked about favourite albums and best concerts attended for a bit.

'That yours?' Fluke said, pointing to a beautiful acoustic guitar leaning against the wall.

'One of them,' Tait said.

'May I? My sergeant and I were in a band when we were at school. Quite fancied myself as the next Joe Strummer back then.'

'Be my guest,' Tait said. 'I was more of a Hendrix man myself.'

Fluke picked it up.

'You didn't stick with it?' Tait said.

'I'd have liked to but there was one thing that stopped me.'

'Oh?'

'Yep. I couldn't play a fucking note,' he said.

Tait laughed.

Fluke strummed his fingers across the strings. Listened to the racket he'd made.

'That need tuning?' he said. 'Or am I even worse than I thought I was?'

'I'd say it needs a good tuning, and you need some practice,' Tait smiled.

Fluke's stomach growled loudly. He leaned the guitar back against the wall. If he didn't leave now he'd miss the chef at the local pub. They shook hands again and, by way of an apology, Fluke said he'd buy him a pint when the case was finished.

The drive back was even more treacherous than the journey out. Fluke's BMW was buffeted by strong side winds over the higher ground. He had intended to ring the duty officer from his car and get that evening's interview logged but he thought better of it. He needed both hands on the wheel.

The wind hadn't relented when he arrived home and some of the taller, thinner trees in his wood were bent almost sideways as the wind tested their roots. One of them was actually touching his cabin roof. Something for him to deal with next time he got a chance. Fluke navigated his wet, muddy drive and, eventually, found somewhere he felt was as safe as anywhere from falling branches. He ran to the front door, using his case file to shield his head from the heavy rain. He rang HQ as soon as the door was shut behind him.

There was no immediate answer and he filled the time scraping the congealed pasta into the bin. Eventually, it was answered. Alan Vaughn had drawn the night shift again. Fluke brought him up to date.

'Seems anyone in that department could have done it. We'll take Tait's statement but I think we need to think of another way to get what we need. We can't prove who it was through the databases, according to Tait. He's gonna help us but he's not back from leave for a few days.'

'He won't come in?'

'To be honest, Al, he would have but I didn't want to ask. He's given me his master-password thing though. I'll hand it to Longy when I see him.'

'What's next then, boss?'

Good question. What was next? Ten hours' sleep is what he needed. He'd settle for six.

'Call everyone and tell them to take Sunday off. We'll start again Monday,' he said. 'I'm assuming there are no hits on Dalton Cross yet?'

The name was unusual. If it was in the system, he was betting he would be the only one. Fluke doubted it would be easily found though. Someone that good didn't leave breadcrumbs.

'Nope, but the ballistic test on Diamond is back. As we thought, it's a match with Farrar's. Sowerby did the PM this afternoon and Matt got the bullet down to Manchester as a priority. The report should be with us early next week.'

No surprises there but it was reassuring that there weren't two murderers out there.

'Right, cheers, Al,' he said. 'I'm off to kip and suggest you try to get an hour or two later.'

Chapter 35

By the time Fluke finally woke properly on Sunday morning, he'd pressed his snooze button half a dozen times. The long hours were doing him no good and he knew his blood would demand a price at some point. He'd planned to stay in bed until noon and then go and meet Towler for Sunday lunch; a tradition they had, and one that Abi loved. She was always allowed an adult portion and whatever she ordered had better come with a Yorkshire pudding or there'd be hell to pay.

By ten o'clock, he was restless. Everyone had needed a day off, himself included, but he couldn't help feeling that the killer was being allowed an additional twenty-four hours to get away. He had a shower, made a drink and got out the case file. It was raining so he sat at his kitchen table and spread out the papers.

He didn't have the post-mortem report on Diamond but something was troubling him about the murder. It wasn't until he stopped comparing it with Samantha's that he knew what it was. Samantha's had been a clean kill. She'd probably not known anything about it. At best she may have heard something the split second before the bullet shredded her brains.

Diamond's had been anything but clean. His had been sadistic. Cruel.

Shocking.

Fluke realised that what was troubling him was the fact that they'd only been able to link the murders by accident. If there hadn't been a witness, Samantha would never have been found.

278

Her body had been too well hidden. Diamond, on the other hand, hadn't been. His corpse had been on display.

With the forensic report on the bullets confirming the same gun had been used in both murders, Fluke wondered why they were so different.

One looked like it had been committed by a professional, the other by a psychopath. If it hadn't been for the gun, Fluke would never have believed they were linked murders. The two together made no sense. Even if the torture of Diamond had been to extract information, it was completely over the top.

It looked like a punishment beating but professional killers didn't do that sort of thing. He briefly entertained the idea they were after two killers sharing one gun but that made no sense. A professional wouldn't work with someone who worked that way. Which meant the killer was the same person. And for some reason he had two vastly different MOs.

Fluke closed the file and shut his eyes. Pretended Samantha had never been found. Looked at Diamond's murder in isolation.

There'd been no attempt to hide him.

Why not?

The answer was obvious – they were supposed to find him.

Sticking with the Samantha-had-never-been-found train of thought, he asked himself what conclusions he would have drawn.

Given Diamond's alleged links to the criminal underworld, Fluke would have probably assumed it was a drug-related murder, a warning to other Cumbrians on what happens when the big boys are crossed. They'd have thought Diamond was finding out what it was like to swim in the big pond.

They certainly wouldn't have suspected a professional hit.

Which was the point, he realised. Diamond's murder had been staged to look like a gangland execution. There could be no doubt that Diamond had information Cross needed about the blackmail drop, but to go on to mutilate the body was mindless violence.

Fluke didn't think Cross was prone to wanton acts of mindless violence. *Extreme* violence, yes, he'd killed at least two people, but mindless? Fluke didn't think so. Everything Cross did, he did for a reason.

Without Samantha, Fluke knew they would have looked at Diamond's mutilated corpse completely differently. As a way of disguising the true motivation for the murder, it was perfect.

Towler had once told him about a serial killer who'd operated in Northern Ireland during the Troubles. His victims were killed in the same style as the sectarian murders. When a Black Watch patrol caught him red-handed shooting a young Catholic in the back of the head, something didn't quite add up. The killer was a respectable man, a dentist with a large private practice with no known affiliations to any paramilitary organisation. Although it was never proven, he was suspected in the killing of a dozen young men, on both sides of the religious divide. Because of the way he dispatched his victims, no one had ever considered they were anything other than sectarian murders.

He'd been hiding in the carnage of Belfast, and Fluke wondered if Cross had been doing the same with Diamond; hiding his murder in the carnage of the drug wars.

He shuddered. Who the hell was Dalton Cross . . . ?

A car pulled up and the sound of small footsteps on his front porch told him his Sunday ruminations were over. He put everything back in the file and went to greet his friend and his goddaughter.

He was still feeling tired when he entered HQ on Monday morning. Most of the team were already there. He asked Alan Vaughn when he could expect the PM report and was told later that day.

'Has Longy taken today off?' Fluke asked. He hoped he wasn't avoiding him because of his error with Gibson Tait. The man had been awake virtually non-stop since he got back.

'No, boss,' Vaughn replied. 'He went off somewhere. Said he'll be in later.'

Fluke let his team manage themselves as much as he could. It wasn't a pissing contest. The one who worked the longest hours didn't win a prize. He expected them to be able to function when they came in. He was only strict on everyone being in when the investigation was either in the very early stages or a big break had been made; the rest of the time he expected them to manage their downtime. If they needed rest, he didn't need to be asked.

He'd take Jiao-long to one side later and explain the mistake had been his fault, not his. He should have insisted he get some rest.

Jo Skelton entered the incident room, holding a document. She caught Fluke's eye and grinned. 'Got it, boss.'

Fluke knew she could only be talking about one thing, and he was genuinely surprised. He thought she'd have about as much chance of finding a one-ended stick.

'The warrants?'

'Yep, both of them. Signed, sealed and delivered. Everything we need. Dalton Cross's file and any CCTV relating to him or the investigation.'

It was exactly what Fluke had asked for, but with no evidence to back it up, he couldn't see how she'd achieved it. He thought he'd sent her on a fool's errand.

'How?' he said.

'Longy,' she said simply. 'Boy's a genius. We've got the warrant but that's not the only thing.'

Frustrated with his lack of success tracking down the name of Dalton Cross, Jiao-long had decided he was working his Sunday. He'd come in and fed the name into every database he had legal access to and, when that didn't work, he went home and tried databases he *didn't* have legal access to. Still, he drew a blank. In desperation, he rang home and spoke to someone who knew someone who knew someone.

Eventually, he was put through to someone in Chinese Intelligence.

An hour later, an email had arrived. Dalton Cross was known to them, as he was to all security services apparently.

'I'm surprised the Chinese were OK with helping a British investigation,' Fluke said. 'I know we have a Beijing boy on the team but it seems a bit too helpful.'

'Yeah, I thought that,' she replied. 'But Longy reckons there's one overriding thing that would make them share.'

Fluke thought about it. It was possible that Cross was wanted in China for something. Possible but unlikely. Contract killers tended to work in their own ethnic groups. He wouldn't be able to hide in China. He was the wrong colour, the wrong size and, in all likelihood, didn't speak the language. Or if he did, he wouldn't be able to pick up on the local nuances and subtleties. No, it was something different. He tried to think of it from the Chinese perspective. What would make them share something they had no reason to? What would be in it for them?

When he thought of it like that, the answer was obvious. 'It's to embarrass the US, isn't it? What do they know about him?'

Jo Skelton nodded.

'He was US Army,' she answered. 'A Ranger, whatever that is.'

'Yank version of the Paras. Matt's worked with them before, I think,' Fluke replied automatically.

Towler confirmed he had, and that they were good. 'Still a bunch of fucking crap hats though,' he added, just in case anyone had thought he'd been disloyal to the maroon beret.

Fluke hadn't needed Towler to tell him that they were one of the world's elite forces. Tough, resourceful and fearless. Exactly what you needed for special-forces soldiers and exactly what Fluke had been dreading.

Most of Jiao-long's file was in Chinese but there was enough in English. It was purposefully incomplete. Some years were blank and Fluke knew that wasn't because he'd been at the beach. It was because there were things in his record that were classified. So, in all likelihood a US Ranger with spook training.

Perfect.

Part of Fluke, the part that cared deeply for Cumbria, hoped that Cross was already out of the country. That no one else here was going to get hurt.

'According to Longy's contact, he went bad a few years ago,' Skelton said. 'He was caught having an affair with an officer's wife but before he could be court-martialled, he slaughtered the entire family: the wife, the officer, even their three-year-old daughter. Set up someone else for it. He'd left no trace forensics; he was wearing bags on his feet, gloves on his hands and a hairnet and had used an unregistered weapon. He knew what he was doing. He was only discovered because the husband had set up a secret camera as he suspected his wife was carrying on the affair. The whole thing had been caught on tape. By the time they found the cameras, Cross had disappeared.

'A few years later and his name starts to crop up in some contract killings. Nothing has ever been proven but the Yanks are desperate to get their hands on him, as you can imagine. China only know about him as he was photographed in North Korea a few years ago.'

'Christ, no wonder they were keen to share the intel,' Fluke said. 'A Yank working for the Koreans? No way they're gonna pass that up.'

'Exactly what Longy said,' she said. 'You want to know how we got the warrants?'

Fluke nodded.

Skelton explained that as well as the summary of Cross's heavily redacted service history, the information emailed across also included his fingerprints. All US military personnel are fingerprinted when they join, and Cross was no exception. She and Jiao-long had spent all Sunday night with the duty SOCO team and the charity box Fluke had grabbed from the coffee stall at the hospital.

There was a clear match on two of the coins.

He'd asked if there had been a photograph on the printout. She confirmed there was but the face had been pixelated out. More evidence of classified operations. She handed Fluke a copy of the printout.

He'd have liked to know who he was looking for, but just getting the warrants had been worth them losing a night's sleep. Because Skelton had been able to link the coin at the hospital with the name of the suspect, she'd got her warrant as soon as the court sat that morning. She'd neglected to put in the application that the name Dalton Cross had originated *from* the hospital but that was just creative police work as far as he was concerned.

The latest development seemed to clear the Monday morning blues. Fluke could feel his fatigue wash away. He handed out a few urgent tasks. Jiao-long was to go and speak to Gibson Tait as soon as he'd been home and rested. Together, they could devise a strategy to identify who the IT leak was. He followed the adage 'If you wanted something done quickly, give it to someone who's already busy.'

Although Fluke had already read the file, he'd go and speak to Doctor Weighman. He'd wanted to help before, Fluke had been sure of it.

The general noise of an office gearing up gradually stopped. Fluke looked up. The chief constable had entered the incident room.

'DI Fluke, can I have a word?'

Chapter 36

Although Fluke was firmly of the opinion you were either a police officer or a bureaucrat, he'd always liked Travis 'Action' Jackson, Cumbria's chief constable.

He hadn't always been a senior manager. He'd once been a tough, no-nonsense copper. He'd been part of the unflinching thin blue line in the darkest days of football hooliganism and stood toe-to-toe with the rest of them when Millwall fans had marauded all along Botchergate in Carlisle, smashing pubs and shops along the way.

His role might have changed, but the man hadn't.

The chief took the seat opposite Fluke's.

'I gather the investigation is progressing?'

Fluke told him it was and updated him on the morning's developments.

'Good. Superintendent Chambers showed me the HOLMES summary. This has been an excellent investigation, Avison. Absolutely top-class.'

Fluke said nothing.

'I'm paying you a compliment, Detective Inspector Fluke.'

'Yes, sir. Thank you, sir.'

'You know it's going to be taken from us, don't you?'

The initial excitement Fluke had felt that morning had worn off. As soon as he found out who Cross was, the investigation heading higher up the food chain was inevitable. They might get some local arrests. The IT leak. Whoever supplied Cross's weapon, that type of thing. But Cross himself would be hunted by people who specialised in international terrorism. There'd be no part for FMIT.

The chief sighed. 'Did you know Superintendent Chambers closed the robbery this morning?'

The lucky prick.

Fluke wondered who'd actually done the real work. 'No, sir, I didn't.'

'Do you know why you weren't involved in the investigation?'

Fluke shrugged. He knew why. It was because Chambers didn't want to be upstaged by a subordinate. He wasn't about to say that though.

'It's because you're not playing well with others at the minute, Avison.'

Fluke looked up.

'I'm the one who kept you off it. There was no way I was letting you near a multi-force investigation. Not with your attitude. I told Cameron to keep you in reserve and to let you manage anything that cropped up in the meantime.'

Fluke said nothing.

The chief stared at him for long enough to make him feel uncomfortable.

'Look, you two are going to have to find a way of working together. This week, FMIT has closed an armed robbery that spanned four force areas and now it looks like it has brought as much closure to these two murders as we're likely to get. You think Cameron doesn't deserve any credit for that?'

As far as Fluke was concerned, the only thing Chambers should take credit for was keeping out of his way. 'Yes, sir.'

'"Yes, sir,"' the chief mimicked. 'Fuck off, Avison. I know you think he's a prick.'

Fluke decided the best policy would be to stare slightly above the chief's hairline and say nothing.

The chief appeared wise to that tactic. 'I'm telling you that Cameron is a good manager. Yes, he's a bit pompous. Yes, he likes the cameras, and yes, he likes the sound of his voice a bit too much. But he knows how to get the best out of his officers and this week he's closed two major cases. And you, Avison, are not an easy man to manage.'

Fluke was about to protest but the chief stopped him.

'Don't argue. You came out of hospital with a chip on your shoulder the size of Helvellyn. You should have heard the way you were speaking to people. You had some sort of PTSD, you must have. You've always had an anti-authoritarian streak but for the last few months you've been taking the piss, quite frankly. You know why you've not been in trouble?'

'No, sir.'

'Guess.' He'd stopped smiling.

As far as he knew, he had no friends in the ACPO ranks. 'You stepped in, sir?' he said after a pause.

'You're the most intelligent man in any room you're in, Avison, but sometimes you're also the stupidest. No, it wasn't me who stepped in. I wouldn't interfere in the chain of command like that. It was Cameron. He knows your worth to FMIT. He knows only you can manage that team of oddballs you seem to like working with. Time and time again, he fends off other departments. Fenton complains at least once a month about the way you speak to him. Don Holland put in a complaint last week, said you humiliated him at the deposition site.'

Fluke snorted. 'Holland. The man couldn't find his arse with both hands,' he said, before adding a 'sir' on the end.

'Yes, I know he'd messed up the cordons, and Cameron told him if he proceeded with his complaint he'd be on capability by the end of the day, so he dropped it. But the point is every time they go to Cameron he bats it back. Tells them to let you do what you do best.'

Again, Fluke said nothing.

'You don't believe me, do you?' the chief said. 'Here, have a read of this.' He thrust a report under Fluke's nose. 'Read the top section, I've highlighted the relevant part.'

It was Chambers's daily briefing to SMT.

> The double murder is progressing faster than could
> reasonably be expected. DI Fluke has been doing a
> remarkable job and has developed lines of enquiry that,
> in my opinion, will close this case. As discussed with
> Chief Constable Jackson, DI Fluke is being left to work
> this case with minimal oversight as this way achieves
> optimum results with this officer. He has total control of
> his team, sufficient resources and I have no doubt he will
> make an arrest within acceptable timescales.

Fluke didn't know what to say. He felt his neck burning.

'Embarrassed, Avison?' the chief said. 'You should be, the way you speak to him sometimes. He's a good man, essentially. I know you think he's an idiot but he's the one who convinced me to let you run that team of yours. He's the one who's making your life tolerable. Anyone else wouldn't have you as SIO. You'd be exhibits officer or something. How long do you think you'd last doing that?'

'Not long, sir,' Fluke admitted.

His tone softened. 'Look, don't worry about it. The three of us will sit down after this is all over and talk it through.'

'Thank you, sir.' Fluke got up and offered his hand. The chief remained seated.

'I'm sorry, Avison. That wasn't why I came to see you.'

Fluke sat back down. The chief's expression was serious. It could only mean one thing.

Fenton.

* * *

Fluke refused his federation rep so the chief insisted that Chambers sit in with him. Fenton was preening. If he'd been a cat, he'd have purred. He had a sergeant from Professional Standards with him. Someone to carry his briefcase.

'Can we get on with this, please, Alex?' Chambers said.

He didn't look happy, Fluke noticed. The chief's words were still reverberating round his head, and he was seeing Chambers in a different light now. It was clear he was getting no satisfaction from this.

Fenton pressed record on the digital interview camera and spoke into the table microphone. 'Detective Superintendent Alex Fenton interviewing DI Fluke on suspicion of misconduct in a public office. DI Fluke is not under arrest but this interview is being conducted under caution. You have waived your right to representation, is this correct?'

Fluke said nothing.

Fenton looked at him but couldn't hold eye contact for very long. Eventually, Chambers saved him.

'Let's just get this over with, Avison, can we? I'm sure we all have real work to do.'

Fluke nodded.

'For the record, DI Fluke has nodded,' Fenton said.

'We're on video, you moron!' Fluke snapped.

Ignoring him, Fenton got out a file. He removed the letter Fluke had forged and put it on the table. 'Have you seen this letter before, DI Fluke?'

As Chambers craned his neck to read it, Fluke said, 'No comment.'

'You must have seen it, Fluke. It was CC'd to your address.'

'No comment.'

At that point, Chambers seemed to lose patience. 'Look, Alex, I know you have a job to do but can we have some context here. This investigation has come from nowhere as far as I'm concerned, and if you're going to interview one of my men, you're going to have to spell it out for me.'

'Certainly, sir. On Tuesday, someone from PSD happened to be at the Cumberland Infirmary visiting a relative and observed DI Fluke on the oncology ward. He appeared to be having a blood transfusion. He was about to make himself known to DI Fluke when Fluke's mobile phone rang. I believe it was a call from you, sir, and was in relation to the body found in West Cumbria. My man clearly heard DI Fluke say that he was at home. On that basis, I opened a file on DI Fluke on suspicion of lying to a superior officer. I accessed his personnel record and found the letter from Doctor Leah Cooper stating that DI Fluke was fit to return to duty. This is a copy here, sir.'

He handed it over to Chambers, who didn't look at it.

'Yeah, I've seen it. So what?'

'I asked Occ Health for their copy, sir, and they sent it to me. It is exactly the same.'

'I'm not following you, Alex,' Chambers said.

Fluke grimaced. *Wait for it, it's coming.* Fenton may not be a good detective but he had a sixth sense for officers in trouble.

'The thing is, sir, this letter was unsolicited. Normally HR ask Occ Health to request medical reports. This one just turned up. I showed the letter to Doctor Cooper and in my opinion it was the first time she'd seen it.'

'I see. Avison?'

Fluke breathed out slowly. Time to come clean. It was a shame as he was sure he could've closed the case given a few more days. It didn't look like he was going to get the chance. He could try to bluff it but that wasn't going to be a winning strategy and it also risked getting Leah into trouble. 'Last year—'

He was interrupted by a loud and urgent knock on the interview-room door. Towler walked in without being bidden. He bent down and whispered something into Chambers's ear.

Chambers looked up and then across at Fluke. 'We're going to have to stop this for a couple of minutes, Alex,' he said.

'But, sir,' Fenton protested. 'Fluke was just about to admit everyth—'

'I'm sorry, Alex. Please stop the tape.' He left the room with Towler.

Nearly ten minutes passed. Ten minutes of Fenton pretending to read his notes, doing everything he could to avoid looking at Fluke.

When Chambers returned, he wasn't alone.

There was a woman with him. She was carrying a brown leather satchel-type briefcase. She was also wearing a black leather jacket, black jeans and had a motorcycle helmet tucked under her arm.

Fluke gasped.

It was the woman Fluke had met at the dinner party. The woman who'd given him a lift home.

'Hello, I'm Bridie Harper-Tarr, Mr Fluke's solicitor,' she said to a bewildered-looking Fenton.

Not half as bewildered as he was, Fluke thought.

'DI Fluke's waived his right to representation,' Fenton said weakly.

'Actually, Alex, he hasn't,' Chambers said.

Fenton protested. Fluke said nothing. He knew he had. He'd nodded and it was on video, as he'd pointed out to everyone earlier.

Chambers seemed to have been paying closer attention to the chain of events than either Fluke or Fenton. 'When DI Fluke nodded earlier it was in response to my point about us all having better things to do. He hasn't actually answered your question yet,' he said. 'Is this correct, Avison?'

Fluke decided he'd best do what he was told for once.

'Yes, sir,' he said. 'I most definitely have better things to do.'

'He can't have a civilian solicitor without prior notice,' Fenton said.

'I'm allowing it, Alex. Miss Harper-Tarr has information that should clear all this up. Not only is she a solicitor, she's also a friend of Doctor Cooper. Miss Harper-Tarr, over to you.' Chambers said it with such assertiveness that everyone sat back down and waited.

Fluke had no idea what was happening but, by the look of things, neither did Fenton. He was also impressed with the new, assertive Chambers. He was beginning to see what the chief had been talking about.

Bridie Harper-Tarr cleared her throat and reached into her briefcase. As she did, her sleeve rode up and Fluke could see that the lower part of her arm was heavily tattooed. Scarred too. She put a document on the table, turned it the right way round, and slid it to Fenton.

'Doctor Cooper wanted you to have this, Mr Fenton. She was too busy to come herself and she said she'd rather not see you again in any case. She said you were quite aggressive when you came to her office.'

'I wasn't!' Fenton blurted out.

'Regardless. She may put in a complaint later on today. She may not. It depends what happens here, I suppose. What you have in front of you is a hospital printout of the letter Doctor Cooper sent to the police's Occupational Health department. You have the original, of course. Is this the letter you asked for?'

Fenton said nothing as he read it. He put it down and got out the original, and put them side-by-side. For a full minute, he studied them.

'Why didn't she tell me she had it?' he said. There was a whine creeping into his voice.

'Doctor Cooper doesn't work for you, Mr Fenton.'

'But she's legally obliged to assist the police in their investigations in a timely manner,' Fenton said, not ready to give up just yet.

Bridie Harper-Tarr smiled at him. It was the smile a shark gives a seal that's found itself in open sea.

'Mr Fenton, I worked at the UN for six years. I've represented countries. Do you really want to challenge me on the law? On medical ethics?'

By the looks of things, he didn't.

Chambers clearly decided enough was enough. 'Alex? Are we good here?'

Still Fenton said nothing as he desperately tried to find a discrepancy between the two documents. Fluke held his breath, mystified.

Chambers raised his voice. 'Alex. I said, are we good here?'

Fenton conceded defeat. 'It seems fine, sir.'

Fluke didn't think he'd ever heard anyone sound so miserable.

'Do you have any more questions for DI Fluke?'

Fenton looked at Fluke with genuine hatred in his eyes, and he knew he'd made an enemy for life. Fenton was renowned for holding grudges over the smallest things, and this one wasn't small. He'd had Fluke dead in the water, everyone in the room knew it. A clear disciplinary offence with, in all likelihood, criminal charges to follow. He could have taken down a detective inspector, in his eyes a massive feather in his cap.

Now he had nothing. Worse than nothing – he'd been made to look stupid.

'Not at this time, sir, although I reserve the right to re-interview him if the need arises.'

Everyone in the room knew it was a last effort at saving face. Even the sergeant with him winced in embarrassment.

'Yeah, you do that, Alex,' Chambers said. 'Now, why don't you run along and find some paperwork to shuffle? Let Avison here get on with his job.'

'Yes, sir.'

Fenton got up to leave. He was trying not to catch anyone's eye. As he walked to the door, Chambers stopped him.

'Oh, and Alex, I'll have a written apology to DI Fluke on my desk within the hour, yes?'

Fluke thought Fenton would refuse. That Chambers had pushed him that one step too far. He didn't have it in him though. He nodded once then left the room.

Chambers stood up as soon as the door shut.

'That was rather fun, I thought,' he said. He offered his hand to Fluke.

Fluke stood up and took it.

'I'm a ridiculous figure sometimes, Avison, I'm fully aware of that. But know this, I've always liked you a lot more than you think. Now, orders from the chief. You're on leave for the rest of the week. No arguments. Sergeant Towler is more than capable of coordinating what needs to happen now. Cross will be out of the country by now. Let someone else deal with him. You've come closer to catching him than at least three different intelligence agencies. You should be proud of what your team's achieved.'

At a loss for something to say, he mumbled a weak 'thank you'.

'Miss Harper-Tarr, it's been a genuine pleasure,' Chambers said, and with that, he left.

Fluke was left alone with Bridie. She busied herself with putting various papers back in her briefcase. When it was clear she wasn't going to say anything, he couldn't contain himself. 'What the hell's just happened?'

She looked up from what she was doing, smiled and said, 'I think you owe me a drink, Mr Fluke.'

Chapter 37

Fluke had some things to tie up at Carleton Hall before he could get away. Once he'd finished there, and was confident Towler had everything he needed, he went to see Chambers. He wanted to apologise for his recent behaviour.

'I can't promise not to wind you up in the future, Avison,' he said. 'I want to be chief constable one day and you don't. Sometimes we're going to see things differently.'

They were never going to be friends but it seemed there was at least the early form of a truce on the table.

He'd agreed to meet Bridie at a pub they both knew in Threlkeld, a small village just outside Keswick. She had to go to her office first to drop off some files, and as they were travelling separately anyway, Fluke decided to just head off.

With the forged letter half-resolved – he still had to see Leah – he felt as if he could relax for the first time in over a year. If it weren't for the looming threat of eviction, he might have actually smiled.

He left his phone on in case his team needed to get hold of him, but the investigation was about to go global. FMIT's part was effectively over. Towler would liaise with Interpol and make the arrangements. As soon as the intelligence community took an interest, a small rural force such as Cumbria got pushed to the sidelines.

It was four o'clock when he arrived at the Fox and Pheasant, too late for lunch but he could do with a decent coffee. He walked in and found a quiet table in the lounge bar. The barmaid walked over and pulled out her pocketbook. He ordered an Americano, black.

She wrote it down in that peculiar style left-handed people tend to have – wrist arched and twisted clockwise so she could see what she was writing. Crab claw, he thought it was called.

'The coffee machine's free so it won't be long,' she said when she'd finished.

'Thanks,' he said, frowning. For some reason it had jarred him. Then again, lots of things jarred him these days. And he was on leave now. He would make an effort to cheer up and enjoy it. He didn't get to take leave that often. He ran through the brief conversation he'd had with Bridie before she'd left. He'd asked her how she had a copy of his letter when the only hard drive it was on was back in his log cabin. She'd told him to ask Towler.

He had.

Towler, it turned out, had been contacted by Leah Cooper. She'd told him everything. She'd wanted to help. Towler had given Jiao-long Fluke's spare key and asked him to hack into his desktop computer. That was what he'd been doing when Skelton was telling Fluke about how they got the warrants for West Cumberland Hospital. It had taken Jiao-long less than two minutes to find the right file and email it to Leah. With the right text, it was a simple case of printing off an identical copy of the letter.

He felt as though both Towler and Jiao-long deserved some sort of punishment but for the life of him he couldn't think why.

Fluke had then asked Bridie about Michelle's dinner party. It was obvious she hadn't been there by accident.

Bridie had explained that Leah had been doing some match-making for her oldest friend who was sick of going out with boring men. She'd decided Fluke might just be the right man. The mysterious detective who lived alone in a wood. A man who caught killers for a living.

She'd told Bridie that he was at the wrong end of a failing relationship and that she might want to engineer a way of meeting him to see what she thought. As luck would have it, a solicitor she knew from court, a lecherous man in his fifties, had been invited to the infamous dinner party. He couldn't believe his luck when Bridie had asked to go with him. Although she'd driven them there, after the party ended, she'd told him to walk home. She wanted to give Fluke a lift. She'd enjoyed his brief company and decided she wanted to see a bit more. She'd intended to wait until the investigation was over but Leah had called and told her Fluke was in trouble. They hadn't had long to come up with a plan and, in the end, they'd called Towler for help with the letter, as she'd already explained.

Fluke had been lost for words before. This was different. A lot of people had put themselves out for him and he wasn't really sure that he deserved it.

Leah, Towler and Jiao-long had all risked their jobs. He didn't know enough about the law, but Bridie probably had too. He wondered how he'd ever pay them back.

The arrival of his coffee brought him back to the present. It was served in a huge cup, more a bowl with a handle, with a tiny Italian biscuit. A group of farmers sitting at the bar with their pints of Jennings and bowls of soup turned to look at the decidedly un-Cumbrian drink. He smiled apologetically, pointed to his keys and mimed he was driving. As one, they turned back to the bar and continued talking about whatever farmers talked about.

Fluke picked his phone up and checked his emails. There was nothing that couldn't wait. He checked his watch. Bridie wasn't due for another thirty minutes. He picked up the menu, picked out what he would have had if they'd still been serving. He put it down; all it was doing was making him hungry.

Instead, he did what he always did when he had time to kill: he people-watched. Tried to work out their stories from the context clues around him.

The three men at the bar talking about Herdwick sheep were clearly fell farmers. No challenge there. The lounge bar allowed dogs and a Border collie lay at the feet of the farmer on the left. As if the dog sensed it was being watched, it got up, stretched and wandered over to the open log fire, before slumping back down.

The only other person in the bar was the barmaid who'd taken his coffee order. She looked about sixteen but Fluke knew she was at least two years older than that. You had to be eighteen to serve alcohol in an English pub. She was wearing the required black polo shirt with the pub logo, along with a black skirt and flat black shoes. He watched as one of the farmers ordered a whisky 'for the road, lass'.

'You want to pay your tab now, Frank?'

'I'll settle up now, lass. May not have it later.'

She laughed. Fluke watched her write out their bills. Same crab-claw action. The jarring feeling was back.

She saw him staring.

'What?' she said.

Fluke said nothing. A memory was rushing back, something that had happened recently. Something to do with being left-handed. But what? To the best of his recollection he hadn't met any left-handed people recently.

Another alarm went off in his head. Something that hadn't felt right. No, something that hadn't *sounded* right. He scoured everything that had happened recently, desperately trying to make the connection. He shut his eyes to blank out all external stimuli.

The case had already thrown things at him that had been just out of his reach. The numbers on the notepad he should have recognised. The odd number of paracetamol tablets. He knew that sometimes things came to him immediately and sometimes they never came at all. Sometimes he had to simply learn to live with not knowing.

This was important though. Didn't know why, just knew it was. Something to do with being left-handed.

Why was it evoking such a strong reaction?

And why was it making him think of something that hadn't sounded right.

If he tried to focus on it, it would disappear. He would scare it away. Like all cases, clues became questions. Questions became lines of enquiry. They had been overrun with them. Clues and questions.

But few answers.

And then it happened. The debris of the collision in his mind cleared and he could see it. He could *hear* it.

But it couldn't be . . .

He reached for his phone and googled something. Desperately hoping he was wrong, knowing with absolute certainty he wasn't.

A picture came up. Fluke enlarged it. Studied the arrangements.

And there it was.

The answer.

The answer to the question no one had thought to ask.

Chapter 38

Why would a right-handed man keep his notebook on the *left* of his computer keyboard? Fluke had watched Tait write down the master-access password and he was definitely right-handed. Why make things harder for yourself?

And if you've taken a week off work to rehearse with your band, why would your guitar be so badly tuned? Unless of course the guitar Fluke had strummed wasn't badly tuned, it was just being held wrong. The guitar he'd picked up wasn't a right-handed guitar, it was a *left*-handed guitar. And that meant when he held it as a right-hander the strings were upside down. The longer and thicker bass strings were at the bottom instead of the top. A musician would have known just by looking at it but Fluke had needed to *hear* it to know it wasn't quite right.

There was no reason at all why a right-handed man would have a left-handed guitar *and* keep his trackpad and notebook on the left side of his computer keyboard.

Fluke immediately knew three things.

The man calling himself Gibson Tait was right-handed.

The *real* Gibson Tait was left-handed.

The man calling himself Gibson Tait was Dalton Cross.

By the time he'd finished processing this, he was already in his car, gunning the accelerator and roaring out of the car park. The big BMW tyres spat gravel. It rattled against the pub windows. He'd left an upturned table and a smashed coffee cup in his wake as he'd jumped to his feet and ran to his car.

The farmers and barmaid had stared at him in astonishment but he didn't care; he'd sent Jiao-long out there to take Tait's statement. And it wouldn't take Jiao-long long to work out Tait had been lying about the IT. He'd challenge him about it.

And Cross would kill him. He'd have no choice.

'Bastard!' Fluke shouted. 'Fucking bastard!'

Bassenthwaite was ten miles away from Threlkeld. After the A66, the road wasn't great; little more than a chain of blind corners.

Fluke pressed his foot to the floor and watched the needle creep up to one hundred.

When he reached the first straight bit, he took one hand off the steering wheel and autodialled the office.

Jiao-long answered.

'Longy, thank Christ!' he said, easing off the accelerator a bit. 'Listen, I need you to—'

'Boss, Gibson Tait's talking shit!' Jiao-long cut in. 'There's no such thing as a master-access level—'

'Longy—'

'And another thing, boss. Why would—'

'Longy!' Fluke shouted. 'Shut the fuck up and listen!'

As he raced along the narrow, bending road, one hand on the steering wheel, he left instructions for Jiao-long to get armed response out to Tait's house. Told him to get back to him with confirmation they were on their way.

Jiao-long got back to him in less than a minute.

'Armed response are on a joint exercise with the nuclear police, boss,' he said. 'They're leaving now but they're at least an hour away.'

Shit!

For possibly the first time in his career, Fluke wasn't sure what to do next. He knew the sensible thing would be to wait for armed response. He wasn't armed and Cross was. And even if he wasn't he doubted he would stand a chance against him. Waiting for the armed cops was undoubtedly the right thing to do.

It just didn't *feel* like the right thing to do.

He decided that a lesson learned when he was a Royal Marines Commando – time spent on reconnaissance is seldom wasted – might be the compromise he was looking for. He might be able to tell if Cross was in just by driving past his house. Could be something useful to pass on to armed response when they finally bothered showing up.

He touched the accelerator again and watched the speedometer creep back up.

His phone rang.

The caller-ID said it was Chambers. Fluke ignored it. He didn't need to speak to the superintendent to know what he was going to say.

Back off and let armed response handle it.

Fluke knew the real Gibson Tait was dead. He would have been killed sometime in the last week. Cross must have found out it had been him doing Samantha's checks on Kenneth Diamond. He'd have hoped Tait could have led him directly to Samantha, but she was far too careful for that. He'd have had no choice but to do it the hard way: abducting Diamond and forcing him to reveal where the drop was.

But when Samantha's body had been discovered he decided he needed to hang around and monitor the situation. Make sure he hadn't made any other mistakes. And while he waited, he knew of just the place to use as a base.

A small cottage in the middle of nowhere . . .

Fluke slowed as he turned onto the quiet lane where Tait's cottage was situated. Cross couldn't have picked a better place. The marine in him appreciated the location. A long drive. No obvious cover. No chance of approaching unnoticed. Thick gravel that would make a noise whether you were driving or on foot.

302

A superb defensive position.

He crawled past the entrance to the drive and surreptitiously glanced at the cottage. There were no lights on. No car in the drive.

He braked and stopped. The cottage looked empty but that didn't mean it *was* empty. But then again, if Cross was in, why would he be sitting in the dark? He didn't know they were on to him. Cross was out, Fluke was sure of it. If he could confirm that to armed response it would save a lot of nervous energy. Reduce the likelihood of an accident.

He put the car into reverse and navigated the unlit lane. Turning a hard left, he reversed up Tait's drive. If Cross came out shooting, Fluke would just duck and drive straight out.

Cross didn't come out though.

Fluke reversed all the way up to the front door. He stopped but didn't turn off the engine. He put the BMW into drive and stayed there for a full minute watching the front door through the rear-view mirror. Looking at the fully drawn curtains for a twitch. The hint of a light going on in the back of the house.

Anything to suggest Cross was inside.

There was nothing. The house remained unlit and still. He picked his phone up off the passenger seat but there was no signal. Cross had mentioned that when they'd drunk coffee together. Said he had to walk into the village for a signal.

There was no point sitting there, exposed. He had to either get out of the car and take a closer look or leave and wait for the armed cops. Let them risk their lives instead of his.

Neither option was attractive.

He punched the steering wheel, frustrated at his own indecisiveness. He was scared but that didn't bother him. A dark creepy cottage in the middle of nowhere and a deadly killer nearby. Being scared was the rational response.

He decided to back off and wait. He was about to take his foot off the brake and get out of there when he thought about what Towler would say.

'What, you didn't even go and have a fucking look? Typical fucking marine. Takes a step back when the range becomes two-way.'

He'd never live it down.

Fluke put the BMW in park and got out of the car. He left the door open and the engine on. He was stupid but he wasn't that stupid.

He opened the boot and took out a heavy-duty torch. It had been there since he'd taken delivery of the car and he'd not once used it. He pressed the on button and nothing happened.

'Damn,' he whispered to himself.

He was about to put it back when he realised that the weight of the torch was surprisingly reassuring. In a tight spot it could make an effective blunt instrument. No match for an expert with a gun but better than going inside with nothing.

He crept round the back of the cottage. Fluke knew what the back garden looked like as he'd seen it through the kitchen window. Fluke approached the window and cupped his eyes. Peered into the house. It was too dark to see anything.

He moved past the kitchen window and further into the back garden. Like the rest of Bassenthwaite's gardens, it was immaculate. Large borders, heavy with snowdrops and the green shoots of the first daffodils of the year. There was a small pond. It had a tennis ball floating in it to discourage ice, and what looked like a solar-powered fountain. Probably turned off for the dark winter months. Natural paving stones led around the outside of the lawn, providing a natural barrier between plants and grass. There were a couple of leafless fruit trees. Three or four evergreen shrubs. A wooden compost heap in the corner, full and ready for spring. The garden providing its own nourishment, year on year.

He turned and surveyed the back of the cottage. There was a set of garden furniture on the patio. A small round table and three chairs. Cast iron, painted white. Available everywhere. The table had a glass ashtray. It was full of water, stained brown by the cigarette butts floating in it.

A place to sit and relax in the evening. Much like his own.

Fluke walked back towards the house and stood in front of some patio doors. He tried looking in but again couldn't see anything in the gloom. He tried the handle gently.

It was open.

This was it. Once he was in the cottage, he was committed. If Cross was inside, there'd be no avoiding him.

He thought about Kenneth Diamond's mutilated body.

He thought about the way a beautiful young woman, criminal or not, had been discarded like a fly-tipped fridge.

And he thought about Gibson Tait. A man who'd been killed just for checking a name on a computer.

Fluke didn't want to leave Cross to someone else. He was his. He gritted his teeth and opened the door. Stepped inside the cottage.

Past the point of no return.

The lounge was empty and he walked straight through, his torch raised as if it were a police baton. He stopped at the door and listened.

The cottage remained silent.

He softly opened the lounge door and peered into the hall. He could see the kitchen but he already knew it was empty. Three other doors led from the hall. They were all closed.

Judging by the time it had taken to walk round it, it wasn't a big cottage. As it was just a single storey, Fluke guessed the closed doors led to bedrooms and a bathroom.

He walked towards the first door and put his hand on the handle. He paused. For some reason Russian roulette popped into his head. He thought about the people who played it. How they felt being an instrument in their own death, never knowing if their next action would be their last.

Fluke raised his torch and opened the door.

It was the master bedroom. A double bed, roughly made. A wardrobe and a chest of drawers with a flat-screen TV on top. The remote was on a bedside cabinet, along with a couple of books and a half-drunk glass of water. The room was otherwise empty. It was similar to his own bedroom. Functional rather than elaborate. It didn't smell musty and he guessed that it was where Cross had slept.

A small canvas bag lay on the bed. Fluke opened it. He could see clothes and three passports. He didn't pull them out and look for a gun; that was a job for a full forensic team.

One thing was obvious though. Cross hadn't left the country yet.

So where was he?

Fluke backed out into the hall and opened the second door.

It was the spare bedroom Tait had been using as a study. Nothing had changed since the last time he'd been in the room. The notebook and trackpad were still on the wrong side of the keyboard for a right-handed man.

One room to go. The bathroom. He stood in front of the door and reached for the handle.

And froze.

There was a noise. A very faint noise. The sound of material rustling. He carefully pressed his ear to the door. This time he couldn't hear anything.

He was sure he hadn't imagined it – Cross was on the other side of the door.

Waiting for him.

Fluke gripped the door handle and pulled the door towards him, made sure it couldn't be opened from the other side without a struggle. He'd been quiet searching the house but there was no way Cross wouldn't know he was there.

He'd been quiet but not *silent*.

Going back wasn't an option now. As soon as he turned his back Cross would put a bullet in the back of his head. But going forward meant coming face-to-face with a contract killer, armed with nothing more than a heavy torch.

In films where Russian roulette had been portrayed, one thing had always bothered Fluke. There had been occasions when they'd been firing a revolver and the rules of the game had not permitted re-spinning the chamber after someone's turn. Fluke had seen one film where it had fired on an empty chamber five times. The person going next had known with absolute certainty that he was about to fire a bullet into his head. Not one-in-six odds, but one-in-one. A 100 per cent chance of death. *Yet they still pulled the trigger.*

He'd never understood that.

He did now.

This was something he had to do. There was no logic to it. He could turn and run. Knew he'd have better odds of surviving if he did just that. He also knew that he was opening that door. That running had stopped being an option the moment he got out of the car.

He had to move fast. The longer he stood there, the greater the chance that Cross would simply start shooting through the flimsy wood.

He didn't want to die wondering. Fluke had been trained in room breaches and knew that going in fast and noisy was better than timidly sticking your head in. Speed, aggression, surprise. SAS. Maybe disorientate Cross for long enough to grab his gun.

It wasn't the best plan but at least he now had an objective to aim for.

Fluke silently counted down from ten, braced himself. He took a step back then shoulder barged the door. He charged in after it screaming obscenities and wildly swinging his torch.

He stopped.

The bathroom was empty.

A shower curtain flapped lazily in the breeze coming from the open window.

Fluke collapsed to the floor in relief.

After a few seconds, he reached for his phone. Still no signal.

He picked himself up and waited for his heart to stop racing. He was drenched in cold sweat. He turned on the sink's cold tap and splashed his face with water. Rubbed the back of his neck.

Breathed out in relief. His legs were wobbly, a price for the adrenalin he'd just used.

He made his way out of the cottage, using the front door, which was also unlocked.

He blinked in the bright evening sun and walked back towards his car.

And stopped.

At the end of the drive, staring at him, was Dalton Cross.

Chapter 39

Cross was on foot. He'd obviously seen Fluke's car and had parked his own out of sight. He was holding a small handgun. He was pointing it at Fluke. A two-handed grip. Steady.

He was about sixty yards away.

He walked towards Fluke.

Fluke stood still, frozen to the cold ground.

Death was on its way, he had no doubt about that. He was out of range of Cross's small handgun but the distance was closing fast. He looked at what he was carrying and laughed, the sound tinged with hysteria. Never bring a torch to a gunfight.

He needed a weapon and he needed one now.

Towler popped into his head again.

The bullet'll penetrate the skull at twenty feet but only just.

Fluke was damned if he was simply going to lie down without a fight. He wasn't pulling the trigger when he knew the chamber was loaded. There would be no Russian roulette for him.

He ran towards his car.

Cross fired. A faint pop at that distance. Fluke heard the bullet hit the stone walls of the cottage behind him and, even though he knew the bullet had already missed him, he ducked. He kept running.

Cross fired again.

Missed again.

Fluke reached the driver's side of the BMW. He dived through the open door.

Cross fired at the car. The bullet hit the windscreen but bounced off. A star-shaped chip appeared. The type TV adverts urge you to fix before icy weather turns it into a crack.

Cross must have reached the same conclusion as Towler. He lowered the gun and ran towards the car.

Fluke struggled to get himself into a driving position. The BMW was already idling.

He pressed his foot on the brake and pulled the gearstick into drive.

Cross stopped running. He paused for a second. He raised the gun again and pointed it directly at Fluke's head.

Neither of them moved.

Now it was a bit more even.

Car versus gun.

Stalemate.

Someone had to make the first move. Fluke decided it would be him.

He took his foot off the brake and slammed the accelerator to the floor.

Like all automatics there was a slight pause but the BMW was new and German engineering is unrivalled. The engine screamed as the turbo kicked in. The thick tyres bit into the gravel and the car shot forwards.

Cross didn't fire, but he didn't seem to be panicking either. He was clearly waiting for Fluke to get nearer. To get within his gun's effective range. He simply stood with his two-handed stance and waited.

The gap narrowed to forty yards.

Fluke kept accelerating.

Still Cross didn't fire.

Fluke was now close enough to see he was smiling. Looked like the bastard was enjoying himself.

It was now a test of nerves. The longer he stayed upright, the greater chance he had of hitting Cross. But it also meant there was a greater chance Cross would be close enough to finally pierce the windscreen and put a bullet in his head.

Twenty yards. Fifteen. Fluke continued to accelerate.

There was an almost imperceptible change as the automatic engine moved up a gear. Fluke kept his eyes fixed on Cross, his right foot pressed to the floor.

Ten yards.

He was now in Cross's effective range.

A flash from the gun's muzzle and a hole appeared in the windscreen. The bullet grazed Fluke's ear. A sharp burning pain, instantly forgotten.

Fluke braced himself as Cross's face filled his vision. The smile still etched onto his face. A split-second before impact, he tried to dive out of the way.

He was too late.

Far too late.

Fluke felt the sickening thump as the car smashed into him.

He heard a scream of pain as Cross was thrown in the air like a discarded ragdoll, arms and legs flailing helplessly.

The BMW kept moving forwards. He watched the airborne Cross smash off the windscreen and disappear behind him.

And still the BMW moved forwards, bouncing uncontrollably on the uneven drive. Fluke's visibility was virtually zero, the windscreen white with cracks. He leaned back in the seat and braked hard.

Nothing happened. He was going far too fast for the tyres to grip the loose gravel.

Time slowed as he went into an uncontrollable skid.

Fluke looked up.

The stone pillars either side of Tait's drive filled his vision. The car was still going forty miles an hour as it glided towards the one on the left. Fluke wrenched the steering wheel to the right but it was useless.

It was like driving on sheet ice.

He flung his arms in front of his face as the car smashed into the pillar.

The BMW had crumple zones designed to absorb some of the impact of a car crash. The bumper and grille collapsed immediately.

The rest of the car wrapped itself around the slate pillar. The sound of metal and stone was deafening. The forward momentum caused the rear of the car to lift off the ground.

Milliseconds after impact, the airbags deployed, the hard plastic cover in the steering wheel striking Fluke in the face, breaking his nose instantly.

Fluke's torso, cushioned slightly by the airbag, struck the steering column but his unrestrained head kept moving forwards. It bounced off the broken windscreen.

He started to lose consciousness.

He felt the rear wheels fall back to the ground. The car's ruined engine finally gave in and stopped. Fluke could hear it tick as it cooled.

Jumping into the car to coming to a dead stop had taken less than ten seconds.

Fluke fought to stay awake.

There was an unwelcome smell. Burning rubber and diesel. Even this close to passing out, he knew the BMW was on fire.

He had avoided being shot but he was going to burn to death instead. As his brain started to close down, Fluke had an auditory hallucination.

The sound of men shouting something he didn't understand.

'Armed police! Armed police! Armed police!'

Chapter 40

At the third attempt, and only after adding a full can of lighter fuel, Fluke managed to light the fire pit. Flames shot up into the clear winter sky. He could smell his own eyebrows.

Abi cheered.

'What are we doing, lighting a fire or summoning the Rohirrim?' Bridie asked.

'Ha, ha,' Fluke answered with a smile. Sarcasm *and* knowledge of *Lord of the Rings*. There were worse character traits.

He lowered the mesh lid, gently pulled Abi away from the flames, and sat in one of the chairs surrounding the fire. With his good hand, he reached forwards and enjoyed the heat.

'How's the arm, Ave?' Towler asked.

'Better. Can't say the same for the nose. Still hurts when I breathe through it.'

Apart from the broken nose and a badly sprained wrist, it was only the cuts from the broken glass that had caused him any problems. He'd needed several pints of plasma to stop the bleeding but Leah had been waiting in A & E when he arrived, and despite the protests from the trauma consultant, had overseen his immediate care. All things considered, Fluke had come out of the crash relatively unscathed.

A veteran of countless broken noses, Towler said, 'It'll get better, probably be another week.'

A silence settled over them. Even Abi seemed to sense it was time to be quiet.

They'd discussed the remnants of the case before they sat down for a winter barbecue. Cross had been badly injured but had survived.

'Typical marine, can't even crash into someone properly,' Towler had said.

Fluke nodded. He felt the same way. Cross had got off lightly. Far more lightly than the real Gibson Tait. He'd been found in his own compost heap. A .22 bullet hole in the middle of his forehead.

'Looks like he's going to get away with it,' he said.

Bridie and Towler looked at him with a start.

'You gonna tell us what happened then?' Towler was the only one who knew Fluke had spoken to Cross.

It was a concession the chief had secured before he was extradited back to the States. He'd had to make a full statement detailing the crimes committed while in the UK and the chief had argued that Fluke was the only one who'd be able to tell if he was leaving things out.

'Not really supposed to, Matt.'

'And?'

Fluke grinned. He'd already told Jo Skelton, Jiao-long and Alan Vaughn.

Fluke had woken in Cumberland Infirmary with a headache that only morphine could dampen. Leah had been there within five minutes of him waking; business-like as there was actual work to do. Towler had been second through the door. He'd told Fluke that Cross was on the floor below. Two broken legs, a cracked spine and severe concussion. Everything else had been superficial. He'd probably limp for the rest of his life but otherwise he was expected to make a full recovery.

'Has anyone interviewed him?' Fluke had asked.

'You're fucking joking, aren't you? No one's getting in to see him. It's all gone political. We have no chance of getting in. The

Yanks want him isolated. Reckon he's a threat to national security. Cousin-shagging wankers.'

Bridie had arrived within the hour.

'All you had to do was say "no" if you didn't want to go out, Avison,' she said, her grin hiding genuine concern. 'You didn't have to go to such extreme measures.'

Within a week, he was discharged. Instead of going home as directed, he'd driven straight to HQ and entered the chief's office without knocking.

'Ah, Avison,' he said. 'Right on time.' He was sitting at a table with Chambers and a man in a suit he didn't recognise. 'I was telling Mr Mortimer here that you wouldn't do as you were told and would be on your way here instead.'

The man in the suit stood up and offered his hand. Fluke awkwardly reached with his left. His right arm was still too sore.

'Mr Mortimer was just laying out the ground rules for your interview with Cross.'

'Sir?' Fluke said.

'What? You didn't think we'd let him out the country without getting something back, did you? The Home Secretary might bend over for the Americans, but we won't. Part of the extradition agreement is that he makes a full statement of what he did here. If he misses anything out then he stays. He thinks he can cut a deal over there so he's pretty keen to get back, as you might imagine.'

Fluke looked at Mortimer. He didn't look happy. Fluke realised he hadn't been told who he worked for. One of the intelligence agencies, then.

'Mr Mortimer will sit in with you. If Cross tries to tell you anything about his life before he got here, the interview will be terminated.'

'Why me, sir? Why not a spook?'

'You're the only one who'll know if he's missing something out.

We are only being allowed to speak to him the once; we have to get it right first time.'

In the end, it had been easy. Eager to make sure his extradition didn't fall through, Cross was keen to talk.

He was being held in a secure hospital room in the Cumberland Infirmary. Armed guards were outside the door. He was immobile but alert. One of his wrists was handcuffed to the metal bed frame.

Fluke took a seat near the bed. Mortimer took one near the door.

'Who hired you?' Fluke said.

Cross told him.

It was as he'd suspected. A nobody thinking he was a somebody. A 'dot.com' millionaire who couldn't stand losing. He'd been a victim of a Samantha sting. Instead of taking the easily affordable option of paying, he'd tried to kill her at the drop. She wasn't as helpless as she looked though and 'dot.com' lost an eye in the ensuing melee.

With her card marked in the States, she'd fled to the UK. Cross had been hired by 'dot.com' to find and terminate her. His fee had been ten times what Samantha had asked for.

The FBI had already arrested 'dot.com'. Some of the crimes in the case had been committed in the States. Cross had recorded all his meetings with 'dot.com' and he'd been charged with soliciting murder. He'd never see the light of day again.

'How'd you find her?' Fluke asked. 'She'd changed her appearance. You had no idea what she looked like.'

'No. But I knew what she did. As long as she kept on doing it I knew I'd catch up with her. It's what I do: I find people and I kill them. It was time-consuming but the result was inevitable.'

'I want more details,' Fluke said.

Cross said nothing.

'If I walk, the deal's off,' Fluke said. 'You can rot here. See how you like British prisons. No conjugal visits here.'

'Empty threat, Mr Fluke. We both know as soon as I can walk, I'm going home.'

Fluke stood up.

'We're done here.'

Cross sighed.

'I knew she was in the UK. I came over and started tracking her. I monitored police databases for drugged rapes, ones where the victim had disappeared. Every time I found one I had someone search your systems for me. I was looking for name searches in the same town with no hits. It was laborious but, eventually, I found one of her victims. He refused to speak to me, but at least I knew my methods were working. The next victim I found was in Birmingham, the one after that in Glasgow. All rich men with too much to lose.'

Fluke sat back down and nodded. It was a variation on how he'd thought it had happened. He understood how Cross had tracked down old victims. He didn't yet know how he'd managed to get ahead of her though.

Cross got to that part next.

'The next man I spoke to was a landowner in Norwich. Landed gentry, I think you call them. He was with her when she got a phone call. Before she could hide the screen he'd seen the number. He recognised it as a Cumbrian area code: 01539 apparently. Kendal. He knew the code because he has a friend up there he goes grouse shooting with.'

'So?'

'So. What if this was her researching a potential victim? She must select them somehow. She'd get most of her intel before she arrives in a city. That's how I'd do it anyway.'

'So you came to Cumbria to look for her?'

'How do you catch a ghost, Mr Fluke?'

Fluke shrugged.

'You can't,' he said. 'The only way is to wait for the ghost to come to you. So yes, I came to Cumbria. A calculated risk but I had nothing else to go on. Nothing at all. This had been the only slip she'd made and even then it could've meant nothing. I monitored all drug-assisted rape allegations up here through a contact I made in your police force, hoping for a break.'

'Gibson Tait?'

'No, not Gibson Tait. He was *her* contact. I had someone else. I don't think they even knew they were breaking the law.'

'And she did go back to work?' Fluke said.

'Yes. A rape, drug-assisted, was reported. The victim couldn't remember her attacker. It fit the profile. I now just needed to identify him before she could get paid. Before she became invisible again.'

'Bit of a stretch,' Fluke said.

'I could only work with what I knew about her. What I knew about her methods.'

'How'd you find him?' Fluke knew how FMIT did it but it wouldn't have worked for Cross. They found Samantha first, but he'd have needed to find Kenneth Diamond to find Samantha.

'I persuaded my man to search your PNC to see who'd made searches without hits. Searches for men in Cumbria who weren't on the computer.'

Fluke understood. Samantha had asked Gibson Tait to see if Kenneth Diamond was on the PNC. He wasn't, but the computer recorded the search anyway. Cross had simply got someone to check who was looking at names without results. He could probably narrow it down to a couple of days before the rape was reported. Fluke knew Samantha had asked Tait for one final check to make sure nothing had changed.

Cross continued and confirmed Fluke's suspicions. 'There were eight names in the period I specified. I spoke to four of them. Pretended I was a detective from the rape team. The first three didn't know anything.'

Shit. Fluke remembered getting an email a few days ago about a man impersonating a police officer investigating a rape. Two separate complaints if he remembered correctly. Nothing had been stolen and CID hadn't been putting too many resources into it. Fluke hadn't given it a second thought.

'The fourth man was Kenneth Diamond. As soon as I explained what I was there for I knew it was him. He tried to tell me he was being blackmailed and that he was innocent. I removed him from his property without difficulty; he thought he was being arrested. I took him to the empty house next door and into a cellar they used to store cheap wine.'

'You tortured him.'

'I got what I needed.'

'You're a psychopath.'

'Probably,' Cross conceded. 'But I needed reliable information quickly, I didn't have the time to finesse it out of him. Samantha didn't wait long to get paid. She approached her victims, demanded cash and expected it straight away. I needed to get to the drop before her.'

Fluke reached for the water jug and poured himself a glass.

'Kenneth Diamond told me he was a powerful man, although I've since found out that it's his youngest son who leads the organisation. He threatened me, he begged me. He told me his family were out looking for her too, and I knew she'd disappear if those idiots got within a mile of her. I had to be sure he was telling me the truth first time. I was only going to get one chance at this.'

Fluke's jaw tightened. Nathaniel Diamond was anything but an idiot. If he ever found out who'd killed his father he didn't think there was a cave dark enough or a safe house so remote that he wouldn't find Cross.

'You smashed his feet and knees with a hammer. You crushed his testicles. All you had to do was tell him you had a shared goal. He'd have told you all you needed to know.'

319

'I did and he did.'

Cross was showing no remorse. He'd stopped smiling at least. He was explaining it the way a TV repairman might explain why a diode wasn't working correctly. Calmly, using small words.

'As soon as I showed him my Ruger, he told me everything I needed.'

'So why torture him? You don't strike me as a sadist. Psychotic, obviously, but you seem to be in control.'

'I think you know the answer, Mr Fluke.'

'Humour me or humour Durham nick for the next forty years. Your choice.'

Cross raised his eyebrows and rolled his eyes.

'Very well. When I found Diamond, I was improvising. He threatened me with his criminal underworld contacts so I decided to make it look exactly like that. An underworld execution. If you hadn't found Samantha, you would have looked no further than a drugs connection. You certainly wouldn't have linked it with a rape allegation.'

'What about Tait though? You used the same gun. We were bound to link them. He's not involved in the same business as Diamond,' Fluke said.

'I'll help you there, Mr Fluke. I hadn't decided what to do with him, that's the simple truth. I considered setting him up for Diamond but couldn't make it work. I could have made him disappear for a while but someone would have started looking eventually. In the end I put him in the compost heap to hide the smell. You found Samantha shortly after and I decided moving him was too dangerous. I waited to see how close you were getting. And then you came knocking. You've no idea how close I came to killing you. How'd you like my English, by the way? Courtesy of the CIA linguistics department.'

'Stay on topic, Cross,' Mortimer warned. The first thing he'd said during the whole interview.

Cross ignored him. 'I got through your interview with my fake accent and a bit of computer nonsense. I knew it wouldn't hold, though, and that I'd have to leave.'

'What did Diamond tell you?' Fluke said, deciding that he needed to move on.

'Everything.'

'Talk me through it.'

'You already know. She phoned him. Told him that she'd reported him for rape. Laid out all the evidence the police had and explained the only thing they didn't have was his name. Fifty thousand pounds would make the whole thing go away. Told him she'd ring with the where and when.'

'He had that kind of cash?'

'Not to hand, no, but his family did and, in the meantime, they went looking for her. He put his son in charge of finding her. I don't know what their intentions were but I suspect her passing would have been cruel and unusual compared to mine. I took Diamond's phone and when she rang it was me she spoke to, not him. I'm good at accents.'

'She told you where she wanted the money?'

'She did. I had an hour to get there and set up observation. I only had one chance. If I failed, she'd never have resurfaced.'

'Where was the meeting?'

'The library in the mall in Carlisle. If you can call something so small a mall.'

The Lanes was Carlisle's indoor shopping centre. Not big compared to other towns and cities but it had a reasonable selection of cafés and shops. It was also home to the council-run library. A decent place for a cash drop. Busy but not crowded. Large windows covering the main approach. Fire exits that led to the shopping centre but also into the delivery areas.

'You got there first?'

'Oh no. She was good. She would've already been there. That's where she would've called from. She'd have been able to slip out quietly if she sensed trouble. If Diamond turned up with help or the police showed.'

'So how did you get in without her seeing? You didn't even know what she looked like.'

'I didn't know what she looked like but I still knew *what* I was looking for. I also knew what I'd have done. All I had to do was cover the exit she'd use. No way would she leave by the main exit. If there was someone waiting, that's where she'd have expected it. She'd be slipping out through the staff exit, into the delivery areas. I waited there for her.'

'And?'

'Fifteen minutes after the agreed time, she came out. She was good. Very good. I nearly lost her twice, but I was better, it seemed. I've been trained to follow the best.'

He paused and looked at Mortimer.

'Sorry,' he said. 'Bit too much information again, Mr Fluke. Where were we? Ah yes, she was careful but I followed her home. I watched her flat all night and all the next day.'

Fluke hadn't yet made any notes. Up to then, everything Cross said fitted with the facts.

'I waited until she went out. I got into her flat quickly enough. I avoided the crude anti-intruder alert under her doormat and the lock wasn't challenging. I waited in her living room. Two hours later, she came back. She came in carefully but the potato chip under the mat was undisturbed. She wasn't expecting anyone. She ground some coffee and filled her filter machine. She came into the living room while she waited for it. I treated her with respect. She was dead before she knew I was there. One shot to the back of the head. I caught her before she fell. No noise.'

Fluke had heard nothing comparable before. He'd heard killers confess. Normally crimes committed in anger or passion. The perpetrator wanting to talk, to get it off their chest. Sometimes he'd heard confessions from murderers whose lies had pushed them into such tight corners, they only had the truth left. Cross was different. He could have been telling him how he got rid of the weeds in his lawn. Descriptive rather than emotive. No pride, no remorse.

He was just describing what happened.

'You've seen the golf bag I'd brought with me,' he continued. 'Marvellous invention for my trade. No more rolled-up carpets for contract killers.'

He smiled. Fluke didn't join in.

'When did you write down your blood test results?' Fluke said.

Cross looked surprised.

'So that's how you found me? I was wondering about that. I got the phone call when I was waiting in her flat. Jotted them down, more habit than anything else. I'm cured now. Well, in remiss—'

'You transported her body in Diamond's car?' Fluke cut in. He didn't care about Cross's health.

He looked mildly hurt. 'No, Gibson Tait's.'

There was a natural pause in the conversation.

Cross spoke again. 'How *did* you find her, by the way? I've been doing this a long time and not once has a body been found that wasn't supposed to be. And not once did I have anywhere as good a place as that.'

It wasn't quid pro quo. Cross could die wondering.

'Why does it matter?' he said. 'We found her.'

'Call it professional curiosity.'

Fluke ignored him.

Cross looked thoughtful.

'There must have been a witness,' he said finally. 'It can't have been that boy who lived opposite her. He didn't see me, I know that. Even if he did, he didn't know where I was going. It could only have been someone on the site. It must have been that office.'

Fluke said nothing.

323

'Oh, well. Sloppy work on my part but I thought the site was ironclad. No way was she being found. At least not until she became an archaeological curiosity.'

He reached for his glass of water. Because of the angle of the handcuffs, he struggled to get a proper drink. He coughed. Fluke thought the restraints were a bit of overkill but it was pointless asking for them to be loosened. Cross didn't deserve his sympathy anyway.

Fluke yawned, a big one that he couldn't stop. He hadn't realised how tired he was.

'Who was your contact in the police?' he said.

Cross gave him a name that meant nothing to him. For the first time, he made a note. It would be someone for the team to arrest later.

Mortimer looked at his watch and stood up. 'Time's up, Inspector. You got everything you need?'

'One more thing, Mr Mortimer.' He turned to Cross. 'Do you know who she was? What her real name was? Where she was from?'

Cross looked at Fluke. 'I have no idea. I told you she was a ghost. English is my bet. Scared people flee to where they feel safe. In my experience that's somewhere they know.'

Fluke had expected that. He suspected her real identity would always remain hidden. It didn't matter; he'd always remember her as Samantha.

'That it?' Mortimer said.

'For now.'

Cross smirked.

'There is no *for now*, Mr Fluke. This is it. As soon as I can get on a plane, I'm out of this shithole of a country. Time to get Stateside, see what type of deal they're offering.'

'Waterboarding and black sites would be my guess,' Fluke said.

'Ah, Mr Fluke, but you don't know what I know. I have things my country wants and I only want my freedom in return. And access to my money, of course. They'll deal, we both know that.' He smirked again. 'You never know, we may meet again one day.'

Fluke turned and walked out.

'Nice place you have here,' Bridie said. The first thing anyone had said since Fluke had finished telling them about his interview with Cross.

She was hugging her knees to her chest and staring into the fire. She wore a black vest and her tattooed arms seemed to be alive as the flames danced in the darkness. Her skin was a creamy white. She was beautiful. More *Guns & Ammo* than *Vogue* but stunning nonetheless.

He nodded sadly. 'Yep. Not sure for how long though.'

She raised her eyebrows.

'Oh?' she said.

Fluke explained the situation with his illegally built cabin. To his surprise, she laughed.

'Is that all? I thought you were going to say something serious.'

'It is serious,' he protested. 'I've got a court date.'

She burst out laughing.

'You've just singlehandedly taken out an international assassin and you're worried about the county council. You crack me up, Avison.'

'You think he has a case?' Towler asked.

She stopped laughing. 'You're serious? Are you telling me the pair of you have been worrying about this?'

Fluke nodded. Towler did the same.

'Listen. I think I can handle the county council's planning department.'

'Yeah, you do international law. This is local. It's different,' Fluke said.

'The only thing that's different is that they're terrified of a court

325

case with someone who knows what they're doing. They can't afford it for one thing. I'll send them a letter first thing tomorrow saying I'm representing you, and I've instructed Mr Tinnings to act on our behalf.'

'Who?' Towler asked.

'My secret weapon. A barrister friend of mine in London who owes me a favour. Charges ten thousand pounds a day.'

'I can't afford that!' Fluke said.

Bridie smiled. 'We won't need him. Just the name will terrify them. They can't risk losing and having to pay his fees.'

She looked at them both.

'The law's not always about who's right and who's wrong,' she said. 'Sometimes it's about who has the most to lose. And anyway, I've only just got here. You think I'm letting them take it away? Not a chance.'

She smiled at Fluke.

They fell into silence once more. Fluke felt a weird peace settle over him. He might even sleep tonight, he thought.

Abi broke the silence. 'What's a stalker?' she asked.

'Where did you hear that word, Abi?' Fluke asked.

'Daddy says that Bridie's yours.'

What could have been an uncomfortable silence was broken by Bridie roaring with laughter. Before long, Fluke had joined in. Towler, embarrassed, eventually grinned as well.

'Yes, I am, Abi. Your daddy's right,' Bridie said when she'd stopped laughing.

Fluke offered Towler a cigar and they lit up. A sense of peace settled over them all.

'This is beautiful,' Bridie said. 'I bet you get a different view every day. It's a shame about that dead tree there, if you took it down you'd have an uninterrupted view across the lake. I have a friend who's a tree surgeon. She'd take it down for you for a cup of tea. I'll give her a call if you want.'

This time it was Fluke and Towler who laughed and Bridie who looked confused.

'You want to tell her why we can't chop that tree down, Abi?' Towler said.

'That tree?' she said, pointing. 'That's where Owly McOwlface lives.'

She giggled delightedly at Bridie's obvious astonishment.

'There's a tawny owl that lives there. He's out hunting at the minute but he'll be back later,' Fluke said. 'He's out getting a nice fat mouse for Abi's dinner.'

'Yuk,' she shrieked.

Fluke got up to pour more wine. Towler put his hand over his glass.

'Driving, mate.'

As they sipped their drinks and looked out across the lake and fells, it dawned on Fluke that Bridie hadn't covered her glass. He already knew she didn't drink and drive. She must be planning to stay the night. Apparently Towler had come to the same conclusion. He tipped Fluke a crude wink.

Bridie looked at Fluke and raised her glass in his direction. He looked back at her and raised his own.

In the distance, an owl hooted.

Epilogue

Six weeks later, HMP Durham

Dalton Cross was wearing a suit. He was still on crutches but he was fit to fly. He was being held in HMP Durham while a specially chartered flight was arranged.

'Cross. This way, please. Grab your things. Follow me!' the prison officer barked.

He picked up a bag containing prison issue toiletries, blankets and a pillow and followed the prison officer.

'Now, you've been told that our remand wing is full? You're going to have to go onto general population with convicted prisoners for now. We're putting you on the lifer wing as it's a bit calmer. And remember, you're still a remand prisoner so you still have remand rights. You can wear your own clothes, you're entitled to more phone calls and more visits. You can spend more money. With any luck, you'll be where you need to be by the end of the week.'

Cross wasn't worried. He'd been in worse places than this and he'd be back in the States within the week. He hadn't been lying to Fluke. He had information he hadn't told anyone about yet. More than enough for a deal. He had passports and funds tucked away in case of emergencies. If he played it right, he might even get a nice CIA pension.

The wing he was brought onto wasn't new. It actually looked like how a film company imagined a prison wing would look. Still, he wasn't expecting to be there long and, anyway, it was better than that gulag in the Ukraine he'd once spent a month in.

The prison officer stopped outside a cell halfway down one of the landings. He took a bunch of keys out of a leather pouch on his belt and unlocked the door. He stepped aside and waited for Cross to walk in.

'There's a button to call if you need something. This red one here. Press it for anything less than a fire and you're in the shit. We're locked down for the night. Your breakfast's in the bag you've just been given. Eat it tonight and you go hungry in the morning. Don't eat it tonight and someone'll try to take it off you. Your choice. Doors will be unlocked at eight a.m. Sleep well, Cross.'

He watched the heavy door clang shut. A sound only a prison door can make. A sound that made good men despair and brave men cry.

Cross smiled. This was going to be easy.

He turned and surveyed his cell. To his surprise he wasn't alone.

Someone was getting up from the bottom bunk. A small, shaven-headed man. He was wearing a pair of shorts and nothing else. Crude tattoos covered his body. He had the look of a man who'd spent a lifetime in institutions.

'Nice place you have here,' Cross said. He might be on crutches but he was still capable enough to put the idiot down if he tried anything.

The man smiled. 'Want a brew, mate?' he said. He had a thick Geordie accent.

With nothing else going on, he said 'Yes'.

While the man busied himself making the drinks with the in-cell kettle, Cross put his meagre belongings on the top bunk and tried to put the sheets on the rubber mattress. They seemed too small and he eventually gave up.

'Here ya gan, mate,' the man said.

Cross turned and reached for the drink he was being offered.

Before he could take it, the man hurled it at him. It struck him on the bridge of his nose. The cup smashed.

Cross screamed.

Boiling water covered his face. Some went down his throat and he instinctively swallowed. Excruciating pain exploded in every nerve ending. He tried to wipe it off but something wasn't right. It was sticky. Sticky and blistering-hot. Even through the pain, he knew what it was.

Sugar and boiling water.

Prison napalm.

The front of his face melted. He tried to scream again. Nothing happened. The liquid had scorched through his vocal cords. His throat swelled and he gasped for breath. He clawed at his face, tried to remove the terrible mask he was now wearing, the mask that was eating his face.

The vision in his left eye darkened as the red-hot sugar bit into his eyeball. He heard it pop and it went black. He fell to the floor, still frantically tearing at his face.

He was completely incapacitated.

The man stood over him, watching calmly.

Cross could see he was holding something. Even with only one eye, he recognised what it was.

A prison shank.

The one in the man's hand was crude but deadly. He tried to get up so he could reach the red panic button. The man was on him before he could even get to his knees.

The man held the sharpened toothbrush so Cross could see it clearly.

'What do you want?' Cross tried to rasp through his ruined vocal chords. His voice was barely a whisper.

Still the man didn't say anything.

Cross saw rather than felt the first blow. He thought he might have just been punched until he felt a warmness that could only be blood. The pain of the wound wasn't able to compete with his burning face. Half a dozen quick stabs followed. All in the same place. Not deep, but deep enough.

He tried to say something, anything, but the words wouldn't form. He stared at the man with his one good eye. The man looked down without expression.

He showed Cross the toothbrush shank up close. Cross shrank back as it was held up to his eye. It was razor sharp and bloodied. Beyond fear, he watched as the man lowered the shank to his throat. He felt it press into his skin, just hard enough to break it.

'I'm going to kill you now, Mr Cross,' the man said.

He gently but firmly pushed the sharpened toothbrush into Cross's neck. He felt it pierce his skin and flesh before finally meeting resistance in the muscular wall of the great jugular vein.

The man grunted and he plunged the shank in. Cross felt warm liquid gush around the wound. His shirt was drenched in seconds. He immediately felt weak and lightheaded.

His bowel and bladder emptied.

The man removed the shank and watched as he died.

Cross had cut enough throats to know his wound was fatal. Of all the places he thought he might die, on the floor of an English prison cell, drenched in his own piss, hadn't even come close.

When his heart struggled to find enough blood to keep him alive, he went into the first stages of cardiac arrest. Death was coming, he knew that.

Not minutes away, seconds away.

The man leaned over him and whispered into his ear.

'Nathaniel Diamond says hello.'

Enjoyed *Born in a Burial Gown*? Check out book two in
M. W. Craven's Avison Fluke series: the gritty and thrilling
Body Breaker.

Read on for a sneak peek ...

Prologue

Although only one was needed, two men carried the coffin. They walked slowly, concentrating on not getting under each other's feet, tears streaming down their faces. These men were no undertaker's lackeys, paid cash-in-hand as and when required; these men knew the family.

They struggled with their grim task; the smallest coffins really *are* the heaviest.

The funeral cortège silently followed them. There was a pause as the few with foresight put up their umbrellas. It had been overcast, but dry, when they'd entered the church an hour earlier, and the thick walls and high roof had muted the sounds of heavy rain.

The woman was the last to leave the sanctuary.

She had stayed behind to have a quiet word with her God. Despite all that had happened, she remained devout. Her husband was waiting for her. He raised his eyebrows and offered her his umbrella. She stopped him with a small smile and a shake of her head. Together they joined the procession taking their child to his open grave.

The moment she left the shelter of the church she was drenched. Her hair became plastered to her skull, her light makeup ran. The rain bounced off the earthen path and before long her shoes and stockings were spattered with mud.

She didn't notice.

Her husband held her as they crossed the uneven graveyard to the pitifully small, dark slash in the ground.

The priest waited, head bowed.

As soon as they arrived the committal began.

'Fear not; I am the first and the last. I am he that liveth, and was dead; and behold, I am alive for evermore . . .'

She barely heard the familiar words, words that had offered succour in the past but did little to quell the burning rage she felt. A rage that would take her back to places in her past.

Dark places.

She made no attempt to rub away her tears. Her husband reached into his pocket and offered her his handkerchief. She ignored him.

Over one hundred mourners had gathered around the open grave. Standing in solidarity with her. She appreciated the gesture, and would thank them all later, but the intense feeling of isolation was overwhelming.

Her son had died while she'd slept peacefully.

She didn't know if he'd cried out or struggled for breath. She didn't know if he'd been scared, if he'd cried for his mother. That morning she'd woken in a bright and sunny room, far brighter than her bedroom usually was. She'd looked at her bedside clock and been shocked at the time. Nearly eight o'clock. He'd never let her sleep so late before. Instinctively, she'd known something was wrong and ran to his room.

He was already cold.

From the moment she'd touched his cold hands, a piece of her was missing. She was in raw, excruciating pain but felt hollow at the same time. Since his death, her body had been encased in a relentless fatigue, but restorative sleep felt like cheating and she embraced the exhaustion like an old friend. Sitting in his bedroom for hours at a time, she would read from books she'd bought for when he was old enough to have bedtime stories. Other times she would play with his toys. Most of the time, however, she would simply sit and try to remember him. What he smelled like. How soft his skin had been. The sound of his cries and of his giggles.

She embraced the demons that came at night just as she embraced the clumsy friends who came during the day. They arrived with food she didn't eat and cards she didn't open. They left as soon as they could and soon found reasons to stay away, some even crossing the street to avoid her. She neglected her appearance and wore the same clothes for days; the world of vivid colours she'd shared with her son became drab and grey.

When she lost her child she lost her future. She grieved for the lost dreams she'd had for him, for the unfulfilled potential and for the experiences they would never share. The pain she felt was now a part of her. It would define who she was.

It would define who she had to become.

Again.

The coroner had ruled her son had died from natural causes, and although she'd been told that nobody was to blame, she knew otherwise. As she stood on the wet, hallowed earth, she looked to the east.

To where those responsible lived.

As the interment neared its end, the rage she'd felt for days left her, replaced by a cold chill. Some mothers set up foundations in their dead child's name.

This woman had other plans.

One man stood apart from the funeral party. He had never known her son, hadn't seen her for twenty years. But when she called, he came. He hadn't made his presence known yet, but he knew she'd know he was there.

Waiting.

He left her alone with her grief although she never left his sight. He would wait until she was ready. There was no hurry.

3

The priest said the last words with a grim finality. A few quiet handshakes and the crowd began to disperse, anxious to get out of the rain but not wanting to rush off and leave the woman. She turned to her husband and spoke a few words of comfort to him. She nodded and he joined the group who were now getting into black funeral cars.

As rainwater streamed from her sodden hair, she stared at the handcrafted wooden casket, partially hidden in the shadows of the grave. It was raining and her son was in the ground.

Eventually only she and the man remained in the graveyard.

She turned.

Ready to command him.

Chapter 1

Detective Inspector Avison Fluke knelt on the third green of Cockermouth Golf Course and pressed his ear against the closely mown grass. 'Thrombosis Hill' was one of the most difficult holes on the course. It had an uphill approach and a fast, undulating green. From his worm-eye view he could see breaks to the left and to the right. As today was the monthly medal competition, the grain of the grass had been cut back to front, making downhill putts even more treacherous.

The lip of the cup was directly in front of him. There were three markers within two yards of the hole, indicating where balls had been removed to avoid distracting the man putting.

Lying on its side, just off the green, was the flag. The group had removed it as they'd lined up their putts. Hitting the flag when putting meant a two-stroke penalty.

As well as the three markers, there was a ball on the green and it was this that interested Fluke. It was the reason he and the rest of the Force Major Incident Team, FMIT, were there.

The golfer taking the shot had faced three challenges. First was the downhill putt on a green that had been cut closer than marble. The type of putt even pros dreaded. Second, he was on the biggest break on the green. He would have needed to aim at least a yard to the left of the hole to compensate for the slope and, on this green in particular, anything more than a cup to the left or right was guesswork.

However, it was the third challenge that had caused the day's

5

problem, and the reason Fluke was now getting grass stains all over his suit.

Because lying on the green, directly in between ball and hole, was a severed human hand.

Fluke stood and brushed grass clippings from his knees. A green stain remained.

He looked down the hill to where DS Matt Towler was speaking to the golfers who had discovered the hand. If they weren't involved, and if it hadn't been left behind by the group playing ahead of them, then it had been placed there by someone else and, on monthly medal day, the time window between one group leaving the green and the next approaching was narrow. No more than two minutes. Probably less.

Fluke looked at the back of the green. There was a path and a dry stone wall. Was it possible someone had hidden behind it, and nipped onto the green? He walked up to the wall and peered into a farmer's field. A Herdwick sheep stared back.

Someone *could* have hidden behind the wall, waited for one group to leave the green, then nipped out before the next group arrived. He looked beyond the third and fourth holes, however, and saw a problem. The farmer's field was in the centre of a U-shaped part of the course. The golfers on the third and fourth holes might not have been able to see behind the wall but, due to the course's natural elevation, Fluke could see at least four holes on the back nine that had a clear view of the field and anyone in it.

A noise from behind made him turn. Towler had finished with the group playing the green and had joined him.

'You thinking it was thrown from behind there, boss?'

'Too exposed,' he said. He pointed at the group Towler had just finished with. 'What's the consensus? Still saying it came from above?' He frowned as he said it; body parts didn't just fall from the sky.

6

'Yep. They all swear it wasn't there when they arrived. Geoff Yates,' – Towler pointed towards a middle-aged man sitting on a golf bag – 'says he was lining up his putt when it just landed in front of him. Said he almost shat himself.'

Cockermouth was an affluent market town so the golf club wouldn't be short of professional, middle-class members. He'd be prepared to bet, on a Saturday, in this weather, at least five doctors would be out on the course at any one time. A prank, that was a possible explanation. Someone who had access to medical waste who thought it might be a bit of a laugh. Probably hadn't expected a team of detectives to take it so seriously. It was a flawed theory; it didn't explain why, after the joke was over, they hadn't picked it back up and got on with their round. No one would have been any the wiser.

'You think he's telling the truth?'

Towler looked back down the hill and shrugged. 'He seems a decent enough bloke. Semi-retired. Been a member here for years and plays at least three times a week.'

'But we have no one who can verify he didn't take it from his pocket and put it there?'

'You want me to bring him in?'

'We'll have to. Don't arrest him though. Take him to Workington nick and make sure we get his clothes and his golf bag. If he brought the hand with him, that's where he'd have kept it. Get statements off the others then let them go.'

Fluke watched Towler walk back down the hill. Two uniformed officers had turned up to help although, in truth, the course was emptying. Those behind the group playing the third had either gone home or were back in the clubhouse, and those playing ahead of them were on the back nine by now.

He wasn't sure the green was a crime scene yet. If it were a practical joke then he'd pass it on to local CID. He wanted to be sure though; someone was very definitely missing a hand.

He bent down for a closer look. Like a child demonstrating what a dead spider looked like, it was lying palm up. The index finger was raised slightly higher than the rest as if the hand was flipping him the bird. One final, desperate act of defiance.

The hand wasn't in good shape. There were bloodless puncture wounds on the palm. Possibly defensive wounds? Too small for a knife. Maybe a screwdriver? It had been removed from the arm at the wrist. Not hacked off; the cut was clean but not so clean it looked surgical. More of a butcher's cut than a surgeon's. Fluke bent down and sniffed. He couldn't smell chemicals. If anything, he smelled putrefaction. The hand was rotten, like bad meat.

He was interrupted by the sound of an engine and he got to his feet. A blue tractor was making its way up the hill. It was dragging a complex-looking mower. A greenkeeper.

Fluke watched him approach; surprised none of his team or any of the uniformed officers had stopped him. Fluke walked out to meet him; he didn't want the green disturbed. He held his hand out in front of him. The universal sign for stop.

A spry old man climbed off the tractor.

'How do, lad,' he said, holding out his hand.

He was ancient and gnarled and, despite the sweltering heat, was dressed in several layers of green.

Fluke shook his hand and introduced himself.

'Sam Wilson. Head greenkeeper,' the old man said. 'Gather you've got a hand there.'

Fluke said nothing.

'Fellas down at the clubhouse are saying it fell from the sky.'

'That right?' Fluke said.

Wilson continued. 'Bet it's got you city boys stumped, eh?'

Fluke lived in a log cabin in the middle of a wood. It was hardly Manchester.

Wilson continued. 'They're saying you'll be taking Mr Yates

in for questioning soon. Thinking he put the hand there or knows something about it.'

'Seem to know a lot, these "fellas" of yours.'

Wilson smiled. 'Reckon they do. There's nowt worse than golfers for gossip, and this has got them fair excited.'

Fluke was pressed for time. He needed to recover the hand before the sun cooked it.

'I'm sorry, Mr Wilson, but I need to get on. If there's something you'd like to let us know, you should speak to one of the officers in a suit. They'll take a statement from you.'

Wilson didn't move. 'You in charge?'

He nodded.

'Can I look at the hand?'

'Why?'

'I'll be able to tell you if you need to lock up Mr Yates or not, that's why.'

'How?' Fluke asked. Wilson undoubtedly knew things the 'city boys' didn't, and he never ignored local knowledge.

Wilson didn't answer. He simply stared at Fluke, waiting for permission.

'Fine,' Fluke said, 'but you follow me and you don't touch anything. And if you're wasting my time I'm taking the handbrake off that tractor. You can walk back to the clubhouse.'

Wilson grinned. 'Fair enough. It won't take long.'

Wilson bent down and stared at the hand. Fluke was expecting him to get down on his knees and look at it from different angles. As it happened, he didn't look at it for long. He stood up and wiped his hands on his thick coat.

'You can let Mr Yates go,' he said.

Fluke didn't know what to expect but a two-second examination followed by an acquittal didn't come close. 'I'm going to need slightly more than that if you don't mind.'

9

He nodded. 'The hand wasn't placed there. Nor was it chucked from that wall ova' yonder,' he said, pointing at the dry stone wall Fluke had only just dismissed as a hiding place. 'This came from the air, just as Mr Yates said it did.'

'And you know this how?' Fluke wasn't being sarcastic.

'You see those marks on the hand?'

Fluke nodded.

'Those are the marks that mean it was dropped from the air.'

Fluke bent down and looked closely. 'What are you seeing that I'm not?'

Wilson scanned the sky. Eventually he saw something and pointed towards it.

Fluke looked but couldn't see anything. There was a white line in the sky. An aeroplane had passed recently. Was that what he meant?

Did he think it had been thrown from an aeroplane?

It wasn't impossible, but he failed to see how Wilson could know after such a short examination.

But Wilson didn't think the hand had been thrown from a plane. Far from it.

'Those marks are from talons. A buzzard dropped that hand, Mr Fluke.'

Help us make the next generation of readers

We – both author and publisher – hope you enjoyed this book.
We believe that you can become a reader at any time in your life,
but we'd love your help to give the next generation a head start.

Did you know that 9% of children don't have a book of their
own in their home, rising to 12% in disadvantaged families*?
We'd like to try to change that by asking you to consider the role
you could play in helping to build readers of the future.

We'd love you to think of sharing, borrowing, reading, buying or talking
about a book with a child in your life and spreading the love of reading.
We want to make sure the next generation continue to have access
to books, wherever they come from.

And if you would like to consider donating to charities that help
fund literacy projects, find out more at www.literacytrust.org.uk
and www.booktrust.org.uk.

Thank you.

 hachette
CHILDREN'S GROUP

little, brown
BOOK GROUP

*As reported by the National Literacy Trust